Praise for
Nicole McLaughlin

"Nicole McLaughlin had a new fan by chapter two!"
—*New York Times* bestselling author
Erin Nicholas on *All I Ask*

"Nicole's fun, sassy stories and sexy heroes are not to be missed!" —*USA Today* bestselling
author Julie Brannagh

"A wonderfully fresh voice in contemporary romance—
sweet, sexy, and immensely satisfying."
—Lauren Layne, *New York Times*
bestselling author

Also by Nicole McLaughlin

All I Ask
Along Came Us

Maybe I Do

Nicole McLaughlin

St. Martin's Paperbacks

This is a work of fiction. All of the characters, organizations, and events portrayed in this novel are either products of the author's imagination or are used fictitiously.

MAYBE I DO

Copyright © 2017 by Nicole McLaughlin.

All rights reserved.

For information address St. Martin's Press, 175 Fifth Avenue, New York, NY 10010.

ISBN: 978-1-250-13998-6

Our books may be purchased in bulk for promotional, educational, or business use. Please contact your local bookseller or the Macmillan Corporate and Premium Sales Department at 1-800-221-7945, ext. 5442, or by e-mail at MacmillanSpecialMarkets@macmillan.com.

Printed in the United States of America

St. Martin's Paperbacks edition / September 2017

St. Martin's Paperbacks are published by St. Martin's Press, 175 Fifth Avenue, New York, NY 10010.

10 9 8 7 6 5 4 3 2 1

For my Mother. Thank you for being
wonderful. I love you.

One

Weddings were a touchy subject for Charlotte Linley. Not that any of her photography clients would know that, since she prided herself on making her couples feel important on their wedding day. She encouraged them to live in the moment, to have fun, not to stress. Treated each couple's day like it was the event of the year. Despite her own personal history, she knew a wedding day was *supposed* to be a happy occasion. And thankfully in her experience as a photographer, it always was. Today's wedding was no exception.

Glancing around the bumpy trolley, Charlotte smiled to herself as the bridal party laughed and sang along to the music blaring through the speakers. They were having a great time, and she knew that was partly because she'd made their on-location portrait session fun and easy. Sure, at every wedding she worked, she couldn't help but have a small underlying feeling of dread until the words *I do*. But she took comfort in the fact that today she was shooting her 234th wedding, and she'd yet to have a bride or groom bail. Not that it couldn't still happen in the future, because if anyone knew that it was possible, it was Charlotte.

With a sigh, she steadied herself in the aisle of the

trolley as it bounced over a dip in the road. Widening her stance for leverage, she wrapped her arm around a pole and then slowly lifted her camera to her eye. It was critical she make no sudden movements, since today's bride was one of those women hyperaware of her photographer at any given time. Charlotte really preferred that her clients forget she existed until portrait time. Not because she was antisocial, but because she loved candid images. The moments like the one before her, the bride and groom cozied up in the back of the vehicle, cocooned in post-wedding-ceremony bliss. The groom leaned in and whispered something sweet—or naughty, who knew—and his bride giggled before tilting in to kiss him, her hand lightly cupping his jaw. They looked content and happy, their foreheads touching as they shared a few intimate seconds before arriving at their reception.

Experience had taught Charlotte that a few weeks from now, when this couple viewed their gallery of photos, they would have forgotten this playful kiss in the back of the trolley. When it popped up on their computer screen, they would smile and "ahh," and maybe even tear up. They'd likely thank her for capturing these little moments that allowed them to relive a day that had zoomed by at lightning speed. That conversation, that feeling of satisfaction, kept Charlotte shooting weddings. And hey, if she contributed just the tiniest amount to a couple staying in love forever . . . well then, that sufficed.

She looked at the back of her camera, pleased with the image. Commotion from the rowdy bridal party pulled her attention, followed by her camera's focus, back to the action. The bridesmaids were passing out Jell-O shots that had been stored in a cooler. Charlotte clicked a few shots of them laughing, throwing them back, and things began to happen in slow motion as one of the guys lifted his hand to give his buddy a fist bump, effectively knocking his neighbor's arm in the process.

Charlotte grimaced as the bridesmaid screeched. "Dang it, Jason, you just made me drop some on my dress. How embarrassing."

A fountain of peach satin fell upon her, fellow maids pulling out homemade wedding day emergency kits and trying to get the bright blue stain out of the lace overlay as if their lives depended on it. After catching some of the drama on her camera for posterity's sake, because *someday* it would be funny, Charlotte turned around to look out the front window.

"Everything okay back there?" Frank, the trolley driver, asked Charlotte.

She met his eyes in his large rearview mirror and stepped down closer so he could hear her. "Neon-blue Jell-O shots. When will they learn?"

Frank chuckled with her. They'd worked together many times over the years. Same drama, different weekend.

"On to the Stag then?" he asked.

She nodded. "Yep, portraits are done. Thank goodness."

The Stag Whiskey Distillery was her favorite venue. Just the thought of it made her grin. She liked this couple and the wedding had gone well, but all day she'd been excited to get to the reception. If Charlotte was a wedding kind of gal, she'd definitely book the Stag for her festivities. But since she'd been there done that, and it would never happen again, she made sure to recommend it to every bride she worked with.

Production of whiskey and vodka was their main gig and very lucrative, but three years ago when the business was still young, they'd started renting out the upstairs space for weddings and other events. Charlotte was one of the very first photographers to shoot there, and she'd loved watching it evolve in to what it was now: one of the most sought-after venues in the Kansas City metro area. What with their delicious spirits, awesome building, and killer branding, they were set. It was just the cherry on top that the three owners, TJ, Jake, and Dean, were all super hot. Charlotte liked to tease them that reality television would eventually knock on their door—something they all balked at.

Frank drove the trolley through the town square of Maple Springs, Kansas, a suburb of the Kansas City metro. Charlotte had lived in Maple Springs her entire life, but it wasn't quite the same town she'd spent her childhood in. There were now *two* high schools, and instead of Mama's Kitchen being the only option for a meal out, there were a handful of chain and independently owned restaurants. Something she had no complaints about.

The town square had been undergoing a revival over the past couple of years as well, which the community seemed to be excited about. As they headed for the Stag, Charlotte took in the mix of small shops that had opened up. Several of the bridesmaids behind her were also pointing out their favorites as the vehicle rolled through town.

She personally loved the Craft Shack, but also Nana's Toy Box, Yellow Brick Coffee, and even Totally Nuts, a boutique nut-roasting shop run by a little old man named Pete Jenkins. Charlotte had gone to high school with his granddaughter, and she could recall that the man had been, well . . . one might say the name of his shop was very appropriate, but he sure could roast a perfect bag of pecans, almonds, or cashews.

Charlotte had many great memories in Maple Springs, and despite its population doubling in size over the past decade, it still felt like a small town. The Stag Whiskey Distillery in the old brick building on the corner of

Hickory and Sterling Avenue only added to the town square's charm.

Over the years, the building had housed everything from a furniture store to offices. It had even sat vacant for a time, but luckily the Stag guys had come along and snatched it up. To their credit, they'd made the space functional for their business but also managed to maintain its historical integrity. The upstairs venue space was simple yet elegant, perfect for weddings, and depending on how the bride chose to decorate, it could work with a variety of styles. Spacious yet intimate, its mix of industrial and antique gave a timeless look and feel. It also always looked gorgeous in photos. Brick walls weren't normally conducive to good images as they tended to soak up all the light, but the beauty of the place—the giant chandeliers, stone fireplace, and wood beams—made up for that. Plus, Charlotte had shot there so many times she knew exactly what settings to use, and where to place her flash the minute she walked in.

As the trolley pulled to a stop at the front door, her stomach fluttered in anticipation. She glanced down and took inventory of her black slacks and cream-colored blouse. Thankfully she'd managed to get through the day without getting dirty, which wasn't always the case. Pulling out her phone, she shot a quick one-word text to her assistant Lauren, alerting her that they'd arrived.

She glanced at the clock, pleased to see they'd timed things perfectly. After working together for almost seven years, she and Laruen were like a well-oiled machine. Once she'd received Charlotte's text, Lauren would alert the DJ to their arrival; he should then be ready to announce the bridal party. From that point forward the reception would proceed as normal, because they were all so similar it was almost laughable. Charlotte could shoot a wedding in her sleep.

After tossing Frank a cheery wave over her shoulder, she was the first person off the trolley as the bridal party gathered their things.

Before stepping inside, Charlotte took a quick swipe at her lower lashes, hoping her makeup hadn't melted too much during afternoon outdoor portraits. She fidgeted with her hair then opened the door and inhaled the now familiar scent of fermenting alcohol. Heading into the expansive first floor, she relished the chill on her arms from the air conditioner as the muffled bass thumped from the floor above.

The black-and-white octagonal floor on the first level of the Stag always drew her eye. It never ceased to impress her how the guys had struck a perfect balance of original and modern in this space. In addition to the original floor tiles, stainless-steel piping, copper trim, leather furniture, and wood beams created a masculine yet elegant feel. The main floor was devoted to the distillery side of their business. Once you entered, a large front desk—always vacant on the weekends—sat to the right, and there was a nice seating area in the center of the room. To the left was a hallway that led to offices and restrooms; to the right, a giant elevator and a hall to the large supply room and back staircase. The pièce de résistance of the room was the back wall. Floor-to-ceiling glass encased the distilling room, which housed their beautiful copper distiller.

Charlotte stepped around the front desk to find the one person she'd been hoping to see tonight. Stepping off the old freight elevator was her favorite of the three Stag owners.

Dean Troyer.

Her heart rate cranked up instantly.

The minute their eyes met, he smiled and headed her direction. She took him in, hands casually tucked into the pockets of his khaki pants, gait sure and smooth. The man wore a dress shirt as if it were tailored to his firm chest, the top button open to reveal his neck and the sleeves rolled to show off his masculine arms. Charlotte particularly liked the bones in his wrists. Something she'd never noticed before on a man, but when it came to Dean, she seemed to miss nothing. His leather belt urged her eyes to wander over his narrow hips. All six sexy feet of him— from his cognac oxford shoes, to his lightly mussed dark hair—was a sight to behold. He was a bit older than her, but not even that seemed to matter. Dean was without a doubt the best part of shooting at this venue.

The first time she'd laid eyes on him she'd fallen a little bit in love. Not real love, of course. More of a deeply unhealthy infatuation. The kind that made you imagine what kind of house you might buy together, practice writing your name as *Mrs. Charlotte Troyer*, or consider what you'd name your first child. Run-of-the-mill female insanity. Charlotte had even been known to *accidentally* find him amid the crowd inside her camera lens during a wedding reception, and then zoom in on his face. There might even be a secret folder on her computer labeled *Dream Man* to contain those special images. She had a bit of a problem, and that problem was currently looking her up and down—an adorable smirk on his face—as she met him halfway.

"Always right on time to greet me," she teased quietly. "I tell myself it's because I'm your favorite photographer and you're miserable until I get here."

Dean chuckled, an embarrassed smile on his face, always the best part. A lot sexy and a little surprised, as if it always shocked him when she was forward. He looked directly at her. "You can continue to tell yourself that because it's absolutely true," he said, voice deep and low.

Charlotte warmed inside at his words, but before she could take the flirting any further, the bridal party entered the front door. Nothing if not professional, Dean changed the direction of the conversation with ease.

"How's the day been going?"

"Good. Ceremony was perfect, portraits amazing. What more can we ask for?"

She turned to the girls, who appeared uncertain where to go as they shuffled into the main room. Charlotte called out. "Ladies, the restroom is that way if you want to freshen up before intro."

The herd of peach made their way toward the indicated hallway down the left side. Charlotte turned back to Dean to find that he hadn't taken his eyes off her.

"Do we like them?" he whispered after they were alone again. She loved when he referred to them as a *we*. Just like she did in her dreams.

"The couple is fantastic. Wedding party is crossing over into drunk territory, so yeah, they're fun."

"How late are you here?" Dean asked as some of the guys dragged in their cooler and various bags the girls had left behind. At least they weren't too intoxicated to be gentleman.

"We're here until midnight."

His lips turned down a bit. "That's a really long day for you."

"You're not kidding. They booked an unlimited day. Started at ten o'clock this morning." Charlotte made a face. "Don't ask me why I offer that option. I'm mad at myself every time someone chooses it."

"Well, I guess I shouldn't complain. I like you in my building. Means I get to stare at you longer."

It was Charlotte's turn to blush. Dean always flirted back with her, but his style was normally much subtler than hers, so when he said something bold, it sent tingles through her entire body. It didn't hurt that his good looks were enough to melt the panties off any female in the vicinity. The proof came when some of the bridesmaids caught sight of him as they exited the restroom. Their eyes went wide with shock and admiration, and these girls were young. More evidence that his age did not factor when it came to his sex appeal. In fact, she believed it worked in his favor.

It wasn't that he looked *that* much older. His hair wasn't gray . . . except for the tiniest pieces at his temples. And his face wasn't wrinkled . . . well, except for the slight lines that appeared at his eyes when he smiled. Although she knew he was older than Jake and TJ, she'd never gotten up the courage to ask anyone his exact age. She really didn't care. It almost made it a little hotter, this air of maturity about him. Not in a stuffy way, more just . . . powerful. Knowing. Stoic, maybe. When she compared him with guys her own age, he was just . . . *more*.

"Oh my God." One of the tipsy bridesmaids made her way across the room toward the elevator where Charlotte and Dean stood. The bride and the rest of her attendants followed. "Are you one of the owner guys?"

"I *am* one of owner guys. Welcome to the Stag." He gave a warm smile to the young woman and other ladies who had circled around. When Sonya, the bride, walked over, Dean politely held out his hand and congratulated her on her nuptials.

Charlotte watched him laugh with the group of women, so confident and handsome, but always professional. He was playful, if a bit reserved, so Charlotte always made it her mission to make him laugh. She loved nothing more than when they found themselves alone so she could flirt with him unabashedly. Teasing him was one of her

favorite things, because his smile was so handsome. Dean
was just flat-out beautiful, like a movie star. Not the ones
that played the young heartthrob, yet definitely not the men
playing the fatherly roles. He was more along the lines of
sexy middle-aged leading man. The inexorable bachelor,
the man that women of every age lusted after and hoped
to bring to heel.

On top of that, Dean was just a really good guy. Always
kind and thoughtful, and he clearly worked hard. Time and
again Charlotte had witnessed him do the sweetest things,
like help old ladies and talk to children. Once he'd even
spent an hour serving food for a short-staffed caterer. Dean
was the ultimate catch, and she liked to daydream that he
was all hers.

"I can see why you booked this place," one of bridesmaids said with an eyebrow waggle toward Dean. The
girls all laughed and the bride blushed, apologizing to him.

"No worries, Sonya," Charlotte interjected. "Dean's
used to having all the ladies' attention."

Dean gave her a playful scowl. "Hardly. The other guys,
yes. I try to just blend in."

From the dreamy looks on the girls' faces, he was failing miserably. This wasn't the first time Charlotte had seen
women flirt with the Stag guys. In fact, it pretty much happened every time she shot a wedding there. They seemed
to take the flirting in stride. Dean was good at politely di-
verting the attention, TJ always appeared adorably flustered, and Jake usually seemed torn between doing the
right thing and dragging the perpetrator into a dark corner
and having his way with her. He was the wild one of the
group, hands down.

Realizing they were killing precious time, Charlotte
called the guys over from where they'd congregated on the
sofas and rounded up her troops.

She quickly explained that Dean would take them up the freight elevator and then they'd do the intro straight-away. As everyone began to make their way onto the lift, Dean leaned over and whispered into Charlotte's ear, "That blond guy given you any trouble today?"

Ah, so he'd noticed the way the best man stood in her personal space and didn't stop staring at her. It happened sometimes. She'd earn an admirer over the course of the day, and by this hour, with alcohol flowing, it could occasionally get a little weird.

"Nothing I can't handle, but I love that you're jealous," she teased.

He gave her a look she couldn't quite decipher. "I'm definitely jealous. Only I get to flirt with the photographer during a Stag reception."

"Don't worry. I'm all yours." She gave him a quick wink.

Knowing Dean would get the group upstairs in two trips, Charlotte headed up the back stairs to prep and find Lauren. She was greeted by the sound of a party in full swing. Thumping jazz music, the tinkling of glass, the murmur of conversation, and the occasional hearty laugh. From the makeshift kitchen room came the tantalizing scent of garlic, and Charlotte's stomach growled as she passed a server with a tray of stuffed mushrooms. How she would have loved to nab one or five.

She spotted Lauren taking group shots of the revelers as they eagerly awaited the bride and groom. Charlotte made her way in that direction.

"How'd it go?" Lauren asked when they were within speaking distance.

"Portraits went well. That park you suggested worked out perfectly. I hated the thought of going to that field again."

"I'm glad it worked." Lauren nodded to the long bar. "I've got a glass of water for you hidden behind that flower arrangement."

Charlotte realized then how thirsty she truly was. "You're amazing."

Heading over to the bar, Charlotte gave a quick wave to the bartender Jen, downed her glass of water, and began to prep for the bridal party's introduction. Twenty minutes later they'd shot the intro and the servers began setting down dinner plates. The cue for Charlotte and Lauren to take a well-earned break.

Another great thing about shooting at the Stag was the little room off to the side of the bar. Basically, only the vendors or an occasional nursing mother went in there. With seating, a table, and a bathroom, it made for a nice little retreat to eat dinner and store gear. It was also close enough to the action that they could be alerted quickly if anything exciting happened.

"My favorite part of the day," Lauren said as she plopped onto the nearest couch. "Dinnertime."

"Absolutely," Charlotte said, gently laying her massive camera down on the table. She removed the second camera from around her neck, removed her heavy bag of equipment, and instantly felt the relief of being twenty pounds lighter. She sat on the opposite couch. "It's been a pretty easy day, though. Considering how early we started."

They both sighed as they leaned back in unison. It was always nice to just sit for a moment and reflect on the day. At their dinner break, Charlotte could take a deep breath and relax, knowing that all of the critical moments were over with. The getting ready, ceremony, kiss, and portraits were all done and behind her. The rest was cake. Literally, because she and Lauren always sampled the cake. Speaking of which . . .

"Who made the cake?" she asked Lauren.

"Jill Fontaine," a masculine voice said from the doorway. Her body instantly went on alert as she turned to find Dean holding a stainless domed plate in each large hand.

Lauren sat up. "That just made my whole night. Jill's cakes are like little fluffy orgasms with frosting on top."

Dean laughed and laid the dishes down on the table. "I think what I have here looks pretty orgasmic also."

Charlotte smiled as she thought of all the ways she could reply to that adorable comment, but she refrained. Instead she sat up, excited to see what was for dinner.

Dean pulled off the lids, revealing breaded chicken breasts coated in a cream sauce, whipped cheesy potatoes, green beans with bacon, and a giant roll.

Charlotte couldn't hold in her gasp of pleasure. "This looks amazing. Thank goodness wedding day calories don't count."

"Absolutely," Lauren replied as she stood up. "I'm going to run to the restroom and then grab a soda."

"Grab me one?" Charlotte called after her. Lauren nodded and headed for the door.

Dean waited until Lauren was gone and then sat down beside Charlotte. Not too close, but enough that she felt his warmth immediately.

"I was surprised when I saw the dinner," Dean said as Charlotte picked up a forkful of mashed potatoes and brought them to her lips. "I wasn't sure about a caterer with a name like Gary's Catering."

After swallowing the creamy bite of heaven, she replied. "Not the most original name, right? But Gary's is one of my favorites. He's consistent and he seasons well. So many of them are afraid of a little salt and pepper." Charlotte loaded up her fork again. "And he's a nice guy, which makes a difference."

"So he's reasonable?" Dean asked.

Charlotte shoved a second bite of potatoes into her mouth, starved after shooting for almost eight hours. All she'd had was a granola bar before the ceremony. She nearly groaned. "Sorry, what did you say?"

Dean's smile—and his eyes on her mouth—made her aware of how she was chowing down. She was so hungry she couldn't find it in her to care. He leaned forward, elbow on his knees, still watching her. "I asked about Gary's. He's reasonably priced as far as caterers go?"

She swallowed and considered his question before answering. "Yeah. I'd say he's the best in his price range, which is right in the middle. After that I'd go with Gourmet Granny. She makes the best chicken Kiev and spaetzle."

Dean nodded. "Good to know. Are Jill's cakes expensive?"

"Very. But totally worth it. Problem with Jill is that popular dates are sometimes spoken for years in advance. I think women have been known to book her before they have a ring. She's in really high demand."

Charlotte cut a bite of her chicken. Part of her just wanted to sit here and enjoy Dean's company, but on the other hand she was ravenously hungry and they had to get their dinner eaten while the bride and groom ate—which usually didn't take long. A sudden thought came to mind, and she quickly glanced over at Dean.

"You getting married or something?"

She wished the thought weren't so devastating. Charlotte was kind of surprised he wasn't already taken, but she'd looked for a ring the first time she'd ever met him and hadn't found one. Flirting had ensued.

"Oh no. Not me. My little sister just got engaged. I told her I'd start getting some information together for when she comes home on leave in July."

Relief flooded through Charlotte's chest just as Lauren walked back in and sat down to her own dinner. "Oh, congratulations! I had no idea you had a sister. She's in the military?"

"Thank you, and yes, army. Tried to talk her out of it . . . but she's pretty tough. I'm really proud of her." His smile was warm as he spoke of his little sister, which only made Charlotte like him more.

"Of course you are. So she comes back in July? When's her wedding?"

"They're talking next summer, but I'm really not certain."

Just then the door flung open and the DJ poked his head in. "Hey you two, thought you might want to know that the bride's brother is giving an unannounced speech."

"Damn," Charlotte muttered, and Lauren groaned before shoving one last bite of chicken into her mouth.

"Lauren, you stay. I'll go get this." She turned to Dean and stood up. "No rest for the weary."

He just shook his head. "You girls amaze me every time."

"Hey, good luck with the wedding, and if your sister needs a photographer, I might know of a really good one." She grinned, grabbed one of her cameras, and was out the door.

Two

Four hours later they had photographed the dances, the toasts, the cake cutting, the groom and his buddies singing their fraternity song to the bride, the bride and her sorority sisters reciting a chant, and finally the sparkler send-off. By now Charlotte's feet ached, her back was stiff, and if the best man hit on her one more time she was going to very calmly punch him in the face. She was also in desperate need of hydration.

"Do you want to go to the bar and get some water? Or a soda?" she asked Lauren. "Normally I'd say we could leave now that the couple's gone but . . ."

"I know. The groom's mom has practically shadowed us all night. It's only eleven forty-five."

Even though there wasn't much left to shoot once the couple left, they were contractually required to stay until midnight. "Right? She's driving me crazy. She's acting like she paid for this. I'm certain all of the checks came from the bride's father. But I've learned that one bitching family member is like a cancer. They start creating doubt in everyone's mind, and before you know it you're trying to defend every shot that didn't get taken."

Lauren waved a hand. "It's fine, let's just hang for fifteen minutes."

Charlotte agreed and they headed for the bar.

"I can't believe you guys are still here," Jen said. She was Charlotte's favorite bartender at the Stag, and worked almost every wedding. There was no missing her big personality, her sleeve of colorful arm tattoos, or her dark-as-night hair. And she was funny as hell.

"Crazy, isn't it?"

"It was a pretty good night, though," Jen said. She was restocking the row of Stag shot glasses on the bar. Guests could take them as a favor. Charlotte had snagged a few for herself over the years.

"It was. Can't complain. Still, it will be better when I'm in bed," Charlotte said.

Jen winked. "Isn't everything better in bed?"

"Stop being inappropriate," Dean warned, walking down the bar behind Jen. Charlotte loved how he always seemed to appear when she stopped and took a time-out. After they'd left him in the break room, she hadn't seen him at all. She'd figured he'd disappeared to the offices, which had been a little disappointing. It was one of her favorite things when he came up and chatted with her while she photographed people making fools of themselves on the dance floor. And she'd scored no new photos for her *Dream Man* stash, either.

"Please, you're the most inappropriate person in this place," Jen said to Dean. She took a damp bar towel and flicked him on the butt.

And just like that a sinking feeling came over Charlotte. Did Dean flirt with everyone? He didn't seem like the type at all. Actually, she'd always had the feeling that she'd managed to pull that side out of him despite himself. Not that she truly thought he liked her in any serious way, but . . . she'd always hoped and assumed he was attracted to her even if he was too much of a professional to act on it. She liked to think that the flirting between them was something he did only with her. But why should she assume that was the case? He was an insanely handsome single male. In his prime, some might say. Other photographers came here. They had other employees, bridesmaids, vendors. He probably had endless opportunities to flirt and even hook up with women.

Thankfully her worries were eased just a little when Dean turned and instantly scowled at Jen after the towel flick to the rear. He pointed a finger at her. "Don't do that again."

Charlotte had never seen that side of Dean. The angry, employer side. It suited him somehow, and she had to admit it was kind of hot.

Jen turned and gave Charlotte and Lauren a wink. "Ignore him, he's decided to be Boss Dean today, which means he's grumpy and no fun." She grabbed two pint glasses and began to fill them with ice. "Charlotte, do you have any new sexy man photos?"

Dean's head jerked toward Charlotte, his attention obviously caught by Jen's question. She felt her face warm in response. It was a little embarrassing that Jen had mentioned it in front of him. Not that Charlotte was ashamed of the extra photo work she'd started taking on recently, but still, it was a bit awkward, even for her.

"She absolutely does. She did the hottest guy on Thursday," Lauren said, adding to Charlotte's discomfort in front of Dean.

Charlotte wanted so badly for him to see her in a certain light, although she wasn't quite sure what that light was. Hopefully the one that led to him asking her out one day. Or at least making out. Part of her feared that maybe he saw her as too young, but the truth was, for a single woman of twenty-nine she was incredibly successful, and she'd always been mature for her age. She owned her own business, had a five-digit savings account, and hadn't bought anything in the juniors clothing section in at least a year.

Charlotte glanced up to find Dean's eyebrow raised in assessment of her. She'd love to know what he was thinking, and of course because she was infatuated with him, she feared the worst. He stepped a little closer to their end of the bar but continued to count liquor bottles and write things down on a clipboard.

"It's not how it sounds," Charlotte said quickly in her own defense. Not that she needed one.

"I'm so jealous. What an amazing gig." Jen poured Charlotte and Lauren a soda out of her fountain gun.

"I keep begging her to let me come over and help her with them, but she never does," Lauren said, giving Charlotte a teasing scowl. "She's stingy with her sexy guys."

"It's just photography."

"Of . . . men?" Dean asked. His face was neutral, but there was a bit of an edge to his tone. Interesting.

Charlotte opened her mouth to speak, but Jen beat her to it. "She photographs hot guys for book covers. Like ripped abs, big pecs, cut hips. The *whole* package. If you know what I mean."

Lauren and Jen giggled like teenagers, but Charlotte couldn't take her eyes off Dean, whose lips had tightened. What was he thinking, knowing that she did this? It wasn't like they were pornographic. Just . . . sexy. A little raw sometimes.

"So these guys are *naked*?" Dean asked.

"No!" Charlotte said immediately. "They're not naked."

"Well . . . they might as well be," Lauren said. "Show him."

"Yes please, show us." Jen leaned on the bar, waiting.

Charlotte pulled out her phone and opened up the Cloud app, which accessed her online portfolio. The truth was, she loved taking these photos. For the obvious reason, hello, hot guys. But also because it was artistically challenging. The light, the muscles, the emotion.

It had been a complete accident that had landed her the first cover gig. Another of her specialties were boudoir shoots, which were often booked by her brides as a surprise for their fiancés. A year ago, one of them had shown her album to a friend who happened to be a romance author. That was all it took for her to build up a little bit of a side business to her wedding clientele. Plus, she really enjoyed it, and wouldn't mind if she could start supplementing her wedding income with this work.

Opening the most recent set of photos, Charlotte held out her phone to Jen, who eagerly snatched it from her. Dean leaned forward a little to glance over Jen's shoulder.

"Oh damn, look at him," Jen said. She swiped through several photos and then paused on one. "Good Lord."

Charlotte was pretty sure she knew which it was, because it was her favorite, too. Kye, the guy in the photo, had the most insanely gorgeous body. They'd done the session in an empty, filthy warehouse. He was in dangerously low-hung jeans, his abs dirty, chest sweaty (although that was courtesy of a spray bottle), and he looked up at the camera through hooded lids, his lips slightly pouty.

"He nailed that one, didn't he?" Charlotte found herself asking.

"Yep, and he can nail me while he's at it," Jen said as she lifted the phone to her face and imitated licking the screen. Dean's head jerked back and he stared at Jen with unveiled disgust.

"Oh, sorry." Jen smiled and held the phone out to him. "Did you want a taste, too?"

Dean just shook his head and walked back to the other end of the bar.

"He's just jealous," Jen whispered, loud enough for anyone within ten feet to overhear. Just then her eyes went wide, and she gasped. "Oh my God. Dean! You should do Dean. Dean, you should let Charlotte do you!"

Grateful that most of the guests had left for the evening, Charlotte's eyes darted from the bartender to the guy who was glaring back at her, his lips parted in shock.

She laughed nervously. "Don't worry, Dean. I wouldn't ask you to do that."

"I hope not," he replied, sending a wave of embarrassment through her. What did *that* reaction mean? Did he think her work was stupid? Or did he mean in reference to the innuendo? She wasn't sure which would be worse.

"But you should," Jen urged, clearly inspired by the idea and not willing to let it go. "I'm telling you, it's the best idea ever. I mean, I know a lot of these guys are super young and hunky, but Dean is . . . you know, *middle-aged* hunky. And he is built like a brick house."

"Wow, you really know how to make a guy feel good, Jen," Dean said. His glaring eyes were insisting that Jen shut the hell up.

A twinge of jealousy came over Charlotte as she wondered how and why Jen had any knowledge of Dean's body. But the idea of photographing him did intrigue her, there was no denying that. She was already imagining what she'd do to him. Or . . . with him. Or to him. God, she was just imagining him shirtless and it was scrambling her brain. Clearly this was all wishful thinking that was never going to come to fruition if the horrified look on his face was any indication.

"Tell her," Jen said to Dean, her voice revealing her irritation with him. "You could totally pull that sexy stuff off."

"Hush, Jen."

"Sorry, Dean, I know this totally isn't your style," Charlotte said, hating that things were getting uncomfortable for her and obviously for him, too.

He stared at her for a long moment, and she desperately wished she could read his thoughts. Secretly, she hoped he would counter, say that he did indeed think it was a good idea, that her talent was obvious and he wanted to be a part of it by stripping off his clothes and playing the part of sexy alpha male. But that was her living in Dean Dream Guy Land again. The truth was that having a scantily clad Dean in front of her lens could be the worst kind of torture.

A light touch on Charlotte's shoulder had her turning to find the mother of the bride standing there with a smile. She surprised both Charlotte and Lauren by handing them fifty-dollar bills and thanking them for putting in such a long day. They rarely got cash tips, but it was always a treat when they did.

When the conversation ended, Charlotte disappointedly found the bar empty. It wasn't like him to let her leave without a good-bye, and now it frustrated her to think their conversation about her work had possibly turned him off.

She and Lauren headed back to the little powder room to get the rest of their gear packed up. Trying to focus on a hot shower and sleep, Charlotte forced herself to look casual as they made their way toward the old metal elevator. Of course she was hoping to catch sight of Dean before they left. He was nowhere.

When they stepped out of the elevator and into the lobby, it was also void of Dean and his handsome face. How had such a fun evening taken such a depressing turn? With a heavy sigh, she recalled she had another job at the Stag for the following weekend. There was always another wedding.

Three

Dean Troyer sat down in his kitchen and propped his laptop on the scarred wood table in front of him. As soon as he opened the Skype window and saw his own reflection—and the cluttered counters behind him—he cringed. *Not gonna work*.

Grabbing the computer, he stood and went around to the other side of the table. From that angle, a harsh light hit his face from the living room window. Groaning, he glanced at the clock. Three minutes. Computer in hand once again, he sat on the couch. He turned and quickly fluffed the pillows, arranged the blanket his sister had knitted him years ago behind him—she'd like that—and then blew out a deep breath. He glanced at his watch. One minute until his impromptu call with his little sister.

The computer alerted him of the incoming Skype call and a giant grin instantly broke out on Dean's face. She'd promised in her email last night that she was completely fine and not to worry, but he couldn't help wondering what she needed to tell him that could not have been said in the original note. When it came to his little sister, worrying had always been a full-time job.

He'd been fifteen when Alexis was born. Full of pubescent male rage and attitude, all made worse by the fact that his mother had divorced his father and married a man nearly twenty years his junior and eight years hers. Dean had hated his stepfather, if he could even have been called that, so when his mother got pregnant he'd been prepared to hate their offspring, too. That had proved to be impossible, because the minute he'd held tiny baby Alexis, he'd loved her.

She was now an adult and serving her second tour in the Middle East, and he couldn't wait for her to come home. Three more months and she'd be back safe for good, finally done with her commitment to the army. He was proud as hell of her, always had been, but it was crazy nerve racking for her to be doing something so dangerous.

They hadn't done a video call in several weeks. Not since she'd told him about her engagement to Nathan, her boyfriend of two years. He clicked to accept her call now, and the minute she came through he breathed a sigh of relief at seeing her whole and healthy. Her dark hair was pulled back into a ponytail, her eyes bright with excitement.

"Bean!" She'd called him Bean since she could speak. "How are you?"

"I'm good, Buzz. How are you?"

"I'm wonderful."

They chatted briefly about unimportant things. The weather, how the Stag was doing, and she asked about Dean's father.

"I'm counting down the days till July. Ready to have you both home," Dean said.

"Nowhere near as ready as I am. *However . . .*" She

smiled but it quickly went solemn. "Dean, that's what I wanted to talk to you about."

He sucked in a breath before responding. "Alex, don't even tell me . . ."

Her face was pained. "I'm so sorry. I know you'll be disappointed, but Nathan and I both decided that while we're young we might as well let the government pay for us to travel."

Dean's head nodded repeatedly—a nervous reaction. He sure as hell wasn't yet in agreement, just . . . processing. He'd been afraid this might happen. "Where?"

"Italy. The air force offered Nate a job there and . . . well, I asked if I could be assigned there also. They said yes."

"Well, of course they did. If you're willing to give the army more years of your life, they aren't going to talk you out of it."

"Dean," she whispered. "Please don't be mad."

The sadness in her voice forced him to get it together. "I'm sorry, Buzz. I'm not mad. I just . . . worry about you. And I miss you."

She smiled. "I miss you. But *Italy* . . ."

He sighed. "Yeah, I guess that's somewhat of a relief. Why does the US military need to be in Italy anyway?"

She laughed. "The US military thinks it needs to be everywhere, and with attacks on the rise—"

"Uh-uh-uh. That's enough. I'd rather imagine my little sister eating pizza and going to the Love, or whatever."

Alex grinned and shook her head. "It's the Louvre, and it's in Paris, France, genius."

"Ah, well, I was just testing you." Dean scratched at the back of his neck. "How long?"

"A year. And then we're out for good. Both of us. We'll be ready for kids by then. It will be perfect timing."

"I'm not sure if perfect is how I would describe it but I will choose to trust your judgment. You tell Nathan he'd better keep you safe."

"He always does, although you do know I outrank him?" She smiled and then reached off camera. "He's here with me."

Dean sat up straighter as Nate's face leaned into the camera's view. The guy looked a little like a young Jamie Foxx and had the charm of a southern gentleman seeing as he'd grown up in Georgia.

"Hello, Dean," Nate said with a small wave. Then he drawled, "I promise to take care of Alex as I always do."

"Oh please." Alexis teasingly shoved Nate out of the screen, then leaned over and kissed his cheek.

Dean chuckled as he watched them grin at each other, feeling old and very alone. He remembered being that happy and in love. Blissful ignorance he now realized. He could only hope that his sister and Nate would be luckier than he and his ex-wife had.

Alex was now twenty-five. Seemed like just yesterday Dean was twenty-five himself, watching her in a dance recital. Teaching her how to fish. Eventually taking her in during her teen years after their mother and her father had died. He'd raised her after that, and in many ways Dean felt less like a fun and cool sibling and more a combination of bossy big brother and Dad.

"So, there's only one problem with this change in plans, Dean."

"What's that?"

"Our wedding."

Dean shrugged. "So you postpone things, right? It will be fine, Alex. We'll do whatever we need to do."

"I was hoping you'd say that. And while we could wait, we don't want to. When we move to Italy we want to live on the base as a married couple. Use married housing."

"Well, okay . . . then you get married before you go."

"Right, but that means we have to get married while we're home in July." Her expression implied that she thought Dean was a little slow on the uptake. "We will only have two weeks' leave. And currently I'm on the other side of the planet, Dean, and we start a month-long mission in a week. Soo . . . remember how much you love me . . ." Alexis made a worried face.

"Alex, whatever you need me to do, I'll do it."

"Bean, I need you to plan my wedding."

"So you're playing bride for her?" TJ asked Dean. They headed for the old freight elevator that led to the second floor of the Stag. Normally they would have taken the back staircase, but a rolling cart of Forkhorn White Whiskey and Ten Point Vodka bottles needed to go up to the bar for this evening's event. Usually their bartender Jen did the stocking, but she was late. Not a surprise.

"I prefer the term *doing her a favor.*"

"Okay, a favor where you play bride for her."

Dean sighed. "It appears so."

"You know three months to plan a wedding is sort of unreasonable, right?"

Dean shrugged as he slid the metal door open and held it while TJ rolled the cart in, the wood and metal clanking beneath it. Pulling the heavy door closed, Dean pushed the UP button. "I have to do the best I can. I figured with Tara's help—"

TJ winced as the lift jerked to life. "Shit, I forgot to tell you. Tara found out yesterday she has pre . . . something or other. Some serious pregnancy issue. She has to take some time off to go on partial bedrest until she can deliver in July."

"What?" Pregnancy complications always pulled at Dean's heart, reminding him of all the struggles he and Amy experienced trying—and failing repeatedly—to conceive. He didn't wish it on anyone. "How did this happen? I thought she was doing great."

Tara had been the first bride at the Stag. She'd been responsible for spreading the word early on, which had snowballed out of control. It had made sense to hire her as their resident wedding coordinator and front desk helper. When she'd announced the news that she and her husband, Ben, were expecting, Dean, Jake, and TJ had been thrilled for them. The thought that something could go wrong left a pit in Dean's stomach.

"Her doctor says it's not completely uncommon but it has to be taken very seriously. She must be off her feet to ensure everything is okay. Obviously, whatever is best for her and the baby takes priority, so the three of us are basically going to have to step in where she left off and pick up the slack until this fall when she comes back. And considering Jake will be on the festival tour for a good chunk of July and August, that pretty much leaves the two of us."

"Shit," he muttered to himself, his anxiety going on red alert at that thought. Although he attended his share of their wedding events, he'd never had a hand in working with the couples or any of the planning. His main job had always been the spirits. Part of the reason he'd so easily agreed to grant Alexis's request was because he'd just assumed he'd have Tara's help.

After TJ opened the lift, Dean pushed the cart off the elevator and followed him to the bar. "Do we need to hire someone temporary to do Tara's job?" Dean asked.

"I thought about that. But who wants a temporary job that has such a learning curve? She offered to do the work from home but Ben called and informed me that the doctor had emphasized how important it was that she relax and not stress to keep her blood pressure in check."

"Yeah, no, I'm completely in agreement with Ben. Tara has to focus on herself. If anything happened to that baby . . ." Dean turned away, rubbing at his chin. His co-owners knew he'd been married, and knew Amy, but they had no clue how painful their life together had been. Something he had no intention of sharing.

"It will be fine," TJ said as he began to move the bottles of vodka to the back of the bar. Dean hated that they all saw him as the worrier of the group, but it was just his nature. "I think I can handle the wedding side of things, but that will take me away from helping you, so I will say again, you need to hire a distilling assistant. Especially now that you're playing bride. Putting it off is really no longer an option."

His co-owners had been bugging him to do that for a while, and Dean wasn't sure why he kept resisting. The three of them had set up their roles in the business early on, and while they all had learned to help one another when needed, they mostly stayed in their own lanes. Didn't micromanage one another, and that had worked.

TJ was the business and money mind. He kept the books, dealt with banks, and made sure all the bills were paid. Jake oversaw their marketing, and for the first time, this year they were sending him on a music festival road trip in a vintage RV they'd decked out and affectionately named The Stag Wagon. They hoped it would help get the word out about their product in other regions.

Dean's job was to make the product. Sure, they all loved the spirits and brainstormed together, but he was the one overseeing production day in and day out. The one who knew how to tell when the mash had cooked long enough, properly use the distiller, and sniff out the heads from the tails. TJ was a great helper, but Dean knew that someone else needed to be trained to do what he did. For some reason, he just wasn't making that happen, although his body was urging him to cut it some slack.

"I do want to hire someone. I know it's necessary. I just keep thinking I'll know when I find the right person. Plus, I'm not sure this chaotic time is the right time to introduce someone into the fold."

"We've been in controlled chaos since we started, so that's not an excuse. You're stalling. And you're never going to find that right person if you don't put some feelers out."

"Yeah, maybe." Dean inhaled deeply, the scent of fresh flowers filling his nose. He looked around the room and took in the scene. Gleaming wood floors ran the length of the entire second floor, and at least twenty circular tables dotted the perimeter. Hanging above the beautiful room was a massive and intricate chandelier made of deer antlers. They'd paid nearly three thousand dollars for the handmade piece from a guy in Tennessee they'd found online. There was a tiny replica downstairs that had cost a third of that, and they'd both been worth every penny.

The left side of the space housed a large stone fireplace that was bracketed by rows of floor-to-ceiling windows that overlooked the town square. This room—the second floor of their turn-of-the-twentieth-century building—was rustically beautiful and elegant. As soon as they'd purchased the space and seen the expansive upstairs, they'd known it could be used for something. When someone suggested renting it out as an event venue, they'd figured it would be a good way to bring in additional revenue for the business, especially since their premier product would take five years to age in oak barrels before it could turn a profit. None of them had anticipated it being so popular that brides booked them two years in advance. They'd continued to make vodka and white whiskey, neither of which required the aging process, and with those products in addition to the wedding events, they'd done quite well for themselves.

Dean had been hesitant at first about promoting themselves as a true wedding venue, but for all his concerns, it was no doubt a large reason they were still in business. For one, the weddings brought in revenue that made it possible for the company to be highly profitable while ensuring their core product was the best it could be. Plenty of start-up distilleries had gone under before their highest-quality offerings completed the aging process. Plus, they served their unaged liquor at the wedding receptions, meaning every weekend they earned new fans. It really was a perfectly symbiotic marketing scheme.

On top of that, even Dean could admit that the Stag offered a beautiful location for a wedding reception. He was grateful to be able to give that gift—a lovely wedding—to his little sister. If only the planning of it didn't terrify him. Of course his little sister had offered her own suggestion, one that made him very uncomfortable.

"Alexis thought I should ask Amy to help me plan her wedding."

TJ froze and met Dean's eyes. He set a bottle down on the bar with a little too much force. "Tell me you're not considering that."

"Well, I hadn't been, but now without Tara, maybe I should."

"Ah, man. I think that's bad news, because she *would*

do it, you know," TJ said, shaking his head. "Anything to be with you. I've seen it with my own eyes. You give that woman an inch and she'd climb you like a tree."

"I'm not so sure." Although they both knew his words were false. "She left me, remember?"

"Oh no. Don't give me that nonsense. You've said yourself she's been trying to get you back for years. Woman found out the grass on the other side is only greener because it's full of dogshit."

Dean couldn't help laughing at that as he and TJ walked around to the front of the bar.

"Alex and Amy are still close."

"I get that, I do. So why didn't she just ask Amy to plan the wedding?"

Good question. "Probably because Amy's a little controlling. I'm sure she also didn't want me to be upset."

While Alexis didn't know all the details of Dean's divorce, she knew it hadn't ended well. There'd been a lot of fighting and bitterness at the end.

"I suppose you're paying for this wedding?" TJ asked.

Dean sighed, moving a tray of pint glasses. "Alex and Nate have about seven thousand, and his parents are contributing here and there. I'll cover whatever else needs to be done."

"You're a good brother," TJ said, and he meant it— Dean could see that in his expression.

"Thanks, but you would have done the same."

"Maybe. But I'm the youngest, remember, so I would have been the one hoping that one of my siblings would have stepped up. They're both selfish as hell so thank God I never had to put their love for me to the test."

"They love you," Dean said, but only because it seemed like the right thing to say. TJ came from an odd family. Not that Dean had much room to talk, but TJ's family was wealthy, cold, and always seemed to compete with one another. Something Dean could not relate to at all.

TJ grunted and moved some stacks of shot glasses around beneath the bar. It was still funny to Dean that he ran this business with two other guys so unlike himself. They'd met at the brewery he used to work at. The two younger guys—who had been buddies in high school—had come for a tour, which Dean had guided.

Afterward they'd sat around the bar tasting blond ales and unfiltered wheats, while discussing their shared true love of bourbon and whiskey. When Dean informed them that he knew how to make spirits, had actually built a distiller once with his grandfather, Jake had joked that he should quit the brewery and they should all open their own business. An odd silence had followed; then they'd begun to throw out ideas. One thing led to another, information was exchanged, and nearly seven years later, here they were, that crazy idea now a successful business.

"Your budget will go fast when you're planning a wedding," TJ said, pulling Dean's attention back.

"I know. I thought of that."

"Obviously she gets the Stag for free, lucky for her because we aren't cheap. Also bar drinks at cost, but everything else is going to be expensive. Matter of fact, these caterers here right now?" TJ nodded to the uniform-clad servers shuffling from table to table setting up water glasses. "Forty dollars a head."

"Are you kidding me?" Dean muttered. "Well, I'm just going to have to do some research. Go through Tara's desk and hope she has resources."

"She does. And I'll do what I can for you, but with the other weddings, and the uncasking party to think about . . . it's gonna be tough. *Helping* a bride plan a wedding is one thing. *She* makes the decisions based on what she likes.

She keeps track of a lot of things on her own. What you're doing changes the game. You're going to have to think like a bride."

Dean glared at his friend, who was trying not to laugh.

"One suggestion I can make without question is that you should ask Charlotte Linley to be the photographer. She's good and she likes us. Might be willing to work something out for you on such short notice if she has the date you need open."

"Good idea." Dean's insides warmed at the thought of Charlotte. He liked *her*, that was for sure, and although he wasn't the most confident guy, he knew she liked him. The thing he couldn't figure out was why. He was much older than she was, part of the reason he'd never taken things further in the past three years. God, he'd wanted to. How many times had she found him at the end of the evening just to say good-bye? It was always so tempting to ask her to stay or invite her to come back when the building was empty. He never had because Dean was a realist, and reality told him Charlotte was not for him.

In addition, hooking up with a vendor could be bad for business. Actually, sleeping with women you worked with in any capacity was never a good idea. Even if you went into it with an understanding, things were always awkward afterward.

"Sorry I'm late, bossholes," a snarky female voice said behind Dean and TJ.

Speaking of awkward.

Jen was a cool girl, but once upon a time they had taken things a little too far and had both regretted it. Once and once only. Dean had been lonely, and she'd been . . . available. All it had taken was a few shots after work. It was something neither of them ever spoke about, and Dean hoped it would always stay that way. Especially considering he was pretty damn sure TJ was infatuated with her. His friend would never admit it, but Dean knew him well enough to know the guy had a hard-on for her. But he was sure Jen was completely oblivious to that fact. Or maybe she just didn't feel the same way.

"Your mom this time?" TJ asked, concern showing on his face. Jen's mother, Diane, had cancer and was currently going through chemo and having a rough time of it. "She doing okay?"

"Oh, my mom's great today." Jen shoved her purse under the bar and gave them a naughty grin. Today her nearly black hair was in a high ponytail and her top was a little on the tight side. "I'm just late because I was lucky enough to score some afternoon delight."

Dean's eyes immediately cut to TJ, who looked stricken. *Damn.* Poor guy. Jen was a little on the wild side. He figured it was partly her way of dealing with her mother's health problems. Regardless, Dean knew it drove his buddy crazy. Jen laughed at the look on TJ's face.

"News to TJ: Women can like casual sex, too, you know," Jen prodded.

"Thank you for assuming I know nothing about women. I'm outta here," TJ said, his eyes darkening. "You guys have fun tonight."

They watched him walk through the giant room, hands shoved into his pockets as he dodged tables and scurrying catering staff on his way toward the back stairs.

"You should tone it down with the sexcapade talk," Dean said.

"Oh please. Not my fault if TJ's a prude." Jen waved a hand in the air and then began to stack glasses, prepping for the night to come. What was left of the job anyway. "Sorry if I find it amusing to make him uncomfortable."

Her nonchalance pissed Dean off. He also didn't really

buy it. "He's not a prude. And it's not funny. Or appropriate at work, so cut it out."

Jen looked up, surprised at Dean's tone. And that look
on her face . . . *that* was why you never slept with your
co-workers. Especially ones who worked *for* you. When
you had to truly act on the role of authority, things got
weird. Then he recalled her statement from the other night
in front of Charlotte.

"And speaking of inappropriate, what did you mean the
other night when you called me the most inappropriate
person here? That was such bullshit."

Jen just stared at him for a moment, a look of full-on
female angst and annoyance. Men usually did everything
in their power to avoid that look from a woman. He held
his ground, knowing that he was in the right. "What is
your problem these days?" she said at last. "I find it funny
that you have no idea how inappropriate you are, Mister
Undresses the Photographer with His Eyes."

"Seriously, Jen?" Okay, so much for holding his ground.
And was he really that obvious around Charlotte?

"Whatever." She put up a hand, her fingernails painted
black. "I'll tone it down. I was just trying to lighten things
up around here. TJ's so uptight all the time. Did you know
freshman year of high school he wore a belt every day?
Who does that?"

Okay, he had to admit the belt thing was a little out
there, but Dean was tempted to point out that she'd obviously noticed TJ every single day. He didn't, knowing she
wouldn't appreciate it. Dean wanted to just yell out the fact
that the guy was half in love with her, but that wasn't his
place, and talk about inappropriate. "He is not uptight. He
just takes this business very seriously and he works his ass
off. And I'll be honest, coming in thirty minutes late and
blaming it on a nooner is not cool, Jen. Not cool at all."

"Fine! I get it, okay? Consider me reprimanded. But I'll remember this moment the next time you pretend to give a shit about what's going on behind this bar just so you can stalk poor Charlotte from the shadows like the Phantom." Jen raised her eyebrows, daring him to argue with her.

Dean glared at her. "The Phantom?"

She gave a long-suffering sigh. "Of the Opera? Good gracious, you need some culture in your life."

He should have known. Jen was always singing show tunes, and he recalled TJ mentioning she'd been really into theater in high school. Made Dean wonder how long his friend had been harboring his crush. Right now, he could only focus on the fact that his lusting after Charlotte was way more obvious than he ever imagined. He'd have to be more aware of that.

"Who are tonight's vendors?" Jen asked, then quietly started humming to herself.

Dean welcomed the subject change and glanced down at the clipboard on the bar. "Delicious 2 Go is doing dinner."

"Meh," Jen said, wiping down the stainless sink. "Last time they did a pasta bar and I wasn't a fan."

"Divine Desserts made the cake," Dean said.

"Hm, haven't heard of them, but I doubt they top Jill's. Did you taste last week's? It was chocolate with a chocolate ganache filling."

"Didn't try it, but it looked good."

"Did you know she built a special kitchen on the back-side of her house just for cakes? Has been making them for forty years."

"Huh, I didn't know that." Dean flipped to another page on his clipboard and made a star next to Jill's name on his list. That was two recommendations for her.

He let his eyes wander back down the list of vendors

tonight's bride had chosen, and Christ, there were probably twenty companies named. Was that really how many people it took to make a wedding day happen? Were they really *all* necessary?

"DJ or band?" Jen asked.

"Uhhh, looks like a friend of the groom is doing it."

"Oh gosh. That should be interesting. The voice of the evening's entertainment is not where you want to cut corners. Don't people realize a good band or DJ can make or break the mood?"

Dean raised an eyebrow and made a quick note. *Get a good DJ.* He needed to start a master list of notes obviously. Suddenly the task seemed so daunting. How could he have agreed to such a thing? And yet . . . how could he not have? This was for Alexis.

"Who's the photographer?" Jen asked. He didn't miss the chiding in her tone.

"Charlotte," Dean said, feigning indifference. He wasn't in the mood to give in to Jen's teasing.

"Lucky you," she crooned. "I should have known that's why you're here two weeks in a row. Try to keep your creeping to a minimum. I hope she has some new sexy man photos for me."

And just like that Dean's mood plummeted. He knew his jealousy in regard to Charlotte was ridiculous and ill founded. He couldn't help it. She was gorgeous, with big trusting eyes and shiny blond hair. Guys constantly flirted with her while she worked. He watched it every time she shot here. Last week it had been the best man and it had taken everything in Dean not to confront the punk. Eventually he'd had to leave the room because he couldn't stand it any longer.

The half-naked-man photo shoots had been the ultimate kicker. Several times over the past week the photo of that

buff young asshole had come to Dean's mind and pissed
him off. How often did she photograph men like that?
Sounded like it happened with frequency. Did she ever
hook up with them? She didn't seem like the type, but
damn, if he was forced to stare at a nearly naked woman
giving him bedroom eyes for any extended period of time
it would affect him.

And jealousy hadn't been the only thing that had been
bothering him. Her reaction to the idea of shooting him
had been quite a blow to his already fragile ego. *Sorry,
Dean. I know this isn't really your style.* What the hell had
she meant by that? It wasn't his style because he was old?
Or because he couldn't pull off hot even if he tried? He
took good care of himself, hit the gym with regularity,
and tried to eat healthy. Not that he wanted to try. But
spending alone time with Charlotte . . . that didn't sound
bad at all.

"Did you know Charlotte told me she shoots about
thirty weddings a year?" Jen interrupted his thoughts. "I
can't even imagine all of the insane stuff she witnesses.
She's like the master of great wedding stories."

"Huh, I bet." Charlotte would be a good reference for
wedding info. He remembered last week, how much she'd
known about every vendor. Maybe he could talk with her.
It would be no hardship to spend a little time with Charlotte in order to seek her advice. He would just have to
keep things professional.

Dean glanced at Jen as she continued to ready the bar
for the cocktail hour, which would begin in about . . .
twenty minutes, he realized with a quick gaze at his watch.
The creak of the metal elevator caught his attention and
he turned to see Lauren, Charlotte's second shooter, step
out of the lift holding a tripod and a giant black bag.
That meant guests would arrive anytime. Lauren waved

hello, and he waved back, but she was not the photographer he was anticipating. Just knowing Charlotte would be here soon had him thinking thoughts he'd be better off avoiding.

She was a colleague and a friend. No more. She was also too young for him. Yep, he'd just keep pushing his thoughts of anything happening between them way to the back of his mind.

Four

The DJ at this wedding had not gotten the memo that playing "Single Ladies" for the bouquet toss was the ultimate cliché and so overdone. Charlotte met Lauren's eyes across the dance floor. Her friend wrinkled her nose just slightly enough that no one but Charlotte would catch it. She smiled in return, giving her agreement to Lauren's feelings. Shooting together for many years, they'd acquired their own sort of facial sign language in order to communicate across the room during loud receptions and silent church sanctuaries alike. It was wedding photographer 101 that you try to never draw attention to yourself.

Except of course when your crush was in the room. Then you definitely wanted to be noticed. But as the bride's friend ran to retrieve the toss bouquet, Charlotte quietly watched Dean speak with one of the wedding guests. A woman. A rather attractive woman who looked to be somewhere in her mid-to-late forties. She'd almost bet money Dean wasn't the type to fraternize with guests, but one couldn't deny that receptions made hookups ripe for the picking. It was Charlotte's experience that attending weddings sometimes had the power to make the single guests behave in interesting ways. Almost out of panic and desperation. She'd witnessed hookups a million times.

The lady in question wore a tight black dress, her hair pulled off her neck and pinned in a loose chignon. Charlotte's stomach tied in knots as she watched the woman laugh and then touch Dean's arm. As they often were, his hands were in his pockets, his entire hot body evoking a look of ease and confidence. He hadn't taken his eyes off the woman's face. Until he did, and he looked straight at Charlotte, as if he'd known exactly where she was in the room the whole time.

Based on his expression, he didn't seem surprised to find her watching him, and he winked at her before giving the guest his attention once again. It was almost imperceptible, like an eye twitch—or would be to anyone else. But to Charlotte, who was fluent in subtle facial expressions, it was unmistakable.

Biting her bottom lip, and trying not to overanalyze what the wink had meant, Charlotte turned back to the bride who now had her bouquet in hand, ready to toss to her only mildly eager single maidens. Silly girls. They should run as far as they could from the offending bunch of flowers.

Charlotte glanced over at Lauren to make sure she was ready with the flash, only to catch Lauren giving her a slight eyebrow raise and a small head tilt toward the door.

Damn, Lauren was also fluent and had obviously witnessed the exchange between Charlotte and Dean. Oh well, they'd discuss it later. Right now she had a job to do.

Lifting her camera to her eye she focused on the bride and shot a few of her with the flowers held over her head, ready to aim and fire.

"One, two, three, go!" Charlotte called. The bouquet shot into the air as the front bridesmaid soared into a jump that would make a basketball star envious. All the while Charlotte's shutter rapidly took frame after frame. As the bridesmaid landed, stems in hand, someone else's arm flung into her face, effectively startling her and sending the flowers to the floor. A third woman—somewhat older—surprised all the bystanders by quickly swiping it off the floor.

Charlotte laughed as she took a shot with the bride and the gloating bouquet winner, and then immediately got back into position as the DJ started up "Another One Bites the Dust" for the garter removal. She inwardly groaned. This guy needed some new material.

When the groom was done sticking his head under the bride's skirt and making a spectacle of himself, he lined up, ready to send the little scrap of lace and elastic into the—somewhat small—mass of young men.

"You ever notice how the guys always look as if they're participating under duress?" a deep familiar voice said close to Charlotte's ear. Goose bumps rose on her neck and arms.

She grinned but didn't lower the camera from her eye. The music and conversation in the room were loud enough that she knew they wouldn't be heard. "Can't say that I blame them."

The words had come out without any thought and Charlotte really wished she could see Dean's reaction to them, but the groom released the garter right at that moment. The male recipients were nowhere as enthusiastic as the ladies had been, but one guy did reach out and snag it, almost as a reflexive action.

Yep, the shocked look on his face said that's exactly what it had been, and he glanced around like he wanted someone to throw it at.

Charlotte laughed and looked at Dean. "He looks like he's wishing he'd sat this one out right about now."

"Yes he does." Dean crossed his arms and smirked as Charlotte stepped forward to set up the customary shot of the groom and the reluctant garter catcher.

She was happy to find that Dean was still waiting for her on the edge of the dance floor when she was finished.

"I've missed talking to you tonight," she said.

One corner of his lips quirked up. "You have?" His tone was all teasing, but she could have sworn there was a hint of uncertainty. Surely he knew she was into him.

"Of course. I would assume it was because you were busy, but you had time to talk with black dress lady for a long time."

"Charlotte," he whispered, shaking his head. One of his go-to body movements when they spoke. He huffed out an embarrassed laugh. "What am I gonna do with you?"

"Well, you can start by not making me so jealous."

His eyes flicked to hers, his lips parting. She could tell he wanted to respond, that her words had taken him by surprise. She continued to watch him as the music filled in the silence between them. It was hard to believe she'd let the teasing between them just go where it had, but she didn't really regret it. She liked this man, and she'd done everything she could to tell him that except physically coming on to him. Was that what she needed to do? Finally, he appeared to mentally shake off her comment, his lips pursing as he inhaled a deep breath. *Damn.*

"How much longer are you here?" he asked.

She pulled out her phone and grimaced at the time. "Over an hour."

He nodded. "Can you spare me a minute? I wanted to talk to you about something."

Oh God. He was going to finally make a move. She could feel it. Her brazen comment about jealousy had worked.

Or maybe he was going to finally let her down easy. *Shit*.

She swallowed. "Of course. I'd love that."

Following him toward the bar, Charlotte caught Lauren's attention and sent her an I'll-be-right-back look. Lauren nodded but Charlotte could see the curiosity written all over her friend's face.

Dean stepped behind the bar, grabbed a pint glass, and proceeded to fill it with ice, lemon-lime soda, and then the tiniest splash of grenadine. Her favorite, and she couldn't help melting inside that he always remembered. She couldn't decide if it was a good sign or not. He slid it across the bar to her and then angled his head toward the little break room. Suddenly panicked, Charlotte dug in the bottom of her bag for a piece of gum and stuffed it into her mouth.

Dean stepped into the room and held the door open for Charlotte. She followed and then turned to face him, her heart pounding in her chest.

But instead of walking toward her, he headed for the sofa. "Have a seat."

"Oh, okay." She did just that, and when she sat down, he took the sofa across from her.

Ouch. Definitely *not* a good sign. Was he . . . *mad* at her? First she'd embarrassed him with the sexy photos, and then she'd just now crossed the line with the jealousy comment. Oh shit. He was totally going to confront her about it.

"So, first I should apologize for what I said out there. That was so completely inappropriate and I should have known better," she blurted.

Dean froze, his eyes meeting hers. "What are you talking about?"

"When I said you should stop making me jealous. I was out of line and I—"

Dean began to chuckle. "Did you think that's what I brought you in here to say?"

Charlotte exhaled, relief washing over her. "Yes. I did."

He grinned. "Charlotte, I'm going to be the one to cross the line here when I say . . . my . . . inappropriate conversations with you are my favorite thing about working weddings here."

"They are?" she asked with a smile.

"They are. In fact, I probably like them a little too much."

Okay. That wasn't great. So, while it was a relief he hadn't brought her to this room to confront her, it also sucked he hadn't brought her here to make out. "Then what did you need to talk to me about?"

He reached up and scratched at the back of his neck before leaning his elbows on his knees. "It's actually something I need to ask you."

A wedding party of butterflies came to life in her stomach. "Oh? Okay, shoot."

"You might recall last weekend I mentioned my sister was engaged."

Charlotte's happiness deflated a bit. If all he needed was to hire her for photos, such a production hadn't really been necessary. It was what she did for a living, for goodness' sake. "Of course. So do you need a photographer?"

"Well, yes. But I need more than that."

"Oh? Well, I'm afraid my skills beyond that are incredibly limited. Unless you want me to enter a wedding cake-eating contest. I could probably help you there."

Dean chuckled and she preened under his genuinely appreciative gaze. She loved making him laugh.

"Well, there is a possibility that eating cake would be required. You see, my sister's re-enlisted and will be going to Italy after her two-week leave in July."

"Oh, I'm sorry, I know you were eager to have her home. But Italy, wow. That's exciting."

"Yes, it is. At least they're excited. Anyway, she still wants to get married when she and Nate are home. And . . . well . . . she's asked me to plan her wedding so she can basically just show up and tie the knot."

Charlotte's eyes went wide. She knew how much work went into planning a wedding. "*You?* Will your mother not do it?"

"She would have, but my mother and Alex's father passed away several years ago."

"Oh, I'm so sorry, Dean. I didn't know."

"Thanks, but like I said, it was years ago. A small-plane accident."

"That's awful." She didn't know what to say, but felt like she should acknowledge this tragedy. "Even if it was a long time ago, some parts of you never heal completely." She gave him a small smile as he studied her intently. Would he ask her who she'd lost? Would she be honest if he did? The thought that she might want to share scared her a bit because she'd never shared it with anyone. Not friends, not even her own mother.

"That is true, yes, but I still have my dad. Alex . . . she lost everyone."

"She lost her parents, but she obviously still has you. You're pretty great."

He gave her a sad smile, which Charlotte reciprocated. She desperately wanted to move to his sofa, put a hand on his shoulder, wrap her arm around him. But she stayed put. She'd wanted to come in here and kiss him, but in a small way she was more grateful for this moment of intimacy. It suddenly occurred to her that she had a very surface relationship with the man she'd crushed on for so long.

"So I guess you *agreed* to plan her wedding then?"

Charlotte asked, sitting up straight, trying to ease them out of the deepness they'd found themselves in. Because while *she* was appreciating their newfound connection, she couldn't tell if he was.

"I did. Alex is much younger than I am. I practically raised her after the accident, so . . . you were right when you said she has me. But Nate's family is in Georgia. So basically . . . I need help."

He stared right at her, and there was a certain pleading in his eyes that she couldn't look away from. That was when she caught on. "You're asking *me* to help you plan your sister's wedding?"

An almost pained expression crossed his face, and he cursed under his breath. "Hearing it out loud, I realize what a stupid thing that is to ask of you. I just thought . . . I don't know. I enjoy your company and I just need a woman's perspective, I guess."

Charlotte's lips twitched. He was so adorably disconcerted right now. She'd never seen him this way. "I *am* a woman," she teased, happy when he smiled and appeared to relax.

"*Yes* . . . you definitely are." The warmth of his words, and the way his eyes drank her in, made her inner butterflies spring back to life.

"And I do know quite a bit about weddings." She left off *but I hate them* at the end of that sentence. Not necessarily a selling point under the circumstances, because although she thought marriage was overrated, the opportunity of working alongside Dean was too great to pass up.

"That's what I was thinking, too." He smiled, his voice turning playful. "Your expertise would be very appreciated."

"Hmmm," she said. In her heart, she already knew she

was going to say yes. This was *Dean*. But her one concern was her lack of time to devote to such a project. She was already stretched thin between weddings, countless hours of editing, and of course trying to promote her other shoots . . .

And that was when the most brilliant idea popped into her head. It was almost too perfect. If she could convince him of the same it would be anyway. Spending a few months overworked and exhausted would be worth it.

"So, I just thought it over," she said with a head tilt.

"Are you sure? You can let me know—"

"I'll help you plan your sister's wedding, but you have to do something for me."

He sat up, his eyebrows raised in surprise. "Of course. Anything."

"Anything? Even if it might make you uncomfortable?" She smiled and lifted an eyebrow. "And required you to take your shirt off?"

The shocked look of understanding on his face made her laugh. "Did it just come to you?"

"I hope I'm wrong, Charlotte." His voice was wary.

"Oh, come on, Dean. Unfortunately, I haven't seen you shirtless, but I have a feeling that Jen was right, you would be good at it."

"Oh shit." His large manly hand scrubbed down the length of his face and then lingered on his chin for a long moment. Finally, his eyes homed back in on hers. "You're serious about this."

"I've never been more serious in my life." Or more excited, she realized. Her heart pounded and her mind began processing all of the possibilities. *Please say yes.*

He quickly stood up and walked slowly toward the far end of the room. Then back. He sighed and eyed her again, his hands settling on his perfect hips. He was truly contemplating doing this for her. Which meant his sister's happiness must really be important to him. All the better for Charlotte. And some lucky book cover, of course.

"You promise there's no nudity."

"Only if you want to," she said, laughing when his eyes bugged out. "I'm kidding, I'm kidding. No, no nudity. Promise."

"So you've *never* taken photos of a guy naked?" The tone of his question implied that the answer was important to him. She wondered why.

"No. Never."

His shoulders sagged a bit. He nodded. "Okay. I'll do it."

Charlotte gasped and stood up also. "Seriously?"

She was almost embarrassed about her shrill reaction but he seemed to enjoy her enthusiasm, an embarrassed smile showing on his face. The truth was she probably would have helped him no matter what. Saying no to a request from Dean would have been almost impossible for her, but this was hitting the jackpot.

"You do know you'll probably be regretting this once it happens," he said.

"Not a chance, pal. I'm ready to compare your real naked torso to the one in my fantasies."

A low groan emitted from his chest, and he smiled down at the floor. "You tease me too damn much, Charlotte."

If he only knew all the ways she wanted to tease him. "You want me to stop?"

His eyes met hers and it appeared he was actually considering his answer, but he finally replied, "Absolutely not."

Five

Tuesday morning Charlotte parallel-parked alongside the downtown square and walked across the small section of park green to the Stag. It was a beautiful early-May morning, warm enough to finally show some skin so she'd taken advantage, choosing her favorite chambray shirtdress and yellow crocheted ballet flats. She'd decided to wear her hair down after it occurred to her this morning that Dean had probably never seen it that way. For weddings she preferred it off her face so she usually styled it in a ponytail or bun.

It was still bizarre to think about what she was doing coming here so early. She was going to plan a wedding with Dean Troyer.

The past three days she'd worked the idea over and over in her head and it surprised her—the hater of weddings—how much she'd enjoyed coming up with ideas, imagining color palettes and reception décor. It was probably because she'd seen so many weddings, and it was nice to put those ideas into practice. She was a creative and motivated person, so it made sense that the idea of implementing her skills was what had her excited.

She waved to an oncoming car that gave her the

right-of-way and crossed the street. As she made her way up to the Stag building, she glanced up to the symbol etched in stone above her head. The Freemason emblem. It always seemed rather fitting that a former Masonic lodge building was now occupied by three strapping men.

Charlotte stepped inside and was instantly greeted by the scent of baking bread. She knew that meant it must be vodka day, which was made out of 100 percent wheat at the Stag.

Surprised to find the front desk empty on a weekday morning, Charlotte walked over anyway to wait for a moment. She quickly spotted a note on the counter with her name.

Charlotte—Text me when you get here. Dean

His phone number followed so Charlotte did as he instructed and pulled out her phone to shoot off a message stating that she was waiting in the lobby.

She lifted her heavy bag onto a small sofa and stared out the window while she waited for him. Looking around, she considered that she'd never been to the building this early. The sunlight filtered into the windows so beautifully. It would be a wonderful place to shoot an engagement session this time of day.

The thought made her think of her upcoming shoot with Dean. She was so looking forward to it and couldn't decide which concept she should use him for. So many great choices came to mind. Football player? Firemen? Fighter? Good Lord, the thought of any one of those scenarios sounded insanely hot, and she didn't want to waste this opportunity.

"Hey you," a sexy familiar voice said behind her a moment later.

Charlotte turned, unable to conceal the easy smile that spread across her face. Goodness, he was a handsome man.

Today he was in jeans, this time with a gray polo-style shirt.

"Sorry, I was in the back building. You look amazing today," he said quietly. It was obvious he hadn't wanted anyone to hear, although as far as Charlotte could tell they were alone.

"Thank you." Charlotte tucked a piece of her hair behind her ear. "You're just used to seeing me on wedding days when I look ragged."

"Maybe, but you always manage to make ragged look beautiful."

"Well, thank you."

He gave her a wink. "Follow me."

She leaned down to grab the strap of her bag just as a large hand slid against hers. "Let me get this. Looks heavy." He lifted with a mock grunt. "It is heavy. What the hell do you have in here?"

She followed him through the first floor to the offices on the left side of the building. "I went ahead and picked us up some bridal magazines. I also had a couple of books and some pamphlets that were lying around my office."

Dean led them into a small conference-style room. A table for eight people sat in the middle. The room was flooded with warm light from the windows that ran along the top of the left wall.

"Does Tara have the day off?" Charlotte inquired. She enjoyed working with Tara although it was usually over the phone, but she'd been one of Charlotte's brides many years ago, and she was very excited—if not a wee bit envious—of her pregnancy.

Dean set her bag down with a heavy sigh. "I wish. Apparently, she's developed pre . . . uh . . ."

Charlotte's eyes widened. "Preeclampsia?" Dean

nodded and she gasped. It broke her heart every time she heard of any woman having complications with her pregnancy. Hit way too close to home. "Oh no, that's so awful. So she had to take some time off early, I assume."

"Yeah, I'm afraid she won't be back until after her maternity leave this fall. Part of the reason why I bartered for your services."

"We were supposed to do her maternity shoot before too long. I should call and check on her. That is nothing to play around with. A friend of mine ended up in the hospital for the last two months of her pregnancy."

Dean's eyes widened at that. Charlotte knew the guys had a great relationship with Tara and were probably worried.

"Ben will baby her, I'm sure. So will her mother. But in the meantime we are sort of fending for ourselves where the wedding side of our business is concerned. TJ has taken over most of her work, leaving me to deal with the distilling alone . . . and my sister's wedding. As I explained Saturday night."

Charlotte smiled. "I've already said yes, Dean. You don't have to convince me I'm needed. I'm here."

He sighed. "And I'm so grateful, I want you to know that. I still can't believe I'm doing this." He ran a hand through his hair and stared at the bridal magazines Charlotte pulled from her bag and arranged on the table.

"But it's such a nice thing you're doing. Obviously your sister trusts you. So many important and personal decisions to make. Every bride wants her day to be just right. Perfect."

"You're making me even more nervous, Charlotte." His smile did little to hide the panic in his eyes. She needed to reassure him.

"I'm sorry, I mean, she's trusted the right person. You,

her brother. And now *you're* trusting the right person. Me. This will be great."

"Have you ever planned a wedding before?" Dean asked.

Oh shit. This question could be handled one of two ways. She could just be honest. Admit that, yes, she had in fact planned a wedding before. A beautiful affair to which she'd invited 150 people, paid many deposits, and ended up the fool of the century when her fiancé realized she wasn't the one. Or she could just lie.

She met Dean's eyes. His expression was wary and waiting, one eyebrow up, revealing that he wasn't sure why this was a difficult answer for her.

"Um, yes. I have planned a wedding before." She smiled and pulled out a chair. Maybe he'd leave it at that. Guys didn't usually want meaningless conversation, so they rarely probed for more. Charlotte reached into her bag and pulled out the fresh notebook she'd bought yesterday. Every new project required one.

"Whose wedding did you plan?" Dean sat down right next to her, and she could sense his eyes on the side of her face. He'd opened up a bit about himself the other night. If she liked this man, she owed him the same.

She turned and looked him right in the eye. "Mine."

His eyes widened, his gaze darting to her left hand. "You're married?"

Charlotte shook her head. "No. Definitely not, but I . . . almost was." She pulled out the next magazine and slid it across the table in front of him as if to bring his attention back to the task at hand.

"*Almost?*" He scooted closer, obviously not ready to abandon the discussion. "So . . . what happened?"

"It's kind of personal," she said, trying for coy, but fearing it came out bitchier.

She was sure that indeed it had when his head jerked back a little in surprise. "You're right, I apologize. I'm prying. Honestly, I just can't imagine anyone having the chance to marry you and not taking it."

Her cheeks flushed at that. She glanced over at him. "Thank you. But crazy things happen every day. It's not really something I like to talk about."

"I understand. I guess I should 'fess up, too. I was married. Divorced now."

"You were?" That surprised her. "I had no idea. I can't imagine anyone being married to you and letting you go." She countered his previous comment with a little smile.

He chuckled. "Thank you for that, but like you said, crazy things happen. To all of us, apparently."

Damn, now *she* was curious. When was he married? How long? What happened? But she couldn't pry herself when she'd just made it clear that she didn't welcome him doing the same.

"Well then, I guess I was right. We are the right people for the job, since between us we have a little experience with weddings. Surely the two of us losers can give someone else a happily-ever-after."

Dean laughed. "I hope so, and seeing as this is the last one I'll ever be planning, I want to get it right. Alexis deserves a beautiful wedding."

Charlotte swallowed. So *that's* where he stood on relationships. She couldn't really judge him on the marriage part since she felt the same, but although Charlotte had no desire to have a wedding, she did want more than what she had now. Much more. Did he not want that?

She'd often heard other vendors joke that their name, the Stag, was a nod to their status as single men and the fact that they intended to keep it that way. Maybe there was truth to the rumors. It had seemed to make sense for playboy Jake, and even TJ. But Charlotte had always thought Dean was a little more . . . traditional. Maybe she was wrong. Or it was just wishful thinking.

Silly that it made her pause. It wasn't like they were dating. They barely knew each other outside of flirting once or twice a month. But still, she'd liked him for years. How long had she daydreamed that maybe—eventually—he'd make a move and end up being the one?

At the same time, if it was going to happen, wouldn't he have made that move by now?

"Okay then, we should get to it." Charlotte opened her notebook up to the list she'd made the night before, carefully avoiding his gaze. "I went ahead and started making some notes on the basic things we need to accomplish."

Dean was silent, and she finally glanced up at him. He appeared panicked, staring down at her list. Charlotte gave it a second glance. It did fill the entire page from top to bottom. Two columns' worth. She watched as he blew out a breath. There was no way to make this easier on him.

"Now, I'm going to be honest with you. Two and a half months to plan a wedding is kind of insane."

"TJ said the same thing." Dean lifted an eyebrow and gave her a look somewhere between worry and amusement. "Regretting this already?"

"No! Not at all, I'll hang out with you any chance I can get." Charlotte gave him a playful wink, loving the way he smiled and shook his head in response.

"I just want you to be realistic about our options. Our resources will be limited at this point. We won't get top pick . . . or maybe any pick on vendors. We'll probably just have to take what we can get and expect to do some of the work ourselves. But I'm hoping that since both of us have connections, we can use that to our advantage."

"I understand. We'll do the best we can."

Charlotte needed to ask him a few questions. "What's the budget?"

She wrote down his answer but couldn't help grow a little concerned. It was very tight. She hoped Alexis wasn't hoping for a fantasy wedding.

"I know it's not a lot, but I'll do whatever I can to make it happen. Alex understands this, she's not expecting extravagance and it helps that she gets this building for free."

"You're right, that does help a lot. Do you know how many people she's inviting?"

"Less than a hundred. She's sent me her list and Nate's mom is emailing hers this week. Nate's mom is also going to choose the tuxedo and will deal with the rehearsal dinner, which I told her we could have upstairs. It's hard for her to do more because she's out of state, and I think their funds to help are also limited."

"Understandable." Charlotte made a few notes. "Attendants?" Dean looked confused so she clarified. "Bridesmaids, groomsmen?"

"Oh . . . I'm not sure. Probably one each if any."

"What's Alex's favorite color?"

"Green." He didn't hesitate.

"What kind of girl is she? Glamorous? Frilly? Tomboy?"

"God . . . I don't know. I don't think she'd be considered glamorous or frilly. She's . . . feminine, but she's got a tomboy side. She liked makeup and buying clothes when she was a teenager but she also played basketball. I mean she is in the army, so whatever that tells you."

"I understand. I'm just sort of trying to get an idea of what kind of a woman she is."

Dean pulled out his phone and showed Charlotte a couple of photos of his sister. One of her standing outside the Stag, and another of her and her fiancé, Nate, in front of a Christmas tree. She was very pretty and somewhat petite, with a wide engaging smile.

"They're a very attractive couple."

Dean nodded. "They are. Nate's good to her, also. And Alexis is just a really great person. She's had to deal with a lot in her life, which is why I really want this day to be the best it can be."

"Of course you do, and I want to help you give them that. Which was why I brought up the time line earlier."

Charlotte realized she had slid into using her "sales voice," the one she implemented with brides when she was trying to talk them into doing things her way. Always for their own good, of course.

"Have you checked the Stag's bookings for the two weeks they'll be in town?"

He looked panicked. "God, no. Guess I should have thought of that."

"There's a good chance you guys are booked solid, July is busy. So my initial thought is that we should have it on a Friday evening. They're getting more popular, but they're still way less so than the traditional Saturday wedding. Might also save a little money with other vendors."

Obviously taking in everything she'd just said, Dean stared down at her to-do list with a glazed expression. His head slowly began to nod. Then he finally met her eyes. "Okay, let's do that. I trust you. I'm sure one of them is open. I can only recall a handful of Friday weddings happening here."

Charlotte smiled. "Perfect. See, you keep agreeing with me and we'll be golden."

Dean laughed, and she could see some of the tension leave his shoulders. She liked that, knowing she could help him feel better.

"So a Friday it is. You check the schedule and let me

know which one is open and we'll go from there." Charlotte marked a big dark check next to DAY on her list. First decision was simple. Planning another wedding shouldn't be too bad.

A week later, Dean pulled his 4Runner into a beat-up lot and parked in what he considered his best guess at a designated spot, since the stripes had all faded. Gary's Catering was located on the east edge of town, on the back side of what used to be the DMV, and was now an empty building that had seen better days. He wasn't sure what to make of that, but decided to hold his final judgment until he'd at least met the man.

Charlotte had made this appointment and texted Dean to meet her here today, so he went ahead and waited in his car for her to arrive. Unfortunately, Mother Nature chose that exact moment to drop buckets from the sky.

A few moments later her car pulled up beside his, which made them the only two in the lot. Again, he was reserving judgment. Dean got out when she did and together they dashed for the overhang that ran the length of the building. Short of breath from jumping puddles in the crumbling parking lot, Charlotte grinned up at him.

"Well, that sucked," she said on a laugh.

Dean had to force his gaze away from her breasts, which were so clearly defined by her damp top that he didn't even need a good imagination to see how amazing she would look if he just stripped it off her. "It's that time of year."

"Yes, it is." Charlotte twisted her lips a little, the movement drawing attention to how moist and full they were. She was wearing bright-red lipstick, and her eyelids were done up with shades of brown that highlighted the blue of her eyes. The best part was she had her hair down again. Many times he'd imagined what it must look like.

She'd always looked cute with it up, but down, damn, she was a stunner.

"Thanks for meeting me here," she said.

"Don't thank me, you're the one helping."

"Well, I didn't really give you the option of saying no, I realize."

He smiled. "I would never say no to you."

The grin on her face was wicked. "I bet someday I can find a way to make you regret saying that, Mr. Troyer."

He had a feeling she might be right but brushed it off. "Should we go in?" Dean managed to say coherently as he soaked in how gorgeous she looked standing there wet and wide-eyed.

"Yes, let's. This should be fun. Free food and spending someone else's money. It's the perfect outing."

Dean laughed. Something he did with frequency when he was with Charlotte, more than with anyone else. It was partly because she was funny, but also because he just found himself feeling lighter in her presence. Something about the proximity of her took his mind away from all the stressors in his life. The woman clearly had superpowers, although he'd become very good at not allowing himself to even consider what all of them might be.

They stepped into Gary's and right away were greeted by the decadent scent of garlic and lemon. A round, middle-aged fellow came through a door at the back of the small room that housed two little tables, a desk, and a soda machine.

"Charlotte, my dear, I'm so happy to see you." The man walked right up to them with a huge grin.

"Thanks so much for seeing us on such short notice, Gary."

She looked back in his direction. "This is my friend Dean. It's his sister's wedding we're here in regard to."

Gary stuck out a large hand and Dean shook it. "It's nice to meet you, Dean. You're one of the owners of the Stag, yes? I don't think we've had the pleasure of meeting yet. Why don't you two go ahead and come back to the kitchen. It will be easier that way. And we're all friends here."

They followed Gary through a swinging door, and based on the nondescript front room, Dean feared the worst. Thankfully he was instantly disappointed. Impressed even. The kitchen was large, stocked with modern, stainless-steel appliances, and best of all it was immaculately clean. From the ceiling tiles all the way to the linoleum floor. Although the building was decades old, Gary had made the most of the space. There were various stations that appeared to be prep space, two commercial ranges, and at least four ovens. A woman in an apron waved at them as she stirred something in a large pot, and for the first time this morning, Dean felt like they might actually get this food thing taken care of today. What a relief that would be.

"Okay, how about you two have a seat here, and we'll just get right to it."

Charlotte pulled out one of the stools Gary had indicated, laid her purse on the seat next to her, and sat up to the stainless worktable. Dean did the same, and before he could get comfortable, Gary was setting several laminated sheets of paper in front of them.

"So, Gary," Charlotte began. She had already pulled out the same notebook she'd used the other day and flipped it open. "We have a modest but doable budget. I think our overall theme will stay casual, and the guest count is just under a hundred. All of that considered, I do think buffet-style will get us more for our money. What do you think, Dean?"

His mouth dropped open a little. She wanted his opinion? He wasn't sure why, because she seemed to be really good at this. "Uh, sure. Sounds good."

He sat silently and listened as Charlotte and Gary discussed meal options, servers, and venue. Earlier that week he'd messaged Charlotte the final head count of ninety-two people. He was waiting on a friend of Alexis in Chicago to email him a list of the last few addresses so they could get invites out. Where did one get wedding invites, a party store? Target? He had no idea. There were just so many little things to remember and think about.

Thankfully it wasn't long before Gary was setting in front of them a plate on which sat three smallish servings of chicken. One breaded, one in a mushroom sauce; the last appeared to be lemon with capers. Gary slid them each a fork while Charlotte snapped a photo of the dish with her phone. Apparently they were to share the plate. No big deal.

"You first." Dean nodded to Charlotte.

"Don't be silly, we can both try at the same time." She cut off a little bite of the lemon-flavored chicken and lifted it to her mouth. Instead of getting his own bite, Dean just watched in fascination as her lips closed around the fork. She chewed slowly and then her eyes widened, a tiny moan coming from the back of her throat. When she finally swallowed she looked right at Gary.

"Oh my God, that is amazing, Gary."

The big guy grinned. "Thanks, doll."

"Eat." Charlotte tapped the top of Dean's fork with her own and then began to cut a bite of the mushroom chicken. He went for the breaded. It was good. Not amazing. He definitely didn't have the urge to moan about it, although he wouldn't mind if she did it again. Charlotte made her way to the breaded chicken as Dean tried the mushroom. He liked that one a lot.

They both finished chewing about the same time. "That's really good." Dean pointed to the mushroom chicken.

Charlotte nodded and cut another bite of the lemon. "It is, I agree. But this piccata is to die for. Here, taste it." She lifted her fork to Dean's mouth. He stared over the bite of chicken at her, hesitating. She was going to feed him, right here in front of Gary?

She grinned. "Seriously, try it."

Her eyes widened just a fraction as if she'd just realized something and felt foolish. She began to lower the fork. "Oh, unless you don't wan—"

Dean reached up and grabbed her hand that held the utensil, guiding it up to his lips before taking the bite of chicken into his mouth. Their eyes met, and the minute his tongue came in contact with the lemon caper sauce, he understood. It ranked high on the list of most delicious things he'd ever tasted. His thoughts must have shown on his face.

"Right? I told you," Charlotte said, her blue eyes twinkling.

For a moment her smile made him question what she was really asking. *You are right, Charlotte. You feeding me makes everything taste better, although I'd rather have my mouth on you.*

She looked over at Gary. "Definitely the piccata."

The next hour was spent trying vegetables, potatoes, and salads, and discussing their order. When they'd finally made all of their decisions and officially booked Gary for the job, Dean and Charlotte said their good-byes and headed to the front door. One major thing checked off the to-do list.

"Well, there goes fifteen hundred dollars of our budget," Dean said as they stepped outside. The rain had cleared and the sun was trying to break through the clouds.

"I'd say feeding nearly a hundred people for that price is pretty darn good. Especially since he is providing servers, tablecloths, and cleanup." Gary had thrown that in as a favor to both of them. Dean had also taken some of his menus to pass out to brides who consulted at the Stag.

"I'm sure you're right. It just feels crazy to spend this kind of money on one day."

They stepped off the curb and began to walk to their vehicles. The rain had stopped, leaving the air heavy and the ground saturated. "You're not kidding. Weddings are insane. Good thing for us in the biz, right?"

Dean chuckled. "Yeah, I guess so. You must do pretty well shooting weddings."

Charlotte shrugged and then opened the back door of her little hatchback to drop her bag into the backseat. "I can't complain. My average bride spends about four or five thousand with me. Including products, so there is some cost. I also have to pay Lauren, and of course all of the overhead no one ever thinks about when I quote them a price."

Five grand, wow. He knew Charlotte was one of the most sought-after photographers in the area, and he'd seen how amazing her work was, but he never would have guessed she could pull that kind of price. He was impressed, yet at the same time frustrated. There went another huge chunk of the wedding budget. "Speaking of which, I should have said it right up front, but . . . are you willing to shoot this wedding? I was really hoping you would."

Her throaty laugh sent shock waves through his body, and he was still thinking about how entertaining it had been to sit and eat with her for an hour. They'd ended up feeding each other several times, and by the end of the tasting it had felt like the most natural thing in the world to eat off each other's fork. It had him seriously wishing they could just go out for real, enjoy each other without Gary looking on.

"Well, I was sort of planning on it, yeah. I mean since I am planning this thing with you."

Dean stepped a little closer to her. "Good. I'm glad you'll be there all day with me."

Flirting with her like this, now that they were working together outside the Stag, seemed much more dangerous. Somehow this arrangement had taken their relationship to another level. As much as he knew it was a bad idea, he still couldn't seem to help himself, and the fact that she seemed to have no problem teasing and flirting with him made it even harder.

"I'm glad, too. It will be nice to see all of our hard work come to fruition." Her eyes searched his for a long moment.

It *was* going to be hard work, reminding him how much he was asking of her. His brow furrowed. "How much do I owe you, then? To be the photographer."

"I'm not sure. You might be worthy of a discount." She gave him a little wink. "Why don't we not worry about that right now?"

"Well, I am paying you, just so we're clear about that."

"Remember, you're doing me a favor, too."

"Yeah, but that's for this, the planning part."

"True. But maybe we could work something else out." She bit at her bottom lip and then grinned. "I'll let you know what I come up with."

Well, if that didn't get his mind working overtime he wasn't sure what would. He wouldn't mind giving her a few suggestions of his own, which was a bad, bad, idea all around. "Okay. So are we still on for next Thursday?"

She'd mentioned doing his photoshoot the following

week while they'd been in the tasting and he'd agreed quickly, not wanting her to elaborate in front of Gary. Dean figured he might as well get the damn thing over with.

"Yes, we are absolutely on, and I'm really excited."

"Yeah, me too." He wasn't, really. Not because he didn't want to spend more time with her—he definitely did—but he'd never tried to be sexy on purpose. Wasn't sure if he could pull it off despite her belief in him.

"I'll be in touch with you tomorrow and let you know the details. I actually had an author contact me a couple of days ago, and I think you'll be perfect for what she needs."

"So she specifically asked for a middle-aged guy, huh?" He knew his smile was forced but he couldn't really help it. This whole thing had his anxiety on overdrive.

Charlotte sighed. Her eyes drilled right into his. "Dean, I'm not really sure how else to make this clear to you. You are insanely good looking. You have to know I think so by now. Besides, there is no way I would have asked you to do this shoot if I wasn't entirely certain that you would nail it."

Dean swallowed hard, staring right back at her. Yes, he made health and fitness a priority. But he knew plenty of fit, muscular guys who would still have no business slapping their mugs on a book cover. Not only that, but he didn't want to let her down, as a professional . . . or as a woman. Her confidence in him helped, but his confidence in himself was seriously lacking in so many ways. "Okay, I'm going to trust you. But you should know, I lied. I'm not excited. I'm scared shitless."

"What?" she cried. Smiling, she reached out and grabbed his hand. His heart nearly stopped. Had she even realized she'd done it? "Don't forget, this is me, and I'll be there to take care of you."

Yeah, that's one thing he was afraid of. Standing in front of her half naked, pretending to be some sort of hunky sex object. Would she touch him while they worked? Did she touch other guys? He forced the negative thoughts away, they didn't do him any good, and as much as he hated the idea of those things it really was none of his business.

"I'm planning on it," he said, giving her hand a squeeze.

She grinned in return, finally letting go of him. This was the "them" he liked the best. The teasing, flirting, and seemingly innocent innuendo. Was that a bad idea now that they were seeing each other more often? Probably. But he'd just have to force himself to keep things like they'd always been. Just fun. They'd done it for years; surely they could continue. He'd try to remind himself of that when he stripped off half his clothes in front of her.

Six

The following Saturday's wedding was one for the books. The mother of the bride was having a meltdown over a rip in her dress, the groom's stepmom was not so subtly mumbling about how ridiculous the MOB was acting, the ring bearer had started vomiting in the bathroom, and the church lady had already lectured Charlotte three times on where she was and wasn't allowed to stand in the sanctuary. Basically she might as well shoot the whole damn ceremony from the front yard; the photos would be just as good. It was tempting.

Thankfully, the bride, Paige, was taking it all in stride as she and Charlotte finished up a few portraits on a shaded patio on the back of the church. The day was made slightly easier by the fact that Paige was one of those rare women who genuinely wanted everyone around her to be happy. Put her friends and family first. Even the sweetest women could get a little crazy on their wedding day, but Paige had remained a saint, and she also looked achingly beautiful in her designer dress.

"Charlotte, I'm so sorry about all of this. My mom is a little overdramatic."

"There is no need to explain. Weddings have a tendency

to bring out the best in us," she said with a smile. "And besides, this is your day, so no apologizing to me. Remember, I'm just here for the cake."

As Charlotte had hoped, Paige laughed. "I hope everything with the guys is going much easier."

Charlotte gave her a warm smile, knowing that even if the groom was MIA, she would lie through her teeth and then call in a manhunt before she burdened her bride with any more unnecessary stress. Thankfully she could be completely honest. "Lauren's been with them all morning, and she texted me five minutes ago. They've had a blast. Golf, beer, and the Royals on TV. They're on the way here now."

Paige sighed. "Oh good. Hopefully once my mother's dress is mended everything will be fine."

Giving Paige's arm a little squeeze, Charlotte spoke quietly. "Everything will be fine no matter what. Trust me, every wedding has its share of drama." Charlotte left out that this one had more than its fair share, because who was really keeping track? "Someday all of this nonsense will be forgotten, but the moments you spend together—the first time your eyes lock in the church, your first dance, stuffing cake in his mouth—those are the moments that you will remember. And when it's all said and done, the only thing that matters is that you and Will are going to end this day as husband and wife."

Paige grinned, her eyes glassy. "You're right," she said in a high-pitched voice. "You're so right. Thank you."

Charlotte's phone buzzed on her hip. "Oop, I bet that's Lauren. Let's get you inside so Will doesn't have a premature sighting."

Carefully pushing the two cameras around her neck out of the way, Charlotte leaned down to lift the train of Paige's dress so they could shuffle indoors.

She blew out a deep breath, impressed with her impromptu speech on the beauty of a wedding day. Even she, the most jaded and bitter woman, could fake it. It was doable because although she never wanted to marry herself, she still knew some people wanted that and truly valued each other enough to keep their promises. She saw it happen weekend after weekend, but she was certain that not even witnessing a million weddings would heal the trauma of being abandoned at her own.

There was not a chance in hell she would subject herself to that kind of pain, humiliation, and fallout, ever again. Now . . . finding herself a man? A relationship? She *did* want that. But a wedding and marriage? No thank you. Those things weren't necessary to have a family or to be happy.

Once they were inside, Charlotte was pleased to find that the universe seemed to have received her message to Paige, because the mama drama had righted itself. The mothers hugged before the ceremony, a slightly pale ring bearer walked down the aisle and then quickly fell asleep in the front pew, and the service was lovely. What Charlotte and Lauren could see of it anyway, being confined to the back quarter of the sanctuary as they were. After that the early-evening light had led to gorgeous portraits with the bridal party, and now the limo pulled up to the Lone Oak Country Club for the reception.

This wasn't her favorite venue, but it was a nice change of scenery. She and Lauren met in the lobby and rushed to prepare for the bridal party's entrance. Once that was over they headed toward the corner of the room.

"Let's hurry and get some food. I feel like I haven't eaten in days." Lauren slid her gear under the makeshift stage the band was playing on. Charlotte did the same. Contractually, they were fed by the couple. It was industry standard, and it was easiest when the reception had a buffet as this one did. They just slipped into line with a wink and smile, and in no time they were sitting on some chairs in a hallway devouring their dinner.

"We haven't shot here in ages," Charlotte said. Lone Oak was on the outskirts of Kenwood, a nearby town. Nice, but nothing too special. In fact, for as much as people paid to have their weddings here, Charlotte thought it lacked amenities, but who was she to judge? Everything always came up lacking when compared with the Stag.

"I would never want to have my reception here. The dance floor area is so small. And I'm not ever really that impressed with their food." Lauren made a face down at her plate.

Charlotte agreed but knew they'd eat it all no matter what it tasted like, that was for sure.

"How are wedding plans going with Dean?"

"Good. We've already chosen the date and the caterer. We went with Gary's."

"Nice. I get to shoot it with you, right?"

"Of course. I'll email you the date this week."

"I still just cannot believe you two are planning a wedding together."

"I know, it's crazy. At first I thought it was going to be weird making decisions for another woman, but the more I think about it, the more it kind of makes sense. I'm not emotional about it. Or bogged down by a family member's expectations. It's way easier than the last time."

The slip was accidental and Charlotte was grateful that Lauren let it go unnoticed.

"I can see that. Maybe you're onto something." Lauren pointed her fork at Charlotte and lowered her voice. "Ready-made weddings by Charlotte. Just show up and say I do."

Charlotte laughed. "A good idea. But no, not gonna happen." She quieted her voice down to a whisper. "I don't even like weddings. And can you imagine the bridezillas?" She shuddered in mock horror.

"You don't have to like weddings to be good at planning them. I mean . . . you're good at photographing them. Making money is its own motivation."

"Anyway." Charlotte waved a hand, hoping to change the subject. "Things are going well and I'm excited to do the rest. And I mean everything. Cake, flowers, his ring."

"What about her dress?"

"I don't know, and I'm afraid to ask Dean for some reason. But obviously it will have to be done. I mean, you can't really pop into a bridal shop in the desert."

Lauren's eyes went wide. "Can you imagine you and Dean shopping for wedding dresses together? Are you going to try them on for him?"

Charlotte hesitated. She hadn't thought that far ahead. "I don't know. But he'll definitely have to come along because I'm certainly not going to pick her dress on my own. I don't even know her."

"And you know Dean is not going to walk into a bridal shop and do it by himself. Wow, it's like *you guys* are getting married."

Charlotte blanched at that. "It's so not even close to that. This is a business arrangement."

"Yeah, but . . . you like him. And you're planning a wedding together. I think it would be hard not to imagine it."

"Lauren, you know how I feel. I can separate my attraction to him from this process."

"Yes, I do. But I can't help hoping that you might eventually change your mind. You have so many painful emotions wrapped up in that breakup, Charlotte. You know it will never happen that way again."

"Do I? It's not impossible."

Lauren gave her a long look. "Okay, nothing is certain. You're right. But you need to learn to trust yourself. You're not the same person you were then, and if you meet a new guy, he won't be just like John."

Charlotte decided Lauren's last comment didn't warrant a response. They'd had the conversation too many times, and nothing was going to change. Lauren was right, that year was littered with pain, and while Charlotte had recovered in many ways, she also hadn't in others.

One thing she knew: Getting jilted by her fiancé John five years ago had hardened her heart on the matter, and there was no going back.

Taking a bite of her dinner, Charlotte sighed. She'd truly believed he was the one, the great love of her life. Her parents had loved him, too, and she'd always believed his parents had loved her. Everything had seemed perfect.

Back then they'd known they were young, that high school sweethearts weren't always meant to last a lifetime, but Charlotte had believed that they were each other's soul mates. They'd talked openly about how they would defeat the odds. What a crock of shit.

When John had begun to pull away, he blamed her business, which was growing fast and taking all of her weekends. She understood that and vowed to be better, make him a priority.

And then she'd gotten pregnant.

A complete surprise, and yet for a while their problems seemed to be resolved. John had appeared to be happy about the baby, and Charlotte—having always dreamed of being a mother—was beyond thrilled. Of course the timing had been less than ideal, but their surprise and happiness had outweighed all the downsides. Plus, what did it matter, they were getting married.

They'd decided to tell their families they were expecting at the wedding breakfast, the day after the festivities. That way the news didn't distract from the excitement of their big day. And a little part of her didn't want her parents to be disappointed—although she knew they could do math—but still.

Sadly, the choice was made for them when Charlotte suffered a traumatic miscarriage. Sitting in the hospital bleeding, vomiting, and feeling physically and emotionally empty inside, Charlotte had let John convince her not to tell their parents what had happened until after the wedding. He told her it would upset them. For some stupid reason it made sense, even though no one could possibly hurt the way she did those next few days. She still occasionally had nightmares. The kind where she woke up crying, drenched in sweat.

Looking back on that time was painful. John pulled away even more, and Charlotte grieved mostly alone when she wasn't busy keeping up the appearance of a bride looking forward to her wedding day. Secretly she was hoping and praying that marrying John and solidifying their relationship would help them to heal and move on. Make them soul mates again.

Time and reflection had now taught Charlotte she'd been too wrapped up in her own pain to see that he'd stopped loving her long before they'd lost their baby. That the days leading up to the wedding day had been full of signs she should have been paying attention to if she'd been in the right frame of mind.

Not that she blamed herself. Not even a little bit, because the way John handled calling off their wedding—like a cowardly and selfish jerk—had been inexcusable.

And yet, eventually, a blessing.

But the blessing came with a price. Her beliefs on love,

men, and forever-after had been changed that day. She now approached the opposite sex with newfound insight and expectations. A man was never going to be her everything. She could care for him, be attracted to him, but if they grew apart, it wouldn't upend her life. Not like it had with John.

Human beings were fickle creatures. How could anyone expect another person to stay with them forever? If Charlotte ever entered a relationship with a man again, her needs were overall very simple. Because of that fateful day, marriage was off the table for her, but she had also realized how much she wanted to be a mother.

She wanted a child. Or maybe even two.

Surely there was a man out there who was okay with that. For a while she'd hoped that man would be Dean, but as time went by, it was looking like it wasn't meant to be.

Seven

Dean had never jumped on the whole hating-Monday bandwagon. In fact, it happened to be his favorite day of the week, and this particular Monday he was determined not to let the dark sky and constant raining get him down.

It was mash day at the distillery, which meant he spent hours babying a small batch of milled corn and rye cooking in a metal vat of hot water. When it was finished, the mash would go into a fermenter and begin its six-day process before finally ending up in the copper distiller. He loved this part, always had.

Dean had learned the art of distilling grain alcohol from his grandfather who had done it in very small quantities in his barn, using a distiller he'd crafted himself out of an old soup pot and some copper piping. By the age of sixteen, Dean was already taste-testing the "hearts" and helping to transfer the distilled whiskey into small charcoal barrels. He still recalled the first barrel his grandfather had given him to take home and keep. It had sat aging in his parents' garage while Dean waited patiently for his legal birthday, when he and his grandfather planned to uncask it together.

Unfortunately, that day came six months shy of his

twenty-first birthday when his grandfather died of a sudden heart attack. The night of his funeral, Dean had opened the barrel, filled a flask, and gone out to the old man's grave site at dusk. He'd emptied that flask, finally appreciating the smooth caramel taste of his hard work, all the while lying on the grass next to a fresh mound of dirt.

To this day he couldn't start a new batch of mash without thinking of his grandfather. Still couldn't feel the milled grains slide through his fingers without remembering the sight of strong wrinkled hands, or smell the yeasty scent without hearing the old man's deep gravelly voice.

Today those fleeting thoughts brought a smile to his face, but he tried not to linger on the ones that made him sad. Like the fact that his grandfather would have been so damn proud to see his grandson running—and succeeding—at a full-fledged distilling operation.

Ronald Troyer—Grandpa Ron to Dean—had also been a hunter, a total man's man. Hence the name the Stag. Dean had been grateful that neither TJ nor Jake had questioned him on that. They'd liked it, or pretended to. It had also matched the tone of the building they'd found, which with all the brick and exposed wood beams had sort of a masculine, lodge feel to it.

Standing on a tall stepladder, Dean watched the vat fill from the hot-water tank next to it. The water began to get murky as it covered the milled grains, and he turned the agitator on to keep things moving. If the grains set too long and got waterlogged, the machine could clog—which was a major headache.

He checked his clipboard and smiled as he wrote on the little dry-erase board that hung on the big metal tub. *Lockdown Whiskey batch 100*. Hard to believe that was true, but sure enough it was. They'd been in business for five years now, which was about how long it took to age a solid, smooth whiskey or bourbon. They'd gotten started quickly after setting up shop by making their signature Ten Point Vodka, which could be made and sold within months rather than years. Next they'd introduced Forkhorn White Whiskey. White, meaning it wasn't aged, and basically moonshine. A white whiskey was a harder liquor, and not really meant for drinking neat. It was a mixing alcohol, as was their vodka, but they'd sold the hell out of them to both regional and Kansas City bars and liquor stores on their local appeal alone. All the while they'd continued to produce and barrel their Stag Signature Bourbon and Lockdown Whiskey, the first barrels of which would be ready to open in just a few short months.

Dean could not wait.

Once the mash looked like it was cooking along just fine, he headed out the back door to their secondary building. A year into business they'd purchased the old warehouse across the alley and used it to store their barrels. Just walking inside the door sent a rush of pride through him every single time.

He flipped on the somewhat ineffective overhead light and sucked in a breath. It was May, and since they didn't regulate the temperature inside the massive space for the sake of the product, the heat was starting to settle in nice and thick. The barrels reacted to the change in temperature, expanding and tightening throughout the year, causing that great oaky flavor to seep out of the wood and penetrate the liquor even further.

Dean walked down the first row of barrels, a Stag logo burned into each lid. Row after row of Lockdown Whiskey and Stag Signature Bourbon, just waiting to be drunk by some lucky person at some point in the future. Some in a few months; many others, years from now. They'd built a solid customer base on their vodka and white whiskey, and all of those customers' excitement for the new products had put a lot of pressure on Dean. But if there was anything he was certain of, it was his ability to make a good spirit. He had no intention of letting any of them down.

Dean's phone buzzed. Pulling it from his pocket, he saw a text from TJ who must have shown up for work while he was working on the mash. Dean read the text and swore under his breath. He typed a single *Ok* in reply and then shoved the phone back into his pocket with a deep sigh. And today had been so pleasant up until this point. The last thing he needed was a visit from his ex.

He decided dealing with that news could wait for a moment and headed to the back to open the bay door for the shipment of bottles he was expecting anytime this morning. Once the door was open, he checked a couple more things and then headed back through the rows of barrels and toward the door that lead to the alley and the main building. A sluice of light entered the darkened room from up ahead, and a feminine voice sent a chill through his spine as he rounded the final row of barrels.

"Dean? Are you in here?" Amy called out.

"I am, but stay where you are, there's not a lot of light in here." He figured she could see just fine, but he really wanted to keep her out of his sanctum.

"This is very impressive. No need to stop working for me."

Dean walked around the large metal shelving unit and locked eyes with the one person whom he would have been happy to avoid for . . . probably the rest of his life would be just fine. Today her brunette hair had auburn highlights surrounding her temples, and her pretty face was caked in makeup that was a little much for a Monday morning.

"Amy, this is a surprise."

"A good one I hope." She grinned but Dean could only muster up a tight-lipped smile in response because no, it was never a good surprise to see her. Instead it was always jarring and a harsh reminder of his past failures.

"Anyway, I'm here to discuss Alex's wedding."

"Ah, I wasn't aware the two of you had discussed it."

"She emailed me last week. I'm so excited. She asked me to check in on you."

"That was sweet of her, but unnecessary. I'm doing fine with everything." Which was the truth, thanks to Charlotte. And clearly he and Alex were going to have some words next time they spoke because he'd made it clear to her he did not want his ex-wife involved. He knew Amy would be invited to the wedding—no doubt about that, since the two women had maintained their relationship—but he'd hoped Alex would respect his wishes on this matter.

Amy laughed. "Dean, seriously? You don't know the difference between a peony and a petunia, let alone manage a seating chart. Surely you want some help planning Alex's wedding. It might be fun to do it together."

He had several thoughts on that but he didn't dare voice them. Needing to get some air, Dean gestured for the door. "Why don't we discuss this outside where it's cooler?" He held the door as she stepped through and out into the alley.

"You know, I'll just admit it," Amy said behind him as he locked up the building. "I'm a little hurt that you didn't reach out to me. This is our girl, getting married."

Dean wasn't expecting that. He turned to face her, taking in the weak smile on her face. Yes, at one time, they'd considered Alex *their* girl, in a way. She'd been young, grieving, and in need of a lot of love and attention when she'd moved in with Amy and him at thirteen. They'd become a family unit, the three of them, and he still had many fond memories of those times. Holidays, vacations, both of them helping Alex with school projects. But at the same time, he and Amy had been going through their own private hell, their marriage and their dreams of a family slowly eroding. But all of that was in the past, and while he wouldn't discount those good memories, he refused to indulge Amy by pretending that was still their reality.

"I'm sorry. Really I am." Dean hesitated, knowing this was not going to go over well, but there was no other way. "But I honestly didn't want us to work on this together."

"But why?" She looked stricken, just like he knew she would.

Dean sighed. Over the past year or two, Amy had made it very clear that she regretted the way things had ended. Ironic, considering *she'd* ended them. Had she come crawling back in the first year or two after leaving him, he might have taken her back. Forgiven her cheating, lies, and blame. He'd have been insane, but he might have done it. Thankfully, he'd eventually found a new life for himself. Accepted that the two of them hadn't been meant to be. But while he'd forgiven her, he had not forgotten.

"Amy, Alexis is my sister. Not yours."

Her mouth dropped open, her eyes full of hurt. It had been a mean dig. Especially after all Amy had done for Alex. Many wives might have thrown a fit or been put out at the thought of unexpectedly adding a teenager to their lives, but that had been one of the few ways Amy had surprised him.

"I'm sorry. I know you're close to her. It's just . . . I don't think it's a good idea for you and me to work together on the wedding. It would only make things awkward and I want Alex's wedding to be smooth and happy."

The hurt on her face quickly turned to anger. "Wow,

Dean. I know I've messed up in the past, but I wasn't aware your opinion of me was so low."

"Amy . . ."

She cut him off with a raise of her hand. "I know what you're thinking. But you're wrong. I didn't come here to seduce you. In fact, I stated right from the beginning that this was about Alex."

Dean knew when a conversation with her was about to spiral out of control. It wasn't worth it. Clearly Alex wanted Amy involved somehow. Maybe she hadn't wanted to admit to Dean how much just to spare his feelings.

"You're right. I understand you wanting to help, so why don't you tell me what you'd like to do and maybe you can be in charge of that. On your own." Trying to give her the hint that he was very busy today, Dean began to jot a few things on his clipboard.

"Fine. I want to pick out her wedding dress."

Dean's pencil instantly stilled. His head jerked up, eyes wide. How had he forgotten the wedding dress? He knew nothing about choosing a dress, and Amy knew Alex well enough to hopefully know what she would like and look nice in.

"Perfect. I'll leave that up to you then."

She smiled. "Good. What's my budget?"

He thought quickly, blowing out a breath before finally saying, "Three hundred?"

A laugh bubbled up from her chest. Not one of her forced flirty laughs. No, this one was throaty and genuinely amused. "Oh, Dean. That's cute. That might be enough for a veil or jewelry."

Dean frowned. "How much were *you* thinking? The rest of this wedding is on a fairly tight budget so the dress has to be also."

"Even an economical wedding requires a pretty dress.

I'd say at least fifteen hundred, but I can't promise anything. Two thousand and I'm sure I can make it work?"

His eyebrows nearly hit the sky. "Are you kidding me?"

"I wish I was. But no. Besides, this is for Alexis. How can you put a price on her happiness? And since you'll never have your own daughter, this will be the only wedding you'll ever have to pay for."

Dean's jaw locked and his entire body went on alert. It was a low blow. About as low as she could go, and she knew it. Looking away, Dean tried to get his emotions in check.

Yes, he'd failed to give Amy children, but she always seemed to forget that their wedding vows had stated *as long as we both shall live*. Not, *as long as we have a baby*. It was painful enough for a man to be unable to give his woman everything she wanted. But to find out your wife had gone seeking it from another man was just flat-out unbearable.

Dean's nose flared as he inhaled a deep breath. He'd given her a job for the wedding. Now he needed her gone.

"You start looking and let me know what you find. But I'll tell you right now, not a penny over two thousand, and that includes everything. Shoes, jewelry . . ."

"Bustier, panties, garter . . ."

Dean held up a hand. "Enough. I don't want to hear anymore. You deal with it."

Amy just blinked at him, knowing full well she'd pissed him off. Finally she spoke. "Shall I just let you know when I find the dress or would you like to give me a check?"

Dean nearly laughed. "No. I will not be giving you a check. You keep me posted and we'll make arrangements then."

"I'm not a thief, Dean."

He sighed. "I know you're not. I'm sorry I'm being a

dick. I'm just . . ." If he said stressed, it would give her more ammunition to insist she help him. "Never mind."

"Well, I guess I'll go. My car's just around the corner. But . . . if you change your mind, get overwhelmed, call me. We could go to dinner. Chat about the wedding. I could just help give you ideas. Talk it out."

Dean met her hopeful gaze. He'd spent a lot of years angry as hell at this woman, but he also felt sorry for her. There'd been enough pain to go around throughout their marriage. At the same time, there was no way he had the strength to put up with this kind of proximity to her for the next few months. Choosing a dress was one thing. Showing up here regularly was another, and if he didn't nip this in the bud right now, he'd regret it. "I actually have someone helping me, so I'm good. But thanks."

"Oh? Like . . . a wedding planner? I figured on a budget—"

"Not a wedding planner. A friend."

Her lips twisted. "A friend?"

Dean nodded. "She's a photographer who shoots a lot of weddings here at the Stag."

"So, a woman friend."

"Yes. If that's how you want to see it."

Amy sucked in a breath and then let it out on an embarrassed laugh. "Well, my goodness, you might have said that from the beginning."

"Didn't think it was necessary."

Amy stood a little straighter and fidgeted with her hair. "Are you sure she's just a friend?"

He hesitated. But there was only truly one answer. "Yes, I'm sure. But I might add that it's really not any of your damn business."

Her head jerked back at his blunt response and he swore there was a hint of skepticism in her expression. "Okay, fine. But it seems ridiculous to have a woman friend you're not even dating help you with Alex's wedding. I know her. I'm close to her. She trusts me."

"She does, which is why I'm grateful you're buying her dress. But I trust Charlotte to help me with the rest of it."

Amy balked. "*Charlotte*, huh. How old is she, seventy?"

"Amy. Enough." Dean could tell when the woman was on the verge of getting worked up, and he would not allow her to stand in front of him and insult Charlotte. Not for a second.

"Well, I guess I'll just be in touch when I find the perfect dress." She gave him a tight smile and then walked around the building toward the square.

Dean's shoulders sagged and he looked up at the sky. Every time he saw Amy it frustrated and exhausted him. Maybe Mondays weren't so great after all.

Eight

It had continued to storm on and off for the next twenty-four hours, so Charlotte was beyond relieved when Thursday turned out to be lovely. A clear sky, warm air, and she'd located the most perfect—and practically abandoned—road for their photo session.

Good thing her plans had come together, because tonight Dean Troyer was going to be a full-fledged, badass bike-club hero, and she could not wait.

The extra work for this particular shoot would be well worth it, she was certain. She'd located a legit bike club in the next town over through Facebook crowdsourcing, and talked one of the guys into riding his vintage Harley over. In return she would be taking a few shots of the bike alone for him personally and having them printed. No big deal, although she found it ironically funny that biker novels were so popular yet according to Facebook photos the guys in this little midwestern club were about as far from physically sexy as one could get. Ah well, it was all in the fantasy, right?

"Booker," also known as Dr. Bill Hanson, equine veterinarian, was going to meet them at seven o'clock on an old country road on the south side of Maple Springs. Right now Charlotte waited for Dean to arrive at her place. She wasn't sure if he'd actually come in, she'd meet him at the door, or how things would play out, but she'd cleaned up anyway.

She'd curled her hair but at the last moment decided that was silly since she'd be shooting, and so she'd pulled it into a messy bun and thrown on some cutoff jean shorts and one of her favorite halter tops. It did some nice things for her boobs, which she shouldn't be worrying about, but it was Dean after all and she couldn't help but think about their last meeting. She'd fed him with her own fork, for goodness' sake.

Checking over her equipment one more time, Charlotte's heart sped up when her doorbell sounded. She glanced in the mirror by her front door, which was unnecessary since she'd already done that several times, and then opened the front door. Her mouth dropped open.

Holy shit.

She'd texted Dean some basic guidelines for how to look and what to wear. He had done exactly as instructed. A well-trimmed five-o'clock shadow dusted his chiseled jaw, he sported some mirrored aviator sunglasses, and his hair was gelled into a perfectly tousled "undone" look. He should definitely do that more often. His chest was molded by a black T-shirt so perfectly sized she could see the outline of his beautifully formed pecs and indented biceps. The look was rounded out with well-fitted jeans and black boots.

He lifted his hands from his sides and glanced down at himself. "How'd I do?"

Charlotte clapped her hands together and brought them to her mouth to conceal her now ridiculous grin. Or at least try to. She knew it hadn't worked when Dean managed to blush and smile down at the ground.

"You look so hot right now," Charlotte said, dropping her hands and looking him up and down openly one more time. "This is definitely going to work."

"Yeah?"

She nodded, loving the hint of embarrassment in his voice. God he was adorable. "You're perfect. But wait. Did you . . ."

Without her having to ask, he grabbed the hem of his shirt and slowly lifted it up to expose himself from waist to chest, and oh my, with his pecs bare she nearly passed out at the sight of his perfection.

Jen had been completely right. Dean's body was wonderful. He wasn't an overly beefy gym rat, but his stomach muscles were taut and defined, his hips indented, and his chest just the right size.

"You owe me for this one, babe. And you better take advantage and get a million photos because I'm never shaving my chest again." He pointed to a couple of red spots, one very close to his nipple. "I cut myself. *Three* times."

She laughed out loud as Dean lowered his shirt. "You poor thing, I'm sorry. No, actually I'm not. Not sorry at all. The ladies are going to love it. And you wouldn't believe how annoying it is to clone out body hair in edits, so I also love you for it."

Dean scowled but she could tell it was all for show. "Well, let's get this over with. I can only take so much blatant sexism in one day. It makes me uncomfortable."

Charlotte laughed. "I'll meet you at the car, I have to grab all my gear."

He offered to drive them in his SUV so within a few minutes they were pulling up alongside an older guy wearing dirty jeans and a polo-style shirt that said SUPERIOR EQUINE CARE, DR. HANSON. What a rebel.

A pickup was parked on the shoulder of the road behind his Harley and an older woman waved to Charlotte from the driver's seat. She waved back.

"Hi, Bill, thanks so much for meeting us out here."

"No problem at all. I'm honored to have Gertie here used on a book cover. And to get some pretty pictures of her."

"Gertie?" Dean asked.

Bill patted the seat of his bike. "This old girl. Had her for forty years. Driven me all over the country. Even been to Sturgis sixteen times."

"That's so cool," Charlotte said. "I really appreciate this."

Bill lifted a black vest covered with patches out of the saddlebag on the side of his bike and handed it to Charlotte. "Brought this like you asked. Take good care of it. It's special."

"I promise we will." She held it up and turned to the backside. It read BOOKER across the shoulder blades. She'd probably have to Photoshop that out, but that one would be no problem. Otherwise it was perfect. She turned to Dean. "You ready to become a biker?"

She could see the skepticism clouding his expression, but he turned to Dr. Hanson. "Thank you, sir, we'll take good care of your things."

"I appreciate it. And goodness knows you'll look much better in that than I do. Don't let my wife see these photos, she'll never be satisfied by the likes of me again."

Charlotte laughed. "Now, I'm sure that's not true."

"Well, we'll be back in, say . . . an hour?" Bill asked.

"An hour should be just fine."

"I left the key." He glanced at Dean. "You familiar with a machine like this?"

"I've ridden before."

"Okay, good. Well then, I'll just let you get to it."

And with that Mr. Hanson and his old lady—Charlotte had been waiting for him to say that and was disappointed he hadn't—drove away, leaving them alone with an old Harley named Gertie on a deserted country road.

"So, how do we start?" Dean asked. His voice seemed a little off, and she could feel his anxiety from three feet away.

"First of all, don't be nervous."

"That's much easier said than done. I'm just really not sure I will be good at this, so I hope you've shown up with very low expectations."

On the contrary, her expectations were incredibly high and just by looking at him she was certain they'd be met. It really surprised her that Dean had such little confidence. She'd just always assumed the opposite based on the way he carried himself. It was endearing for a super-handsome man to not have a big ego. "You'll be great, I know it. And I'll help you. Remember, I've done this many times."

He scowled at that. "Are you usually on deserted roads with these men? Alone?"

Her eyes met his and she had to keep from rolling them. "Stop. I'm a big girl."

"What does that have to do with anything? And you're not a big girl. You're . . . tiny. And young."

Charlotte's mouth dropped open. "*Young?*"

"I just mean, compared with *me* you're young."

She made a sound of annoyance. But finally, a good opener to ask the million-dollar question. "How old *are* you?"

He hesitated for a long moment, swallowing hard before finally answering. "I'm forty-one."

Okay.

Yes. There was an age difference. He was . . . *over* forty. She'd guessed *maybe* forty, but knowing for certain made it real. Did it matter? Not to her. Not even a little bit. But obviously, he had an issue with it. She wished she knew why. It wasn't like they had something going on between them. And it wasn't as if she were twenty, for goodness' sake. They were both grown adults, but she couldn't help wondering if the age gap was what had held their flirting at bay for the past few years.

"Dean, forty-one is nowhere near old." She fiddled with the vest, draping it across the seat for the time being.

"But it's older than you'd expected. Isn't it?"

How did she answer that one? "No, not at all."

Dean chuckled. "Jesus, don't tell me you thought I was older."

Her eyes jerked up to his. "No! And can we please drop this conversation?"

His lips quirked up. "We can, after you tell me how old you are."

"I'm twenty-nine." She stared up at him and he nodded slowly, taking the information in. His lips pursed a bit. She wished she could see his eyes, read his thoughts, but his glasses remained in place and his expression was impassive. "Is that going to be a problem for us?"

Okay, now his expression changed. She could tell by the furrowing of his brow that his eyes narrowed, and there was a distinct new intensity emanating from his body. "What exactly are you asking, Charlotte?"

Good question. And how embarrassing. They'd flirted for a long time, but that was all it had been. She'd leave the Stag and they wouldn't speak again until the next time she did a wedding there. Sometimes that would be a couple of months. They'd never even exchanged numbers. But now . . . tension hung between them thick enough to cut.

"I don't know, never mind. Let's just start."

He didn't respond so she took that as agreement.

"Can you move the bike to the middle of the road?" she asked. "I'll take this time to get a few of just Gertie, get my settings right."

After she'd taken a few at different angles and was satisfied she had enough to give Dr. Hanson some good images, she had Dean lean against the Harley carefully. He watched her as she instructed him on where to put his hands, how to position his legs. When she stood back and took him in, she smiled.

"You look great."

"I feel ridiculous." His words were toneless, as if he was afraid to make any movement at all.

"Well, don't. You're oozing hotness. Now look right here." Charlotte backed up a little and lifted her camera. She adjusted a couple of settings and then looked through the lens. This was good. Too good. But his face . . . he was nearly scowling at her. Lips tight and jaw severe. Was he really that uncomfortable? Maybe she shouldn't have asked him to do this. She lowered the camera.

"Your expression needs a little work. Broody is good, but it needs to slide into the sultry zone. More sex, less fury. Feel me?"

He muttered something she couldn't quite catch. Then he took a deep breath while he leaned his head to the right and then the left in what appeared to be a neck pop, and then he looked at her once more.

And that was it.

She was a goner. He had the smoldering sexy look down. Immediately Charlotte lifted her camera and captured it before it disappeared. "Oh my goodness. That's amazing, Dean. Don't change a thing."

She moved to the side, switching up her angle, catching

a different ray of light that perfectly reflected off the metal of the bike. For several moments she made minor adjustments to his body, the direction of his gaze, and shot away. She continued to talk him up, knowing from experience that the more positive feedback she gave, the better the results.

"This is amazing, Dean. You pull sexy off effortlessly. I knew you would," she called out. And if any model had needed a confidence boost, it was Dean. It was also fun to have a good excuse to tell him what she thought about him. She was rewarded with some genuine, sexy smiles.

When she took a break to look at the images, he spoke. "How many more do you need?"

"As many as you're willing to give me. And you thought you wouldn't be good at this. What a tease."

"I appreciate you saying that."

"Well, I want you to know I mean it."

Their eyes met and Charlotte took a moment to just stare at him. It made her sad that he wasn't enjoying this as much as she'd hoped. Something was off today, and that age conversation hadn't really helped things. She didn't know what to do to get them back on course with the fun banter that usually took place between them. Maybe now that they were seeing each other more frequently, he'd decided it was no longer appropriate. What a shame that would be.

Charlotte reached into her bag and pulled out a white tank undershirt.

"What do you think about putting this on? I think it would look good under the vest."

"I think that you're the boss," he said, holding out a hand. She tossed him the shirt.

"Okay. We'll do a set of those and then just a few other things. Shouldn't be too much longer. You're doing great."

Not wanting to be too obvious in her ogling, she forced herself to focus on her camera equipment while he changed. Once the top and vest were in place, he looked like the real deal. Tough, sexy, and full-on biker.

For the next fifteen minutes she directed him to lean into the front of the bike, lean back, to the side. She shot from behind him, lying on the ground and angling upward as he gazed into the distance through the aviator glasses. She was probably taking way more than necessary, but she couldn't bring herself to stop. Some of them weren't even suitable for a book cover. They were just . . . hot.

"Should we take a break? And then, uh, maybe we can do some without the shirt. If you're willing."

"I'm good. Let's just keep on going so we can get it over with."

Okay.

Without hesitating he ditched the vest and carefully laid it back in the leather saddlebag before he immediately pulled the tank over his head and tossed it toward the side of the road. Charlotte held her reaction in check, but her entire body was responding to the sight of Dean Troyer shirtless. It was beyond breathtaking. Prophecies might have been written about this moment. Maybe she should have written one.

When Charlotte Linley sees Dean Troyer with no shirt on, she will never again settle for less than a four-pack.

His was a solid six, but she'd settle for four, because reality was still a bitch.

"So . . . okay." She could barely remember what should happen next. Which was ridiculous because this was not the first time she'd photographed a beautiful man. But this was the first time that beautiful man was Dean. The same man who had starred in her fantasies for almost three years. Some of them innocent, many of them not. "Why don't you go ahead and get back on the bike."

She had him repeat a few of the poses they'd already done, because honestly, shirtless they'd become something completely different. Then she had him do a few standing next to the bike, leaning on it, some with glasses, some without, and then eventually she lowered her camera.

He stepped away from the bike and, thank goodness, didn't immediately put his shirt on. The sun was slowly setting behind the trees, and because it was only May, a hint of a chill was on the breeze. Nobody ever talked about a man's nipples hardening. That was a shame, because she realized it was a complete turn-on. She glanced down at the screen on her camera and began to scroll through the images she'd taken.

"These are going to be so good. The light is amazing right now. Too bad we don't have a female here."

He made his way toward her. "A female. Like in the photos *with* me?"

"Yeah, you know how romance covers are, right? A lot of times there's a couple."

He seemed to be processing that. After a moment he lifted his chin in her direction. "How about you?"

Charlotte laughed. "Uhh, I'm sort of *taking* the photos. Plus . . . I'm not really cover material."

"You can't be serious. Charlotte, *you* . . ." He looked her up and down. "Are sexy as hell. And I have a feeling that fancy camera has a self-timer."

Had he really just said that to her? She was pretty sure she'd heard him right, but oh how she wished she would have known that was going to come out of his mouth so she could have listened very carefully in order to savor the sound of those words on his lips. *You are sexy as hell*. She'd be adding that line to her fantasies, no doubt about it.

"Thank you, that was nice of you to say."

The corner of Dean's lips quirked and he looked at the road. "I probably shouldn't have said that."

Nothing like a metaphorical splash of cold water on your ego. She wasn't sure how to respond to that.

"Not that I don't mean it, I do. I just . . . you know, shouldn't have said it."

"It's fine. Not like we don't flirt with each other."

"Well, yeah. But that's all for fun. While we're working."

And now she wanted to crawl in a hole. Of course it was all for fun, but his words still stung a little.

"Sure," she lied. "But this is also working."

His brow creased a little. "Anyway, I still think we should do it," he said. "Get as much out of this chest shave as possible." He winked at her.

Charlotte pursed her lips, considering it. "I actually do have a remote. I use it during wedding ceremonies sometimes so I can hide a camera."

"Nice. Well, get it out, set it up on the hood of the car, and get in this shot."

"What about my hair?"

Dean took the three steps that separated them and reached toward the back of her head. With a quick movement her bun was dislodged, allowing her hair to fall down around her shoulders. "I think that pretty much takes care of it."

Charlotte sucked in a breath, nervous about her proximity to his bare chest. She'd stood near Dean in the past. During wedding receptions, the music was so loud they had to get close to hear each other, and he'd always smelled of musky cologne. Today she still picked up on that, but there was more. It was mixed with the scent of his skin warmed by the setting sun, and maybe a hint of . . . shaving cream? That made her smile.

"So set it up," he repeated.

"Okay," was all she could say at that point, because she wanted to do this. She might never get another chance to be so close to him.

Charlotte got into her bag, found her remote setup, and got it all rigged and ready. She situated it on the hood of his car and looked through the lens to frame the shot.

And now she had to decide how she was going to position them together. Several things instantly came to mind, but of course they all required them to touch . . . intimately. Not inappropriately, but she was talking about romance novel covers here. Obviously he knew that when he'd suggested it, but did a forty-one-year-old man know anything about romance novels? She guessed there was a good possibility he had no idea.

"Ready?" Dean asked. Charlotte nodded and walked over to him.

"Sure, um, okay. Let's just start with something basic. You stand closest to the front of the bike, and I'll sort of just . . ." She grabbed his left hand and stepped into him before settling it on her hip. "Now I'll grab onto you like this, and then you sort of cup my face with your right hand."

"Like this?" His hand came up and caressed her face. It took everything inside of her not to curl into him like a cat. Instead she nodded and rested one hand on his chest and the other around his waist. His skin was slightly cool and dry to the touch. And yet the contact sent warmth surging through her body. She did what came naturally to her when things got awkward: She tried to lighten the mood.

"Your chest is so smooth." She grinned up at him while

she rubbed her hand over his perfectly formed pecs. "Like a baby's bottom."

Charlotte giggled when Dean scowled down at her. "Not funny at all."

"It was very funny. Now don't be grumpy. We need to be sexy."

When she looked up his gaze was leveled down at her. He seemed to be analyzing things. "Should we look at each other?"

Was this not affecting him at all?

Charlotte nodded. "To start."

Their eyes met once more and she felt his left hand pull her into his body even tighter, so much so that her thighs pressed into his and their chests touched. When he breathed out she felt the warmth on her cheek.

"I photograph a lot of couples, and it's all about the gaze." Her words were quiet, and Dean listened intently. "They look longingly into each other's eyes. So let's give that a try."

Eyes meeting, they stared at one another for a long moment, and then out of nowhere Dean crossed his eyes hard, making Charlotte laugh out loud.

They were grinning at each other now, their faces a breath away. She pushed the remote and heard the shutter close and release.

"Okay, now, no more silliness. Just look at each other."

Dean's lips went tight and his eyes molten as they gazed on her lips. Her nose. "You're pretty easy to stare at," he whispered.

Charlotte couldn't help the hint of a smile on her face. They were having fun. Acting. But she wanted to pretend this was real. Pretend that he was holding her, looking at her with hungry eyes because he wanted to. That his thumb slid over her cheek because he was desperate to know how her skin felt. Was he aching to drop his left hand lower and cup her bottom?

The rise and fall of his chest matched her own, and as she continued to push the button, his lips gave the tiniest of quirks, his eyes never leaving hers. Without the sunglasses, his stare was so intense it was nearly uncomfortable. Suddenly there was no more playfulness, only heat. The question was, how much of it was real?

After snapping about five more images, Charlotte forced herself to slide out of his arms. "I better see what those look like. Make sure the focus is good. It would suck if we did this all for nothing."

Dean made a sound under his breath that implied that he agreed with her on that. But she couldn't disagree more. There was nothing about that moment she regretted, usable photos or not. She'd have been fine being held by him all day long for absolutely no reason at all.

Nine

While Charlotte scrolled through the images on her camera, Dean turned away from her and tried to inconspicuously adjust the growing problem in his jeans. When he heard her shoes shuffle on the asphalt he cleared his throat and stepped on the other side of the bike, hoping like hell he didn't have his thoughts written all over his face. Or anywhere else.

Having Charlotte in his arms, her lips a breath away, that sweet scent enveloping him . . . it had been all he could do not to pull her against his body and show her exactly what she did to him. Thank goodness he'd kept his cool, but still. Just thinking about it was keeping things from settling back down, so to speak.

"Those are actually really good," she said. "Can we do a few more?"

Holy shit. Dean cleared his throat. "Sure. Whatever you need."

She smiled and resumed setting up her camera. Dean tried to use the few precious moments to think about Booker, the old bike owner. *There we go, that's doing the trick.*

He stepped back around the Harley and continued to

force flashing thoughts through his brain to keep things in check. Work, Alex's wedding, what he was going to have for dinner. However, as soon as Charlotte walked back toward him, her blond hair catching the highlight of the sun, her tan thighs in those cutoffs and her shapely hips swaying as she stepped up to him and put her hands on his chest. Yep, he was back to having a problem.

Damn.

"Okay . . . so, this is going to be a little awkward, but this time I'm going to tilt my head toward the camera and you lean your head down and just sort of . . ." She trailed off, her hand waving toward her neck area. Was she too embarrassed to put what she meant into words?

Didn't matter, because he knew exactly what she was asking for. She wanted him to nuzzle into her neck. Make it more romantic. Without waiting for her to finish, he leaned in, wrapped his arms tightly around her waist, and tilted his head down so that his lips were just shy of her skin. Inhaling deeply, he then blew out as he spoke. "Like this."

"Yeah, that's good," she said, laughing a little. Her hands slid up around his neck. "See, you're a pro."

"It's pretty damn easy with you."

He felt her tense for a fraction of a second before she melted against him. It almost felt real. Nails raked into his hair and then began sliding up the back of his skull. There would be no distraction strong enough to overcome the sensations, especially when the only thought he was capable of having was how good she felt in his arms. If she only knew how many times he'd imagined her just like this. How often he'd watched her across the room during a wedding reception and fantasized about pulling her into an empty alcove and devouring her.

She's twenty-nine. God, it sounded so young. She was so vivacious and fun. A woman like that had needs and desires. Dreams for the future. He needed to remind himself of that.

Then Charlotte shifted against him, her face tilting toward his. If he lifted his head, they would be nose-to-nose, so he didn't dare move. "It will be good if we get a variety of looks so . . . you know, whatever comes to mind that you think would be sexy."

She laughed softly against his ear, the sound full of uncertainty. Could she feel how close he was to snapping? Was it possible that she wanted him the way he wanted her? Dean cleared his throat and then forced himself to pull back and look at her. Their eyes met and her lips parted the slightest bit.

Here he was, a grown man, in the perfect position to seduce a woman he'd lusted after for years. There would never be an opportunity so perfect, a situation so expertly contrived to give him permission to touch her as he'd always wanted to. Pretend that she was his. It didn't have to mean anything. He swallowed hard.

"Whatever comes to mind, huh?"

She nodded.

"Sexy is what you're looking for?" His eyes roamed across her skin, her lips, trying to decide what he should do.

"It is for a romance novel," she said with a little grin.

He slid his hands—which had been resting on her soft hips up till this point—up her arms and then to her face, cupping it gently. "How sexy are we supposed to get for these shoots?" he whispered.

"Very." She swallowed, her chin tilting up toward him.

His mouth ached to cover hers. He could nearly taste it, the fruity scent of her shiny lips reaching out and begging him to suck on them. Holding on by a thread, he warred with the temptation and pulled her hair the slightest bit, exposing her neck to him once more. This time, though, he gave the camera what it wanted. Something real.

Opening his mouth over the taut skin of her neck, just above her pulse, Dean let his tongue taste her before pulling his lips together in a light sucking motion. She gasped, her body bowing further, pushing her harder against him. He repeated the action. Then again. Gently he placed open-mouthed kisses all over her throat, under her jaw, beneath her ear.

"Oh God . . ." The breathy exclamation that fell from her lips was not for the camera. It was all for him. Of that he was certain.

Charlotte's left leg began to shift, her foot slowly snaking up his calf, her opposite hand gripping the back of his head, pulling him harder against her.

He sucked her earlobe past his lips and let one of his hands grip her butt, giving her leverage to lock her leg up over his hip, and in that very moment the air around them shifted. There was no doubt the motion gave her a very obvious idea of what she was doing to him and it had nothing to do with these photos.

Should he stop? Apologize?

He'd wanted to give her a taste of what he could do to her, but now . . . he wanted to give her more than that. Three years of being professional was long enough.

"Charlotte," he breathed into her ear.

It was a question. A request for permission. She answered by turning her head, her lips meeting the corner of his mouth. "Dean," she whispered, and as her lips closed, they caught the corner of his just the slightest bit.

Shit. There was no stopping this. Right or wrong, it didn't matter. He was no longer capable of thinking through the decision. The softness of her plump mouth meeting his even that small amount was too much to deny.

The request now appeared to be hers, and he gave her what she wanted as her parted lips pushed against the edge of his once more. It took only the slightest movement of his head, and he kissed her.

Finally.

Their first few touches were gentle, their lips exploring, and hesitant, teasing each other. It didn't take long for them to become bold, needy, and frantic. She tasted like strawberries and mint gum, her lips soft and wet. He sucked the pout of her lower one between his and then chased it with his tongue. Not one to be outdone, Charlotte responded eagerly and let out the faintest whimper.

She broke away just long enough to whisper, "Give me more."

Goddamn. That was it. The kiss deepened into something so carnal, filthy, and wet, he could barely remain upright. Her body rocked against his, her hands gripping his head, and without hesitation or unlocking their mouths he hauled her up against his body, her legs locking around his waist.

They continued to kiss, her arms going around his neck. This was better than he could have dared to hope. She fit against him like her body was made for it, and all he could think about was how bad he wanted to get her somewhere soft and horizontal, so he could strip off her clothes and have her in every way possible.

Something knocked into his neck. Charlotte broke the kiss and then laughed against his mouth. Dean looked up to find her smiling down at him.

"Sorry, my remote."

"That's okay," he said, his breath short.

They stared at each other for a moment. He still held her in his arms, her feet digging into his ass.

"Wow," she whispered, leaning her forehead onto his. "That was amazing."

The look on her face suddenly had him panicking. Now what? "It was. I hope you got what you needed."

Her lips parted a bit, and she looked surprised. Shit. He didn't mean to sound cold, but he wasn't ready to take this to another level. The kiss had been unexpected. Amazing, but now what? That was when he heard the sound of a motor running. Charlotte must have heard it at the same time, both of their heads jerking up to find Booker and his wife staring at them through their windshield a little way down the road. The old man lifted a hand and waved, an obvious smirk on his face even from a distance.

"Oh my God," Charlotte whispered.

"We gave them quite a show," Dean said.

Charlotte just laughed and began to slide down his body. Dean panicked. He brought his hands up under her arms and tried to place her away from him. Now that he'd just reminded them both that this was a performance, the last thing he wanted to do was reveal his raging hard-on.

Charlotte waved and then held up a finger to alert the older couple that she just needed a minute. Booker just gave another hand lift in reply.

"Should we look at them quickly?" she asked, her voice bright. Was it a little shaky?

Dean ran a hand through his hair and looked at her flushed cheeks and swollen mouth. Bad idea. God, he was a mess over this woman. One minute he wanted to maintain his distance, the next he hoped she was as on fire as he was. He was a mix of lust and confusion, but obviously now there was no returning to what they'd been doing a moment ago.

"Sure," he said as he walked over to his discarded T-shirt and pulled it over his head. When he turned back Charlotte had retrieved her camera from the hood of his car and was scrolling through the images on the back screen. He walked over and peeked over her shoulder.

"These are so gorgeous." She held the camera up so he could see.

The setting was gorgeous, the golden sunlight filtering through the trees lighting the chrome of the motorcycle and the blond in her hair. But that wasn't the part that held him captivated. It was them, her body straddling his, her thighs squeezing his hips as his palms cupped her behind, their mouths fused together. The pose, the light . . . her. All of it was so sexy he couldn't believe it. Never in his life had he viewed himself entwined with a woman in this way, and he loved it. The only problem with it was that he was the only one half naked, and with that thought he was looking at it in a new way, imagining her supple body in his arms completely bare.

Holding back a groan, he watched as she flipped quickly through the images, making them come to life but in reverse. It was like watching a stop-motion capture of himself making out with Charlotte. What he wouldn't give to have that on loop for him to watch tonight in bed.

"What do you think?" she asked, turning toward him.

"I think they're good."

"They're more than good. They're wonderful. You're amazing." She stepped closer to him. "I . . . uh, know you didn't want to do this, but I'm glad you did."

Which part was she referring to? The shoot . . . or the kiss?

"I'm glad, too." Unable to help himself, he touched her elbow, and a hint of longing showed in her eyes.

What exactly did she want from him? Those kisses had been too hot, too intense, to be simply pretend. But Dean knew as much as he'd enjoyed kissing her, it probably wasn't best to try it ever again.

"Wonder how much they saw," Charlotte said tilting her head toward the idling truck.

"They couldn't have been there more than a couple moments." Long enough to get an eyeful, that's for sure, since the two of them had been way too preoccupied to hear the truck pull up.

"Probably not." She grinned at Dean. "Whatever they saw, I'm sure they loved it."

What he wanted to know was had *she* loved it, because he sure as hell had. Way too much.

The following Sunday morning, Charlotte had a wedding hangover. A very real physical ailment brought on by dehydration, exhaustion, muscle fatigue, and a sort of melancholy that only a single woman could appreciate after watching two people in love say "I do."

After trying to sleep in for over an hour, she finally dragged herself out of bed, headed to the kitchen, and peered into the refrigerator. Milk, coffee creamer, and spicy pickles. With a shrug she grabbed the spicy pickles and stood at the counter and ate a couple. Nothing like salty food when you're dehydrated.

After drinking a glass of water and refilling it, Charlotte headed back to her bed and pulled her laptop in front of her. She really needed to go into her office and start culling yesterday's image files. Three weddings came due in the next two weeks, and she still needed to open the photos of her session with Dean.

For some reason she hadn't been able to do that. She

wasn't sure why, because she'd flipped through them during the shoot. However, something about opening them up and looking at the way he held and kissed her in full resolution gave her anxiety. As much as she'd thought about that day—and that had been often—there was part of her that almost wished it hadn't happened. Because what now?

She'd been grateful last night's wedding hadn't been at the Stag. A breather had been necessary. How would they act around each other the next time? Unsure of what Dean had been thinking, she'd made a conscious decision to be nonchalant about the whole thing after it happened. Now she wondered if that was a mistake, because she really liked him.

The attraction was there. She knew he was sweet and funny. There was a hesitance on his end, she knew that, but she'd hoped after that kiss he might be closer to taking things to the next level. Maybe ask her out. Or ask to come in when he'd dropped her off at home. But he'd done neither, and his uncertainty had made her overthink the entire thing.

Her phone began singing ABBA's "Does Your Mother Know," and Charlotte reached over to her nightstand and picked it up. She debated not answering, then forced herself to just get it over with.

"Hey, Mom."

"Hi, sweetie. Did I wake you?"

"No, I was up."

"Oh good. I just had something to discuss with you. I saw Mary Sue Willis yesterday."

"That's nice." Charlotte wasn't sure why that was news. She'd gone to school with Mary Sue Willis's daughter Shelby, but the two of them hadn't really been friends. Friendly, sure. But not close.

"Well, I figured you weren't aware of it, but . . . apparently Shelby and Jason Reynolds are getting married in a couple of weeks."

Oh.

That was interesting news. Jason was John's older brother.

"Good for them." Charlotte shifted on the bed, her skin feeling tight all of a sudden.

"I'm sure you don't love hearing about it, but Jason was always such a sweet boy. And, well . . . I hate to bring this up, but according to Mary Sue, they've run into a problem. She was so upset as she told me, I just immediately knew that even though it may be difficult, you'd want to help."

Charlotte sat up in bed, her heart picking up speed. Her mother was a do-gooder. If there was a problem, she wanted to be part of the solution. She found her value in that way. Charlotte liked to be helpful also, but she wasn't nearly as giving with her time as her mom. "Help with what, Mom?"

"Well, she said their photographer canceled on them. Can you imagine such a thing?"

She couldn't really imagine, as she would never do that to a client. But there were always horror stories. "Why would their photographer cancel?"

"His excuse was that he'd double-booked without realizing. Although Mary Sue suspects there's more to it. Said he'd become difficult to reach."

Unprofessional, but she'd almost overbooked once, by accident. But waiting until two weeks from the event to tell your bride was outrageous.

"Now, I told her you'd probably already be booked, but secretly I'm really hoping you can help them."

"Mom, why? Did you even consider how awkward that would be for me?"

"I know, Charlotte, I really do. But it *was* five years ago. You're a successful, strong woman now. It might make you feel amazing to show them how well you're doing. That it didn't break you."

"But . . . it did break me, Mom." In ways her mother didn't even know.

"Charlotte . . ." her mother whispered. "It broke you for a time, but you're healed."

Charlotte knew that a large part of her mother's "fix-it" and helper mentality was because she just hated for anyone to be unhappy. Because of that, she tended to wear the weight of the world on her shoulders. And although she always had the best intentions, sometimes her loyalties could be a bit misplaced. A big reason Charlotte didn't always share her woes with her mother.

"You do realize that half of the guests attending would have been invited to my wedding." Need she remind her mother that those same people would have been the ones showing up to Grace Baptist Church, only to be greeted by her father in the parking lot, alerting them the wedding was no longer on? She could still remember standing in the window of the bride's dressing room, in her full dress, makeup, and hair, watching him speak to car after car of people. She hadn't been able to look away. Wondering what their response had been. *"What?" "Really?" "Is Charlotte okay?" "Did he meet someone else?"*

Finally, her mother had forced her to take off the wedding gown and get dressed so they could leave. There had been no plan for going home that evening. All she could do was lie in her childhood bed and cry. At some point that evening, John's mother had come over to check on her.

While Charlotte had known the woman meant well, nothing could have humiliated her more.

What if they assumed she still pined for John to this day?

"Think of poor Shelby, Charlotte. No photographer two weeks before her wedding."

Two weeks. Charlotte's eyes closed as she realized that she did, in fact, have that weekend off. Damn. She could lie. How could they prove otherwise? It was really a miracle she wasn't booked. But a part of her, deep inside, was a little intrigued by the idea of giving John's brother the best wedding photos he'd ever seen. Spending the day acting as though none of it fazed her.

God, she hated that her mother might be a little bit right.

"Where is the wedding?" Charlotte inquired.

"The Methodist church on Newman, and the reception is at that place on the square that makes alcohol."

Charlotte's heart skipped. "The Stag?"

"Yes, that's it. The one with the handsome gentlemen everyone talks about. Would you just consider it? For Mary Sue and Shelby? You've been friends for years."

"Mom, I barely spoke with Shelby in high school."

"Well, she's a Maple Springs girl, and so are you. Maybe you'll meet someone there. How perfect would that be? That would really make him jealous."

"John would not be the slightest bit jealous. And remember, I go to weddings almost every weekend, and I've yet to meet a man while working."

Well . . . that wasn't quite true, but she didn't feel the need to clarify with her mother.

"I'll check my schedule just in case they reach out. But I can't make any promises." She hadn't decided what her answer would be yet so she wasn't ready to let her mother know that she had the date open.

"Thank you, sweetie. I do appreciate it. Mary Sue is such a nice woman."

Charlotte placated her after that, answering her mother's questions about if she, herself, was doing okay and eating enough, and if she needed anything. A few moments later and Charlotte ended the call, confused, and with her wedding hangover nowhere near improving.

She hadn't seen John since the week after their big terrible day. He'd come by to pick up some of his things at her apartment, and bring her some things from his. Thank goodness they hadn't cohabited before the wedding—that would have been even messier. When he'd stopped by that day, Charlotte had been in shock. The pain of losing him and everything she thought to be true had completely shaken her foundation. He'd made it all worse by informing her that he'd wanted to break it off for almost six months, but hadn't because she'd found out she was pregnant.

A pregnancy that he'd been excited about—or had at least seemed to be. She still remembered telling him. Showing him the test. They hadn't been trying, but they hadn't been too terribly careful, being twenty-four and knowing they were getting married soon. She'd been nervous, but secretly ecstatic. They'd spent hours making plans, talking about where they wanted to live, what they'd need to buy. To find out that he'd actually already fallen out of love with her had been a knife to her already broken heart. He told her that the baby had convinced him to try again. Made him believe maybe it was meant to be, but that once it was gone . . . what else was there to stay for? She could still hear the words as they came from his mouth.

Once it was gone . . .

Those words alone told her that, in a way, the death of

their baby was a relief for him. How could she ever forgive that?

What would it be like to see him now?

Her phone ringing startled Charlotte. The caller ID showed a local number. Had her mother really worked that quickly? Good Lord.

She answered and immediately recognized Mary Sue's voice. She was from Mississippi, her drawl thick as syrup even though she'd moved to Kansas decades ago. "Charlotte, dear, it's Mary Sue Willis. How are you?"

"I'm great, Mary Sue. How are you?"

"Well, I've been better. I know your sweet Mama filled you in on the details. Shelby is just fit to be tied over this. Can you believe her photographer?"

"Being in the business, I'm afraid I've heard all kinds of stories although it's unusual. I'm sorry you've found yourself in this position."

"Me too. And, dear, let me be clear. I know what we're asking is no small thing. What John Reynolds did to you is inexcusable." She punctuated every syllable of the last word, and Charlotte had to appreciate her words although it was incredibly uncomfortable.

"Well, thank you, Mary Sue. It was a long time ago."

"It was. But a woman doesn't forget such a thing. Ever. No one does and he should have thought things through way before that day."

"Well, I appreciate that. But . . . the past is the past. I've moved on."

"Good. I just want you to know that we'd be so eternally grateful if you came to our rescue. To Shelby and Jason's rescue. It would mean the world."

Charlotte closed her eyes. Could she do this? Face these people that had witnessed her pain and embarrassment? Be in the presence of John?

"Did your mother tell you, it's all here in Maple Springs, so you wouldn't have to go far."

"Yes, she did. I've worked at your church several times, and I love the Stag." And for that reason alone, she knew she could do it. Spend an entire day in the presence of the guy who'd broken her heart into a million pieces. Her mother was right; she wasn't the same woman she was five years ago. Now she was running a small empire— the same one he'd once bitched about taking all her time. She owned her own home, and drove a nice car. And if there was anywhere she felt confident in her abilities to nail photographing a wedding reception, it was at the Stag. With a sigh, Charlotte went on. "I'll do it, Mary Sue."

"You will? Oh, honey, you've made my day. I know Shelby will be so relieved also." Charlotte almost thought she detected the sound of tears in her voice. She smiled to herself. It wasn't Shelby's fault that her photographer canceled, or that her future brother-in-law was a selfish ass. It also did make Charlotte feel good to help. Maybe she had a little of her mother in her after all.

"I'm glad. Why don't you have Shelby call me, and she and I can set up a time to meet and just go over a few things."

"That sounds fabulous."

They continued to discuss a few details like payment and contract, and when the call was over Charlotte fell back on her bed, exhausted. It felt like she'd relived a life's worth of emotions in the past twenty minutes.

Ten

The following Monday, Charlotte still hadn't heard from Dean about the invites, so she decided to make a surprise drop-in. She couldn't deny that part of her feared he was avoiding her after that kiss, and she knew that meant it was up to her to make the next move.

At the sound of the front door, TJ stepped out of the office hallway into the main room. He gave Charlotte a wide smile and headed over. She couldn't help wondering if Dean had told any of the guys what had happened between them, but instantly she dismissed the idea. It was not at all in his character to kiss and tell.

"Are you here on official wedding business?" TJ asked with a smile. "I still can't believe you let Dean talk you into helping him."

"Well, I had to, didn't I? Since you guys wouldn't," she teased.

TJ feigned a hurt expression before continuing. "It's true, but not because we don't love him and Alex. We are literally all working our asses off. Nearly twelve-hour days sometimes. And Dean's the worst offender."

"Is he? I'll have to give him an earful. I bet things are even tougher with Tara gone."

He nodded. "Yeah, that hurt, but her health comes first. And her baby's."

Their care for Tara and the health of her pregnancy sent an ache through Charlotte. She loved that they were all such good guys, and they worked so hard. All of them. "Maybe you should hire someone."

"We talked about it. It'll be somewhat back to normal once Tara comes back and can take over the wedding side of things, but Jake is struggling with getting all the marketing stuff done along with deliveries and social media. Then Dean . . . well, he needs an assistant. That's for damn sure."

Charlotte knew Dean was their head distiller, having worked for a larger company for several years and then a craft beer company in downtown Kansas City. "Surely he could train someone."

TJ laughed. "I know he could. He's taught both of us how to help him—and we do—but we're all overworked. I think pride has kept him from admitting he can't do it all. And then with this wedding planning on top of that . . . well, I feel for the guy."

"Sounds like you and Jake just need to pull majority and insist he hire help. Is it a matter of money?" One thing she liked about the Stag guys—especially TJ, since the money side was his specialty—was they could talk business transparently. She enjoyed networking and sharing experiences with other small-business owners. It was always nice to hear other perspectives and ideas, even use one another as sounding boards.

"No. I mean, we're not rich, but we were out of the red by our third year, and this has been our best year yet. Once the signature offerings are ready to distribute, things will be even better. Jake's already got about eighteen accounts lined up to carry them and will no doubt sign more when he goes on his festival tour."

"So the distilling won't be slowing down anytime soon."

"Not at all. In fact, if things go as we hope it will increase."

Charlotte nodded. She hated to think Dean was working too hard, but she could see him being a little reluctant to bring someone on to help him. The guy had a lot of pride. Not in an arrogant way, just . . . a wants-things-to-be-done-well kind of way. The type of pride that people respected. Especially her. "Maybe I'll talk to him."

"Be my guest. Maybe he'll listen to you. He's in the distilling room right now."

Charlotte made her way through the main room, passing by the back wall of glass that showcased the row of stainless fermenters and the copper distiller. She saw Dean step through a door at the back, but he'd yet to see her. He was so adorable in his Stag polo and dark jeans, just working away in his domain.

A couple of years ago Jake had given her and Lauren a tour one night after a wedding, so she knew where she was going as she headed through a side door into a small hallway. She passed the room they used for bottling and made her way to the large back storage space. It was utilitarian, with concrete floors, a loading dock, and a large garage door. In the corner was the machine they used to mill grain. The door to the distilling room stood open, and she stepped through.

"Hey," she said.

Dean's head jerked up, and when he met her eyes, the expression on his face was one she'd never seen before. Panic. That let her know she'd been correct in her assumption that he was avoiding contact. Up until the photo shoot they'd had a pretty steady stream of texts going in regard to the wedding planning, and that had gone radio silent since that night. Since the kiss.

"Hi," he said after getting control of his expression. "To what do I owe this surprise?"

He began to fidget with a gauge on the large vat that collected the distilled alcohol. Charlotte stepped farther into the room, noticing that he didn't look her way.

"I just never heard from you on the invite situation and they really do need to go out this week."

"Invites, yeah, God, you're right." His eyes finally flickered to hers; then he quickly bent over to mess with some hoses.

Never, ever, in the years she'd known him, had things been awkward between them. Not when she'd told him he had a nice butt, or when they'd joked about casual sex with co-workers. Okay, when *she'd* joked about it, and he'd played along. Not even the time they stood watching kids dance at a reception and she'd informed him he would make cute babies, to which he'd responded with, "Only if they were with you." Not even that had made things awkward between them. But now they'd gone and made out, and things had changed.

She hated it.

"So, anyway, I went ahead and made a couple of designs in Photoshop, thought you could look and choose one. If I ordered them from my printing company, it would save you some money."

"That sounds like a good idea." His voice came from behind the fermenters, where he was still working on something.

Charlotte had no doubt that Dean was a busy man, especially after the conversation she'd just had with TJ. However, she also knew this was about way more than that. Had she come in like this a week ago, she was certain he would have taken a minute of his time to focus on her. She had to put a stop to this, especially if they were going to continue working together in any capacity, whether planning his sister's wedding or with her shooting as a vendor in his building.

"Dean, can you not look at me?"

He let out a long sigh and then a muttered curse before standing up and meeting her eyes over the stainless-steel vessels. His look of panic had turned into something more resigned. Exhausted. Maybe she'd had it wrong and he was just stressed about work.

Stepping around the equipment, he walked up to her. "I'm sorry. I'm being rude and . . . it's just been kind of a crazy week."

"TJ mentioned how busy you guys have been."

His eyebrows raised in surprise. "Yeah, well, things will be better when Alex's wedding is over."

For some reason that stung a little. "Is it just that?" She nodded toward the distilling operation. "Wouldn't it be easier if you had someone helping you?"

He chuckled. "You've definitely been talking to TJ. He wants me to hire another distiller, but he fails to realize that it's not that easy."

"Couldn't you teach someone? Like an apprentice. I mean, I have firsthand knowledge of your *many* talents, but I doubt even you came out of the womb making whiskey."

Thankfully he laughed, the joke smoothing the way over her not-so-subtle nod to their previous time together.

"No, I didn't. I learned from my grandfather, then went to work for a company in Oklahoma for a while. When I moved back here I worked for Bogey's Craft Brew downtown, which has a similar process."

He didn't know Charlotte had read his bio on their

website maybe a hundred times, since it included a picture of the three guys together. She knew his background well. Or at least what he'd shared with the public. She wished she knew more. The public, and the private.

"So see? The magic can be taught. TJ said you taught him and Jake."

"I did. They help when I need them, but they're not passionate about it like I am. I need someone who really wants to learn for pleasure."

"The world is full of passionate people, Dean. If you haven't noticed, you don't really have an argument for not hiring help."

He smiled and shook his head. "You're stubborn, you know that?"

"I've been told. Plus, I worry about you. You're working too hard."

"That's unnecessary, Charlotte. I'm fine."

"Yeah, well, too late." Their eyes met and held. She desperately wished she knew what he was thinking.

Finally, he nodded. "Why don't we go in the office and you can show me those invitations."

Charlotte followed him through the single door, into the warehouse, back down the hall, and into the main room once again. Jake, the playboy of the group, was sitting on one of the leather sofas with a laptop on the coffee table.

"Another order for Forkhorn and Signature. In Denver," Jake said without looking up.

"Is this our first in Denver?" Dean asked.

"One has halfway committed but it's contingent on the taste test." Jake shook his head as he typed something quickly. "Idiots. As if the Stag would put out an inferior product."

"Hi, Jake," Charlotte finally said. The minute he looked

up, he grinned, and within a fraction of a second he was off the couch and making his way toward her and wrapping her in the always eager, Jake hug.

"The prettiest photographer. Must be my lucky day." His voice was muffled against her hair. When he pulled back he smiled.

Jake was an unapologetic flirt. With every female, so she always took it for what it was, which was innocent fun. Luckily for him, plenty of ladies fell for it, which Charlotte suspected was his intention. Jake never hurt for female attention, and she couldn't blame any of them because he was young, gorgeous, and had a body that was meant for a good time.

But she felt nothing when she was around him. When she turned to Dean his eyes were tight and focused on Jake.

Jake looked quickly from Dean to Charlotte and then chuckled. "All righty then. I was going to ask Charlotte if she wanted to go out on a second date, but I don't want to piss off the old man."

Charlotte shook her head and laughed. She had never gone out with Jake, as he well knew. But it was kind of fun to make Dean squirm. "We haven't done a wedding together in a while. I miss talking to you."

"Yeah, funny, isn't it? Your weddings always seem to fall on Dean's nights." He gave Charlotte a wink. "Wonder how that happens. I might have to insist on having you next time."

"Jake." Dean's voice shot out hard, followed by the sound of Jake's laughter as he sat back down to his laptop.

"Good to see you," Charlotte called over her shoulder as she followed Dean toward the offices.

"You too, babe." The clicking of his typing followed her.

She stepped past Dean, noticing the way his shirt

pushed at his biceps as he held the door open so she could step into the conference room. Charlotte began to lay her bag on the table when his voice came from behind her.

"When did you go out with Jake?"

All right. She'd had enough of whatever this was between them.

She spun around, instantly annoyed at the anger in his tone. "Really? After all the times I've flirted with you, and you'd believe I've gone out with Jake? He was trying to get you worked up and clearly he succeeded. Which is interesting, isn't it? Because as I recall, not fifteen minutes ago you could barely even look at me."

His eyebrows went up and then his eyes went stormy once more as he stepped into her space. Charlotte backed up, the table pressing into the back of her thighs. She looked up at him. This was another thing that had never happened in all these years. She'd never witnessed Dean like this, definitely not directed at her. He'd always treated her gently as a vendor, and with reverent flirtation as a woman. Always straddling the fine line between naughtiness and propriety, even though she constantly strived to push him over the edge.

Right now he was way over the edge.

"I don't need to look at you, Charlotte, because ever since I had my mouth on you Thursday, you're all I see."

She swallowed, her eyes unable to look away. "And obviously, that's a problem for you. Is that what you're telling me?"

His eyes softened. "I haven't decided yet."

With their eyes locked, she willed him to give her more to go on before she answered. Even the slightest expression might help. She searched his eyes, needing to know what he was thinking. Was he frustrated because he feared she didn't feel the same? Or was he irritated because he didn't want to feel what he did? Unfortunately, he gave her no hint to his emotions.

She'd always hoped her flirting with Dean would lead to something, since she'd had a crush on him for so long. But faced with the reality of admitting that, she knew that if it went wrong she'd be devastated. Working at the Stag was a huge part of her income. She loved working with these guys, loved flirting with Dean, and if some misplaced moment of passion between them messed all of that up . . . what would she do? Was it worth that? Why had she never considered the possible fallout between them before?

She nodded. "I don't want you to regret what we did. I think you know I've wanted that for a long time. But I also don't want things to be awkward between us."

He breathed in deep through his nose and stepped away from her. They continued to stare for one long moment. She hated that her photo shoot had forced them into this position.

"I'm sorry I'm being an ass. I'm just worn thin right now." He ran a hand through his hair and then sat down hard in a char.

Charlotte followed his lead and sat, but she couldn't help her sadness over the fact that he hadn't voiced a lack of regret for their kiss. *Damn.*

She wasn't going to be hurt by that.

"Don't apologize. I understand there's a lot on your plate. Planning a wedding alone is incredibly stressful. But don't go bridezilla on me this early in the game."

Dean's eyes shot to hers, and then he let out a chuckle. Charlotte sighed in relief. Laughter always worked. Charlotte pulled the laptop from her bag.

"Let me just show you these invites really quick and then I can quit bugging you."

"You're never bugging me, Charlotte. Ignore me when I act like an idiot," he said quietly as she clicked through files.

"I'll remember that." She gave him a weak smile. Once she'd located the folder where she saved the samples, Charlotte turned the screen so Dean could get a good look at her work. "Here is one option. Simple, sophisticated. We could have this one printed on a beautiful pearl paper that would add a little shimmer."

"That looks nice," he said. Charlotte took that as her cue to click onto the next one. He immediately leaned forward. "I like that one better."

"This one's my favorite also. The font is really pretty and I thought the vines at the top added some interest without being ridiculous. I just had this feeling she wasn't into over-the-top."

"You would be correct. But she does like pretty things. She's still a girl." He sounded a little defensive.

"Of course, that's not what I meant at all."

His eyes flickered to hers. "I definitely think this is the one. How much will these cost?"

"Maybe eighty dollars for all of them. And that includes envelopes."

He reached for his wallet. "Will a hundred be fine?"

Charlotte turned to face him fully. "I said eighty, and there's no need to pay me now. I'll give you a definitive price after I order."

"What about your time?"

She shook her head. "It's fine. I wanted to do this, and honestly this barely took me any time at all." That wasn't true—she'd worked several hours on these designs—but for some reason taking money from him felt . . . weird. It shouldn't, but it did.

"Thank you." He leaned forward, resting his elbows

on the table and lacing his fingers together. "What's left to do?"

Charlotte relaxed, hoping the awkwardness would continue to pass as they conversed more about the wedding. She pulled out her notebook and turned to the checklist in the front. "Quite a bit, actually. But it shouldn't be too hard. We need to order the flowers, the cake, and a DJ if they want one. Discuss décor. I have some ideas for that. Also, what about rings? Do they have that covered?"

Dean sighed. "I have no idea. I didn't even think about rings. I mean, he gave her an engagement ring, but I doubt he thought that far ahead."

"Sometimes engagement rings come with a band, but not always. Is there a way you can ask her?"

"I don't know. They've been busy lately. She's on a mission. But I can email. Sometimes it takes her a few days to answer."

"That's okay. Why don't I put together some questions for her and you can send it all in one email so we can move forward on some of these things."

His face relaxed, eyes softening. "Yeah, that's a good idea."

Charlotte touched his arm gently. "We sort of jumped into this without thinking much through."

Dean chuckled. "No kidding. I knew this would be a lot of work, but . . ." He sagged, his shoulders slumping when he looked over at her. "Thank you, again. You have no idea how grateful I am to you for doing this for Alex."

She smiled. "Well, I don't even know Alex, but I'm happy to do it for you."

It was the truth, but the way his eyes focused in on her, maybe she shouldn't have said it that way. They were both sending mixed signals, which she feared would eventually get them into trouble. But if Dean was feeling anywhere close to the way she was, he fought his own good sense on this one. She wanted Dean, badly. But his friendship and happiness were equally as important.

"So, why don't you tell me what days work best for you and I'll set up some of these appointments?"

He pushed his chair back, as if preparing to leave. "Don't worry about that. You set them up when it works for you and I'll make it happen."

"Okay. I'll let you know."

He nodded and then stood up. Charlotte began to gather her things and stuff them back into her bag when a bridal magazine caught her eye. She turned to Dean. "Oh, I forgot, the most important thing. The dress."

His face tightened and his mouth dropped the slightest bit. "Yeah, I actually thought of that, and uh . . . I think Amy is going to pick out Alex's dress."

"Is that a friend of hers? That makes sense."

He hesitated. "Yeah, I thought so, too. I also found out she isn't having a bridesmaid, or whatever. Just the two of them."

"Okay. Well, that's easy enough." Charlotte smiled. "So we're making progress. I'll be in touch when I have some appointments set up for us."

She slipped past him and was grateful to find that Jake had left the main room, leaving them alone. Dean followed her to the front door. Before pushing it open, she turned and looked up at him. If she left without saying what was on her mind, she would regret it.

"Dean, I'm sorry about the photoshoot. If I'd known it would make things weird between us, I never would have done it."

"Don't apologize, Charlotte. Everything that happened . . . it was my fault."

"What makes you say that? Do you think I didn't want

to kiss you? I thought . . . well, I just thought you'd always known that when I flirted with you . . . I meant it."

He breathed in deep, his eyes trained on hers. "I always hoped you meant it."

She grinned at him, releasing a breath. Here they went again, sending those mixed signals. But before she could speak, he interrupted.

"But Charlotte, I'm way too old for you. We both know that. And this . . . this awkwardness. It sucks. I like you too much to give up this good working relationship we have together."

Charlotte's arms and legs suddenly felt prickly, as if her body was going numb. Her mouth couldn't decide if it should smile or frown, but she finally got control and gave him a forced quirk of her lips. So he'd decided to do what was best. While she'd had the same thoughts, why did she suddenly feel sad that he'd voiced his concerns out loud?

"I understand. You're completely right. You're my favorite person to work with. So . . . yeah, we should not . . . uh, mess that up at all."

Damn it, she could hear the tears in her voice, and the look in his eyes told her he did, too.

"Charlotte . . ."

She held up a hand. "Oh my gosh, Dean. It's fine. I'm grateful that we're close enough to be honest with each other. I'll be in touch, okay?"

She turned and left the building as fast as she could.

Eleven

"I still think you should cash the check," Lauren said as she placed a stamp on the final envelope.

Instead of responding, Charlotte took another sip of her wine. She was on glass three. Or five. Hard to tell.

It was Friday night, and she and Lauren had spent the past two hours binging on Chinese food and addressing wedding invitations to people neither of them knew. Earlier that evening Dean had dropped off a legal envelope that held the final list of addresses. He'd been friendly but hadn't come inside, claiming he had some work to get back to, and Charlotte had forced herself to keep it short and not be weird.

Once she'd gotten inside and opened the envelope, she'd found a check made out to her in the amount of two thousand dollars. In the memo he'd written: *thanks for being amazing.*

Fuck being amazing.

"I plan on cashing the check. Don't worry. He owes me big for all the help I'm giving him."

Lauren just raised an eyebrow and then slid all the finished envelopes into a bag. "How about I drop these off at the post office in the morning."

"Thanks," Charlotte said. "And I'm sorry I'm being a bitch."

"You're not being a bitch at all. I completely understand your feelings on the matter."

Charlotte stared at her. "*But . . .*"

"There's no but. I swear."

"Please, I've been your friend for way too long. I know a but when I hear one."

Lauren leveled her with a hard state. "Okay, fine. I think you're giving in too easily."

"What? Lauren, the man made it very clear that he's not interested."

"No, he didn't. He made it very clear he's *afraid*."

Charlotte rolled her eyes. "Right. A forty-one-year-old man, afraid of me."

"Bingo. A forty-one-year-old man who has the hots for a beautiful young woman with her entire life ahead of her."

"Pshh." Charlotte couldn't believe this. Of course they'd discussed their age difference, but it wasn't like he was fifty or sixty. "Dean is not a normal older man. He's hot."

"Do you think hot people are impervious to fear? You two have spent three years flirting. Finally, you kiss. Then he freaks out."

"Exactly. What part of that are you not understanding? It was a mistake."

Lauren shook her head in exasperation. "I don't buy that. I work with him, too, you know. Dean is a very thoughtful guy. One of the biggest gentlemen I know. If he was completely uninterested, he wouldn't have let himself get in this position. He's torn and fighting it. I think he genuinely thinks he's too old for you. He thinks he is doing you a favor."

Charlotte shrugged. Was it possible that he was interested and just afraid? She'd been with a man before who couldn't own his true emotions. Did she want to go down that path again? "He probably *is* doing me a favor."

"Fine!" Lauren threw her hands up and rose from the table. "If you believe that, then I don't want to hear about it again. Snap out of it."

"Lauren, I'm sorry."

Her best friend sighed. "You have no reason to be sorry. I just don't like to see you sad. I'm trying to urge you to push a little harder if you think he's worth it. If not, let it go. Take his money to the bank and buy yourself something awesome."

"Do you really think he's just afraid?"

Lauren sighed. "I think there's a good possibility. But don't hold it against me if I'm wrong."

"I could never hold it against you. You're always there for me."

"And don't you forget it." Lauren heaved the heavy bag of invites up onto her shoulder. "See you next Saturday then?"

With a groan, Charlotte let her head fall back. "God, yes. Here I thought I'd be in a better emotional state when I was forced to see John again. But once again Charlotte Linley is messed up over a guy."

"This guy is nothing like John. And you'll be fine. Take that money and go get a facial or a wax. Something that makes you feel sexy."

Charlotte stood up to see her friend to the door. Lauren had a point. It had been a while since she'd had a hair appointment. "Yeah maybe I will.

Dean had spent the past five years of his life enjoying a pretty steady routine. He ate cold cereal for breakfast, went to the gym four days a week, spent most of his day at the Stag, and then fell into bed exhausted every night and slept through till morning. Once in a great while there'd be a date or hookup thrown in the mix, and usually when a new *Call of Duty* game released he'd devote a weekend to sitting on the couch and trying to beat it, but basically he was a creature of habit. Conventional and adaptive. Despite the hardships he'd been dealt in his life, he felt like he managed to have a positive outlook, and for the most part his mood remained even-keeled. He considered himself the voice of reason and experience in his partnership with TJ and Jake, and was nearly certain they'd agree with that sentiment. Overall, these days not much got him worked up or interrupted his life.

Until he'd kissed Charlotte.

The past week and a half, he hadn't had a full night's rest, was moody as hell, and he'd been so distracted he'd put in a vodka mash and then forgotten to turn on the agitator, meaning the entire thing waterlogged and ended up all over the distilling room floor.

The fact that he had to see her today had him all kinds of messed up. He'd seen her a couple of times since the kiss, and each time had been uncomfortable. All week he'd been trying to convince himself that he hadn't hurt her feelings the day she'd come to show him the invitations. That she hadn't been about to cry. But the truth was, the look on her face before she'd left had nearly broken him. Still, he knew putting the brakes on this thing between them was the right thing to do.

"Are you sure everything's okay with you?" Jake asked as he used a mop to push a pile of oatmeal-consistency cooked grain into a bucket on the floor.

"Yeah, why?" He didn't meet his friend's eyes.

"Just . . . I don't know. You seem off your game this week."

"I think I'm just stressed about planning this wedding."

That seemed a reasonable explanation. Hadn't Charlotte called him a bridezilla?

"Makes sense, I guess." Jake said. "But isn't Charlotte helping you?"

Dean picked up his own full bucket and sighed. "Yeah, she is."

Without elaborating he hauled the vessel over to the giant plastic tub they were filling and dumped it over the side. What a waste of grain, time, and money. He shook his head and headed back to the mess. They'd almost gotten it all picked up. Normally he'd start fresh with a new mash, but today he had to meet Charlotte at the floral shop across the town square. He'd give anything to avoid it. At the same time, he could hardly wait to see her.

"I figured you'd like working with Charlotte."

Dean looked up at Jake to see him grinning. Here the past three years he thought he'd done a good job at masking his feelings for her, but lately it had become clear that he'd been wrong.

"Working with her is just fine."

"Just fine, huh? TJ told me about your photo shoot."

Dean groaned. "TJ has a big mouth. But yeah. I did it."

After filling his bucket with hot water, Dean began to pour it over the floor. The majority of the mess was picked up so the rest could be squeegeed into the drain on the floor.

"You have to get naked?" Jake asked with a chuckle.

Immediately Dean's eyes flew up to his. "No, I didn't get naked. Of course not."

"Just asking, simmer down. I bet it was kind of hot, though, right? Having her take pictures of you like that."

Dean sighed. "I don't know if I'd use the word *hot*." Which was a complete lie. That day had ended up being one of the hottest of his life, all because of her and that kiss.

Jake nodded and gave a look that implied he wasn't quite convinced. "Well, I think it would be hot. And it would be kind of cool to be on a book cover. Haven't been able to use that line before. I mean, how could the ladies not think that was awesome?"

What the heck was he getting at? Dean's jaw tightened as he filled another bucket with water. "I don't intend to tell the ladies."

"Then you're missing a prime opportunity. Women go crazy for that stuff. You'll be some kind of Fabio. Honestly, I didn't think you had it in you."

"Thanks a lot."

Jake chuckled. "When do we get to see these pictures?"

He had no idea so he just shrugged.

"Maybe I should ask Charlotte if I can be next. I think I could pull it off."

Dean stilled. He was facing away from his friend, but he knew Jake was watching him, so he forced his body back into action and grabbed the squeegee off the wall. He needed to move past what had happened. Stop letting that kiss affect his life and, even more important, his interactions with Charlotte. He hated that she'd had to be the one to make the first move after what they'd done. Even then he'd acted like an idiot. Another good reason to stop letting his attraction to her mess with his good sense. A real relationship with a woman like her was impossible, which meant just fooling around with her was not an option. He definitely didn't want to jeopardize what they had.

But although that all sounded noble and good, one problem remained. He wanted her so damn bad. Fighting that was not easy. He had to try harder.

"Yeah, maybe you *should* ask her. I get the feeling she's looking for guys." Dean hated the words coming out of his mouth. Just that thought pissed him off, but he clamped his teeth down and pushed through the feelings of jealousy that rose up in his gut.

"Why do I feel like this is a trap?" Jake asked.

Dean turned around. "It's not. Ask her. She's a professional."

"Listen, you know I have absolutely no designs on Charlotte. She's so into you."

With a sigh, Dean clamped his eyes shut. "I don't know about that. But she and I are better off just being friends."

"Why?" Jake sounded genuinely perplexed.

Dean leaned his squeegee against the wall. "Because I'm a divorced, middle-aged man for a start."

"Good grief, dude. I'm pretty sure you've got a few years left in you."

Dean knew Jake was teasing, but his buddies didn't know all the reasons he wasn't meant for a young woman like Charlotte. And it was none of their business.

"Anyway, let's drop this," Dean said.

"Fine. Consider it dropped, but I want to go on record as saying that you're fucking nuts not to give things a try with her. Charlotte's not the type to get crazy on you if it doesn't work."

Dean leveled Jake with a stare.

"Okay, okay. Now it's dropped. Promise," Jake said. "But she works with me on Saturday, you know?"

Dean turned around. "You have a funny way of dropping a conversation, you know that? And I thought Trevor Rich was shooting." He wasn't a fan of the guy. Big ego and wasn't all that friendly, as if being the photographer made him important. Wasn't even willing to share images with vendors, whereas Charlotte not only shared them for free with everyone, she'd even had several canvases printed for the Stag.

"Yeah he was. Apparently he canceled on his couple and they asked Charlotte to do it."

"Huh. Well then, I guess you'll be able to ask her about doing a shoot then." Dean glanced at his watch. "You think you can finish this up? I actually have to meet her at the florist across the street in five minutes."

"Sure." Jake pulled out a hose so he could give everything a final rinse. "You gonna start another mash today?"

Dean shook his head. "Not now. I'm actually gonna head home after this appointment."

Jake looked surprised but nodded. "Good for you, man. You need a break."

His friend was right. He needed to try to unwind. His nerves felt fried, and the lack of sleep was catching up with him. Sounded like a good night to just get a pizza and try to zone out for a while. Take his mind off things.

Wouldn't be easy to do since he had to spend the next couple of hours in Charlotte's presence.

It was impossible not to be happy in a flower shop, Charlotte thought as she meandered through Harrington's Floral Design, which sat on the opposite side of the square from the Stag. Mark Harrington was an up-and-coming florist in the area, and considering that beautiful photos of his earliest weddings hung on the walls of his shop all courtesy of Charlotte, she was hoping to exploit his goodwill for return favors.

She didn't doubt that he expected it from her the minute she'd called and made the appointment, but he'd seemed really excited about the job. He'd also not been shy about how much he liked setting up at the Stag so he could check out the "luscious owners." His words, but she'd agreed wholeheartedly.

The bell sounded and she turned. Speaking of luscious owners . . .

"Hey," she said as Dean walked in.

His eyebrows popped up when he saw her. "Hi." He spoke quietly, which was cute. He looked completely out of place surrounded by giant floral bouquets and home décor. "Your hair . . ."

Charlotte touched a piece of hair at her shoulder. Yesterday she'd gotten it cut and highlighted. It was quite a change. Much lighter than before. "Yeah, I was in the mood for something different."

"It's . . ." His eyes wandered over her face. "I really like it."

"Thanks."

He quickly looked away, eyes darting around the shop. "There's a lot to take in."

"Isn't it gorgeous? I love coming in here." Charlotte inhaled. The scent was heavenly.

"I hear a man in my shop," a singsongy voice said from the back room, and then Mark pushed through a white curtain. "And I'm not disappointed."

Charlotte chuckled quietly as Mark eyed Dean from head to toe.

"Dean, this is Mark," she said.

"Hi, Mark." Dean reached out his hand but the man bypassed it, going straight in for a hug—which clearly took Dean by surprise. His eyes widened and darted to Charlotte, who couldn't wipe the grin from her face.

"So happy to meet another one of you Stag men. We're all friends here," Mark said as he pushed Dean away and then embraced Charlotte. She was used to Mark's hugs. He was a larger-than-life guy—in personality and in stature, with a thick dark beard and colorful tattoos going down each arm. He was as sweet as could be, although he had

an intense side as she'd often seen as he set up for weddings. She assumed it was just his perfectionism getting
the better of him, which she could understand.

Mark turned back to Dean. "So, your sister is getting
married. Fantastic."

"She is. I'm sorry to say we're on somewhat of a budget. Time- and money-wise."

Mark laughed and then held a conspiratorial hand to the
side of his mouth. "That's what they all say, in the beginning," he murmured.

"We truly are, this time, Mark," Charlotte threw in.
"But there was no way I could go to anyone but you. Alex
deserves the best, even if we have to use budget blooms."

She hoped to appeal to his ego, and it appeared to work
like a charm. "Of course she does. And you're so sweet.
Love your new hair by the way." He touched Charlotte's
arm quickly and then headed over to his counter and pulled
out his notebook.

"Let's talk details," he said, sliding a pair of tortoise-
shell glasses onto his face.

They proceeded to give him the fast-approaching
date—which had his eyebrows rising—and the location,
which he'd assumed correctly would be the Stag.

"Attendants?" he asked.

"None," Dean said.

"Hmm. Unusual but easy. Very easy." Mark made a
note in his notebook. "Colors?"

"She likes green."

"I also love green." After a few more notes, Mark
looked up. "Okay. Usually there is a contrast color."

"I guess whatever looks good with green?" Dean asked.
Mark turned to Charlotte.

"The invitation I kept neutral. Golds and ivories."

"Okaaay, so what if we really made the greenery pop

by using a neutral color palette. Whites, ivories, maybe just a hint of a peach."

"I love that idea," Charlotte interjected. She glanced at Dean, who just nodded his approval. Had he been staring at her?

"Buffet or plated?" Mark continued.

"Buffet," Charlotte said.

The questions continued and finally Mark led them to the walk-in cooler along the back of the shop. It was bursting with color. Roses, lilies, carnations, and even tropical flowers like birds-of-paradise lined the walls. It smelled so wonderful.

"Isn't it beautiful?" Charlotte said, looking up at Dean.

"It is. Looks expensive, too," he whispered.

Charlotte squeezed his arm playfully, and then quickly pulled away. She didn't want to make him uncomfortable, but God how she loved the feel of corded muscle under his skin.

"Now, now, don't get caught up on the price." Mark turned to face them. "I'll make sure everything is gorgeous and we'll stay in your budget. Charlotte's done many things for me over the past two years while I got this place off the ground."

Charlotte breathed a sigh of relief. "Thank you, Mark. We really appreciate it."

The next fifteen minutes flew by as they discussed different flowers, centerpiece ideas, and thoughts on the setup for the reception. Mark and Charlotte agreed that two main arrangements could do double duty: They'd use them during the ceremony and then move them to flank the buffet table.

Standing in the cooler for so long was making her cold and when her thoughts strayed that direction, the hair on her shoulders began to rise in response. She gave a little shiver as Mark went on about the different varieties of white roses he had available.

Warm hands settled on her upper arms and rubbed up and down. Charlotte sucked in a breath and didn't miss the subtle look and smile Mark sent her when he saw Dean touching her with such ease and familiarity. He didn't break his speech or give anything away, just kept on with his explanation.

Charlotte expected Dean to pull away after rubbing her arms, but he held on, his hands settling just above her elbows, the feel of his skin nearly burning her. His thumbs gently traced back and forth on the backs of her arms, which made her shiver again. That made him stop, and she silently cursed her body's involuntary responses.

She now knew what it felt like to kiss him. Today she saw how her body would react with just the lightest, innocent touch. It was almost too much to imagine what it would be like if he touched her entire naked body with real heat and passion.

Managing not to shiver a third time, Charlotte was relieved when they exited the cooler. The smaller space had forced her to stand way too close to Dean.

They'd decided that Alex's bouquet would be a mix of delicate white roses, green and peach hydrangeas, succulents, and eucalyptus leaves. Nate's boutonniere would be a tiny succulent backed by a single eucalyptus leaf. The overall look would be natural and elegant. Charlotte was beyond pleased with how things were coming together. She had finally begun to picture the wedding in her mind, and it surprised her how excited she felt about it.

"Well, I think we have a plan, my dears." Mark glanced down at his notes. "Let me just run a few quick figures and I'll let you know where we stand on these ideas."

"Perfect. Thank you," Charlotte and Dean said at the

same time. When Mark walked to the rear of the shop and around to the back of the counter, it left the two of them somewhat alone. Within seconds music came on from the speakers in the ceiling, a local jazz radio station. Charlotte glanced over her shoulder to Mark, who gave her a quick wink and then refocused on his notepad and calculator.

She smiled. Did he assume after the cooler that they wished for a moment of privacy? Dean had wandered up to the front end of the shop and was eyeing a dining table made up for a dinner party complete with massive centerpiece and place settings. Hardly something a man like him would find so engaging. Was he back to avoiding her?

Deciding that wouldn't do, Charlotte walked over to him. "This is beautiful, isn't it?"

"Hmm. A little much. Who'd want to eat at a table this full of . . . *stuff*?" he whispered.

She laughed quietly. "It's for inspiration."

He sauntered to another display, this one patriotic, gearing up for Independence Day, which would arrive before they knew it. Dean picked up a packet of designer paper napkins that looked like American flags and then dropped it back down a little too firmly. "I hate that Alex reenlisted."

Whoa. That was out of left field and Charlotte wasn't sure what to say. She could see that Dean felt very protective and paternal about his little sister. But Alexis was a grown woman. "Italy seems like a very safe place to be stationed."

"It is, I think. Especially compared with the Middle East, where she's been."

"Where do they plan to live once they're out?"

"I honestly don't know. I hope around here."

Charlotte smiled. "Just think. A couple of years from now, you could be a grandpa." She said it to tease him, but the way he looked at her showed that he hadn't appreciated it.

"Is that how you see me?"

"Oh my God, no! Not at all." Charlotte regretted the joke completely, considering their previous conversations and the things Lauren had suggested. What had she been thinking? "I'm sorry. I just . . . in some ways you just seem more of a fatherly figure to Alex, and she is old enough for children. I . . . anyway. No. The last thing I imagine you as is grandfatherly. Remember, I saw you shirtless."

She gave him a flirty smile, hoping it would ease things over, but his eyes narrowed. "Speaking of that. I think, uh, Jake is interested in being a model for you."

Her eyes went wide. "Seriously? That would be amazing."

His gaze shot to her and he shoved his hands in his pockets. "You think?"

"Well . . . yeah. I can totally see him as a book cover."

Dean gave somewhat of a grunt and looked back at the table. "Yeah, well, just don't make out with him, too."

Charlotte's head jerked back in shock. "Wow. Is that how you see *me*?" She threw his words back at him.

He shook his head and walked away toward the windows at the front of the store.

"Okay, ladies and gentleman. Here we go." Mark came walking through the store toward them, and Charlotte forced herself to smile. In reality she was stewing at Dean's comment. Why hadn't they been able to find some sort of common ground since that stupid kiss?

Dean accepted the invoice from Mark, so Charlotte peeked over his shoulder to read it. She gasped. The proposed total was a steal. She was guessing not a whole lot over his cost.

"Oh, Mark. Are you sure?" Charlotte asked.

"Very. Now are we in business?"

Dean nodded and stuck out his hand, which this time Mark took. "Thank you, Mark. This means a lot. Really. And Alex will love your work."

"Of course she will. And I want lots of photos, dear," he said in Charlotte's direction.

"Absolutely. And maybe some new canvases for the store."

"Now we're talking," Mark said.

They said their good-byes and Charlotte led the way outside to the sidewalk. As soon as Dean joined her and the door shut, she turned. "Ready to explain yourself?"

"For what?" He tried looking confused, but she knew Dean was no dummy. He sidestepped her, making his way into the street and crossing toward the green space at the center of the square.

"*Don't make out with Jake*?" She repeated his words back to him while following close on his heels.

"Charlotte, just forget it." Dean stepped around a parked car and onto the sidewalk.

Once she caught up, she grabbed his arm, stopping him in his tracks. He turned, a scowl on his handsome face.

"You do not get to make that comment and then walk away. Do you really think I make out with my models? I thought I was pretty clear about that."

He sighed. "You were."

Charlotte held up her hands in exasperation. "Soooo, your words were coming from a place of bitterness or jealousy? Or maybe regret? Just get it out there. Be honest with me, because I'm really over how ridiculous things have been between us since that day."

"You want me to get it all out on the table?" he asked. Charlotte nodded, ignoring the few passersby walking through the park. "Okay, fine. When it comes to you photographing Jake? Yes. I'm jealous as hell."

She swallowed and stared up at him. Here they went again, back and forth. "Why? It won't be the same."

Dean glanced around and then lowered his voice. "He'll still take off his shirt. You'll tell him to look . . . sexy, or hot, or whatever the hell it is you'll want him to do."

"That doesn't mean I'll like it."

Dean gave her a long glance. "I'm not an idiot, Charlotte. And you're not immune to a guy who looks like that."

"Have you ever heard of self-control? Or loyalty, or even trust?"

"You don't owe me anything. This is my issue. I shouldn't have said anything, okay? I'm sorry." He ran a hand down his face. "God, I keep apologizing to you, which is exactly why what we did was a mistake."

Her heart sank. "Was kissing me that big a mistake?"

"Damn it." He jammed his hands into his hair and then dropped them with a heavy sigh. "This is what I wanted to avoid. I didn't want to feel this way. Didn't want things to change between us."

"But they did, so what now? How do we go back?"

"I don't know if we can."

"Then which way do we go? Forward? Sideways? Upside down? Because this weird thing we're doing is bullshit." Charlotte stepped closer to him, her neck bending to meet his gaze. "Dean, I liked kissing you. I don't regret it. After all these years of flirting, it was totally natural for us to kiss. And if that's all it's going to be, then . . . we're both adults. We can move past it."

Dean shook his head. "It's more than that, Charlotte, and you know it. If it was merely curiosity, this wouldn't be a problem. I wouldn't want to rip one of my best friends into shreds when I imagine you seeing him naked."

Okay. Maybe they were getting somewhere. "He wouldn't be naked," she said with a smile.

"You know what I mean. I've always liked you, Charlotte. I'm a possessive guy and after kissing you . . . I'm just having a hard time reminding myself that I have no right to be that way with you."

"But what if I want you to have the right?"

Dean stared down at her, his neck bulging as he swallowed. "You shouldn't. It's a bad idea."

"Why don't you tell me what you're afraid of?" she asked quietly.

His lips pursed and he looked away. Charlotte watched as the wind blew the tips of his hair, the lightest bit of gray sparkling in the sun. His silence told her that Lauren had been close to the truth. Their age difference was a real problem for him, but if he couldn't see past that, then why was she wasting her time trying to convince him she was worth the risk? It was starting to become apparent that he was being a real dick about the entire thing. If he couldn't even admit his fear to her, there really was no use.

"I guess I'll let you off the hook for that one. I have a lot of work to do," she finally said. If he wanted to put up boundaries, she wasn't going to beg. "We have two appointments next Tuesday. Both cake tastings. I'll pick you up here since I know where they are."

Dean nodded. "Sounds good."

So she was right. He was willing to leave things like this, with him admitting he liked her and was jealous, but also unwilling to act on it or even speak about it. Fine. She had better things to do than wait for him to get over himself.

"All right. See you then."

She began to turn and head for her car.

"Charlotte, wait."

She turned back to find him watching her, hands in his pockets. "Thanks again for today. Getting us that deal on the flowers. I appreciate it."

She gave him a pinched smile, because it was really tempting to tell him to go to hell. "Yeah, sure. What are friends for?"

And she walked away.

Twelve

Charlotte hadn't really known what to expect from Shelby and her friends, but she'd been pleasantly surprised. They'd greeted her at Mary Sue's home Saturday morning with hugs and how-are-yous, acting as if no time had passed between high school and the present. The best part was that everyone seemed genuine, which was nice. Shelby had run in a different circle of girls than Charlotte, but they'd all been friendly acquaintances so it wasn't as if she was with strangers.

Thank God, no one mentioned John. And she was trying really hard to forget the fact that she'd have to see him in less than an hour. The girls were close to ready, so Charlotte stepped into the kitchen to get some water and take a breather. Glancing at her phone she saw a text from Lauren, who had headed over to the house Shelby and Jason had purchased together just a few months prior and would be moving into after their wedding. The guys were getting ready there.

LAUREN: He asked about you.

Charlotte bit at her bottom lip and then replied.

CHARLOTTE: What did you say?

She wasn't sure what she hoped her friend had said. Anything but *She's still single*. Which was stupid since it was a shamefully true statement.

LAUREN: That you were doing great.

That was vague enough. She wondered if there was anything Lauren wasn't saying. Not that she didn't trust her—Lauren would never do anything to embarrass her—but still . . .

LAUREN: I might have also told him you have a boyfriend.

She'd said *what*? Charlotte nearly choked, and obviously she hadn't hidden her shock because Mary Sue put a hand on her back. "Everything okay, Charlotte?"
"Oh yes, just fine. Thanks."

CHARLOTTE: What is wrong with you???????
LAUREN: I know! I'm sorry. He just casually mentioned that he knew you weren't married and it just pissed me off.

Huh. How did he know? Charlotte supposed it wasn't that strange. Mary Sue knew she was single, as did Shelby and his brother. But it still sucked that he'd made mention of it. Was he gloating? And was it so bad that Lauren had lied? What did it matter? He'd never find out the truth.

CHARLOTTE: It's okay. I appreciate you having my

back. But please tell me he isn't that good looking anymore.

Because although she used to look him up online occasionally, it had been years since she'd had any desire to
do so.

LAUREN: Uhhhh . . . sure.

Charlotte groaned quietly and stuffed her phone back
into her pocket just in time to see that Shelby was carefully
walking down the main steps. Pulling out her camera,
Charlotte snapped a few of her smiling at her mother, who'd
begun to tear up. It was a sweet moment, especially when
Mary Sue embraced her daughter at the foot of the stairs.

Charlotte lowered her camera and gave them a weak
smile. Happy people were getting married today. Just like
they did every weekend all over the world and the show
had to go on, whether she would see her ex for the first
time in five years or not.

Within a half hour the girls were loading up in the limo
bus and heading to the church, where Shelby and Jason
would have their first look.

John would be there.

On the way over, Charlotte's hands began to sweat. Before they'd left she'd ducked into a powder room to freshen
up her makeup a bit and adjust her hair, which she'd spent a
little more time on today. This morning she'd decided to
style it in a messy low side bun with pieces framing her
face. It said *chic without trying too hard*, which was completely false considering it had taken her half an hour to
perfect. She'd felt satisfied with her appearance fifteen
minutes ago, but as the bus pulled up outside the church,
and the brakes hissed, she felt like a hot mess.

She knew the boys would be hidden away in the church so Charlotte could get Shelby into position in a garden patio to the side of the church, but the minute she stepped off the bus she worried John might be around any corner. What would she say? Why hadn't she prepared better before this moment?

The girls shuffled into the church, carrying their flowers and bags, and Charlotte stepped inside the atrium to see Lauren heading for the door with a smile.

"You made it. Jason's ready when you are."

"Okay. I just . . . I need a minute."

Lauren frowned. "You gonna be okay?"

Charlotte nodded. "I will. But I really don't know what I was thinking taking this job," she whispered.

"Char?"

That voice. *The* voice. The one that use to say things like "*I love you*." "*Forever*." "*You're beautiful*." The voice that calmed her when she was panicked, soothed her when she was sad, and whispered in her ear the first time she'd ever made love. It still sent sensation rippling through her nerve endings.

Looking over Lauren's shoulder, Charlotte plastered on a smile. "John. How are you?"

She didn't miss the way he looked her up and down. Too bad the shape of her body was mostly concealed by the layers of equipment hanging on her body. Nonetheless, he grinned and walked right up to wrap her in a big hug. Her two camera bodies prevented them from getting too close, but still, the feel of him almost took her breath away.

He was bigger than he used to be. In a good way. Muscular and strong, and his arms squeezed her tight as she was shocked into the past by the scent of him. A different cologne, but still the same John undertone.

Pulling back, he was still grinning. "You look amazing."

"Oh." She chuckled, embarrassed and genuinely surprised by his excitement at seeing her. She hadn't known what to expect. Awkwardness, indifference, maybe even irritation. But this . . . this *happiness* came as a shock. "You look amazing yourself."

He laughed, and then awkwardly glanced over at Lauren as if he'd just realized she was standing there watching. She quickly turned her look of shock into a cheeky grin.

"Well, I need to get our couple moving along so we can take some portraits," Charlotte said. "Sorry to cut things short."

"Of course. I understand. We can catch up later," he said.

Really? What was there to catch up on? *Remember that one time we almost had a family together but then we didn't?* Or, *Remember that one time I'd just put on my wedding dress at the church and your mom came into the dressing room crying and told me the wedding was off?* Huh. She really wondered what they had to discuss, and just like that some of her anger and sadness bubbled up from the place she'd buried them deep inside. Maybe he'd been able to move on, but she had a little bit of lingering resentment. Some might say she was justified.

"Yeah, we could totally do that. Later." She turned and headed back outside, letting out a deep breath. She heard the door behind her and knew it was Lauren.

"You okay?"

Charlotte spoke quietly as she stepped around an alcove on the side of the building. "What the hell was that?"

"What do you mean?" Lauren asked.

"Well . . . he acted happy to see me."

"That's good, isn't it?"

"It's just not what I expected."

"He was so nice at his brother's house all morning. Offered to carry my bag and brought me a drink. It's been very unsettling. Would have been a lot easier if he was a dick."

"Right? I agree." Charlotte groaned and looked up to the sky. "I wanted to hate him today. Why was he sweet?"

Lauren laughed. "Let's just get this first look over with. The sooner we get the portraits done with, the better."

Charlotte couldn't disagree with that. Portraits were the time when she'd spend the most time with the bridal party, and by default with John. As she found Shelby and led her to the garden patio, it was strange to consider the fact that in another life, they'd have been sisters-in-law. That Jason, who was currently facing away from them on the stone pavers, ready for Shelby to tap him on the shoulder and reveal herself in her dress, might have been her brother-in-law. She possibly would have been a bridesmaid in this very wedding.

Shaking off those silly and irrelevant thoughts, Charlotte prepared her camera settings, nodded at Lauren who was shooting from another angle, and then instructed Shelby to make her way to her groom.

Charlotte's shutter began to shoot rapidly as Shelby did as instructed, lightly touching his shoulder and alerting him to turn and look at her. The moment he did, his face broke into a wide grin, his eyes going glassy as he took in every inch of her dress, hair, makeup. Shelby did look spectacular today, and apparently his reaction pleased her, since she covered her mouth with her hand to conceal her emotions.

First sights were almost always emotional. Charlotte glanced over at Lauren to find her friend's lips twisted, holding back her own happy tears. Despite her thoughts on the wedding day and all of its unnecessary pomp and circumstance, Charlotte knew it was a privilege to witness a couple in this private and vulnerable moment. That fact never escaped her.

"Babe, you take my breath away," he whispered. He leaned forward and kissed her forehead. "I love you so much."

Though slightly different, his voice was similar enough to John's to make Charlotte pause a moment. She forced herself to continue shooting as they hugged and whispered to each other. When Charlotte and Laruen were both satisfied with their coverage, they made their way to the couple.

"You both look wonderful," Charlotte said.

"Charlotte, hi." Jason reached out and gave her a hug. "It's so good to see you. Thank you so much for helping us out today. I realize it might not have been ideal for you, but I can't tell you how much we appreciate it."

He glanced at Shelby, who nodded her agreement as she wiped at the corner of her eye. Charlotte couldn't decide if she appreciated his acknowledgment of the situation from her perspective, or wished he'd avoided the obvious like everyone else, but either way it was kind of him.

"I'm happy I could help. Truly." She was surprised to find that she meant it. So far the day had gone well. Shelby was a beautiful bride, her family was lovely and sweet, and after the ceremony and portraits, they'd be spending the evening at the Stag. A bummer that Dean wasn't scheduled to be there, but it felt like home, so that would be nice. "Shall we get on the bus and head out for some portraits? We have exactly an hour and a half before you need to be ready for the ceremony."

They agreed it was time to get everyone back on the limo bus, and Lauren made her way inside to gather the troops. The two of them let everyone else load up first and then made their way up the steps and onto the vehicle. After having a quick chat with the driver on how to get to the field they were shooting in first, she turned around to see only one seat left available. The man in the seat next to the vacant one grinned up at her.

She'd have to sit by John.

Thirteen

Dean knew he should be ashamed of himself. There was no reason for him to be at work tonight. He'd set himself up yesterday to leave his most recent mash to ferment until Sunday and had even tried to plan a relaxing evening at home. That had included spending Saturday afternoon working out, picking up a movie from the nightly rental machine, and buying some groceries. But once late afternoon had rolled around, he'd gotten restless. Unable to stand it any longer, he'd showered again, gotten dressed, and headed over to work.

So here he was, the sounds of the wedding reception above him as he stood checking the temperature on his still. Not long ago he'd added the mash into the still and was waiting for the heat to rise. The sound of chairs scraping over his head informed him everyone was sitting down to dinner. Or were they getting up from dinner?

He hadn't even gone upstairs to see how things were going, or even to see Charlotte, but for some reason just being in the building made him feel better. After everything that had passed between them in the previous couple of weeks, it killed him to know she'd be spending the evening with Jake, especially since he figured the guy would be bringing up the photo shoot. And it wasn't that he didn't trust his friend, because he did. But he really wished it was him working with her.

The past few days he'd replayed their conversation on the square over and over in his head. For months, he'd convinced himself that what seemed obvious was his own wishful thinking, but there was no more denying things after she'd made it clear with her statement.

What if I want you to have the right?

She wanted something more. With him. And he wanted it, too, but there was so much fear wrapped up in that idea that all the what-ifs nearly choked him. The fact that she'd flat-out asked him his fear was sobering. Damn, she was intuitive. And his answers abounded.

What if she eventually resented the age difference?

What if it didn't last and she quit working at the Stag?

And worst of all, because Charlotte was young, beautiful, and full of life: What if they did fall in love . . . and she wanted children? What the fuck would he do then?

He was torn with wanting to just see what happened between them and deal with the consequences, or keep trying to put walls up. Sadly, the latter hadn't been working for him. All that resulted was her walking away angry and hurt. It was starting to feel like there was no good answer.

Looking at the thermometer once again, Dean was finally satisfied with the rising temperature. He adjusted the nozzle so the first drips of liquid would make their way into the plastic tub where he would collect the foreshot, which was the unusable bit that came out of the still first. It had to be tossed.

A while later, he looked up and through the glass wall saw two men watching him work. One in a tux and the other in slacks and a tie. It wasn't that unusual for wedding guests to make their way down to check out the distilling equipment, but it was odd for them to find work being done on a weekend. Dean hadn't been working in here on a Saturday night in over a year.

The two guys gave him a small wave and he returned it and went about his business. Five minutes later, he could still feel them watching him so he walked out the back door, then down the short hallway to the main room, and asked if they wanted to come in and see the process up close. He wasn't sure why—he didn't usually do that unless he was leading a guided tour, which they did occasionally— but the tux guy seemed ecstatic at his offer.

Back in the distilling room Dean gave them a very brief rundown of all the bigger equipment: the fermenters, the mash cooker, the still.

"So is this whiskey you've got going right now?" Tux Guy asked.

"This is actually our Stag Signature Bourbon."

The guy's eyes lit up. "The one nobody's tasted yet."

Dean laughed. "Just us owners and a few of our close friends and family. We will uncask our first few barrels next month."

"Wow. How long have those been aging?"

"Five years. We actually made them in my father's basement before this building was ready for us."

"That's amazing. I love this stuff." Tux glanced around the room. The second guy, obviously wanting to get back to the party upstairs, said thanks for the tour and headed out. "Mind if I stay and watch?"

Dean shrugged. "Sure. Not too interesting at this point."

"Ah, I disagree. I find this fascinating. Why did you guys choose copper over stainless?"

It surprised Dean how much he enjoyed sharing his knowledge about how the copper still turned the sulfur into copper sulfates, thereby improving the taste of the product. He proceeded to explain what he was doing, how he had to watch the pressure, temperature, and steam, and how he determined when it was time to make the cut from the head to the hearts.

"Notice how the smell changed?" Dean held up the hydrometer to the man's nose.

He took a sniff and his eyes widened. "Yeah. It's a lot sweeter."

"The foreshots and heads contain things you don't want to drink. A lot of methanol. Now we start to fill this large bin with the hearts. The good stuff, ethanol. Want to taste it?"

The guy laughed. "Seriously? Will I have to sign a nondisclosure?"

Dean grinned. "Nah, the final product will taste completely different after spending five years in oak. This will taste clean but a little harsh. You can taste the corn a bit." He put a small glass under the spout and retained just a tiny bit before handing it over.

"Is this considered hooch?" Tux asked.

Dean laughed. "If you want to call it that." He watched as the guy tipped his head back and swallowed it down before letting out a loud breath.

"Wow. What proof is that?"

"About a hundred thirty-six."

His new friend laughed. "Jesus. Good thing it was just a taste. Thanks. This has been great. Really." He handed Dean the glass. "You've got a great job. I sit at a desk all day. Well, actually I don't sit anywhere but my parents' couch. I just got laid off and moved back home."

"I'm sorry to hear that. Where'd you move from?"

"Chicago. I'm a finance consultant."

Dean nodded. "I'm sure you'll find something around here."

"Yeah, I'm sure. Money will always be a problem for someone, right?" The guy laughed, but there was worry behind his eyes. "I don't know. I'm kind of thinking of treating this as a fresh start. Sucked to be laid off, but I actually hated what I did."

In that moment, Dean had a sudden urge to do something he'd never had the desire to do until now. Maybe this was a sign, and it could solve both of their problems. He hesitated, knowing that he could regret what he was about to say, but this guy was cool, and clearly interested. He was young but not much younger than Jake and TJ. Besides, his youth was an asset, wasn't it? He knew nothing about distilling but he seemed passionate about the process, which meant Dean could mold him to be exactly what he wanted. Teach him how to do things his way.

"Listen, this is sort of strange, but . . . I've been meaning to hire an apprentice for a while now." The guy's eyes widened. He was clearly listening with interest. "I'm sure we couldn't pay a financial consultant's salary, but . . . it would be a job. Seems like something you might enjoy. We're rolling out two new products by next month and if our projections are accurate . . . we'll be doing pretty damn well for ourselves."

A slow smile spread over the man's face. "Are you serious? You're offering me a job making whiskey?"

The words struck Dean as a little odd, and for a moment he felt ridiculous. "Well . . ."

"That would be absolutely amazing."

Dean froze, and then finally laughed. "It is pretty amazing if I do say so myself. Don't feel pressured to answer right now. Think about it."

"I'll do that." He shook his head, a grin on his face. "Wow. Thank you."

Dean stuck out his hand. "You're very welcome, and my name's Dean by the way."

The other man gave Dean a firm shake in return. "Great to meet you, Dean. John Reynolds."

John shook his head again, clearly shocked. "Here I was nervous as hell about coming to this wedding tonight. My ex is here and I'm jobless and living with my parents. Doesn't make you feel great about yourself. But this . . . this is great. Thank you."

Dean could relate. He'd been in a similar situation just after his divorce. "I'm sure things aren't going as great for her as they appear," he said, just to be supportive.

John gave him a long glance. "Thanks, but I think they are. She looks so amazing, and she's obviously very successful. I'm not surprised, really. She was always ambitious." He nodded above them. "She's the photographer tonight. Was willing to do this job last-minute as a favor for my brother and sister-in-law even though she and I didn't part on the best of terms."

Dean swallowed hard, knots forming in his stomach. "Charlotte's your ex?"

"You know her?"

"Uh, yeah. She shoots a lot of weddings here." He pretended to fiddle with the temperature gauge, because all of a sudden he felt sick to his stomach.

"I've been trying to talk to her all night. It's good to see her again." He huffed out a laugh. "Can't help but make a guy wonder what might have been. Especially when you're feeling like a failure."

The same sentiments Dean could relate to a minute ago now sounded like a whiny cry for help. He needed to stop and pull himself together. This John was a good guy, the same good guy he'd just offered an apprenticeship to not five minutes ago. He couldn't renege on his offer, that wouldn't be right. He didn't really want to, either. Meeting John and offering him a job had instantly given Dean a feeling of relief at the thought he might finally have found the help he needed. John was clearly intelligent, good-natured, and curious. All of those things made him a good fit from first impressions.

"Don't be too hard on yourself. You should get back up there. Always lots of single women at weddings."

John chuckled. "Yeah. Except I can't stop looking at the one I let get away. Anyway, I'm sorry for going on and on. I've obviously had one too many cocktails from upstairs. But thanks, man. Can I come by Tuesday so we can talk some more about this apprenticeship?"

Dean began to say yes and then recalled he had appointments with Charlotte to eat cake. "How about Wednesday? That works better for me."

John nodded. "Wednesday it is, then."

After he'd left Dean let out a muffled curse. He'd just offered Charlotte's ex a job. An ex who currently had his eye on her. An ex who was clearly questioning if he could get her back, or maybe just into bed to relive old times. John was a good-looking guy. Young and charismatic. Everything Charlotte should want in a man. Had he broken her heart or had she broken his?

Dean had no idea of the details, she hadn't wanted to discuss them, but he did know that they'd planned a wedding together. He definitely hadn't forgotten her mentioning that, and something told him this had to be that guy.

He'd have to tell her.

As he headed up the back staircase, Dean knew his real motivation in seeking Charlotte out right now, and it was not to give her a heads-up about the fact that he may have just hired her ex. Well, maybe partly. The bigger reason, however, was that he suddenly had an overwhelming urge to claim what was his.

Fourteen

Charlotte smiled as she watched Jason and John's grand-parents cutting it up on the dance floor to a hip-hop song. Their faces were so full of joy. What would it feel like to be with someone that long? Watch your own children marry. Your grandchildren. It wouldn't do for her to go melancholy now, but this wedding, more than any other, had her thinking of all the what-ifs. Especially when the biggest what-if wouldn't stop staring at her from across the room.

Just as Lauren had described, John had been incredibly kind and helpful during portraits. He'd talked to her constantly, even helped her up when she'd needed to get on top of a low stone wall for a shot of Shelby and Jason in a park. When they'd gotten back to the church to prepare for the ceremony he'd brought her and Lauren a bottle of water. Even the videographer who had shown up while they were shooting in the field finally whispered to her, "I think the best man has a thing for you."

Charlotte had only laughed it off, not daring to admit their connection. What was John expecting? What did he want? It was possible that it was just that special wedding magic that overcame single people at the festivities. Or maybe he also had a case of the what-ifs as he witnessed his brother saying I do. Whatever his reasons for showing her so much interest and attention, it was making her uncomfortable.

Five years was a long time to build up anger and resentment for a person, and she'd lain in bed many times thinking of all the things she'd have liked to say on the day she saw him again. None of them had felt right or had even come to mind. The truth was, she didn't feel angry or hurt, so much as . . . sad.

She did deserve to have happiness. A man who loved her enough to do anything. The classic love story. A family.

John had never been that person for her, and she could see that clearly now. He'd never been an asshole; he'd just finally had the courage to do what needed to be done before it caused the two of them—and their families—even more pain. Sure he could have done it sooner, saving everyone a lot of embarrassment and money, but it was all in the past now.

"How's it going?" a voice said in her ear.

She turned in time to see the man of her thoughts looking down on her. Smiling, she lowered her camera and stepped off the dance floor so they wouldn't get trampled. He followed her. "Your grandparents are amazing."

John laughed. "They are. Grandpa turned ninety this year."

"Wow." Charlotte looked on in awe, wondering what else they might have to talk about.

"You want to sit down in the corner? Talk for a minute?" He pointed to the other side of the room, near the bar and away from the DJ's speakers. A couple of tables sat abandoned, their former occupants probably on the dance floor.

"Sure. Maybe just for a moment." Charlotte spotted

Lauren walking back from the restroom and mouthed that she'd be back in a minute. Her friend gave her an eyebrow raise and a nod. Having a stroke of genius, Charlotte turned back to John. "Actually, I'm going to grab Shelby and Jason's rings. I'll meet you at the bar."

He looked confused but agreed and Charlotte made her way through the room to find her bride and groom and collect their wedding rings. It was one of the things she had fun photographing on a wedding day. Right now it would give her something to do while they spoke. Much easier than looking him in the eye.

Earlier in the evening she'd noticed a guest with a beautiful glitter-covered gold shawl laid over the back of her chair. Charlotte sought her out and politely explained what she'd like to use it for. The woman was thrilled to help and handed it over.

Heading back to the bar, rings and shawl in hand, Charlotte caught sight of John standing in line at the bar to get a drink from Jen. She decided to get set up so they could cut things short. After choosing an empty table with some good full candles glowing for her ambient light, Charlotte laid the shawl out flat. Next she arranged the groom's band, then the bride's wedding ring and engagement ring, which was very pretty. Not outrageous, but nice. Once everything was to her satisfaction, she sat down on her knees to line up the perfect angle.

"This looks interesting." John set a glass of what appeared to be a pinkish clear drink on the table, and Charlotte was glad he'd been smart enough to keep it far from the shawl. "The bartender said you'd like this."

"It's my favorite, thank you."

"Seems like I should have known that," he said with a chuckle.

Charlotte ignored his statement and kept adjusting her

settings. Why in the world would he expect to know much about her these days?

"So, do you always do this?" He gestured to the rings and then took a drink of his beer bottle.

"Yeah. It's become very popular over the years."

"Jason did good on that ring, didn't he?"

"He did." Charlotte thought of her own ring. John had purposed on Christmas Eve at the ice-skating terrace in downtown Kansas City. It had been so romantic. People had stopped skating and gathered to watch. When Charlotte said yes, and they hugged, the crowd had cheered and applauded them.

She'd given the ring back that day he'd come to pick up his stuff. Did he still have it? Probably not, that would be silly, but part of her wanted to ask him, although she wouldn't. The last thing she wanted was to discuss their relationship. It would serve absolutely no purpose.

Charlotte lowered her camera and checked her image on the back screen. She smiled to herself.

"That good, huh? Let me see."

She scooted over on her knees and leaned in to show him.

"Wow. How'd you do that? It's so dark over here."

She lifted her camera a little. "I've got six thousand dollars of equipment in my hand that makes that possible. And of course I've got a great eye."

"I guess so. The glitter makes it look like it's sitting on a sparkling ocean."

That was a rather poetic sentiment for John, but he had always had a secret romantic side. And he was right. With the candlelight highlighting the shawl, it did sort of look like a sparkling ocean. Just for good measure she decided to take a couple more from a different angle. She always liked to overshoot, just in case.

"I'm really proud of you Charlotte," John said. He scooted his chair a little closer. "I still remember when you shot your first wedding."

"Me too. I'd gotten my first credit card to buy that camera." It was nice to think of how far she'd come. In college she'd started her business with photos of kids and seniors. Her first wedding had been only a year before what should have been her own.

"I've thought about you over the years, Char."

Charlotte's heart skipped and she was glad her camera was in front of her face to conceal her reaction to his comment. Although she'd already gotten plenty, she kept taking photos.

"Charlotte. Did you hear me?"

She lowered her camera and met his eyes. "Yes I heard you, but I don't know what to say."

"Have you thought of me?"

"Well . . . of course I have. But I'm not sure what you mean. It would have been impossible not to ever think of you again. We'd been together since high school."

"I was scared, Char. Did I ever tell you that?"

She really wished he'd stop calling her that. No one had ever called her that except John. It had felt like a term of endearment, which made it all weird and inappropriate now.

"You don't owe me an explanation John. I'm *almost* over you by now." She smiled, letting him know that she was teasing.

His lips quirked. "Lauren said you were seeing someone."

"Um, yeah. It's kind of new."

His eyes shifted back to hers. "So . . . not serious?"

"Well, I didn't say that." But what was she going to say? From the corner of her eye she saw the door to the back staircase open, and Dean walked through. Her heart picked up speed.

What was he doing here? The minute he stepped into the room he spotted her. The next second his eyes cut over to John, and she could have sworn he frowned.

"So is this relationship the kind that would allow us to get lunch together or something?"

Charlotte's gaze cut back to John. "Why would we do that?"

He looked surprised by her vehemence. "Why wouldn't we?"

Turning her head back to the side door, she saw Dean making his way over to her. He looked so handsome tonight. And intentional. God it was so hot, and when she stood there comparing him with the man sitting next to her, she knew: She was not going to let him get off so easily. She wanted Dean, and it was time she made him decide if they were worth a try or not. No more flirting and wondering. They were professional, or they were more. No in between.

Looking back to John, it was clear there were no romantic feelings left for him in her heart. None at all. What she found being in his presence was nostalgia, nothing more.

"We can't go to lunch because although it's new, the relationship is important to me." As Dean angled his body around the nearest table, his eyes on her, Charlotte spoke completely without thinking. Forget his fears and hesitation. She needed him right now. "In fact, this is him."

Charlotte took two steps and met Dean, grabbing his arm and pulling him toward her and back to where John was now standing, eyes wide. She silently sent him a thank-you for not acting weird at her public display of affection. Oddly, he hadn't seemed bothered by it at all.

"Dean?" John asked, obviously shocked.

"You two have met?" she asked, now panicking. So much for lying. She was already busted. How humiliating.

"Just briefly, downstairs. I was interested in the distilling process . . . and, well, then he . . ."

"Then I offered him a job as my apprentice," Dean said.

What? Was she hearing that correctly? Charlotte felt her body waver and Dean glanced down at her, his eyes darting to her hand gripping his arm. She was certain he would pull away, but instead, he did the unimaginable. He untangled her hands locked around his biceps, put his arm around her, and then pulled her tight against his side.

John let out a choked laugh. "So you guys are seeing each other?" He moved his fingers back and forth between the two of them.

Charlotte instantly poked Dean in the back, secretly begging for compliance. "We are," she said. To her complete shock and gratefulness, Dean leaned down, planted a kiss on the top of her head, and then spoke to John.

"I'm sorry, man. I was coming up here to tell you. I should have said it downstairs when you mentioned her but you just caught me off guard. I didn't know how to say it."

"No, no . . . shit, I get it." John appeared flustered and confused. He laughed awkwardly. "I shouldn't have even brought it up. I just . . ."

He hesitated, his eyes cutting to Charlotte. She was so confused. What the hell had gone on downstairs between the two of them? In just one day, her ex had been thrust back into her sphere, shown interest in possibly making amends, and also been offered a job by her massive-crush-turned-pretend-boyfriend?

What a shit show. Only in Charlotte's world.

"I just . . . man. I don't know. This is awkward so no hard feelings. I understand if you no longer want to work with me."

Charlotte froze and then glanced up to Dean. She didn't necessarily love the idea of John working at the Stag, but she felt bad for what had just happened. She didn't want to be responsible for taking something away from Dean that he so badly needed, and she also didn't want to be the ex who got weird about proximity.

"John, I thought you lived in Chicago," Charlotte asked, forcing her words to sound merely inquisitive.

"I got laid off. I'm back in Maple Springs for the fore-seeable future."

"I'm sorry to hear that."

"Yeah, me too." There was such sadness and confusion in his eyes. It made her sad. Here she was afraid of still being single when she saw him, but he was now single, job-less, and probably living with his parents for the time be-ing. She knew then that crazy words were about to come out of her mouth.

"You should definitely be Dean's apprentice, John. You'd be great at it, and Dean needs the help. He works way too hard." She smiled up at him, like a concerned girl-friend would. He squeezed her tighter like a loving boy-friend, and was there a hint of amusement in his eyes?

"Are you sure, Charlotte?" Dean asked.

"I am. I think it's a great idea. And I actually think John would be really good at it."

Dean turned back to John, and Charlotte felt like she was suddenly in another dimension. Was she seriously praising the man who had destroyed her heart? And why was Dean going along with her lie so easily? Not that she didn't like it. What woman wouldn't enjoy hanging on the arm of the sexiest man in the room while her ex looked on alone and painfully uncomfortable?

John looked at both of them and then took a drink of his beer. Once he swallowed she could tell he'd made a decision "Okay. If Charlotte's okay with it, then I'd still like to give this a try. At least discuss it."

"Okay. I'm glad." Dean still didn't let Charlotte go.

"Well, I better go see if I have any more best man duties to worry about. Dean, once again I'll plan on seeing you Wednesday."

"Sounds good," Dean said.

After John walked away, Charlotte pulled back and looked up at Dean. "What the hell just happened?" she cried.

Dean laughed. "Well, I offered your ex a job and apparently, I'm your boyfriend."

"But you played along flawlessly. Why?"

He looked confused. "I had a pretty strong feeling that's what you wanted. Was I wrong? You know, I'm the one who should be standing here asking questions."

That caught her up short and she snapped her mouth shut for a minute. When he didn't go on, she continued. "You're right. I did want you to play along. But after everything that's happened between us this past week . . . I'm just having a hard time processing the last five minutes."

"I'm with you there. But I want you to know, I had no idea who he was when I offered him the apprenticeship. I'm sorry, I hope this won't be awkward for you."

"Well, it will be. *Obviously*," she said, her tone teasing, though it was also very true. "But I guess I'll get over it. He just looked so pitiful standing there."

Dean laughed. "He's got a good buzz going. Seeing you has made him emotional, I think."

Charlotte knew Dean was right. She could tell, considering she'd dated John for many years, but it was still hard for her to comprehend. What had they talked about downstairs? "Yeah, well, I'm hard to get over. Maybe not for *some* people."

She gently shoved at his stomach and he grabbed her hand, holding it against him. Her face jerked up to meet his eyes, which were now hooded and full of longing.

"Don't try and guess how I feel about you, Charlotte," he said.

When their eyes met, her body fluttered to life, her nerves crackling at his touch. His thumb whispered back and forth over her hand as he stared at her.

"I have tried, but you make it very difficult."

He nodded. "I know. And I'm sorry for that. I've been overthinking us to death. But the truth is . . . I haven't been able to stop thinking about you."

She stared up at him. "Now you know how I feel all the time."

His lips quirked. "Well, you understand . . . now that we're suddenly dating, there's only one thing left for you to do," Dean said. His voice was sultry and low, even over the noise in the room.

"What?"

"Come home with me tonight." With that, he lifted her hand, placed a kiss on her fingers, and then walked back to the stairwell door.

Fifteen

When the DJ called all the single men forward for the garter toss, John was noticeably absent. Charlotte's relief didn't last long when Jason requested the DJ call his brother out by name.

"I'm looking for a John Reynolds. If anybody sees him, you have his brother's permission to kindly drag his rear out onto the dance floor."

Charlotte and Lauren gave each other a look as the room chuckled, and within moments one of the bridesmaids was doing as instructed, dragging John out so he could join the very scant group of men lined up around the edge of the floor.

When the garter was flung over Jason's head, it headed in the exact opposite direction of where his brother stood, landing right in the hands of a tall guy in the back who seemed surprisingly proud to have caught it. A female, obviously his girlfriend, jumped into his arms and kissed his face about eight times. Charlotte stepped back to look through the images she'd just taken. Automatically her eyes went to John, off to the side of the frame. He hadn't been looking at Jason or the garter at all.

He'd been watching her.

But Charlotte had other things on her mind. The next hour flew by, and with every moment she grew more anxious and definitely more excited. It was hard to believe Dean was serious about what he'd said. Surely he wasn't trying to tease her for getting him into such a ridiculous situation.

No. He'd been on the fence about them, but she knew him well enough to know he wouldn't do that. Not after what they'd been through the past few weeks. The thing that kept her mind reeling was the look in his eyes. Nothing about his expression had made her doubt his meaning until she'd walked away and tried to make sense of it all.

Because this was a crazy turn of events. Not that she was complaining. They'd been playing this game of lust and denial. Had he finally decided to throw caution to the wind? It seemed so un-Dean-like . . . and yet something had to give. She'd already decided that they either stop flirting or give this a shot, so he must have decided something similar. If necessary they were mature enough to enjoy each other and then remain business colleagues. People did it all the time. And if something came of it? Even better.

"Are you calling it?" Lauren asked, reading Charlotte's body language well.

"I think so. I'm going to say good-bye to everyone. Want to meet in the break room?"

Lauren nodded and Charlotte felt the butterflies in her stomach kick back to life as she made her way through the reception, saying good-bye to Shelby, Jason, and their parents. They all thanked her again profusely for coming to their aid on such short notice. Even John and Jason's mother, Roxanne, gave her a warm hug and told Charlotte she missed and thought of her often. She purposely avoided John, who hadn't sought her out again since the conversation with Dean. In fact, she didn't see him anywhere.

As she headed to the break room beside the bar, she glanced around, wondering if Dean was going to come find her. That was when she realized she'd never told him what time she was leaving. This happened to be an earlier wedding for them. Normally she and Lauren stayed till ten or eleven, but tonight's coverage was only till nine thirty since they'd started early and the contract was only for an eight-hour day.

She could seek him out, but what would she say? *I'm ready to go home with you*? Besides, she and Lauren had ridden together in Charlotte's car so she had to take them back to her place so Lauren could get home. On top of that, she hadn't even told her best friend what Dean had said.

Opening up her phone, she sent him a text.

CHARLOTTE: We're leaving. I hope you were serious.

"You ready?" Lauren asked, after she'd packed up the last of their gear.

Charlotte eyed her phone, waiting. "Hang on a second," she said to Lauren.

After a moment of no response, she sighed. "Yep. I think I'm ready."

"Everything okay?" Laruen asked.

"Yeah. Just tired."

They picked up their bags and headed for the freight elevator. At the end of a wedding day, even one narrow flight of stairs was asking a lot. When they got to the big metal gated door, Jake was just getting off.

"You ladies already out of here?" he asked.

"We are," Charlotte said as she pulled back. "It was good to see you."

"You too." His smile could light up a room. She'd decided not to say anything to him this evening about doing a shoot together. After finding out how Dean felt, she couldn't get excited about the idea anymore.

They said their good-byes and Jake helped them shut the elevator door. Once they were downstairs Charlotte took a quick look around the first floor. Dean was nowhere to be seen. The distillery room was dark. The offices toward the far side of the room appeared to be also.

"Are you sure everything's okay?" Lauren asked. "Are you looking for him?"

Charlotte turned and headed for the front door. The last thing she felt like was getting a lecture from her friend. "I was just going to say good-bye. No biggie. Let's get out of here."

Looked like despite her excitement, she'd end this night just like she did every other time. Alone.

Dean shut off the lights to the back room and made sure all the doors to the alley were locked. To kill time, he'd made sure all the giant vats of leftover stilled mash were pushed over to the loading dock door for Monday morning when their farmer friend, Fred Simmons, would drive his huge truck into town and pick them up. His pigs loved the stuff, and it kept the guys from having to dispose of it. The cool part was that Fred also supplied them with the corn for their bourbon, so it was kind of nice to see the product go full circle.

He hadn't realized it was so late—nearly ten according to the clock on the wall—so Dean quickly made his way toward the stairs and headed up to the wedding reception. He could tell the noise wasn't quite as boisterous, so things must have been winding down. He wished he'd have asked Charlotte what time they were finishing up for the evening, but it was usually at least ten or eleven. Plus, he'd made his intentions clear, so hopefully she'd be waiting for him.

When he entered the side door and walked into the dim room, he scanned the guests, not finding her or Lauren anywhere. He walked over to the bar, where Jen had started loading up the dishwasher with a multitude of glasses.

"Hey, have you, uh . . ."

"They left already," Jen shot back without even looking up.

Dean's heart sank. "How did you know what I was going to ask?"

Jen's hands stopped on the rag she was using to wipe the bar. She slowly lifted her head and gave him a long-suffering you've-got-to-be-kidding me look. "Please, Phantom. Don't play me for a fool."

"Will you not call me that?"

She just shrugged and continued on with her work.

"Hey, what are you doing here? I saw you at the still earlier." Jake walked up and leaned his forearms on the bar. "Jen, give me a water, will you?"

She scoffed. "I'm not your personal bar wench." But Jake ignored her and she proceeded to pour the drink anyway, slamming it down in front of him.

"So what time did Lauren and Charlotte leave?" Dean asked, nonchalantly.

He didn't miss the knowing smirk Jen and Jake shared. "Just a bit ago. Right after she begged me to do a photo shoot for her."

Dean's jealousy ratcheted back up, but he played it cool. He needed to accept that Charlotte might photograph Jake—or other guys he knew. In fact, he knew she would. But she was right, it was her job and she did it all the time. "Good for you, man."

Jen pointed at Jake. "I see you as a duke or a pirate. Something with a frilly shirt."

Jake's head jerked back. "You've got to be kidding. Only if I was like . . . ripping that frilly shirt open or something masculine like that." He imitated exactly how he would pose.

Jen laughed. "When do we get to see your photos?" she asked Dean.

"I'm not sure. She hasn't shown any to me yet."

Jen grinned. "Probably keeping the ones of you all for herself. Now it only leaves TJ."

"No way," Dean said at the same time Jake said, "Definitely not."

"Why wouldn't he? He's pretty cute, has a good body." Jen focused on loading more glasses into the dish machine. "I can see it."

Dean tried to read her. Could she possibly be as interested in TJ as he was her? Maybe, but Jen was very hard to read. Not only did she not wear her emotions on her sleeve, she stuffed them into a pocket, sewed it shut, and then wore a mask to try to throw you off.

"Doesn't matter," he said. "I don't think that's something TJ would ever be open to doing." And that was just fine with Dean, although he'd much rather Charlotte hang out with a half-naked TJ than a half-naked Jake.

"I'm sure I could get him to do it," Jen said with a wicked grin, and there was always a possibility she was right. If *she* asked him, TJ might give up a necessary organ.

"Hey, I'm out of here." Dean gave a quick wave, but before he could get too far, Jake called out to him.

"Hey, man. I was just puling your chain. She never mentioned me modeling for her so I didn't bring it up, either."

There was no denying Dean's relief at those words. But

then he felt a twinge of guilt. The last thing he wanted to be was controlling. "If she does bring it up, go for it."

"You sure?" Jake asked.

Dean nodded.

After he started his car, he pulled his phone from the center console. As soon as he saw Charlotte's text he cursed. She probably thought he'd changed his mind.

DEAN: I was absolutely serious. On my way soon.

The minute he started driving, he forced all creeping thoughts of doubt out of his mind. This was the right decision. Having his arms around her a couple of hours ago had felt so right.

At home he jumped in the shower, his mind swirling with images of her. He'd wanted this woman for a long time now. He'd had a taste of her, and he was finally realizing that there was no moving on until he'd had more. What happened after that? He couldn't predict, but as much as he wished they could, there was no going back, and things couldn't stay the same.

Everything about her appealed to him, not only on a visceral level, but on a cerebral one as well. She made him think, made him laugh. She challenged him with her witty comments and snarky innuendo. The way she looked at him, talked to him, made him feel like she wanted him physically, and she was honest, without pretense. For a younger woman, that seemed . . . surprising. Then again it was Charlotte, and she *never* failed to surprise him.

Tonight when she'd blurted out that they were seeing each other, his heart had nearly pounded out of his chest, but playing along had felt like the most natural thing in the world. After hearing another man have possible regrets over this woman, it made him realize he didn't want the same.

When he'd found her upstairs, it had felt wonderful to finally kiss and touch her like she was his.

Within ten minutes he'd toweled off, gotten ready, and was out his front door and back in his vehicle. Just as he started up the engine, his phone vibrated. Pulling it out of his pocket, he grinned when he saw her text.

CHARLOTTE: Waiting . . .

DEAN: Good things come to those who wait.

CHARLOTTE: Yeah well I've been waiting a loooonnng time so I'm expecting really good things.

He headed to her house with a grin on his face because finally, this was going to happen. Taking a deep breath, he pulled into her little driveway and parked behind her car. There was a low light on in the living room.

He stood there a minute, hesitating, but before he could knock, the door flew open. Stepping back instinctively, he met her eyes through the screen door. He swallowed as his gaze ran down the length of her body, from her damp hair down to her tiny little pajama shorts.

Christ.

"I was starting to worry you'd been teasing me again," she said quietly.

He smiled. "Not this time."

She opened the door and he stepped in slowly, catching the fresh scent of her shampoo as he passed. When he'd been here for the photoshoot he hadn't come in, but he was unsurprised to find that the space was completely her. Neat and cozy, a little eccentric, with unmatched furniture and a mix of various pillows. A blanket was disturbed on the sofa, a book tossed onto the coffee table as if she'd been lying there reading. Probably how she'd heard him pull up.

Several large, framed photographs hung on the walls, mainly of wildflowers and sunsets. "Did you take these?" he asked as he stepped in and she shut the front door behind him.

"I did. Sometimes when I'm location scouting I like to shoot the landscape. It's relaxing. And I love looking at them."

"I can see why. They're beautiful."

"Thank you."

He turned back to her, realizing he was stalling. For a man in his forties who had been with his fair share of women, he was suddenly unsure what the hell to do next.

She smiled up at him, her hands clasped in front of her. Was she also nervous? She didn't really appear to be, more just . . . waiting. Could she sense his awkwardness?

"It's hard to believe I might finally get my wish," she whispered.

Dean stepped toward her slowly. "What's your wish, Charlotte?"

"You."

And then just like that she was in his arms, her lips on his. He groaned the minute their bodies met, couldn't help himself, and he instinctively hauled her up against him, his hands grasping her butt as her arms locked around his neck in a kind of wild, possessive stranglehold.

Their first kiss had been sexy, slow, and surprising. But this, this was a frenzy. He wasn't sure he'd ever been kissed like this. Charlotte came at him with a maddening intensity he'd never, ever experienced from a woman, her lips and tongue touching every bit of him as her hands explored his shoulders, back, and biceps. Instantly he was rock-hard and grinding her body into him.

"I want to touch you everywhere," she said as she pressed kisses to his jaw.

Dean's eyes rolled back as he tilted his head to give her access. How the hell would he explain the marks she was no doubt leaving on him? When her tongue stroked his earlobe he nearly came right there.

They continued to kiss for a few moments, each enjoying the other's mouth. After a bit Charlotte slid down his body, her arms still locked around his neck.

"Holy shit." He looked down, and the lust in her eyes set his body on fire. She was so hot like this, so uninhibited. "You're so beautiful."

The smile she gave him in response was so happy and pure it took his breath away. She was like a dream come true. Which was absolutely terrifying. Here he thought he could have her and get it out of his system, but as good as he knew this was going to be, it was hard to believe that would ever be a possibility. How could a man experience his ultimate fantasy and not want to come back for more?

"I've wanted you for so long," he said quietly, stroking down the side of her face.

"Why'd you keep me guessing?"

"You were right. Fear."

"And you're not afraid anymore?" she asked.

"My desire for you is stronger than any fear."

She smiled at that, and Dean inhaled through his nose, loving the scent of her this close. Right now, tonight, she was all his. He would forget the decade between them, the fact that they worked together, and all the reasons they shouldn't be together, and just revel in the mind-blowing reality that this absolutely gorgeous and seductive woman wanted him as much as he wanted her.

"Take your clothes off, Charlotte."

Sixteen

Excited didn't even begin to describe what Charlotte was feeling. Dean's command left no room to question or negotiate what was going to happen next. She just obeyed.

Grabbing the hem of her tank top, she pulled it up and over her head, revealing a lace see-through bra. The kind of garment a woman wore when she intended to be admired in it.

Dean stepped back enough to look down and take in the sight of her, and she stood there for a moment, hands at her sides, allowing him the time to appreciate what she had to offer. She'd never felt sexier than she did right now.

His right hand came up and cupped her breast, his thumb gently running over the rough lace that covered her nipple. It puckered beneath his touch, which had their eyes meeting once more.

"Keep going," he whispered. He dropped his hand and watched as she locked her thumbs in the waistband of her shorts and then pushed them down her thighs. She kicked them to the side and then looked up at him.

His lips were parted and a slow—almost depraved—smile formed on his face. She wouldn't have pegged Dean as a dominating or bossy sexual partner—he was usually so easygoing—but she was not going to complain. In fact, she was loving it.

"You are so much better than I imagined." Before she could respond he grabbed her hand and led her to the sofa. When she could tell he was about to sit down, she pulled on their joined hands and stopped him.

"Not so fast. I want to see *you*."

He looked in her eyes, waiting, and she used both of her hands to lift his T-shirt up and over his head, revealing his perfect chest and stomach. As soon as the shirt hit the floor he wrapped his arms around her and pulled her down with him onto the soft cushion. She adjusted herself, legs straddling his, and their mouths met once again in another reckless kiss.

The feel of his warm hands on her butt penetrated through the lace of her panties down to her skin beneath as he gripped her hard, grinding her body against him. Her hands bracketed his face as she kissed him, their tongues sliding, lips sucking. He tasted like cinnamon and smelled fresh, like he'd also recently showered.

His chest was covered with short, coarse hairs, and when she recalled why—that she'd made him shave it—she could only feel amused and turned on, remembering how hot their kiss was that night. She'd spent so much time hating the thought that was all she'd ever have with him. And yet here they were, halfway to naked and no end in sight.

Dean's fingers pressed against her back, urging her closer to his mouth as he lowered his head. The moment his lips touched her collarbone, she shivered. He continued down, to the upper swell of her breast, the outline of her bra, and then finally his mouth closed around her nipple, sucking hard. His tongue fondled the tip, the lace of her bra no match for the wetness of his mouth.

"Oh my G—" she gasped as he released her nipple only to follow lightly with a gentle scrape of his teeth. Her hands drove into his hair and she pushed her body down onto the bulge beneath his jeans, searching for friction.

His fingers went to her bra's clasp, and when it fell away from her body, she waited in rapt anticipation. A heavy sigh escaped her lips when his mouth touched her bare skin. One breast, then the other, licking and sucking as if her body might be his last meal.

"You still have way too many clothes on," Charlotte said, leaning back and angling her body away from him. She smiled as she watched his neck crane forward to chase her breasts with his mouth, like candy being pulled away from a child.

He took a deep breath and dropped his head back on the cushion, running his hands up and down her body. She did the same, letting her hands wander across his chest, loving the prickly feeling.

"That's your fault," he said, obviously aware of what she was thinking by the way she rubbed at him. "Regrowth is a bitch."

"It was worth it for your shoot. But I have to say, I'm excited for when I can see you completely natural and hairy. The way you're supposed to be."

He huffed out a laugh that melted into a groan as he cupped her breast and then lightly pinched one of her nipples. It was as if their hands couldn't help but explore the other's body after being denied so long. "So my natural, *hairy* body wasn't good enough for a book cover? Is that what you're saying?"

"I'm not saying that at all. But I am saying that I'm glad I saved the most perfect version of you just for myself. I don't want to share you." She was teasing him again, as he had been her, but when their eyes met, his narrowed.

He was contemplating what to say, she could tell, but without speaking he continued to stare at her as he scooted forward on the couch. Her body jerked with the motion. He did it again, his head sliding down a little more, and she knew what he was doing. Making it easier for her to remove his pants.

Charlotte didn't hesitate, leaning back so she could reach between them and get her hands on the fly of his jeans. She shimmied back a little, trying to ignore the way his fingers traced a pattern on her inner thighs as she worked at his zipper. Her entire body was a ball of electric currents. So warm and glowy feeling, she wondered how she wasn't putting off light.

Her hands fumbled with his pants and then finally she stood just long enough to tug at them. Dean lifted up his backside to help her pull them off. Once they were tossed aside, Charlotte was unable to help herself. She knelt on the floor between his legs and laid her fingers on the band of his boxer briefs. The outline of his hard erection through the cotton was so beautiful, she felt dizzy.

Stopping for a moment, she looked up at him. He watched her, waiting. She loved that his personality never wavered, even during sex. He was patient and observant, his reserve held just at the brink of breaking fully. She knew the way his nose flared with every breath that he was silently begging her to touch him. It was almost as if she could hear the words on his lips without him speaking them.

Their eyes held as she slid a palm up the length of him from base to tip. His jaw clenched, and when her fingers curled around the head and squeezed, he couldn't hold back. His eyes darted down to where she held him, a muffled groan came from his closed mouth, and his pelvis arched up toward her the slightest bit.

Charlotte bit back a smile, her teeth clamping down on her lower lip as she began to pull his underwear down. This was better than Christmas, her birthday, and getting a new camera all in one.

This was Dean Troyer. The man of her fantasies. The man she loved to tease, hoping that he fantasized about her in return. How many time had she played this out in her mind?

"You know, sometimes when I'm alone . . ." The minute his penis was revealed, she took hold of it, the width and length just about as perfect as it could get. "I imagine a moment just like this. You here, naked, at my mercy."

She gripped firmly, stroking up and down once. Did he shiver?

"Do you?" His eyes were dark. "And what do you do to me in those moments?"

"Everything I can imagine."

His right hand came up and clamped down on top of hers, squeezing, causing her grip to tighten on him.

"Am I the only one of us who has thoughts like that?" she asked, coyly. She continued to stroke him, loving the way he kept his hand steadied over hers.

"You know you're not. I've thought about you a thousand times."

"Then how about *you* tell me what I do to you in those moments."

"Charlotte—" He lifted his hand to touch her cheek softly.

"*Tell me*. Tell me what fantasy me does to you. Or maybe . . . show me."

Dean swallowed. Maybe he wasn't used to a woman being so forward. Quite honestly, Charlotte wasn't always this way, especially during sex, but something about this man made her the most outrageous, wanton, playful version of herself. It was liberating, and it turned her on immensely.

She knew it turned him on, too, when his thumb brushed over her cheek, then her lips, before his fingers slid into her hair, gripping the back of her head. Her heart pounded and her body hummed, because she knew full well what he wanted, and knowing they were both about to bring their fantasies to life only made her hotter. Meeting his eyes, she urged him on with her gaze, and he gently pushed her head down.

Dean's breath caught in his throat as he watched Charlotte go down on him. She'd asked what she did to him in his fantasy, and this was it only a million times better. He was pretty certain that nothing in his life had ever been this hot. He reached out to sweep her blond hair off her face, pulling it around to one side. Her hooded eyes shifted up to him, holding contact as she licked up the length of him.

That sight alone had him gripping the pillow beside him, trying to take this like a man and not a teenager in the backseat of a car getting head for the first time. But goddamn, that's exactly how he felt.

After a few moments of sucking, he knew he couldn't take anymore. He lifted his hand and caressed her face, his thumb touching her cheek once more until she pulled back. "Get up here."

She didn't ask any questions, just stood and pulled his briefs all the way off his legs. She then slid down her own panties, revealing the most beautiful sight he'd ever seen. His mouth went dry as he took in the beauty of her soft skin, her full thighs, and the triangle of hair between them. She let him look at her for just a moment before she climbed back onto his lap.

"Condom?" she asked, once settled.

"Front pocket of my jeans."

She leaned down, fumbled with his pants, and her smile was playful and sexy as she sat back upright with the packet between her fingers.

Dean watched, mesmerized, as she opened it, and then stroked him several times before finally rolling the condom down the length of him. Their eyes locked as she lifted and then slowly . . .

"Holy . . . damn . . ." Dean hissed out a long breath, his hands going to her face, one on each cheek, as she seated herself fully. "Oh God, you feel so good."

Too good. Too tight, warm . . . and then she began to move, and Dean's eyes slid closed as Charlotte let out a breathy moan. His hands still on her face, he could feel her lean forward and then her lips sought his.

The kiss was slow and wet, mimicking the movement of their bodies. They'd waited so long, and he didn't want to rush this, but every movement of her body sent him closer to the edge. It didn't take long for her to pick up the pace, her body rocking and pounding against his. The lust was too intense, and within moments they were both chasing after release like their lives depended on it.

"Touch me," she said against his lips. "Please."

Dean dropped a hand between them and his thumb instantly found its intended destination. She gripped his head in response and tilted her pelvis forward to give him better access. Her change in position altered the friction below and his mouth dropped open, his body trembling.

"Slow down, baby, or I'm gonna come."

"Me too . . ." Instead of slowing down she picked up the pace, rocking her body against his, and within seconds they were coming together.

Seventeen

Charlotte was startled awake by ABBA singing the chorus of "Does Your Mother Know." She reached out to the bedside table and pushed the top of her phone to silence it just as they got going.

There was movement on the other side of the bed. "You have an ABBA ringtone?" a husky yet amused voice asked.

"Only for my mother," she lied. "Sorry to wake you. Go back to sleep."

Which was what she intended to do. Her wedding hangover was in full force this rainy Sunday morning. However, Dean must have had other plans, because he rolled over on the bed before she felt his arms slide around her. One between her and the bed, the other around her waist.

She smiled as he tugged her against his body and his lips found her neck. Maybe this was the wedding hangover cure she'd been searching for. Last night after round one on the sofa, they'd moved into the bedroom for round two before falling asleep. But Charlotte was far from finished with Dean.

As she arched her back and pressed her bottom against him, she wondered if he intended this to be a onetime night together. The fact that he hadn't jumped out of bed and rushed off this morning was a good sign, but she still wasn't certain.

His hand began to snake its way down her stomach and underneath her underwear just as ABBA started up again. The curious fingers stopped and the elastic of her panties snapped as he pulled his hand out.

"That is very unsettling," he whispered.

Charlotte laughed as she reached for the phone. "It is quite appropriate for the situation."

"Too much so."

"I should probably get it so she doesn't show up here to make sure I'm alive." Charlotte pressed the ACCEPT button and lifted the phone to her ear at the same time she gave Dean the quiet signal. "Hey, Mom."

"Good morning, sweetie. I can tell I've woken you but I did wait until ten to call."

Charlotte rolled her eyes. "The day after a wedding that's like calling at seven. But it's fine. What do you need?"

"Well . . . tell me how the wedding was."

That was what Charlotte was afraid of, and here she sat with an audience listening to every word. "It was really nice. Went well."

"Don't be vague. How did everyone treat you?"

"I'm not being vague." *Too* much. "Everything was fine. It wasn't like anything major would be mentioned there, Mom."

And it wouldn't be discussed here, either, not with Dean lying behind her, slowly rubbing his fingertips across her bare back. God, why did her mother have to interrupt this?

"I'm glad to hear it. Actually Mary Sue called me this morning. Told me she could not have been more pleased with your professionalism and organization. Shelby was also thrilled."

"They haven't even seen the images yet, but that's nice to hear."

"Mary Sue also mentioned . . . that you're seeing someone."

Charlotte froze. "She what?"

She looked over her shoulder at Dean wide-eyed. He returned her expression, his brows going up in question. She rolled back to her side, facing away from him.

"Why hadn't you told me, Charlotte? Is it serious?"

"No, Mom. It's not serious. In fact . . . it's not even true."

There was a pause on the other end. "I don't understand."

"I lied, Mom. It wasn't smart and I wished I hadn't done it." She definitely wasn't going to throw Lauren under the bus, not when she'd played right into it and hadn't regretted it. Until now. "I just fell victim to my ego under the circumstances . . . and I lied."

Dean put his arm around Charlotte and pulled her back into his body, giving her a firm squeeze. Was he comforting her? It felt good to be held that way. Too good.

"I guess I understand, but you certainly got my hopes up."

Charlotte smiled. "Sorry. You'll be the first to know when I find Mr. Right."

"I better be. But . . . tell me. Who is this man? Mary Sue seemed to be under the impression that he was there last night?"

"Well . . . uh. He was there. A friend of mine played along." Charlotte felt the shaking of Dean's laughter on her back and couldn't help holding back her own laugh. "But he understood the situation."

"Hmmm. Maybe he likes you if he was willing to go along with it."

Her mother. Always an opportunist. She'd probably be

a mixture of shocked and elated if she knew her daughter was in bed with said man right now. But that was something Charlotte was unwilling to discuss with her parent.

"Mom, please. We can discuss yesterday's event more later on. I'm still tired."

With a sigh she agreed and Charlotte disconnected. After placing the phone back on the bedside table she fell back and looked up at the ceiling.

"What happened between you?" he asked, sliding his arm underneath her back and pulling her into his side.

Charlotte readjusted so her head rested on his chest. She could have pretended she didn't understand the question, but that would have been ridiculous. With a sigh, she answered. "We were high school sweethearts, although I hate that phrase. I feel like the words themselves imply immaturity, and while that may explain my situation, there are plenty of high school couples that last forever."

"Fair enough. Why do *you* believe you broke up?"

Where to begin? Going into detail wasn't really ideal for her, so she decided to give him the version that wouldn't scare him away.

"I guess we grew apart. Our problem was that we weren't on the same page when we discovered this. According to him, he realized it a few months before our wedding. I realized it an hour before our wedding . . . when he called it off. I already had my dress on."

Dean just stared down at her, his brow furrowed. "I'm so sorry, Charlotte. That's complete bullshit, though, the way he handled it."

"Yeah, well, I'm over it."

"If I'd known, I never would have offered the guy a job."

She smiled. "You'd have taken my side?"

"Of course." He ran the back of his middle finger across her jaw, and the expression on his face was so genuine and tender, she had to stare at his chest. "I still will if you want, in fact I—"

"No, please." She pushed up off the bed and rolled toward him, resting her hand on his chest. "I don't want to be that girl. The one who can't handle it. Besides, you need help, and if you felt a good vibe with him, then that's what's important."

"I don't know. I'm not sure I'll be able to get the thought of you standing there in a wedding dress out of my head."

"Ugh, please don't picture that. I shouldn't have said anything."

"Why not?"

"I don't know. It's humiliating. Plus, that was five years ago. Just picture me naked instead. That should do it."

"I've been picturing you naked for years."

Her mouth dropped open. "You have?"

"I have and you know it. Now that I've gotten lucky enough to actually see you naked, those fantasies will be even better."

Charlotte snuggled in closer and wrapped her arms around his waist. "That sounds good. But now that I've lied and pulled you into my web of drama, what will we tell John?"

Dean was quiet for a moment. "I guess we could just . . . pretend a little longer. See what happens between us."

Charlotte's head jerked up to meet his eyes. Dean looked hesitant, as if he was unsure of what she'd say. "Are you sure?" she asked.

He nodded. "Yeah. I'm sure."

"I like that idea," she said.

His lips slid into a sexy grin.

"I'm glad." He began to roll on top of her, his hands going to each side of her head to hold his weight off her body. "I think I have a couple more ideas you'll like."

Charlotte grinned up at him. "If they include your mouth on me then you're probably right."

He turned out to be very right.

Charlotte spent that afternoon uploading the images from the previous day's wedding and starting to cull out the ones she didn't plan to keep. This was always the process she liked the least. It was tedious and boring, but necessary, so she preferred to get it done and out of the way as soon as she could.

Today the task was made slightly better by the fact that she could pass the time daydreaming about the events of last night. And this morning. Not long after her mother had called, and they'd made out a little more, Dean had gotten up and headed home. He'd kissed her lightly at the door, and then reminded her that they'd see each other Tuesday for the cake tastings.

Now that he was gone, she was having a hard time deciding exactly what he might have meant by his *see what happens between us* comment. Did that imply they were . . . dating? At the time his words had been enough, but now Charlotte felt the need to hash out the details.

He hadn't mentioned seeing her any sooner than Tuesday, or calling her. It was probably best if she just played it cool and waited things out. She'd hoped something would develop between them for a while, and since she already knew he had a lot of concerns about them dating, the last thing she wanted was to scare him away.

Charlotte's phone rang on her desk. She picked it up and the caller ID read TARA STILLINGS, the Stag's usual wedding coordinator.

"Tara, so good to hear from you," Charlotte answered.

"Hi, Charlotte. I hope you're doing well."

"I'm doing great, but I heard you've been put on bed rest."

"I have, it's so frustrating. I don't even know what to do with myself besides eat, binge on Netflix, and eat some more."

Charlotte laughed. "Sounds like my kind of life."

"It was nice at first, but it's getting really old. I've actually resorted to reading books."

"Aww, you poor thing," Charlotte teased. "What can I do for you?"

"I actually called for a couple of reasons. First, I did some begging, and cleared it with the doctor to meet you for thirty minutes for my maternity photos as long as it's not a super-hot day. Could we get something in that amount of time?"

"Absolutely. I can get some great photos in ten minutes if I need to, and we'll leave the car running nearby so you can just get out and then back in as soon as we're done."

"Oh good. I thought we could go back to that neat park that you did our engagement pictures at. Do you remember?"

"I do, and I think that's a great spot. What else?"

"The other thing is also photography-related. Do you happen to have July twenty-first available? It's a Friday."

Charlotte clicked out of her photo editing software and opened her calendar. "Looks like I do. What's going on that day?"

"That's the night the Stag is hosting its uncasking party for the premium line. It's kind of a big deal. They've waited five years for this day. I'd love if you could get some photos of it."

"Of course, I'd love to. But do the guys know you're still planning this? They've been so worried about you."

"I know, and TJ did take over the majority of the planning, but I just had some loose ends I hadn't wrapped up before I left. This was one of them. It's killing me not to do more. I won't even get to attend and I've been so excited for it."

"I understand that. But you know you and your baby's health is way more important." Just the thought made Charlotte sad. Sometimes she wondered what she might have done differently to prevent her miscarriage. It was hard not to feel like she'd done something wrong, and worry it would happen again the next time. As much as she wanted it, the thought of getting pregnant was terrifying.

"You're right, but this work is easy to do from my bed, and asking you is the last item on my list. I apologize for not getting in touch sooner."

"Don't apologize, you've had a lot going on. And my answer is without a doubt, yes. I'd be thrilled. But promise me no more working."

"Promise. I heard you're helping Dean plan Alex's wedding. That's so nice of you."

"Not a big deal. It's been fun."

"I was surprised he didn't have his crazy ex helping him with it. She's weirdly still close to his sister."

"*Oh* really? I didn't know that." Why hadn't he told her? Actually, why would he have? But she couldn't deny hearing that Dean's ex was still a part of their lives bothered her. Was he close with the woman?

"Yeah, Dean and Amy practically raised Alex after their parents died."

"He told me a little bit about that. But not everything." Charlotte was being nosy, but she was so curious about Dean, who didn't really offer up much information about himself. Of course, she didn't ask him much, either. Their relationship wasn't really like that. She wondered if it might become that way now that they were "seeing what happens."

"Supposedly, and this is from TJ, but I guess his mother left his dad for some younger guy. They were always traveling and doing adventurous things. They had Alexis, who is much younger than Dean, and when she was about thirteen, they died in a small plane accident on a trip to the mountains."

"That's so awful."

Tara's story basically matched what little bit of information Dean had shared. The big part he'd left out was how close his little sister still was to his ex-wife. Hearing this story helped Charlotte understand Dean's feelings of responsibility for his sister, but she couldn't help wonder how close the ex still was to *him*.

"So do you think he still sees his ex a lot?"

"Not really, I don't think. She used to come into the Stag on occasion. She seemed nice, but . . . I don't know. I think it was hard for me to like her after hearing how they split."

"Was it bad?" It really wasn't right of Charlotte to pry, but she was sooo curious and Tara was practically volunteering her the information.

"I'm not entirely sure, but I get the feeling she was unfaithful."

"Oh my, I had no idea." It was crazy to think a woman would be unfaithful to a man like Dean, and Charlotte felt a rush of sadness that they'd spent time that morning discussing her heartache and not once had she asked Dean about his own past.

"He doesn't talk about it. Like I said, I only know because I was nosy and pried it out of TJ, who also seems to hate Amy because of it."

Wow, all of these people hating a woman they didn't

know because she'd been unfaithful to their friend seemed slightly harsh, but Charlotte couldn't deny feeling the same.

"Don't you think Dean's cute, in that sort of . . . older-man kind of way?" Tara asked with an awkward laugh. If Charlotte recalled, Tara was about a year younger than she was.

"Yes . . . I would agree with that completely." Charlotte had a grin on her face as she spoke.

Tara chuckled. "But I'll never admit to saying that."

It was Charlotte's turn to laugh. "I've already forgotten it."

But she knew there would be no forgetting all the things she'd just learned about Dean.

Eighteen

Tuesday morning, Charlotte wasn't sure which delicious treat she was more excited about: cake or Dean. It had been a long couple of days to go without seeing him, and she was anxious to spend some time together.

She pulled up in front of the Stag and put her car in park before shooting off a text to Dean.

CHARLOTTE: Out front, "boyfriend."

She stared at the screen, biting back a smile, wondering how he'd reply. When she finally saw that he was writing back, she held her breath.

DEAN: Be right there, dear.

She laughed and shoved her phone in her purse. Within a couple of moments Dean came out the front door, dressed in jeans and his Stag polo with the logo on the chest. She admired his body as he walked, the way his belt sat right at his hips and the denim of his jeans hugged his thighs. Now that she knew exactly how beautiful he was underneath, it was hard not to imagine it as he got into the front seat of her car.

As soon as he sat down he leaned forward to grab the lever beneath and then push the seat back.

"Sorry, I forgot I was picking up a big strapping hunk of man."

He laughed quietly and turned to look at her while he buckled his safety belt. "How are you?" he asked.

"Happy to see you." She couldn't help being blunt about it. Why lie?

"Good. I'm happy to see you."

She hoped so. "Ready to eat cake?"

"Always."

She pulled off from the curb and headed for their first stop, Delicious Diva's. She'd had their cakes a handful of times. They were pretty good. Not nearly as good as Jill's cakes—that was their second appointment—but they would do if Dean liked them and their price. Charlotte knew that Jill's would be over the budget, but she kind of hoped the woman might be willing to work with them.

When Charlotte had called and explained their situation, Jill had been kind and excited to hear from her. They'd referred each other several times over the years, and Charlotte always sent Jill digital photos of her cakes for her website. She'd informed Charlotte that she was booked on that Saturday for two cakes, which made her Friday very busy, but to go ahead and come over for a tasting and they'd discuss what she might be able to do.

So that was today's plan, and Charlotte really hoped she and Dean would manage to work in some kissing along the way.

Delicious Diva's was about twenty minutes from Maple Springs in downtown Overland Park, so on the ride she and Dean discussed everything except Saturday night or their new relationship status. Which left her a little frustrated, although she knew that was silly. What was there to say, really?

"So John called this morning to verify that I still wanted him to come in tomorrow. Talked to TJ on the phone," Dean said. Reminding Charlotte of the conversation she really didn't want to have anymore.

Her stomach twisted a bit, but she knew being cool was important. She'd told him repeatedly that she was okay with this. "That's good. He seems eager still. What did TJ think?"

He rubbed the top of his thighs. Maybe the topic made him a little uncomfortable still, also. "TJ seemed to like him. It was only over the phone, but he thought he seemed really excited about the process and the business. And I can't imagine he and Jake won't get along."

Dean was right, Jake got along with almost everyone. Charlotte twisted her lips as she watched the highway zoom by. It hadn't occurred to her how much she'd hate the idea of John becoming chummy with *her* Stag guys. Would he become one of them? Close friends? That idea grated a little more than she'd expected. But it was inevitable. Everyone liked John. Always.

"Does this upset you, Charlotte? Be honest with me."

Clearly he could read her thoughts . . . or her body language was more like it. "It's a little weird, obviously. But truly, it's fine," she said brightly, and she knew her attempt had been unsuccessful when he turned to face her. Well, as much as a man his size could in her little car.

"Seriously?"

"What do you want me to say? It's not like my feelings should affect your business decisions."

"That's not true. You're like . . . part of the family at the

Stag. I hate the thought that someone working with me will make you uncomfortable. I hate knowing he hurt you." He looked out the windshield and ran a hand through his hair. "I hate knowing . . . he slept with you."

Charlotte's hands tightened on the steering wheel, and her gaze flickered to him for a brief moment then back to the road as she merged to get off the highway.

"Why would you even think about that?"

"I can't help but think about it. I know that's messed up, but I'm a man, babe, and we generally don't like to share. Even retroactively."

His words warmed her from the inside out, and she knew her cheeks flushed. It was a very relationship-minded feeling to have, and that made her optimistic about them.

"Would it help if I told you Saturday night was the best sex I've ever had?" Charlotte asked.

She felt his eyes on her. "Yes, it would help. Feel free to elaborate."

Laughing, she pulled into a parking spot outside the Delicious Diva's awning. "Hold that thought. It's time to eat cake."

Once inside the cute little bakery, Charlotte and Dean chose four different flavors of cake and two varieties of frosting to try. They sat down at a small table with a woman named Gloria and dug in. They were good, no denying that, but Charlotte just couldn't help comparing every bite with Jill's.

"They are all really good," Dean said once they'd tasted all of the offerings.

"Thank you," Gloria said with a smile. "Our recipes are all made fresh from scratch."

She proceeded to give more of her spiel on price, delivery, and ordering. When she was finished, Charlotte thanked her and assured her they'd be in touch soon.

Stepping outside, Dean let out a deep sigh as they walked to the car.

"Let it out," Charlotte teased. "What are you thinking?"

"I'm thinking that five dollars and seventy-five cents a serving, for *that*, is thievery."

Charlotte winced. "It is expensive, but so is Jill's. Maybe more so."

Dean shook his head and held out his hand. "Let me drive."

"Why?"

"I'm frustrated." His words were clipped.

She handed her keys over with flair. "Oh yes, please take my life into your hands while you're irritated and want to blow off steam."

His eyes softened. "I'm sorry. I just . . . like to drive."

She was beginning to see that Dean was not always as chill as he appeared to be. They got into the car and he started up the engine before adjusting his seat. Charlotte did the same, but moved the passenger chair back up to where it had been before he and his long legs got in.

"I hope I shouldn't take this as an insult on my driving," she said.

"No, not at all." He sounded convincing. "Now, where do I go?"

Charlotte pulled up Jill's address on her phone and told him to get on the highway. Jill worked out of her home, and luckily it wasn't far. They were pulling into her driveway not ten minutes later.

"So, Jen told me this Jill woman has an entire wing built onto the house." Dean put the car in park and stared up at Jill's cute little bungalow.

"She does, but I've never seen it. I'm so excited." And she was. Jill's cakes were among the most delicious things Charlotte had ever eaten in her life.

"We're supposed to walk around to the back." Charlotte led the way around the side of the house and up to the addition on the rear. A cute little awning topped the glass-paned door. A sign hung off to the side that read JILL'S CAKES BY APPOINTMENT ONLY.

Before Charlotte could knock, she saw Jill wave through the glass, so she waved back and waited. When Jill opened the door she ushered them inside.

"It's getting hot out there," Jill said. Her blondish-gray hair was pulled into a low ponytail. Jill was a beautiful woman, and it was obvious that she'd probably garnered a lot of attention from the boys in her younger days. Her warm personality only added to her charm. "Don't worry, I keep it nice and cool in here so my frosting doesn't melt."

It was chilly in the little space and Charlotte squeezed her arms against her body. Just as he had in the flower shop, Dean laid his hands on her bare skin and slowly rubbed up and down in an attempt to warm her. Lately he seemed to be very in tune with her body, and she was afraid that was something she could get used to in his presence.

If Jill noticed their closeness she made no mention. She went right on and showed them around her bakery, which she was clearly very proud of—for good reason, in Charlotte's opinion.

"My late husband built this entire space ten years ago with the help of my grandson Joshua, who still builds all my cake stands. He's a carpenter."

"This is remarkable, Jill," Charlotte said. The entire work space was maybe the size of a small living room. One entire wall was shelving that held pans, cookie cutters, cooling racks, delivery boxes, and all kinds of baking accoutrements. The far wall had two wall ovens, a full stove, and a giant sink, and in the center of the space was a massive island with three professional mixers and several turning cake stands.

"They did a great job. And it smells wonderful," Dean said.

"Yes. I'm so excited, Jill. I have to be honest, you're really the only baker I wanted right from the start." Charlotte glanced at Dean, who was holding back a grin. With an embarrassed laugh she said what she knew they were all probably thinking. "I sound like this is for my wedding, don't I?"

"A little bit," he teased her. "But it's cute."

Jill smiled, her eyes darting between them. "Well, come over here you two. I've invited my granddaughter Julia. However, she appears to be running a touch behind. I hope you don't mind me including her, I know it was presumptuous, but I think having her involved will make this all possible."

Charlotte wasn't sure what Jill meant by that, but she had no problem with Julia joining them. As she and Dean sat down at a pair of stools, the door connecting the bakery to the house burst open.

"Sorry I'm late, Grandma. Traffic was just so crazy."

"Hurry up, dear." Jill waved her granddaughter over. "We're just getting started."

"Dean, Charlotte, this is Julia Morris."

"So nice to meet you," Charlotte said.

Julia took her hand and then shook Dean's hand with a large bashful smile on her face. Charlotte's senses went on high alert at the look. Julia was quite beautiful, with wavy brunette hair and bright-blue eyes.

"I guess I should explain my thoughts to you," Jill said, sitting adjacent to them at the island. She motioned for Julia to sit beside her, and the young woman plopped her large purse on the counter. With a sigh, Jill grabbed the bag and quietly moved it to the floor. "Food-safe, dear. Purses are filthy things."

Charlotte smiled as Julia quickly grabbed a Sani-Cloth out of a nearby container and wiped at the counter with it.

"So, after our phone chat the other day I was able to get another good look at my calendar. I am sad to say that I'm already incredibly busy the weekend of your event." Jill shifted in her seat, but before Charlotte had time to show her disappointment, the woman held up a finger. "However, I've been teaching Julia here the business. I'm no spring chicken, you know, and I've developed quite a client base, which I'd hate to lose to someone else. Julia's doing really well and I thought maybe she could take on your event."

Charlotte's eyes went wide. "Oh . . ."

"She uses all my recipes," Jill said quickly. "And I'm here if she needs me, but the majority of the execution will be up to her."

Julia was biting at her bottom lip. She began to speak as soon as Charlotte looked at her. "This would only be my third wedding. I have to be honest about that. But I've done several baby showers and birthdays."

"She's also helped me on several of my recent jobs. She has a gift." This was from Jill. "In reality, she's been in my kitchen since she could pull up a stool to the counter. I have complete faith in her ability."

"I don't know why not. We're desperate enough," Dean said. Everyone looked at him. "I mean . . . sorry, that came out wrong."

"What Dean is trying to say is that we are happy to use you." Charlotte tried to help him. "We are asking a lot to give you such little notice. If Julia is using your recipes and has experience, I'm sure it will be wonderful. As long it's delicious, that's all that matters."

Julia smiled. "I promise it will be delicious. And beautiful."

Jill looked pleased. "Fantastic. Julia's prices are also more reasonable than mine."

"Even better," Dean blurted out. Charlotte flicked his thigh under the counter, and he flicked her back. The brat.

"Well, let's taste some cake, why don't we."

Charlotte sat up straighter on her stool, because this was the part she'd been waiting for. She rubbed her hands together with relish and heard Dean laugh beside her.

Julia retrieved a long white platter from a far counter and removed the plastic wrap. Charlotte let out a small gasp when she saw the two rows of triple-layered cake pieces. Dean leaned over and bumped her shoulder with his. "It's your lucky day," he whispered.

"Yes it is." Eating cake with Dean. Nothing could be better.

Jill left to do something else and allowed Julia to take over from there, describing all the varieties of cake they offered. There was chocolate fudge with espresso ganache, strawberry cream with champagne buttercream, sour cream white with raspberry cream, carrot cake with cream cheese, chocolate chip with salted fudge, and pumpkin chocolate chip with cinnamon cream cheese. Charlotte was in heaven.

"All of the cakes and fillings are interchangeable if you'd like. We've just matched the most popular options." Julia handed them both a fork.

Charlotte's instinct was to go at it with abandon, but she glanced over to Dean.

"Ladies first." He nodded at the platter. "I'd hate to lose a finger over it."

Charlotte laughed and went right for the chocolate chip cake. "I know I love this one." She put the bite into her mouth and her eyelids dropped shut.

When she opened them, she looked right at Dean. He was grinning from ear to ear. "I guess it's pretty good."

"It's more than good. It's life changing."

"You willing to share?"

"I guess since I must. But start with that one." She pointed at the flavor she'd just tried.

He took a bite and she watched as he put it in his mouth. She couldn't help remembering how soft and full his lips had felt when she kissed them. His neck moved as he swallowed.

She waited. "Well?"

"It's really good. Not sure about the salted fudge, though."

"Try this then." Charlotte scooped up some of the chocolate chip cake and used her finger to put a dab of the chocolate ganache on top. Dean tried it.

"I like that much better."

Charlotte decided she obviously had to try that combo. "Oh yeah," she moaned and then loaded up another bite. "I liked the salt, but I think that's a winner."

"There's still more." Dean chuckled. "Keep tasting."

Julia jotted down some notes as they went through the pieces, trying them as they were, experimenting with the fillings. Every cake was delicious and there really wasn't a bad choice.

"I want to make sure this has real frosting on it," Dean said after a while. "Not that smooth blanket-looking stuff."

"That's fondant," Julia said. "If you prefer buttercream on the outside I'll make note of it."

"What do you think Alex would like?" Charlotte asked.

"Well, she loves frosting, which is why I mentioned it. As for cake, she loves anything chocolate. But I also think she'd like this white one with the raspberry in it."

"That one is very popular for weddings," Julia said.

"How about that one and the chocolate chip?" Charlotte suggested.

"Can we do that?" Dean inquired, turning to Julia. "Have two flavors?"

"Of course. People have multiple flavors all the time. Once we choose a design we'll just decide the best way to divide it up on the cake."

Dean noticeably relaxed, and Charlotte smiled. "Sounds perfect, Julia."

The woman beamed. "Great. So let's choose the design." She pulled a couple of photo albums from a shelf on the wall and opened the largest one in front of them. The first page of cake photos already had Charlotte swooning. Jill's cakes ran the gamut from simple to over-the-top showstoppers.

"Now, I'll be honest, I'm not yet capable of re-creating all of these cakes."

"That's okay." Charlotte tried to sound reassuring. "The taste is the most important thing, and I don't really think our style is too fancy."

"Perfect. Then why don't I just point out the ones I know I can manage."

Charlotte and Dean looked at each other and agreed with a nod. After a few moments they'd noted several they thought looked pretty. For the most part it was Charlotte commenting and Dean quietly agreeing with her.

"You guys like the same ones I like," Julia said with a laugh. "And you always agree, it's so cute. How long have you been together?"

"Not long, but we've known each other a long time," Dean said, shocking Charlotte. She just stared at him as he finished. "This cake, however, is actually for my sister's wedding. Charlotte and I are planning it for her because she and her fiancé are currently deployed."

"Oh! That's so nice. I'm sorry, I didn't realize. So now a few things make sense. She must be the Alex you mentioned. I should not have assumed."

"Not your fault, this is kind of an odd situation. And the couple is Alex and Nate."

"Wonderful!" Julia made a quick note of the names on her paper and then looked at Charlotte with a wide grin. "I better do a good job then, so you'll ask me to make the cake for your wedding."

Charlotte was stunned into silence at the words, but thankfully Dean saved the moment. He gave Charlotte's leg a quick squeeze.

"I'm sure you'll be great."

Looking over at him, Charlotte gave an awkward smile. Was he not completely thrown off by the idea of them *marrying*?

They'd just slept together, for goodness' sake.

Focusing on the photos once more, it didn't take them long to choose a classic buttercream-frosted design. Some simple piped filigree would adorn the first and third layers, which would be white with raspberry. The second and fourth layers would be chocolate chip cake with a ruffle pipping detail. It was going to be lovely, and Charlotte couldn't help wonder if she was making good decisions on Alex's behalf. Everything would be petty, but would the other woman love what they were choosing for her wedding? She snapped a photo of the cake design with her phone. Currently, she had a slew of photos from their plans saved up for reference.

After Dean had given them a two-hundred-dollar deposit, Julia was kind enough to pack up all of the uneaten cake samples and send them with the two of them. As they quietly walked out to her car, Charlotte began to feel butterflies in her stomach. Ridiculous, considering she was now closer to Dean than she'd ever been, but then again, that was more than likely the problem. What did they do now?

Outside she automatically got back into the passenger seat while he headed for the driver's door. Once they were buckled in and he'd started the engine and pulled out, Dean cleared his throat.

"That went well. I liked their cake much better than the first place," Dean said.

"No one can outdo Jill. She's a treasure."

"But you weren't expecting her granddaughter."

"No . . . but it seems like it will be fine. Don't you agree?"

"Yeah, absolutely. Saving some money was nice also."

Charlotte laughed. "Yes, Scrooge, I'm sure you charmed them both with your comments on liking the cheaper price."

He shrugged as he pulled onto the highway. "Yeah well, four hundred dollars for a cake still seems like a lot. What can I say? I'm stressing about the money."

"Speaking of which, I want you to know I have no intention of cashing that check you very slyly slipped in with the addresses."

Dean frowned. "Charlotte, I'm paying you to photograph my sister's wedding."

"No, you're not. You need to quit worrying about it. I want to do this for you, and that's final."

She was ready for him to argue, but as they pulled into the alley behind the distillery, he just let the car idle while he turned his head to stare at her. "I cannot begin to tell you how much I appreciate you."

"It's my pleasure helping you. You should know that." Her eyes met his and held. She loved the small creases that formed beyond his lashes when he narrowed his gaze on her. His eyes flickered over her face, her lips, and then back up.

"I want you again, Charlotte." His voice was rough.

"Then have me," she said. Unable to resist, she reached up and rested her palm on his cheek. She was rewarded with the rumble of Dean's laughter before he sighed and leaned his head back against the headrest.

"I wish I didn't have so much to do today. Plus I kind of want to jot some notes down on what I want to go over with John tomorrow."

Remaining quiet, Charlotte debated her next move as she stared at Dean's profile. It was so masculine, just like the rest of him. His nose was straight, his jaw defined. The most appealing idea was to just crawl into his lap and cover his beautiful face with kisses, but her car wasn't really made for that kind of craziness.

"Will you maybe . . . call me tonight?" she asked. And for some reason the request made her feel very vulnerable. Sleeping together was one thing, talking just for fun . . . well, that felt like another.

He turned to her. "Of course. I'd like that."

She smiled and then got out of the car. He did the same. When she met him on the driver's side, he reached out and pulled her against his body.

"I like cake," he whispered. "But I like you better."

"I was thinking the same thing all day," she said, her hand reaching up to stroke his jaw.

Dean leaned down and pressed his mouth against hers. The feel of his soft lips stroking hers was like magic, and she let her fingers slip into his hair as they angled their heads to deepen the connection.

He kissed her hard and then more slowly, until finally pulling back to rest his forehead against hers.

"I better get inside."

"Me too. I think I'm going to go home and edit your photos."

Dean's eyebrow went up. "I wondered if you'd done that yet."

"I'm pretty excited. I might frame them to hang all over my bedroom."

He chuckled and placed another quick kiss on her lips. "As long as they're hidden when I come over. Unless they're of the two of us. That, I would enjoy. In fact, I want those printed and hung all over my bedroom."

Charlotte grinned, biting her bottom lip. "Maybe you'll get a surprise text from me later."

"I better."

Nineteen

The following morning Dean headed into work early, still thinking about the pictures on his phone that Charlotte had texted him the previous night.

After they'd talked on the phone for almost an hour, he'd lain in bed looking at the two of them tangled together, the sun setting behind them, as he kissed her for the first time. How many couples had their first kiss immortalized in such a beautiful and sexy photo?

And . . . yeah, he guessed they were now truly a couple. Or at the very least they were dating, although he'd yet to ask her on an official date. Something he realized he needed to remedy. And if they were really going to give this a shot, he knew he needed to be completely open and honest with her.

That was the part he was having trouble coming to terms with. He liked Charlotte. Almost more than was healthy, and if he knew anything about himself, it was that he couldn't give a warm, sweet, *young* woman like that what she needed. How would she take that news? He was jaded, bitter, and afraid of giving his all to a woman, mainly because his all would never be enough.

His insecurities ran deep, and the last relationship—his marriage—had only exploited them. There was a time in the beginning that he'd been able to share his inner fears with his wife. How his mother's abandonment had scarred him, or how he'd been resentful of her leaving his father for a younger man. Amy had been so empathetic and loving at first. They'd been on the same page, wanting to settle down, have a family. But after the third miscarriage, the relationship was strained. Eventually he'd gotten checked by a doctor and given the official news, which had only served to fuel her resentment and anger. It gave her a solid reason to blame him. She'd started going away frequently for "girl weekends," which only made Dean jealous since most of her travel companions were single.

"I don't have any children to tie me down, *do I*? Might as well take advantage of it," she'd say, lashing out at him on so many levels. He recalled the time when one of her clients was some hotshot punk that she "just needed to have a work dinner with." Dean had not hidden the fact that he was jealous, and over and over, Amy had assured him that he was being silly.

He might say the joke was on her, because sure enough, he'd proven that his concerns weren't silly. But no matter who was right or wrong, the joke was definitely on him. Dean flipped on the light to the distilling room and considered what he needed to get started. But his thoughts kept dragging down his mood.

By the time he'd caught Amy cheating, it was almost a relief, because they'd grown to not even like each other. Passion had left the relationship long before that, though. They'd been raising a teenager and sex had become a mechanical affair of temperature taking and calendar watching, which had resulted in nothing but a roller coaster of excitement and then tragedy. Amy's grieving of their lost babies left him feeling alone and helpless. She wasn't the only one who blamed him.

Dean was looking over his logbook and filling out the day's clipboard when a raspy voice came from the doorway.

"Morning."

Dean turned to find a puffy-eyed TJ sipping on a steaming cup of coffee. "Damn, dude. What happened to you?" Dean asked.

His friend chuckled. "I had a date last night."

Dean's eyes went wide. "Nice. Is this obvious hangover because it went well or . . . not."

"Oh, it went well. Two times well."

"Wow. I didn't know you had it in you." Normally it was Jake who came in with a sex hangover.

TJ took another sip of his coffee and lowered his mug. "Honestly, I didn't either. It had been a while."

"Congratulations. Who is this girl?"

"What girl?" Jake asked them both as he stepped in the distilling room and pivoted around TJ. He took in his friend's slumped posture, giant mug of caffeine, and squinty eyes. "Rough night, man?"

"Something like that."

"TJ scored last night." Dean couldn't help himself. He was happy the guy had finally given up on Jen, because he'd have bet money that ship would never sail.

"My man," Jake said, slapping TJ on the back. A bit of coffee sloshed over the rim of his mug, but TJ jerked it away from his body just in time so that it didn't get his pants wet. "It's about damn time. I was starting to worry about you."

"Not sure why the two of you are so worried about my sex life."

"We worry about your lack of a sex life. A critical difference," Jake said. "I don't ever want to see a friend suffer."

TJ shook his head as Jake laughed. The entire conversation reminded Dean that he had something to discuss with the two of them before his apprentice showed up in . . . damn, about twenty minutes.

"Hey, guys, listen, something I need to mention," Dean said. Both turned his way, waiting. "So, you both know I have this new guy coming in to discuss a possible apprenticeship."

"John, yeah. He seems cool." TJ took another sip of his coffee, the other hand in his pocket.

"He is cool, but here's the thing I haven't mentioned. He is Charlotte Linley's ex."

Jake's eyebrows rose. "Seriously? Does she know?"

"Don't you . . . *like* her?" TJ asked, and Dean could tell his friend wasn't trying to make him uncomfortable, just stating a fact.

Jake nodded in agreement. "Yeah, I know you do. So this has to be a bad idea."

Dean sighed and then decided there was no better way than through. "About that. Charlotte and I . . . well, we've kind of been seeing each other."

"It's about damn time," Jake said with a grin.

"When did this happen?" TJ asked. "I mean I'm happy for you. I like Charlotte a lot."

Dean nodded. "Yeah, it's kind of recent, and, well . . . her ex working here is a little awkward. But he knows about us."

"Jesus, man," TJ said. "This sounds like trouble."

"I realize that, and had I known at first, I would have avoided this. But I think they're both cool with it."

"You sure about Charlotte?" Jake asked. "Obviously, our loyalty lies with her."

"I told her the same thing," Dean said, but he appreciated Jake voicing the same opinion. "And she says she's good. It will be a little awkward, but she wanted him to have the job."

"I hope he works out. You need help," TJ reminded them all. "I was relieved as hell when I heard you'd talked to someone."

"I hope it works out, too. He'll be here in about ten minutes."

"So, new distiller is the ex of your new girlfriend. I hope you know what you're doing."

"Me too." Dean just shook his head and headed to the distilling room to get ready for the day. He was grateful that he'd partnered with two guys who were so easy to work with. They all gave one another shit, but they first had one another's backs. It would be interesting to see how John fit in, or if he even did.

A few minutes later, the man himself stepped into the distilling room.

"Morning," John said.

"Hey, glad you're here. I was just getting started."

"Great. Um, before that, I wanted to say something." John shoved his hands into his pockets, obviously trying to not fidget. "I just want you to know that I would totally understand if you'd like to change your mind about this. I mean, I appreciate you standing by your word, but—"

Dean put up a hand. "Listen, thanks for the offer, but we're good." John relaxed, his shoulders slumping. Dean continued, telling him what he'd told his co-workers a few moments before. "I let Charlotte make that call, and she wanted you to have the chance to see how this goes."

"That doesn't surprise me. She's. . . ." He stared at the ground a moment, and then looked back up to Dean. "She's really something. You're lucky you have her. I mean it. Don't make the same mistake I did and let her get away."

Dean inhaled deep, nodding slowly. So, maybe this whole thing might be even more awkward than he'd thought.

Twenty

It was Thursday, only five days since Charlotte had been inside the Stag for Shelby and Jason's wedding. But in that short amount of time, everything had changed. This no longer felt like the same safe, welcoming space it had always been. The full impact of having John back in her life was starting to really show itself.

She and Dean had texted and spoken on the phone several times over the past couple days, and although she'd asked him how things with John were going, he hadn't offered her much information other than that they were moving forward with hiring John.

But mostly he'd given vague responses. Maybe he thought he was being considerate of her feelings. Or maybe it was just a guy thing not to elaborate on work stuff.

Secretly she'd kind of hoped Dean had realized that it wasn't going to work out for whatever reason. It was apparent that wasn't the case as she made her way to the back of the building. The glass enclosing the distilling room revealed Dean and John cleaning up a giant mess on the floor with a hose and a squeegee. They were also laughing.

She stood there in the middle front lobby area, watching them for a long moment. How long had it been since she'd seen John laugh that way? Certainly not the last few months of their relationship. Those had been filled with his looks of concern. Concern for her because she hadn't handled the loss of their pregnancy well. The only thing that had kept her going was their impending wedding.

Suddenly John turned his head and looked right at her. Standing straight, he gave her a smile. She reciprocated quickly and waved. When she looked over at Dean he was watching her. As soon as their eyes locked he crooked his finger, beckoning her to come in.

She did, heading off toward the side hall, through the back warehouse, and into the distilling room.

"Hey you," Dean instantly said. They hadn't discussed how they'd greet each other in John's presence, but thankfully Dean walked right over, wrapped a hand around her waist, and leaned down to give her a quick kiss on the lips. That definitely helped her insecurities about being here.

"What happened in here?" she asked when he pulled away. The entire floor around the stainless-steel masher was covered with a mealy brown substance.

"Basically Dean turned his back on the newb for half an hour and I messed up," John said.

"Honest mistake. The machine can jam fairly easily if you don't keep an eye on it. Jake and I cleaned up a similar mess just a couple weeks ago."

Charlotte smiled. These two seemed to get along well. "Anything I can do to help?"

"No, it's my fault," John said quickly.

Thankfully Dean looked at her and pointed to the wall. "Actually, would you mind pulling that hose down and handing it to me?"

"Of course." For some reason it pleased Charlotte that he asked for her help. As if they were a team, and he needed her. She handed him the hose then followed his instructions to turn the water on so he could wash the residue down a drain on the floor. They had plans to meet a DJ in the conference room any minute, so when she was finished she headed back out to the lobby to wait on him.

As soon as she got to the hallway, an arm grabbed her.

Turning, she found herself looking up into John's face. She jerked her arm from his grasp and sent a panicked look toward the mouth of the hallway. She definitely didn't want Dean to find John touching her like that.

"I'm sorry, I just . . . you didn't hear me over the water."

"It's okay." She stepped back a space. "Did you need something?"

"I just wanted to say . . . thank you. While I had the chance."

Charlotte heard the hose turn off and glanced toward the hallway entrance, but no one appeared. "Thank you? For what?"

"For not insisting Dean change his mind about me. So far I really like this job, but I know you'd have had every right to not want me here."

Considering her words, Charlotte paused. "It was a shock, I'll admit that. But I also want Dean to have the help he needs, and . . . I know you'll enjoy this job. You've always been a hard worker."

He nodded and Charlotte turned to go, but not before he caught her one more time, his fingers gripping her arm. "Next week is the twelfth."

She froze, and then slowly pulled her arm from his fingers. "Don't. Please. I can't talk about this with you."

"Every year, Charlotte . . . every year I think of you."

Charlotte glanced over her shoulder and met his eyes, which were pinched and full of sadness. Some deep and instinctual part of her almost longed to fall against him and cry. But she was stronger than that. It had been five years and he'd proven himself unworthy of her emotions.

There was nothing to say so she just turned away and kept walking to the front of the building. She headed straight for one of the sofas and sat down to try to collect her thoughts. Moments later she heard footsteps, and then two strong arms wrapped around her from behind the couch's low back.

"Hey. Everything okay?" Dean whispered in her ear. Instinctively her body exhaled and she leaned back into his embrace. This felt right.

"Of course. Why do you ask?" Charlotte reached up and laid her hand on his forearm. He was so warm, his muscles so strong.

"Did he say something to upset you?"

"No. He was basically just thanking me for not telling you to boot his ass out."

Dean laughed, but his look of concern didn't go away. "Charlotte, I don't want you to be uncomfortable here." He turned his head and kissed her temple.

"I'm *not* uncomfortable here," she replied. "Especially not right now." She ran her hand up and down his arm.

"You sure?"

She turned to look into his eyes. "I promise."

He finally nodded and then stood upright. With a sigh, Charlotte followed him into the offices, but not before glancing over to the distilling room. It was empty.

Todd, the DJ they were meeting with, showed up a few moments later. Dean greeted him by the reception area and then brought him back to the conference space. Charlotte recognized him immediately. Although she didn't know him that well, they'd definitely been at weddings together before. Unfortunately, she shot so many, it was hard to recall if she liked someone. The two DJs who would have been her top picks were both unavailable on their date, which hadn't surprised her at all.

Dean motioned for Todd to have a seat and then sat down right next to Charlotte. He grabbed her hand under the table, gave it a squeeze, and sent her a quick wink. Smiling back, she listened intently as Todd proceeded to tell them a little about himself and his business—which was rather new. Nothing wrong with that, everyone had to be new at some point—but Charlotte could tell within moments that he was pretty inexperienced. However, they didn't have a lot of options, and his newbie status was reflected in his pricing, which worked with their budget.

After that he asked them to fill out a questionnaire.

"I know it's a little silly, but I think it helps me get to know my couples' style and preferences, and also gets ideas going on song choices."

"Oh . . . okay." Dean took the papers and handed one to Charlotte. She wondered why he didn't mention that they weren't *the couple*, but decided to keep her mouth shut.

She sat up straight and looked down at the first question. *What is one of your favorite songs from high school?*

She heard Dean chuckle and then he looked over at her. "This should be fun," he whispered. Fun, yes, and she was really going to have to think on some of these. They worked on their answers in silence for a bit. The questions were all obviously geared toward Todd creating the ideal playlist for the bride and groom. Charlotte almost stopped them and reminded Dean that their answers were irrelevant, but since the real couple was half a world away, and she was really curious about Dean's answers, she just proceeded. When Todd asked for directions to the restroom, and then exited the room, Dean leaned over her shoulder.

"What do you have down for number six?"

Charlotte hadn't gotten that far yet, but she glanced down at her paper. *If you could only listen to one artist for the rest of your life, who would it be?*

"Oh, I know instantly. Easy for me, but you tell me yours first." She leaned toward him just as he slapped a hand over his paper.

"Really?" Charlotte said, laughing. "We're hiding answers now?"

She reached out and peeled his hand off the paper before tilting in to read his boxy man handwriting. "Led Zeppelin. Nice. Can't go wrong with Page and Plant."

Dean's eyes widened.

"Does it surprise you I know their names? Or that I know classic rock at all? I'll have you know that Lauren and I don't go on a road trip without their fourth album. I know all the words to 'Going to California.'"

"I apologize, then." He leaned forward, elbows on his knees. When his finger reached out and brushed her leg, it seemed to Charlotte that he did it without even thinking. "You constantly surprise me, Charlotte."

"I hope so," she said. It was her turn to lean in, and she swore he came a little closer.

"Your turn to answer," he said.

"Easy. ABBA. You might have guessed from my ringtone."

Dean let his head drop forward for a moment, obviously amused. When he looked up at her he was grinning. "What is your obsession with ABBA?"

"I've just always loved them, ever since I was little and my mother would play their records while she cleaned the house. I think she always wished she was Agnetha Fältskog."

"Is that the blonde or the brunette?" Dean asked. His

chair rolled closer, their faces now a couple of feet apart, and his hand gently grabbed hers. He held on to her forefinger, and Charlotte sucked in a quick breath.

"Agnetha is the blonde, and my answer to the first question on the paper, what is your favorite song from high school, is 'Dancing Queen.' Definitely not popular with the rest of my high school, but it was with me. I listened to it all the time." He watched her as she spoke, his fingers interlacing with hers. She loved this new intimacy with him, the way he casually touched her, like he had every right to do so. "My freshman year we went to New York as a family and saw *Mamma Mia!* on Broadway. My fangirling hit an all-time high after that. I was . . . obsessed, as you so sweetly put it."

He squeezed their palms together. "Wow. I never would have guessed. You should talk to Jen. She sings show tunes constantly. Drives us all crazy."

"Really? I've heard her singing while she worked, but didn't realize she was into musical theater."

He nodded. "She even works at a place teaching kids or something."

Todd came through the door and they quickly unlocked their hands and adjusted their seats back toward the table.

"How we doing?" Todd the DJ's grin was a little obnoxious, and his enthusiasm was slightly manufactured, but he was trying. And weren't all vendors playing a part to an extent as they met with potential clients? She completely understood, because you didn't always feel "on," but you had to sell yourself anyway. Charlotte figured as long as he had the right equipment—which he appeared to have—and a decent personality, then he would do.

She gave Dean a slight nod and they proceeded, giving him what they'd finished on their questionnaires and then taking care of the final details like time, down payment, and contracts. When it was all finished, Dean saw Todd to the door.

There were so many reasons for her to be happy right now. It was finally summer, she was dating the man she'd lusted after for years, and she had enough work to keep her busy for the next year.

But as John had reminded her, the saddest day of the year was just around the corner.

After seeing the DJ to the front door, Dean headed back toward the offices. He inhaled deep and blew out a breath. Right now he was fighting the urge to go back into the conference room, shut and lock the door, and spread Charlotte out on the table like a sacrifice. Or maybe an idol to worship.

That's what this woman did to him.

Hearing her conversation with John in the hallway—seeing them talking that close—had made him worried and a little jealous. He'd heard enough to know there was something between them that he wasn't aware of. Part of him wanted to ask, but a bigger part of him just wanted her to tell him. This relationship thing they were trying was new, not yet to the point of revealing secrets, but he suddenly wished it was. If he wanted her to open up, they needed to spend more time together.

"One more thing to check off the list, right?" Charlotte announced when he walked into the conference room.

"Absolutely. Feels good to have that finished. So what's left?"

Charlotte pulled out her planning notebook and flipped through a few pages. Instead of sitting down close to her, he leaned his hands on the table.

"So, we've got our venue, obviously. Bar service arranged, catering, flowers, the cake, and now the DJ."

"And . . . you, right?"

"Of course. Me. Photographer. I'm also still planning on handling the reception decorations, but what's going on with the dress? Do we know?"

"Oh . . . damn. No. I'd completely forgotten about that."

"About the dress?" she teased. "It's only very, very important."

"Yeah, you're right. Just slipped my mind." Or more than likely he pushed anything that had to do with Amy into the back of his thoughts on purpose. "I'll just text and see what's going on."

Dean grabbed his phone out of his pocket and scrolled through his message threads. Amy's name was near the bottom, which wasn't a surprise. The last time they'd texted was probably the day Alex left for her deployment.

DEAN: Any luck with the dress?

She replied immediately.

AMY: Yes! I found it. Ordered it last week and put it on my credit card. You can just pay me back.
DEAN: How much?
AMY: Don't be mad . . .
AMY: The minute I saw it I knew it was perfect for our girl. When you see it you'll agree.

"This isn't sounding good," Dean muttered.

"What? Why?" Charlotte scooted to the edge of her seat.

DEAN: How much?
AMY: $1700

"Holy shit." Dean let his arm drop as he sank down to sit on the edge of the table.

"What is it?" Charlotte instantly rose from her chair and stepped up to face him. With him seated so high they were eye-to-eye, and on instinct he parted his legs and she stepped between them, laying on a hand on his chest. "What's wrong?"

"The friend picking out Alex's dress . . ."

"Yes?"

"It's my ex-wife."

"Oh. Okay." Her eyes lowered to stare at his chest. She'd been mindlessly fidgeting with a button on his shirt, but when her hand began to slide away from him, Dean reached up and stilled it. Her eyes came back up to his. "That's nice that you can remain friends."

"No, Charlotte, it's not like that. We aren't enemies, but we are not friends."

Her eyes widened as she stared at him. "Okay."

She appeared to be processing everything he'd just said, and Dean realized that he needed to clear this all up. He'd just been wishing she would share more about herself; this was his chance to set the tone. She deserved to know.

"When my mother and Alex's father passed, Alex was only thirteen. Amy and I . . . well, we basically became her parents after that. The two of them are close, and although I have no wish to have a relationship with Amy, I can't deny that to my little sister. Not when she has no other family."

"I understand. That makes sense." Charlotte smiled at him, and the relief he felt was palpable. "I'm glad you told me."

"I should have told you sooner."

She shrugged. "We're seeing what happens, remember? You told me now. That's what matters."

Dean sighed with relief. "You're pretty amazing. You know that?"

Her lips parted into a smile, but she didn't meet his eyes. Instead she was busy watching her hand slide up his chest and then skim along his neck. Dean shivered, couldn't help it. When she stepped closer, her breasts meeting his body, her pelvis aligning with his own, he lifted his palms to settle on her hips.

"I'm glad you think so. But do you know what I think is amazing?" she purred, leaning into his neck. The minute her lips found the stubble under his jaw, Dean dropped his head back.

"Tell me."

"How hot I get every time I'm around you." Charlotte's tongue blazed a trail up to his ear.

A low groan escaped Dean's lips and he ran his palms up the back of her legs, lifting her little skirt along with it. As soon as his fingers met with the firm cheeks of her butt, he sank his grip into each side and pulled her hard against him.

Charlotte's lips found his and he kissed her several times. Playfully first, and then slightly more aggressive, until her arms wrapped around his shoulder and her hands gripped the sides of his face.

"I'd like to have you right here on this table," Dean muttered against her lips.

A throat cleared from the doorway and Charlotte jumped out of his arms, shoving her skirt down in the process. Dean stood up tall, pulling her body in front of his to conceal what had to be an embarrassingly obvious erection.

TJ stood in the doorway, John just slightly behind him.

"Sorry about that, lovebirds," TJ said, smirking. "But uh . . . John wondered if you were done with him for the day."

"I apologize," John said, a mixture of embarrassment and . . . something else on his face. "I should have just waited."

The animal part of Dean's brain loved every second of visibly marking his territory in such a physical and undeniable way. But this just reminded him that Charlotte and John shared something he knew nothing about. Something that had definitely upset her.

"That's okay," she said, turning to Dean. "I was just leaving, actually."

"Not yet. Hang on." Dean turned to John. "Hey man, I'll meet you out front in a second."

John nodded and he and TJ left.

Turning back to Charlotte, he caught her biting her bottom lip.

"That was awkward," he said.

"And unfortunate." She stepped into his space and wrapped her arms around his neck. He instantly melted against her, letting his hands slide up her back. God, she felt good in his arms. "I was really getting into you. When do I get to see you again?"

"As soon as possible." He placed a kiss on her forehead, happy when she tilted her mouth to find his. He kissed her once. Again. "Let's go out this weekend. On a real date."

"I want to so bad. But this weekend I'm going out of town."

Dean stilled, looking down at her. "You are?"

He wanted to protest the fact that she hadn't told him, but he hardly had the right.

"Lauren and I are shooting in North Carolina this Saturday. We fly out tomorrow, and I haven't even packed yet.

His heart sped up. He couldn't believe she was flying across the country and he was just now finding out. "Do you shoot a lot of out-of-town weddings?"

"Not a lot, no. Some years more than others, but I have two this year."

"That's . . . fun. Where's the other one."

She grinned. "Cancun. Awesome, right? That one's in October."

"Wow. So Lauren will go with you to that one also?"

"Yeah, it's always the two of us. Unless you want to be my new assistant." She grinned up at him.

Dean chuckled. "No thanks. But I am going to miss you this weekend." They were both busy people, and while they hadn't been seeing each other every day, the idea that he couldn't see her even if he wanted to this weekend sucked bad.

"I'm going to miss you, too." She tilted her head to the side. "I still can't believe we're finally doing this."

"You glad?" he asked.

"Very. You know that."

He was glad, too, but in this very moment his anxiety about them started to creep back up. She was not Amy. He needed to remind himself that. "When you get back, then we'll go out."

"Of course. I'm all yours."

Dean placed one more kiss on her lips. "Good. I'll see you next week then."

Twenty-One

By the time he was done with work on Friday, Dean was in need of a distraction. He was missing Charlotte like crazy, and he'd seen her just the day before. The fact that he wouldn't see her again until . . . well, he wasn't even certain exactly when, made it so much worse.

This was what falling for a woman felt like, which meant he was in trouble.

After making sure everything was shut down and locked, he headed for the alley where his car was parked.

The week had been long and busy. Teaching someone new was incredibly stressful, although Dean was really impressed with his new apprentice. Part of him had almost hoped John would prove to be unfit for the job—for Charlotte's sake at least—but the opposite had proven true. John was a quick learner and asked good questions. He had an analytical mind, which helped him understand the scientific processes of distilling easily. Dean's initial instincts had been spot-on. John was basically the dream apprentice he'd been waiting for: eager, curious, and driven. If Dean ignored the fact that the guy had slept with Charlotte, given her a ring, and then broken her heart, then he liked John.

The guy was great, even had the kind of sarcastic but friendly personality that Dean could get along with. Yet, despite how well things had been going, Charlotte had figuratively been in the room with them at every turn. They'd both known it, and John had even mentioned her casually a time or two. Or three. Each time had been a reminder to Dean that his jealousy was more intense than he'd expected it would be.

He'd thought of her constantly. Their previous Saturday night and Sunday morning together. The look in her eyes as she'd put that chocolate chip cake in her mouth. Even the feel of her goose-bump-covered skin under his fingers. He couldn't stop, and every time he thought of her relationship with John, he was conflicted.

There was no doubt in Dean's mind that John wasn't fully over Charlotte. At the very least, seeing her again had brought up a lot of fond memories—that was obvious by the look on his face and the tone of his voice when her name was mentioned. It probably didn't help having to watch her with someone new, but Dean refused to feel guilt for that. He'd waited a long time to have her all to himself.

But at the same time, he could hardly fault the guy for his feelings. Charlotte was beautiful, successful, and now off limits.

A small part of him couldn't help wondering if maybe fate was trying to bring two people back together and Dean was standing in the way of Charlotte's happiness. John was young, handsome, and seemed to be a good guy. The way he'd ended their relationship didn't mean they couldn't try again, did it?

Yeah, on second thought, hell no. John could have Charlotte over Dean's dead body.

Once in his vehicle, Dean felt restless and decided to

head over to his father's for a visit. It had rained recently. Maybe his lawn needed mowing. Some manual labor might work wonders on keeping his mind off things. Wondering exactly where Charlotte was. Who she was with. What she was doing.

Pulling into his father's driveway, Dean turned off his ignition and got out. It was still warm even at seven in the evening, and the humidity was starting to kick in. Grabbing some gym clothes out of his trunk, he made his way to the front door and let himself in after a quick perfunctory knock.

"Dad?" he called out.

"In the john," a muffled voice said from within the house.

Dean chuckled to himself at the choice of words. He made his way into the small kitchen where he'd eaten many meals as a child. Across the top of the cabinets was a row of Stag alcohol bottles and Dean smiled. His father wasn't much of a drinker, but he was incredibly proud of his son.

He opened the fridge and found several containers of fruit, a bag of salad mix, and about six or seven packages of pudding cups. Even at eighty-three his father was getting along just fine. Always had. It about killed Dean to think that the man wouldn't live forever. Losing his mother had been hard, and they hadn't even gotten along that well. It was almost impossible for him to imagine a world without his father in it.

The sound of the bathroom sink was followed by a creaky door, and then his dad walked into the kitchen. "You in here making me dinner?"

Dean let the fridge door shut and opened the freezer. "I would, but I'm not sure what I could whip up with forty pudding cups."

"Those are my favorite. Eat one while I watch Jimmy every night."

Dean shook his head and shut the freezer. "How about I order some pizza and then mow your lawn."

"I guess that sounds okay. I don't keep you around to do my chores, though."

"No, I just like to give you a hand once in a while. I get bored," Dean lied.

"You know the cure for that, don't you?" His dad sat down to the kitchen table and let out a sigh. He sure didn't move as fast as he used to, but he was still mobile. Independent.

"I'm sure you'll tell me."

"A man your age needs a wife."

Dean refrained from pointing out that having a wife hadn't done either one of them much good. His father constantly hounded him not to go through life lonely. Dean knew the man was worried about him, but while lonely might not be ideal, it was consistent. Safe.

"What about you? You're not dead," Dean said, just as a deflection. He grabbed a glass from the cabinet and filled it with water.

"Who says I don't have a woman in my life?"

Dean's eyes went wide and he turned to look at his father, who had a bemused expression on his face. "You never know is all I'm saying."

"Hmm." Dean decided not to even go near that comment. He pulled out his phone. "What kind of pizza you want?"

"I'm not picky. Whatever you like."

Joel Troyer had always been a kind man. Accommodating, pleasant, a jokester. He wanted everyone around him to be happy and to feel welcome. It was his nature, which was why Dean had never understood why his mother left.

Except for the fact that she'd married a younger man after their divorce. Not once had his dad acted bitter or angry. Sad, yes. Those first couple of years had been rough on him, and Dean had worried he might never pull out of his funk. But eventually he did, and never, ever had he bad-mouthed or blamed Dean's mother for the demise of their marriage.

Dean hadn't been so forgiving. To a teenage boy, watching his mother flaunt herself, date various men, and then settle on a guy a decade younger than her had stung. He'd been livid, and while he knew his father would have done anything to get her back, Dean's feelings had grown to near-hate. Eventually his ire had thawed somewhat, but the two of them had never been close after that.

His dad had never gotten an apology as far as Dean knew. He'd always wished he'd just made a scene, given her a piece of his mind. But he never had. Even to this day, if he mentioned her name, a smile came to his face. Dean would never understand it. A good man like his father didn't deserve to go through life alone.

As far as he was concerned, his mother had given up the best thing that had ever happened to her. Then again, if she'd stayed there would be no Alex, and that meant Dean had to believe that maybe she'd done them all a favor. His father loved Alex, too. Everyone who met her did. The two of them—his dad and Alex—were similar in nature, both mild-mannered and kind. Made Dean wonder if somehow she'd inherited a Troyer gene through osmosis.

After calling in a pizza order, Dean found his father in the living room, sitting in his favorite chair, watching the evening news. "How's the wedding planning going?"

Dean sat down on the sofa, deciding maybe they'd eat before he went out and tackled the yard. "Good. Better than I could have expected."

Joel laughed. "You got a knack for it, huh?"

"Don't know about that, I just enlisted some help."

"Good idea, I s'pose."

"Yeah. She's a wedding photographer who shoots a lot at the building so she knows her stuff. Best decision I could have made."

"I guess so, if it puts that look on your face."

Dean's eyes went to his father's. He couldn't help laughing. "I have no idea what you're talking about."

His dad just chuckled. "I can always tell with you. She pretty?"

Realizing there was no point in playing dumb, Dean just answered the question. "Of course she is." *She's gorgeous.*

"Is it serious?"

"I don't know yet. It's still new." Dean put a leg up on his knee and fidgeted with the sole of his shoe.

"Gotta start somewhere."

"You're right. Makes me nervous, though. She's a lot younger than I am."

Joel's eyes widened. "She legal?"

"*Christ*, Dad, yes she's legal. She's close to thirty."

"Oh well, hell." Joel waved a hand in Dean's direction. "She may as well be your age then."

"There's almost twelve years between us. We didn't even grow up on the same popular music. Or television shows."

"Pssh. Please. Give the woman some credit."

"You of all people should understand," Dean said, getting defensive.

"You're damn right," Joel's voice bellowed, and Dean's head jerked up in shock. His dad rarely raised his voice. "I understand completely what it feels like to be alone. I don't want that for my son."

"Dad—"

"A few years between a couple never hurt anybody. You're a healthy man. Look better than most guys do at twenty-five. You're welcome for those genes by the way."

Dean laughed quietly. "Part of the problem is . . . I'm sure she'll want kids, Dad."

Joel sighed. "That is something to consider. Have you told her?"

"No. I'm scared to death."

"If it's meant to be, she'll understand."

"Giving up children is a lot to ask a young, healthy woman," Dean said.

"There are lots of ways to have a baby."

Dean hesitated before he went on. "I have an appointment on Monday to test again. Get a second opinion."

His father's eyes cut to his. "You sure about that? The last time . . ."

"I know, Dad, last time was rough."

"That's an understatement."

"Yeah, but it was also close to ten years ago. Maybe . . . I don't know. I doubt things have changed, but . . . I just need to go back in. I want to be able to tell Charlotte I tried again for her when I tell her I can't ever give her a baby."

"You certain you feel that strongly for her?"

"Yeah. I think I do."

His dad ran a hand down his face, leaning back in his chair. "Wish I could change this for you, son."

Dean smiled. "I know, Dad."

"I'm proud of you, though. I was starting to fear you'd never try again."

"Making a baby?"

"No. Not that. Loving someone."

Dean looked down at his lap. He'd been afraid of that, too. Part of him still wasn't certain he'd allow it to happen, but Charlotte made him hope.

"You have to risk the pain." His father scooted to the edge of his recliner, resembling a sprinter about to take off at the gunshot. "Because if you keep going through life trying to safeguard yourself from ending up alone, only one thing will happen."

"And that is . . ."

"You'll *definitely* end up alone."

Twenty-Two

Saturday evening, Charlotte and her freshly married couple stood with their toes in the firm sand on beautiful Sunset Beach in North Carolina. Lauren was back at the resort covering the cocktail hour and getting the details like the cake, table settings, and random shots of the guests mingling. Here on the beach, it was peaceful and lovely. Charlotte kept thinking about how romantic it would be to walk along the shore with Dean.

"Amazing, Rebecca," Charlotte called out to her bride. The sun was setting off to their left, creating a blanket of pinks, purples, and oranges in the clear sky. It was possibly the most gorgeous sight she'd ever seen.

Speaking loudly, with her camera to her eye, Charlotte continued directing them. "Okay, Aaron, go ahead and pull her in tight and dip her back. Yes, beautiful. Okay, now pull her back up and put a little kiss on her temple. Rebecca, you're gorgeous, just drop that shoulder a little bit— oh yes, just like that. Oh my God, you guys! These are going to be so fantastic."

Charlotte's enthusiasm earned her the response she was looking for when her bride blushed, smiled, and nuzzled into her new husband. The shutter of her camera rapid-fired through several photos, catching their private whisper and ensuing laughter. Finally satisfied with the coverage, Charlotte lowered her camera. "That was wonderful. Let's head to the reception!"

Rebecca and Aaron lifted their joined arms, and the bride whooped in agreement as she headed toward Charlotte.

She and Lauren had been looking forward to this wedding for months. Destination and travel gigs were always a treat when they came her way, and this couple had been fantastic to work with. Laid-back, easy to please, and just plain in love.

"I'm starving," Aaron said with a chuckle as he neared Charlotte. "But are you sure we got enough? I want Beck to be happy with this part. Her sunset pictures were what she was most excited about."

"Aw, babe." Rebecca leaned over and kissed him on the cheek.

"Trust me." Charlotte adjusted her camera equipment as they began to head back toward the golf cart they'd taken to the beach from the resort where they were all staying. "We got amazing stuff out here."

"Thank you so much, Charlotte. I know I've said it several times, but I'm just so grateful that you were willing to travel."

"Of course. I'm honored you chose to bring me with you. It's been an amazing day, and your family is all just lovely."

It was all true. Weddings like this made her realize her job had some serious perks, and being able to travel and work with happy people were the biggest ones. When she revealed to people that she was a wedding photographer, the first thing they wanted to know was how crazy the brides were. And while that happened sometimes, most couples were wonderful. Families in general got along fairly well, despite a few hiccups here and there, but for most normal people, weddings were happy affairs. Reason to celebrate.

For the first time, ever, it occurred to Charlotte that . . . maybe weddings weren't so bad. As long as the bride and groom were for sure in love, anyway.

Charlotte smiled to herself as she got into the driver's seat of the golf cart and the couple got into the back. They began snuggling and whispering as soon as Charlotte took off toward the resort.

This was her first time in North Carolina, and the evening was just luscious. Just the right temperature, a hint of salt in the air, and the sound of seagulls overhead. She could get used to jobs like this. Nearing the resort, Charlotte glanced into the rearview of the golf cart to find her couple kissing, their eyes shut in bliss, Rebecca's hands on Aaron's face.

What did it feel like to end the day belonging to someone? Knowing that they belonged to you and only you, forever and ever. To have that someone who would love you no matter what. Who'd grow old with you. Whom you'd have babies with. If you were lucky.

With a sigh Charlotte pulled into the front drive of the colonial building. "You two hang tight. I'll come to the top of the stairs and motion when we're ready for your entrance."

Rebecca shrieked quietly, completely excited to be announced as Mr. and Mrs. Aaron Tiller. She should be excited, and grateful that she'd already lucked out by choosing a groom who had actually wanted to come down the aisle and marry her.

Inside the resort, the reception was in full swing. A three-piece string ensemble played while the guests sipped pretty drinks and ate finger foods. Charlotte spotted Lauren and made her way across the room, dodging laughing women in high-heeled sandals, and men in suit jackets. The room smelled amazing, like crab cakes and shrimp boil, and Charlotte knew it would no doubt be the best seafood she'd ever had. Considering that the dance floor was already filling, it appeared it would be a fun reception to shoot.

Several hours later, Charlotte and Lauren were wiped out and officially off the clock. Rebecca and Aaron had tried to talk them into hanging out and having a drink, but they gracefully exited and went up to their room. The minute they shut the door, they each unloaded their gear, kicked off their shoes, and flopped down on one of the beds. After a moment of silence Lauren spoke.

"I'm exhausted, but we're in a beach town. We can't waste it."

"What are you thinking?" Charlotte asked.

She heard Lauren's mattress creak as she moved. "Want to walk over to that little bar we passed earlier today? The one on the way to the beach?"

Charlotte had her eyes closed, but she considered the idea. Lauren did have a point about being in a beach town. Kansas was about as landlocked as a state could get, so they really should live it up while they were here. "Yeah, that sounds nice. But first I'm going to change into something more comfortable."

She dragged herself out of bed, as did Lauren, and they each dug through their bags. Charlotte took off the capris and blouse she'd been wearing for ten hours and pulled out a light tank dress. The air had cooled a bit so close to the water, so she put on a light three-quarter-sleeved cardigan and off they went. The wedding reception was still going—albeit not as strong as it had been an hour ago—as they passed by on their way to the front lobby and out into the night. The bar was just a few blocks away, and there were other tourists meandering about.

"It's so nice," Lauren said. "I could totally live here."

"I like it, too. It's peaceful. I always thought I was a mountain person, not a beach person, but this one is nice."

Once in the little bar they each ordered the special—something pink and garnished with a pineapple—and found a high-top table to sit down at. A small band was playing at the far end of the room, and there was a decent crowd. It was only moments before a couple of guys came up and introduced themselves. They were actually pretty cute, and Charlotte and Lauren gave each other a quick glance of communication, agreeing it was cool to invite them to sit down, which they did.

The guys were from Atlanta and in town for a conference at a hotel nearby. The four of them hit it off pretty well, and the guys asked them lots of questions about weddings and enjoyed hearing about some of the details from her and Lauren's workday.

"That sounds so stressful," the guy closest to Charlotte said. He'd said his name was Tim . . . right? She felt a little nervous when he leaned in closer to her.

"You get used to it. I find it more exciting than anything. Never know how a wedding day will go."

Charlotte glanced up to find Lauren leaning on her palm, her face angled toward the guy next to her. Her friend was totally giving the guy the look. Panic suddenly took over Charlotte. What if Lauren wanted to take this guy back to the room? Or go to his room? What would she do?

Glancing at her phone, Charlotte nearly jumped when it rang. "Honey, Honey," by ABBA, blared from the device.

She quickly pushed the ACCEPT button before anyone could hear too much of it and held it to her ear. "Hello?"

"Hey, it's me."

A giant grin broke out on her face. "Hi, Me. How are you?" Much to her chagrin, from the other side of the table, Lauren was calling out to her in regard to the ABBA song. Charlotte shot her a look, which only made a slightly tipsy Lauren laugh.

"Are you out?" Dean asked, his tone going a little cold. The music was loud, so Charlotte put up a finger to her companions, excused herself from the table, and headed out onto the wooden porch on the back of the building.

"Yeah. Our wedding was winding down so Lauren and I headed over to a little bar on the beach."

"Ah, okay. I can let you go."

"No way. I'm so glad you called. Lauren's talking to some guy she met. Plus, I've been thinking about you."

"Good, because I've been thinking about you." His tone seemed a little softer now.

"Did you work a wedding tonight?"

"No. It was TJ's night. I spent the day doing laundry and trying not to feel sorry for myself that you're on the beach and I'm not with you."

"Aww, poor thing." She proceeded to tell him about their wedding day, the beautiful beach sunset, and the crab cakes she had for dinner. He listened, asked questions, and laughed at her jokes. She could talk to him forever, she realized.

"But truly, I did think of you often today, and how much more fun I'd be having if you were with me."

"I wish I was. Maybe we should go to a beach."

"And leave your precious barrels of bourbon?" she teased.

Dean's muffled laugh on the other end of the line warmed her. "I'd leave them to lie on a beach with you."

Charlotte leaned back in the chair, put her feet up on the rickety wooden deck, and closed her eyes. "That sounds nice, doesn't it? I can imagine it so well since I'm here smelling the salty air and listening to the waves crash."

Dean groaned. "Stop it. I'm jealous."

Before she could reply, a loud group of people burst onto the deck. "Charlotte, we're walking to the beach," Tim said rather loudly.

"Come with us, Charlotte." That was from Lauren, who clearly had drunk a bit more while Charlotte was outside. There was no way she could leave her friend alone with strange men. She suddenly realized she should have never left Lauren inside and she felt bad.

"Everything okay?" Dean asked, and his voice had lost its lightness and gained a bit of an edge. Charlotte realized Dean had a very strong jealous tendency.

"Lauren's pretty drunk, it appears."

Dean cleared his throat. "This guy she's talking to, how do you know he's safe?"

"Charlotte, we're going," Lauren called from the steps that led to the side of the building.

"Lauren, wait!" Charlotte stood up. "Dean I'm sorry, I'm going to have to go."

"Charlotte—" he said quickly, then paused. "Be careful."

"I will. Bye."

She disconnected and ran down the deck stairs and into the sand. Tim stood in the road waiting for her, but her main goal was to not let Lauren and the other guy out of her sight. She'd really never seen Lauren so intoxicated before, and that worried her. Had she let the guys buy her a drink? How long had Charlotte been out on the deck talk-ing to Dean?

She hurried to catch up to her friend. "Lauren, wait."

The two of them were nearly thirty, both of them. Def-initely old enough to know better than to set out in the dark, in a strange place, with two strange men. "Lauren, stop!"

These guys could have told them any story. That they were clean-cut, handsome, and nice really meant nothing. She couldn't stop replaying Dean's words over and over in her head. *Are you sure he's safe?*

The answer was no. She wasn't sure at all, and Lauren's giggly demeanor was making her nervous. When Char-lotte caught up to her friend and the other guy, Tim was on her heels. "Charlotte, slow down, will you? What's wrong?"

"Lauren, I'm not really feeling good. I think we need to head back." Charlotte gripped her friend's arm and pulled. "Lauren."

"Yeah? We're going to the beach." Lauren turned to Charlotte, her eyes glassy. "What did you say?"

"I said I don't really feel that well," Charlotte repeated. "Can we just go back to the room?"

As she spoke, Charlotte began to steer Lauren back toward the bar and the main road they'd walked down, which was more brightly lit then the sandy road the guys had urged them down.

"Oh, okay, but Trent said they had wine down by the beach." Lauren glanced over her shoulder. "Sorry, Trent."

Charlotte swore she heard a muttered curse behind them as she picked up the pace and led them back toward where they'd come from. The guys continued walking behind them about ten feet. When she and Lauren didn't slow down at the bar, they appeared to quit following. She realized Lauren had become very silent. "Do you feel okay, Lo?"

"Yeah, why?" Her voice indicated she was more drunk then she should have been for as long as they'd been there.

"What were you drinking before we left."

"Trent got us all Everclear shots. Wasn't he cute? And why are we leaving?"

Charlotte grimaced. The one and only time she'd drunk Everclear, she'd passed out in someone's bathroom and woke up covered in her own vomit. She'd been twenty-five and still grieving her many losses. Never again would she touch the stuff. In fact, just the thought of it made her nauseous.

Pulling out her phone, Charlotte dialed Dean back. She was grateful he answered immediately.

"Charlotte? You okay?" His voice was panicked.

"Hey, yes. But . . . we're walking back to our hotel. We're alone and . . . well, can you just stay on the line with me?"

He sighed, and it sounded like relief. "Yes. God, yes."

"Thanks. Lauren's pretty drunk," Charlotte whispered.

"Hey! I heard you," Lauren said.

Charlotte looped her arm through her friend's as Dean spoke in her ear. "Is she okay? What happened?"

"I'll tell you later, but I just decided it was best if we call it a night."

He was quiet for a moment. "I'm glad. I was worried about you."

"That's sweet, but we're okay."

"Where are you? Almost back to your hotel?"

"I can see it up ahead."

"Anyone following you?"

Charlotte turned around, her eyes daring around the road and the lighted areas beneath the lampposts. "I don't think so. It's quiet here at the resort, but there are a few people leaving in the parking lot."

"I'll stay on until you're in your room."

Lauren leaned into Charlotte and spoke into the phone. "Hi, Dean. Charlotte misses you."

Charlotte rolled her eyes. This wasn't typical Lauren behavior at all, which meant she'd forgive her for this.

"I miss you, too," Dean said to Charlotte.

That made her feel good. "You'll see me soon."

"I hope so. Where are you now?"

"We're walking into the building." Charlotte glanced around, not wanting to run into any of the wedding party or their families. Lauren had grown even more quiet in the past couple of minutes, and Charlotte began to feel the weight of her on her arm. "Lauren, you with me?"

"Uh-huh," Lauren said, but her voice was slurring.

"She okay?" Dean asked, his words full of concern. "They didn't slip her anything, did they?"

"I don't think so, but they bought her who knows how many shots of Everclear."

"Holy shit," Dean muttered.

"I know. We're getting on the elevator. I may lose you."

"Call me back if you do."

Luckily she didn't lose him and when she unlocked their room, Lauren headed straight for the restroom. "Okay, we're in."

"Good. Now lock the door and dead bolt it if there is one."

"Done and done."

"You have an outside door?"

"A door to a balcony. We're on the third floor. I'm locking it now."

"Good girl."

Charlotte stood at the balcony door and looked out at the night. She sighed. "Dean, thank you."

"You're welcome. I'm glad you called back. Even more glad you decided to head back to your room."

"Just because you were worried about me?"

He sighed. "You know that isn't the only reason. I hated the thought of you out with some drunk assholes. I don't want to think about any other man touching you."

She was quiet for a moment and so was he.

"Does that make you uncomfortable?" he asked. "Me saying that?"

"Not at all."

"Good, because you're mine now, Charlotte."

She sucked in a breath. *His.* "And you're mine."

They were both quiet for a long moment.

Finally he spoke, low and quiet. "Text me before your flight tomorrow."

"I will."

"And make sure Lauren drinks a shitload of water. She'll probably end up hugging the toilet here real soon."

Charlotte grimaced. "Well, that romantic conversation took a turn."

Dean laughed. "Good night, Charlotte.

"Good night, Dean."

Twenty-Three

That Tuesday Dean led John outside, across the alley, and into the barrel building. They were nearly midway into June and the temperature inside was becoming oppressive.

"Damn," John said behind him, blowing out a breath.

"Yeah, we don't regulate the temperature in here."

"What's the reasoning for that?"

"Taste. The barrels are wood—obviously—which expands in the heat and contracts in the cold. The liquid inside soaks in and out of the wood throughout the process. Gives that caramel, oaky flavor."

"That all makes sense. Every day I learn something fascinating."

"A lot to learn, but it's all pretty straight forward," Dean said, leading John to the back of the warehouse. They were going to use a dolly to move a couple of empty barrels into the main building to fill with bourbon. Dean quickly gave John a rundown of how they filled, stored, and organized the barrels.

The minute they carted the first two barrels back across the alley, Dean's phone buzzed in his pocket. He pulled it out, his insides instantly warming.

"I'm gonna take this real quick," Dean said over his

shoulder before stepping over to a quiet part of the back-room.

"Hey." Dean's voice went low, and he had an odd desire to grin—which he held in check.

"Hi. Busy?" Charlotte replied. He could tell by her voice alone that she hadn't held in her own smile.

"I have a minute. What's going on?"

"I just . . . well, I went to the craft store this morning and bought some more things to make some decorations for the fireplace. Simple, I just . . . I don't know. I really just wanted to call you."

This time he did grin. Glancing back toward John, Dean found the other guy messing around on his own phone, just waiting.

"I'm glad."

"I haven't seen you in five days."

She was right. Their busy schedules had prevented them from seeing each other since she'd gotten back from North Carolina, although they'd talked and texted plenty.

"What are you doing today?" he asked.

"I'm actually doing Tara's maternity session today."

"Oh really? She's able to?"

"We'll have to be quick. Her doctor only allowed her a short amount of time. We're doing it later in the day so it's not too hot, which is fine because it's my favorite time to shoot."

"Let's go to dinner afterward."

"Okay. I would love that."

"Good. I'll be at your house . . . what time? You tell me."

"Eight thirty?"

"I'll be there."

"Okay."

"Okay."

"Bye, Dean."

He chuckled as he spoke. "Bye, Charlotte."

Disconnecting the call, he stared down at his phone. How did this woman manage to make him feel so young and hopeful? It was ironic: All this time he'd been worried she wouldn't seriously be interested in someone his age, and yet it felt like he'd gone back in time emotionally. What he felt for her . . . it was still scary, but slowly it was starting to feel right. It was that heart-pounding, nervous, panicky kind of sensation you felt when you saw the girl you had a crush on in the hallway at school. With all the perks of being adult, of which there were many.

He turned back to John, who was stuffing his phone into his pocket.

"Charlotte?" the other guy asked, which put Dean on alert.

"Uh, yeah. It was."

John nodded. "She doing okay today?"

His tone implied he knew something Dean didn't, which made his skin itch. "Yeah. Of course." Except he was now dying to know why she wouldn't be. "She's got a shoot today. Tara is our receptionist but she's on bed rest. Her pregnancy isn't going as they'd hoped. You'll meet her when she comes back from maternity leave."

Dean wasn't normally one to ramble, but at this moment he found himself annoyed with John's presence. He knew it was petty and immature to have hard feelings toward someone who'd dated Charlotte years ago, but he couldn't help it. Especially after he'd seen how they'd interacted in the hall the week before.

"She's photographing a pregnant woman *today*?" John looked shocked, and then his face quickly crumpled into annoyance and he shook his head. "Why would she do that?" he mumbled to himself.

Dean's concern for Charlotte overrode his frustration with John. "Why would she not?"

John's eyes met Dean's and then his expression almost looked . . . sympathetic.

"Forget it."

"No, no. Why shouldn't she do a shoot today?"

"She didn't tell you." John said matter-of-factly.

"Didn't tell me what?"

John shook his head. "It's not my place. I just assumed since you guys were a couple . . ."

"What did she not tell me, John?" His desire to know overrode the fact that it majorly pissed him off that John had one up on him where Charlotte was concerned. But how could he not? They'd been engaged. Dated for years. He knew things about Charlotte it would take Dean a long time to figure out or learn. God, that made him mad. And the worst part was the concern on John's face.

"Listen, you need to ask her. I won't betray her confidence. I shouldn't have assumed, because . . . well, she may not want you to know."

Dean's head jerked back. That was obviously possible, but the thought had him raging inside. Why in the world would it be a bad thing for Charlotte to photograph a pregnant woman?

"Charlotte photographs pregnant women all the time."

"Yeah . . . but *today*. Just, never mind, seriously. Talk to Charlotte."

An awareness came over Dean. "Charlotte's been pregnant. Hasn't she?"

John's lips pursed, and then he let out a breath. "Don't do this, Dean. I like you, and I like this job, but don't make me say something that makes things uncomfortable between us."

"It's already uncomfortable, so I suggest you just shake your head yes or no. I'll make sure she doesn't know it was you who told."

John's eyes closed for a moment, and then he nodded his head yes slowly.

"Yes, she's been pregnant?"

Another nod.

"Was it yours?"

Irritation crossed John's face. Dean knew he was pushing it, but he didn't care. The only thing that mattered was Charlotte. Finally, the guy nodded.

And yet, there was no baby. Was there? "Did she . . . lose it?"

"Obviously," John answered.

"Shit." Dean ran a hand down his face. All his own demons rose to the surface, playing through his head. The sound of his wife sobbing in the bathroom. The doctor telling them there was no heartbeat. Her screaming at him that he wasn't sad enough. As if every loss didn't rip him apart. The guilt had nearly consumed him. Had John felt that way? "Does this have anything to do with why you two broke up?"

John put up a hand. "Huh-uh, I'm done talking. Nodding, too. She's your girlfriend, you have to talk to her about it. But I'll say this. What we went through . . . it was nowhere as hard on me as it was her, and yet, this day, every year, it kills me. I can't imagine how she's feeling."

Dean turned away. He knew exactly what it felt like to experience a miscarriage. It was hell. And Charlotte had lost a baby on this very day. How far along had she been? Who had been there for her? Something in his gut told him it was related to the breakup between her and John, but he wasn't going to ask any more questions.

And on top of all of that, she was photographing a pregnant woman whose pregnancy wasn't going perfectly. Had she seemed strange on the phone? No, she hadn't, but she had called him just to talk. Knowing that this woman he was so wrapped up in had gone through such a tragedy made him want to punch something.

Dean pulled out his phone and opened a text to her. He just wanted to reach out to her again. Needed her to know he was thinking of her.

DEAN: I'm excited to see you tonight.
CHARLOTTE: Not as excited as I am.

With a tilt of his lips, Dean stared at her words. He cared for this woman, maybe more than was good for him.

"Listen, man, I'm sorry—"

"It's fine, John." Dean said, cutting him off as he slid his cell back into this pocket. "I'm sorry I pushed you, but I appreciate you telling me."

"So are we good then? I don't want things to be weird."

"They won't be."

John hesitated and then gave a quick nod. "I'm glad she has you. Charlotte needs someone who can take care of her. Give her everything. I hope you're that guy."

Dean was frozen in place, his tongue heavy in his mouth. "I hope so, too."

Except he knew for a fact that he wasn't the guy that could give her everything. He could only hope that what he could give her—himself—would be enough.

Fat tears ran down Charlotte's cheeks as she drove home from her shoot with Tara and her husband. She'd known better than to play this song, and yet every year at some point on this day, her fingers seemed to work on their own accord, shuffling through her phone and pulling it up from her playlist. If she was smart, she'd delete it.

The past half hour she'd gazed through her lens at the beautiful Tara, round and glowing in the sunset, her hands around her belly, her eyes full of love for her husband and their unborn baby. The second she'd gotten behind the wheel Charlotte had gone right for her playlist, turned up the volume, and given herself completely over to the heartbreaking lyrics that currently pulled quiet sobs from her chest.

She'd listened to this song on repeat the days after her miscarriage. At the time she hadn't known if it was terribly unhealthy to wallow or part of the healing process. Probably both, but either way she'd been unable to function for days. John had tried to get her up out of bed, tried to care for her, but it had been useless. The loss had been devastating, physically traumatic, and emotionally draining.

Looking back, she should have told her mother. She'd needed help, and John had needed support. Driving Charlotte to the emergency room in the middle of the night with uncontrollable hemorrhaging had been terrifying for him. But he'd kept her secret, as much as he'd hated it.

At first she hadn't wanted to ruin everyone's excitement for the wedding. Or her own, but part of her had just enjoyed the selfishness of mourning her baby in whatever way she saw fit. She hadn't wanted someone to make her feel better. It had been bad enough that she'd had to go through the final weeks of wedding prep silently dying inside.

After her tragic non-wedding-day, she'd remained silent still. The weight of her pain had almost been like a comforting blanket. The overwhelming sadness of both events coalescing into one heartbreaking tragedy. This sad song had been part of that, and here she was, letting it drag her down into its abyss once more.

Charlotte pulled into her drive and let her head fall back against the rest. She needed to pull herself together. Dean would be there in twenty minutes. She needed to grab some bags of frozen peas and hold them on her eyes stat.

With a deep exhale, Charlotte grabbed her gear and got out of the car. Once inside she quickly grabbed the peas from the freezer and headed for the bathroom. The minute she saw her red swollen face, her mouth dropped open.

Racing back out to the living room, she searched her bag for her phone. She'd have to ask Dean to come a bit later. She looked like a mess, mascara streaks under her eyes, her lips and nose puffy.

The minute she located the device there was a knock on the door. She muttered a curse to herself as she froze there in her living room. Surely Dean wasn't early. With shaky fingers she began to wipe at her undereyes, hoping to get rid of the worst of her raccoon makeup. Grabbing a tissue from a side table, she blew her nose and then went to the door.

She took a deep breath and opened it enough to peek out. The minute she saw Dean standing there, her lips quivered. It was as if she couldn't help it. He looked so strong and safe standing there on her doorstep.

Their eyes met and his softened with sadness. For her.

"Charlotte," he whispered. Without hesitation, he yanked open the screen door and his arms instantly wrapped around her, pulling her into the hard warmth of his body. His head bent and his lips found her ear. "Baby, talk to me. What's wrong?"

With just those words, she let herself melt into him, her pain bleeding out of her like a pulsing, open wound. His arms tightened as her legs went slack and a muffled cry escaped her lips.

Suddenly a strong arm slid beneath her bottom and then she was hefted into his arms. She felt him carrying her, his shoes thunking along on the wood floors, and then he was laying her down on the bed. He came down beside her and pulled their bodies flush.

"I'm so sorry," she whispered.

"Don't apologize, Charlotte." He angled his head back and ran a hand through her hair. "Not for this. But I do want you to talk to me."

She clamped her eyes shut and squeezed his shirt inside her palms. Could she hide against him? Just soak up all of his strength and then pretend none of it happened?

His hands continued to brush her hair back off the side of her face. She knew that when she'd opened the front door he must have been alarmed, although he hadn't really seemed to be. This was a side of her he'd never seen before. She was always happy, fun, good-natured Charlotte.

"Charlotte, please tell me what has upset you."

His voice was so full of concern, it was hard to imagine him wanting to pull away from her, but she'd need to be ready for that. Dropping emotional female baggage on a man unprompted had to be frowned upon in a new relationship.

For a long moment she allowed the soothing feel of his fingers sliding through her hair to bring her heart rate back to normal. Finally, she scooted up in the bed so her head could rest in the crook of his arm and she peeked up at him.

"I'm sure this wasn't what you had in mind when you said dinner, huh?"

"Nothing about you is what I had in mind. It's always better."

"Stop being so good at this," she whispered. "It scares me."

"Me too," he whispered back. Their eyes locked and then his head dipped down, his lips brushing against hers. They were soft and warm, and so gentle it nearly brought her to tears once more. Several times he kissed her, never changing the intensity, or rushing. Just savoring every little touch of their mouths coming in contact. He turned his head slowly from side to side, letting his lower lip slide back and forth across hers. A shiver rippled through her.

"Talk to me, Charlotte," he said against her mouth.

"Can't we just keep kissing?"

She felt his lips tilt up in a smile. "We can kiss all night, after you tell me why you're sad."

She pulled back a bit and put a hand on his jaw. A bit of stubble poked at her palm. "Today is kind of a . . . difficult day for me."

His eyes locked onto hers. "Why is that?"

Charlotte shifted on the bed, her leg restless. Sensing her needs—as always—Dean lifted one of his legs so she could slide her thigh between his. When he lowered his leg, he had her locked close. And still he waited patiently, never taking his eyes off her. She let out a quiet sigh. "Five years ago . . ."

Feeling tears press against her eyes, Charlotte stopped and took a deep breath. Dean leaned down and kissed her nose. It was a small action, but it gave her strength.

"Five year ago, I got pregnant. With John."

She looked up at him, but he only watched her with no change of expression. His hand still stroked her hair ever so gently.

"What happened?" he asked quietly.

"We were so excited. The timing was awful because it was right before our wedding. But I didn't care. I was so happy. And then . . . I miscarried." Her voice grew shaky, and she fought to keep herself together. "I was only fourteen weeks. But . . . Ugh, God."

Charlotte reached up and pressed at her eyes with the heel of her hand, hating that she couldn't find the right words to say without losing it. Just saying it out loud hurt so much.

"Fourteen weeks is plenty of time to fall in love with someone."

Oh, how did he know just what to say? It was as if he knew exactly how she felt. Her lips quivered and tears welled in her eyes. "Yes, it is."

"I'm so sorry, Charlotte."

She nodded, unable to continue talking. Her throat felt tight and her lungs pressed against her breasts. Leaning up into him, she sought his mouth once more. He gave in to her, their lips pressing together, but Charlotte no longer felt satisfied with tentative and soft. She wanted to feel all of him. Wanted to forget.

Opening her mouth, just the slightest bit, she nearly groaned when he did the same, their tongues meeting and sliding against each other. She ran her hand up his chest, along his neck, and into his hair, pulling him into her, fusing their mouths together. He was letting her set the pace. Not rushing, but obviously willing to give her what she needed.

After a deep, long kiss, she pushed herself up and over him. The minute her hands began to pull up on his shirt, he broke the kiss.

"Charlotte, we don't have to—"

"I want to. Please."

His answer was to lock his hands on each side of her face and devour her mouth. This was the best way to forget the sad song, the sight of someone else's pregnant belly, and the ache in her heart she let bubble to the surface every year on this day. This was what she wanted. Needed and craved. But not with just any man.

This man.

She rocked against him, his body hard and ready for her, and she lowered her hand to grip him through his jeans. He moaned into her mouth and then flipped them over, pinning her beneath his body.

"Last time you gave me what I wanted," he murmured into her neck. "This time I'm going to give you what we both want."

Charlotte let her eyes drift close, smiling up to the ceiling as Dean kissed his way down her torso. Pushing up her T-shirt, he exposed one breast at a time, slowly sliding down the cup of her bra, freeing each one. His eyes met hers as he enveloped each tip in his mouth, sucking gently, then licking. After he'd paid plenty of attention to her chest, he placed little kisses down her rib cage, her stomach. It occurred to Charlotte that never in her life had she been caressed, kissed, touched, with such reverence.

It had been a warm day, so she had on a pair of flimsy seersucker shorts. The kind so light that when Dean pressed his mouth on her center, she felt the heat of his breath radiating through the material. His hands worked at the button and she reached down to help him, their hands tangling as they frantically worked to get the shorts pulled off, followed by her panties.

As soon as he'd bared her from breast to toe, her shirt bunched under her chin, he pushed her legs apart and settled onto the bed between them.

The first touch was the delicate fluttering of his fingertip tracing her entire opening. It was maddening in its lack of focus or pressure, almost a ghost of sensation. She let her legs fall open wider, pressing herself against his hand. She swore she heard him chuckle, the warmth of his breath only adding to her frustration.

"I've been waiting a long time to get you like this. I plan to take full advantage of it." Dean smiled up at her and Charlotte gripped the sheets hard on either side as his face dipped down past the horizon of her body.

Twenty-Four

Dean held Charlotte against him, his fingers trailing up and down the length of her back as she drifted in and out of sleep. Her arm was draped over his chest, and he watched as one little freckle on her inner arm rose up and down along with their deep breaths.

He hadn't felt this content in a long time, but with that came worry. And fear. This felt right. Good. This woman could not be any more perfect for him if she tried. Charlotte was funny, smart, passionate, and so beautiful it made him ache.

He'd known this was a tough day for her, had wanted to get her to open up to him, but finding her in the doorway obviously fresh from crying had just about done him in. All he'd wanted to do was take her pain away, make everything right in her world. It was still all he wanted, which was why he worried that in the long run, he might not be the man to make her happy. That thought was so terrifyingly sobering, his chest tightened against her arm.

Charlotte had lost an unborn child, something he had had the misfortune to go through himself, four times. But if the experiences had taught him anything, it was that even just one loss was too much.

Tomorrow Dean was expecting a phone call from the doctor. Lab results that would more than likely tell him that he would be wasting his time to try and conceive again. He was prepared for that.

The problem was, what did that mean for him and the woman in his arms? It was a real fear, and the only thing that made him worry that Charlotte might be better off without him. She obviously wanted children, and the reality for him was that he was not only unlikely to be able to give her that gift, but he was also unlikely to be interested in trying. Who in their right mind would knowingly risk putting the woman they cared for through that kind of pain?

He knew he needed to tell her, let her know what she was signing up for if she wanted to pursue whatever this was between them any further. But he just couldn't do it today, not with what she'd just revealed to him.

She shifted in her sleep, snuggling closer into his body. Her breasts pressed into his side, warm and plush, and Dean closed his eyes to savor the feel of every inch of her skin in contact with his. He'd watched in amazement as she'd ridden him just moments ago, her body so supple and perfect. He was weather-beaten, beginning to gray, and starting to feel the creaks and aches of a body that had worked hard for a living.

Nearly twelve years between them. When he talked with her, listened to her laugh and flirt with him, it felt like nothing to worry about. He loved her youthfulness. But sometimes, when he thought of how he might feel or look physically ten years from now—or even worse, what *she'd* feel when she looked at him . . .

His mother had left his father—and in many ways him—for a younger man. His own wife had gone looking for happiness elsewhere. Why in the hell wouldn't Charlotte feel the same eventually?

Why were there so many damn strikes against them?

"What are you thinking about?" a husky voice said against his chest. Charlotte turned her body and rested her chin on his chest. Her eyes were still slightly swollen and red, her lips full.

"Nothing important. Work."

Her eyebrows rose as if she wasn't sure if she believed him. Smart girl. He brushed a lock of hair off her forehead.

"Your chest hair is almost grown." She ran her nails through it until her hand came up to his mouth, and he kissed her index finger. "I like it this length."

"Well, don't think for one minute I'm going to start trimming it to maintain."

"Not even for me?" she teased, her lip going into a pout.

God, he'd do anything for her. He wanted to do everything for her.

"You may have to entice me," he said.

"I'm sure I could do that." Her grin was wicked as she lowered her hand under the sheet.

"I'm afraid you may find me . . . unenticeable at the moment. A perk of reaching your forties."

She yanked her hand up and gently slapped his chest. "Will you stop acting like you're old? I just had the most amazing sex of my life with the hottest guy I've ever met."

Crawling up his body, she dropped her head down and kissed him before continuing with her speech. "Everything about your body turns me on."

Her breasts hovered over his chest and he filled his hands with their fullness, his thumbs brushing over her nipples. "It can't turn you on nearly as much as your body does me."

"You're wrong," she whispered.

They kissed for a long moment, her mouth so sweet and wet.

When she finally rocked back on her heels, he let his hands drop to the bed.

"Can I still take you to dinner?" Dean asked, glancing at the clock beside her bed. It was ten thirty, but there would be something open.

"Well, I don't turn down free food on principle. And I'm starving. Crying and sex really work up an appetite—and no, I don't make a habit of doing them together."

"And here that sounded so exciting," he teased.

Charlotte laughed as she got out of the bed. Dean loved that she was so free and unashamed of her nudity around him as she picked up her clothes and began to dress. She was as lovely as a woman could be, her hips full and breasts lush enough to just spill over his hands. It was hard to imagine a woman as perfect as she was had just let him have his way with her.

"I hope you don't mind waiting about fifteen minutes. I'm kind of anal about downloading my shoot and backing it up as soon as I can. Peace of mind and all that."

"Of course." Dean sat up and began to search for his own clothes.

"Okay, I'll be in my office." She pointed toward the door and what he assumed was across the hall. "Won't take long."

He nodded and watched her go, then began to gather his things. He used the restroom, got dressed, then went in search of her.

"Come look," Charlotte said as he stepped into her office.

She sat at a big desk that held two large monitors. Her office was very her, the walls painted a pale gray, a bright-turquoise antique-looking sofa on the far wall. Above it were several different-sized canvas images of brides and grooms, babies, and even what appeared to be a high school student. Charlotte was incredibly talented.

Walking over to her desk, he saw that the screen was filled with images of Tara and her husband. The photos were breathtaking, Tara in a flowy white dress, Ben holding her close, the sun setting behind them all golden and bright.

"Doesn't she look beautiful?" Charlotte asked.

"She does." Dean forced himself to touch her shoulder. Tara did look beautiful, but he could only think of how hard it must have been for Charlotte to be dealing with this on such a difficult day.

"I was worried about having this shoot today," she said quietly. "But I'm glad I did it."

"Yeah? How come?" he asked, running his fingers through her hair.

"It was a good reminder that miracles happen. I need to stop worrying about being pregnant in the future. It will happen when it's meant to happen."

Dean felt his chest tighten at her words. He forced his expression to stay neutral when she turned to look up at him. He couldn't deny his relief when she quickly smiled and change the subject.

"Want to see something that will make me look ridiculous?" Charlotte asked. She clicked the sorting software shut and opened her photo files. She clicked through a few things until she opened a series of photos. "I can't believe I'm going to show you this."

Dean looked closer. "Is that me?"

She turned and looked up at him, grinning. "Every single one."

He laughed and before he could lean over, Charlotte

stood in her chair and motioned for him to sit. As soon as he did, she rested her butt on his thigh, so comfortable and easy with him, it took his breath away. Even more so when he realized she had at least thirty pictures of him during weddings she'd shot at the Stag.

"You are such a sneaky girl," he said, resting his chin on her shoulder. "Is that one of just my ass?"

"Of course it is." She laughed as she clicked it open, making it take up nearly the entire screen. He was at the bar, talking to Jen. Charlotte had apparently been close to the dance floor, a time he would have no doubt assumed she was photographing the guests dancing. But no, instead she'd been focused in on him. Mostly he appeared to be in the background of her intended shots, but for a few she'd zoomed right in on him, without him having a clue.

"I confess sometimes I like to watch you," he whispered into her ear. "While you're working."

Charlotte turned on his lap, looping one arm around his neck. "Obviously I watch you, too. Constantly."

"For how long?" he asked.

"Since the beginning."

He inhaled deep, their eyes staring at each other.

"What about you?" she asked.

"Since the moment I first met you."

Charlotte bit at her bottom lip, holding back a smile as her hand found its way into his lap. "Do you think you're still unenticeable?"

He chuckled, leaning his head against hers. There was no letting this woman go. At least not willingly. But how in the hell could he convince her he was enough, damaged and all?

Twenty-Five

Dean walked into the office he shared with his two co-owners and sat down next to TJ's desk.

"Did you see that order that came in this morning?" he asked.

"I did. Crazy."

"I expected Pete to order, but I never dreamed it would be so big," Dean said. Pete Schumer was the owner of Schumer Liquor, one of the biggest liquor store chains in the metro area.

"I was going to ask you if you thought we'd be able to fill it."

"I think so, but I told Jake to inform suppliers from here on out that we're probably looking at a month out on reorders."

"You don't think we should limit him?" TJ asked. "He wanted two cases per store. We could tell him just one. Or maybe he will only do certain stores for the first month."

"Irritating Pete seems like a gamble."

TJ shrugged. "Agreed. But if I know Pete, the idea that demand is high and supply is low will keep him on the hook no matter what. Especially if people like the product."

Dean glared at TJ, who was grinning. "You know damn well the product is solid."

"I do. Or I wouldn't be here. So what do we do? We've erred on the safe side and figured a hundred cases for this first batch. I planned on one for the uncask party, and since we limited our bar and restaurant account to only three bottles on the first batch, that will leave us with less than seventy-five cases."

"How many stores does Pete have?"

"Twenty-two."

Dean nodded, his brain spinning. "We need at least twenty cases to get Jake started with his first trip this summer." Jake was taking The Stag Wagon—which was currently being renovated as a whiskey-tasting party bus—on a tour of summer festivals starting in July.

"That answers our question then. We'll have to tell Pete one case per store until the next batch. It won't be that long, only a month."

"Yeah. Maybe we can convince him to let us do some special promotion. Let him be the only liquor store with it for the first few days or so."

"I think he'll go for that. Want me to call Mel?"

Mel was Pete's daughter, and buyer. "Yeah, do that and let me know what she says."

"My answer is *Only if you show me yours first*," a flirty voice said from the doorway.

Dean and TJ both turned at the same time to find Jen walking toward them. She dragged Dean's desk chair over to where they were seated and joined them.

"Don't act all weird, I was just kidding." Today Jen wore a tank top, showing off her ink-covered shoulder. Sometimes he almost forgot she had those tattoos, and as brassy as her personality was, you'd have thought that amount of ink showing would make her look tough, but on her it seemed to have the opposite effect. She looked really pretty today—soft, almost.

"We were talking about Mel Schumer," TJ said. He turned to Dean. "I'd be happy to call her. She's always fun to talk to."

Dean raised an eyebrow at TJ. He was obviously trying to make Jen jealous, and by the way she glared at him, lips twisted, he'd done a fine job. *Interesting.*

"Okay then, that's settled. Let me know what she says," Dean replied. He was just waiting for what would come out of Jen's mouth next. Maybe he could distract her. "What are you doing here on a weekday, Jen? Paychecks are tomorrow."

"I know. I actually needed to talk to you." She looked around. "Is Jake here?"

"He has the day off. Why?" There was a hint of concern in TJ's voice.

"Well, I had an idea." Jen shifted in her seat, which was unlike her. She gave a sideways glance to TJ. "I know I'm not always . . . super fun to talk to. But what would you guys think about letting me take Tara's job until her leave's over?"

Dean's eyes widened and he quickly turned to TJ, who appeared just as shocked as he was. "Don't you work at the community theater during the week?"

"I did. It's closing. Funding was cut off."

"Damn, I'm sorry. I know how much you loved that job." TJ's voice was full of real concern. So much for sticking it to her.

"Yeah, well, shit happens, right?"

Dean looked at TJ once more, who was staring intently at Jen. If he knew his friend, it was killing him to see the woman he cared for so upset about her situation. Jen was obsessed with musical theater. It was her passion, and she'd mentioned several times just wanting to drop everything and move to a bigger city where she could pursue it. But Dean knew that with her mother's health in question she never would. Jen might be many things—loud, mouthy, frustrating—but she was loyal and had a soft side when she wanted to show it.

"I don't know what you made at the theater, but Tara's hourly wage wasn't anything to brag about," TJ said. "Ben's income pays their bills."

"Well, a small income is a far cry better than none." Jen looked nervous, something Dean wasn't sure he'd ever really seen before. Even in her sweet moments she never lacked confidence. "Besides, it wasn't like I was working at the theater because I was making a fortune."

"I know that, but you loved it," TJ said. He met Dean's eyes, and the look on the guy's face left no doubt. He wanted to give Jen the job.

"Jen, what will you do when Tara comes back?" Dean asked. It was a valid question.

"Well . . . I guess there's the possibility that . . . my mother will have passed and then I'll move to Chicago or New York where theater is only *slightly* more lucrative. Not that I want that. I don't. I mean, not until we've done all we can."

"Jen, we know you love your mother." TJ leaned forward, and Dean could tell the guy wanted to touch her. He wouldn't, but how could *she* not tell?

"I'll let TJ be the bad guy if he's so inclined, but I'm for it." Dean knew TJ was grateful when he sighed with relief.

"The job is yours."

Jen sat up straighter in her chair, a little of her Jen fire gaining some brightness. "Thank you, guys. I promise I'll leave my bullshit antics at the door."

"Nothing you do is bullshit. We wouldn't employ you if that was the case."

Dean could call bullshit on that statement, but he didn't contradict TJ. They did love Jen—some of them more than others—she was just . . . high-maintenance.

"When can I start, then? How about today?"

TJ looked at Dean, who just shrugged.

"Awesome!" Her grin was wide, and Dean couldn't help smiling back. It felt good to do this for Jen. Tara would also have approved. "I'll need one of you goofs to come train me. I'll be at my desk."

She was gone. Dean gave TJ a long glance. "No bullshit, huh? Isn't that what you said?"

TJ shook his head. "Jen is Jen."

"Yes, that is true, which is why I was happy to do this for her. You gonna be okay working with her every day?"

"Of course, why wouldn't I?"

Dean tilted his head. "Come on, man. It's me, here."

TJ sighed. "I know, and yes. I will be fine. I've been fine this long."

That was hardly an admission, but even those words surprised Dean. "You have. But honestly, I'm not sure why you don't . . . tell her."

"Right."

Dean was about to argue with him when Jen popped her head back in.

"Who is the super-hot new guy?" she asked, her eyes alight.

TJ gave Dean an I-told-you-so glance before he answered. "It's actually Charlotte Linley's ex. Dean gave him an apprenticeship."

"What? Are you kidding me? She let *that* guy get away? Dean, you're crazy for letting your girl be around that kind of eye candy."

She darted off, presumably to find a way to put herself in John's path. Dean looked at TJ, who was practically scowling. Yep, now they were both pissed.

Dean's phone rang. When he picked it up and saw the name of his doctor's office his heart sank.

Charlotte ended the call with an author looking for someone to shoot her next cover. She was ecstatic to get the job, which required a male and a female in a rather compromising situation. Tasteful, of course, but super sexy. She knew she could do it, and the author was wonderful and charming so far.

Now she just needed to pick the models. Strangely enough, the way the author described the hero, she'd immediately thought of John. Handsome but somewhat boyish good looks. She wasn't sure if she'd be able to pull that off, or if he'd even want to. The other problem would be finding the female. But she'd worry about that later. The cover didn't need to be done for six months so she had plenty of time.

Her phone began to buzz and play "Honey, Honey." She grinned from ear to ear, knowing it was Dean. Things had been going so well between them, and she realized she hadn't been this happy in a long time.

"Hi, you." There was no keeping the excitement out of her voice.

"Hi, you back. Busy?" he asked.

"Well, I just booked another cover shoot so I'm very excited about that."

"Good for you. I wondered if you could be free this afternoon?"

Charlotte couldn't help but notice he sounded a bit down. "Of course. What do you have in mind?" She asked, going for sexy.

His voice lowered. "I like what you're implying. However . . . I need a favor."

Sitting up straight, her brow furrowed. "Okay, what?"

"Well, I just got a call from Amy. My ex. I guess Alex's dress is in and she wants me to come and look at it."

"Oh, that's wonderful. Why do you sound irritated? Don't you want to see it?"

"Definitely. I just . . . I don't want to see her. And it's been kind of a rough day. That's all. But seeing you will make it better. Plus I thought you might like to see the dress."

"I'm sorry to hear you're having a bad day. Want to talk about it?"

"No, it's fine. Just work stress."

She considered pushing because she didn't quite believe that. He always had work stress, but he sounded so sad. Maybe she could get him to share once they were face-to-face. "I would love to see the dress. I'd also love to see you, and I'd be lying if I said I'm not a teensy bit curious about seeing Amy as well. Don't judge me."

Dean chuckled. "At least you don't have to work with my ex."

"So true. I don't think I could do it."

"I have two calls this afternoon. Do you mind if we meet?"

"No problem." Charlotte wrote down the time and the name of the shop.

Once she hung up, she sighed down at the paper. She truly was excited to see Dean, but the location made her pause.

She'd unfortunately been to this dress shop before. About five years ago.

Twenty-Six

Charlotte hadn't known what to expect when she finally saw Amy Troyer. It did irritate her just a little bit to hear that the woman had kept Dean's name. She couldn't help it. A name felt like it implied some kind of ownership. Some lasting, unbreakable connection. On top of that, Amy was very attractive, in the perfect-makeup, polished-outfit, super-white-teeth kind of way.

Maybe it was the air of maturity about her, the easy way she laughed and familiar way she touched Dean's arm at the same time, or possibly the slight smirk she'd given Charlotte when they were introduced. But something about her made Charlotte feel uneasy.

And childish.

Oh right, it was jealousy. Pure and simple green-monstered envy. And she couldn't help being annoyed that Dean had introduced her as just Charlotte. Not *my girlfriend, Charlotte*. Not even *my friend Charlotte*. He hadn't touched her yet, either.

She really needed to stop being ridiculous and overanalyzing everything he did or didn't do. It was clear that this entire situation made him uncomfortable, probably for a variety of reasons. He was in a bridal shop with his ex-wife and the woman he'd recently started seeing.

How bizarre.

"It really is very kind of you to help Dean with this wedding planning," Amy said as they waited in the front room of the shop.

Charlotte was tempted to mention their trade, her help with the wedding for Dean posing like a sexy hero, but she had a sinking suspicion he wouldn't appreciate her sharing. "Well, the Stag guys have become friends, so it was my pleasure to help him."

Dean gave Charlotte a warm look. "I couldn't have done it without her. That's for sure."

Amy looked perplexed at that comment, but before she could respond, the woman helping them at the front counter peeked her head out from the back room. "If you'd all like to head through the curtain to the back, I've got the dress ready."

Amy led the way, and as they fell into line, Dean then Charlotte, he hesitated outside the curtain. Turning, he lifted her hand in his, brought her knuckles to his mouth, and placed a quick kiss there. "Thank you for doing this."

He dropped her hand and held the curtain aside for her. With a little smile, she passed by.

So was that an official declaration? They could touch, but only in secret? If so, she was a little pissed, but they could discuss that later. Especially when she had other things to bring her down, like the fact that Lydia Jane's Bridal Shop still looked exactly as it had when she'd been in here trying on her own wedding dress.

The back of the shop was open and spacious with high ceilings that were peppered with pot lights. In the center was a beautiful crystal chandelier that highlighted the beads and shimmer of the dresses dotted around the room. The damask-wallpapered walls were mostly covered with mirrors, so a woman standing on one of the five platforms could see herself reflected at any angle. It was a little disconcerting to see your own face every which way you turned. It forced a reminder not to look stricken, so she pasted a smile on her face as their saleslady, Shirley, led them to the gown, which hung on a display rod.

"Oh my goodness," Amy said wistfully. "Dean, can't you already imagine our girl in this dress."

Dean cleared his throat. "My sister, Amy, who is a grown woman. And, uh, yes. It looks nice."

Amy turned. "Nice? It's gorgeous." Touching the lace sleeve, she spoke to Charlotte. "Don't you agree, Charlotte?"

Honest truth, it wasn't something Charlotte would have chosen. Not for herself, maybe not for anyone. Not that it wasn't lovely . . . it just wasn't her style. "It's very pretty, but since I don't really know Alex, it's hard for me to judge it."

"And yet . . . you've planned her entire wedding." Amy laughed, but it was on the bitter side.

"Amy." Dean's word was a warning. "Don't be like that."

She definitely didn't need or want Dean fighting her battles. "Actually, I believe a dress is a much more personal and subjective thing than, say . . . choosing the kind of chicken to serve a hundred people. I wouldn't have been comfortable with the job, so Alex is lucky to have you."

"Thank you, Charlotte." She turned to Dean. "*See*, I told you."

He reached out and shocked Charlotte by giving her hand a quick squeeze before sitting down in a plush ivory chair. Charlotte could tell he was already over the errand. She also noticed that Amy hadn't missed their interaction.

The saleslady came back in with a notebook. "I realize we're working with some unusual circumstances so I've discussed it with one of our seamstresses. She just so happens to have a son in the marines, so she is sympathetic with your time line."

Dean nodded, leaning forward in the chair. "That's kind of her."

"It is. She agreed to last-minute alterations on the bodice part of the dress if we could just fit for the length. That way she can get some of the work completed ahead of time. So hopefully you know how tall the bride is?"

Charlotte glanced at Dean, who looked at Amy, his expression a little panicked. "Not exactly, no. Does it need to be exact?" he asked Shirley.

She quirked her lips. "It's certainly better if it is. Is there a way to ask her?"

Dean shook his head. "I'm not supposed to speak with her for another week. She's been on a mission. I can email but there is no guarantee she'll get it or respond."

"Certainly we can get close." Amy stepped closer to the chair Dean sat in. When she laid her nails on his shoulder, Charlotte flinched. "If you stand up, Dean, can you imagine how tall she is compared with you? I mean, worst case we have to adjust with her shoe choice, right?"

"You could." Shirley looked skeptical.

Dean stood with a sigh. Instead of discussing it with Amy, he walked right over to Charlotte and stood directly in front of her. "She's a little taller than Charlotte. But she definitely isn't taller than me."

Charlotte tilted her head up and looked into Dean's

eyes. He gave her his quick, almost imperceptible wink before stepping back.

"I guess we'll ballpark it and hope for the best. What size dress are you, dear?" the attendant asked Charlotte, whose mouth dropped open.

"Uhh, well—"

"This one was ordered in an eight. Do you think you could slip it on so we could take some measurements?"

Charlotte's face became flushed. She'd say she was a solid ten jeans, an eight dress if she'd been running consistently. But her boobs . . . they could pose a problem. "I can try."

"Are you sure, Charlotte? I didn't kn—" Dean started.

"It's fine." She smiled and put a hand out. "All girls love to try on dresses. Right?"

Dean gave her a sympathetic expression and Amy looked like she didn't know how things had gotten away from her so quickly as Charlotte followed the woman into the large dressing room.

"Didn't expect to be doing this today, did you?" Shirley said with a grin, as if Charlotte should be excited. The woman had no idea that this was the last thing she'd ever want to do, so she just gave a slight smile as she began to remove her clothes.

"This dress will definitely require some kind of strapless bra or bustier."

"I don't know, I'm kind of worried about fitting myself into this one." Charlotte tried to joke, but the woman turned and analyzed her breasts. Weird.

"Hm. Maybe we will try it without. Just see how it is. I guess it doesn't matter since we'll be doing that measurement at a later date. I just wanted to make it a real wedding gown experience for you. Just for fun."

"Oh, that's quite unnecessary," Charlotte said as she

turned to fold her shorts before laying them in a chair.
She'd already had that experience, thank you very much.

Charlotte removed her bra and covered her breasts as
she stepped into the gown. Facing away from the mirror
in the fitting room, she held the material up to her chest
while Shirley worked at the back zipper and the tiny but-
tons.

"Oh, this is going to be just breathtaking. It's a little
tight in the bust, but it's nearly perfect."

Charlotte sucked in her belly, tempted to argue when
she felt the dress cut into the skin under her arms, but she
kept her mouth shut. A few minutes later, the dress was
on and Charlotte dropped her arms.

"I can't wait for you to stand on the dais to see yourself," Shirley said, her voice full of excitement. Ridiculous,
Charlotte thought, since she wasn't even the bride. Shirley
really should crank down her enthusiasm. The woman
peeked her head out the door and spoke to Amy and Dean.
"Are you ready? She looks gorgeous."

Charlotte looked up to the ceiling and sighed before she
felt the gentle tug of Shirley grabbing her hand.

"Turn gently and step on out."

The skirt of the dress was slightly fuller than it had
looked on the hanger, and it gave a delicious swish around
Charlotte's bare legs as she stepped forward. Glancing
down, she saw that her cleavage looked quite nice from her
view. The sleeves of the dress were three quarter, off-the-
shoulder, with a delicate lace overlay. Flower appliqués ran
across her chest, making it appear as though her décolle-
tage was surrounded by blooms.

Taking a deep breath, she stepped around the large
doorway and followed Shirley into the main viewing room.
Dean was staring off in the other direction, but suddenly
their eyes met in an angled mirror across the room and he

jerked his head around to face her. Charlotte sucked in a breath when she heard Amy gasp.

Dean stood up and walked toward her.

Reluctantly, Charlotte picked up the skirt on each side and headed for the platform. She felt lighter when she realized Shirley had lifted the back of the dress. Dean held out a hand to her as she stepped onto the dais.

She let the skirt drop in a whoosh and Shirley flittered around her circumference, arranging it. Charlotte looked up and felt her legs wobble.

Oh my . . . this dress. It was the most beautiful thing she'd ever had on her body. Now she knew why people always said, "Sometimes you have to just try it on." She'd completely dismissed this exquisite creation out of hand after just one glance at it on the hanger. That was silly, because she'd never felt more beautiful than she did right now. Not even her own dress had made her feel so wonderful.

Dean stepped beside her, his eyes roaming all over her reflection in the mirror.

"Do you think Alex will love it?" Charlotte asked quietly.

His mouth dropped open a bit as if he was at a loss for words. "I'm sure she will."

"Does it make you think of her?" Charlotte asked, meaning . . . she wasn't sure what. She supposed, *Does it look like something she'd wear*, but how does anyone know what kind of wedding dress someone would pick? Not even a bride knew most times until she had it on. When his eyes narrowed, Charlotte realized what a silly thing it was to say.

"Right now it's hard to think of anything but you," he whispered, but Charlotte knew that as quiet as the room was, Amy would have heard every word.

She smiled. "Hand me my phone." He did as she asked and she took a quick photo of the dress for the planning folder.

"What type of shoes do you think Alex will want to wear? A heel? A ballet?" Shirley asked.

The sound pulled Dean's focus away from Charlotte. As she turned toward the conversation, Charlotte's eyes met Amy's for a moment. She knew. Her expression wasn't angry, more . . . observational. When she caught Charlotte watching her, she gave her a tight-lipped smile and turned to Shirley.

"Alex isn't much of a heel girl. I'd guess a ballet would be more her speed."

Dean nodded. "I'd agree about the heel, but I'll be honest, I don't know what you mean when you say ballet."

"A flat shoe," Shirley clarified. "Charlotte, dear, didn't you have flats on when you came in?"

"I did. They're in the dressing room."

Dean was still staring at Charlotte when Shirley went to retrieve the shoes.

"I told you the dress was beautiful, did I not?" Amy interjected, stepping somewhat in between Charlotte and Dean. "Alex's arms and, uh . . . upper body are smaller, so it will lay nicely."

Charlotte bit her lip to keep from commenting. This wasn't about her at all and she knew Amy was trying to get a dig in since the comment was completely unnecessary.

"It looks beautiful on you, Charlotte," Dean said.

"Thanks." She loved it, too, and in that moment, she had a fleeting thought, the likes of which she'd never thought to have again. She could clearly imagine walking down an aisle in this dress. Dean smiling and waiting for her at the front in a handsome, perfectly fitted suit. Was it possible that she'd reached a turning point? That she might finally be willing to give marriage, and even a wedding, another try?

Her thoughts were shaken by the sound of Dean's phone ringing. He dug it out of his pocket and glanced at the screen, his brow furrowing.

"What's wrong?" Amy asked.

"It says PRIVATE NUMBER. I've only had one other call like that before." He quickly accepted the call and said hello.

Amy and Charlotte watched as he turned away from them, seeking privacy he wasn't going to get in the big open space. Shirley continued working as she knelt down on the dais. Charlotte kept her eyes on Dean as she lifted the dress on instinct and then her foot.

"Alex? Hang on. Slow down, tell me what's wrong." Dean's voice was panicked, but Charlotte couldn't help feeling that if Alex was physically speaking to him, things couldn't be too bad. She was alive, at least, but something was wrong.

When Dean dropped his head and leaned a hand onto a nearby chair for support, she knew she was right.

"Aww, God . . . no, Al. How?" The instant raw heartache in his voice made Charlotte's breath catch. The sound urged Amy to his side, which made Charlotte curse the fact that this stupid dress had her weighed down. She watched as Amy wrapped her arms around his hunched shoulders. "Alex, did they do everything they can?"

Charlotte lifted a hand to her mouth, and now even Shirley stood up, her eyes full of fear.

"Her fiancé," Shirley whispered. Charlotte could only nod in response, never taking her eyes off Dean.

"I'm so sorry, Al. I'm so . . . so damn sorry." His voice came out so wrecked, Charlotte felt like she couldn't breathe.

She lifted the dress off the floor and clumsily made her way toward Dean, coming around the chair to face him. His eyes were pinched shut as he listened, and this close even Charlotte could hear Alex's tearful panicked voice, although she couldn't make out her words. He sucked in a deep ragged breath.

"I know, sis, I know."

A sob came from the other end of the line, and Dean's eyes squeezed shut hard. "Don't cry, Al. God, I'm so damn sorry."

A pause and then Dean turned away from everyone once more. It felt like all of them were eavesdropping on something sacred and private. "I love you, Alex. We will get through this. I promise. You won't be alone."

The conversation wrapped up after a few more murmurs, and when he disconnected, all three women began to inch toward him. Dean lifted his right arm to the side and sent his phone flying into the cushioned chair across the room with a booming *"Fuck!"*

Charlotte flinched. He lifted his hands to his face and dug the heel of his palms into his eyes, and in that moment she had never wanted to touch anyone so badly. Before she could lift the blasted dress and move, Amy rushed to his side.

"Babe, what happened to Nate?"

Dean's arms flopped to his sides, and his head went limp. For a long moment he was silent, obviously fighting back emotion. Charlotte took quiet steps toward them.

"She doesn't deserve this, Amy." His head shook back and forth, still facing the carpet. "We got her through one loss. I don't think she can handle it again."

At the admission, Amy began to well up with tears. She latched onto his limp arm. "She will. We'll help her. She's stronger than you think. Tell me what happened."

"A helicopter accident."

Dean allowed Amy to wrap her arms around him, even put his own across her back as she began to openly cry.

Charlotte stood there for a moment, tears filling her own eyes as she watched the man she loved take comfort from his ex-wife. Alex was . . . theirs. He'd told Charlotte that he and Amy had practically raised her. Been her makeshift parental unit through adolescence. They were all Alex had now. Charlotte had never even met the woman and yet the pain of her loss was so acute, her own chest clamped down in fresh sorrow.

Turning, she motioned for Shirley—who was frozen to the floor, eyes wide—to follow her back into the dressing room. Once the door was shut they began to undress Charlotte in complete silence. There really was nothing left to say. If Nate was dead, the dress was no longer needed.

Dean's and Amy's voice could suddenly be heard through the dressing room curtain, and on instinct Charlotte froze. Shirley did the same so they could listen.

"Is she coming home?" Amy asked.

Dean sighed. "Yeah. With Nate's body. They'll go to Georgia. Damn . . . Nate's poor family. God, I can't fucking believe this." His words were full of frustration and anger, and so much sadness.

"We need to make arrangements then. Meet her down there."

Charlotte continued to eavesdrop, her palms holding the lace material to her breasts. She met Shirley's eyes, and the other woman gave Charlotte a warm but sad smile then patted her arm.

"I'm gonna need you, Amy," Dean said quietly. Charlotte wondered if he was trying not to be heard. "Alexis is going to need you."

"I'm here. Here for both of you. We're a family."

Charlotte's eyes pinched shut and she quickly began tugging the dress down her body. She refused to stand here, another minute, in another wedding dress, while another man realized he no longer needed her.

Once again, there would be no wedding.

Twenty-Seven

That Saturday Charlotte followed her bride and groom off the limo bus and toward the entrance to the Stag. Although their wedding day was going well, she couldn't help feeling down after the week's events, which still weighed heavily on her mind. She'd barely slept a full night or been able to get much editing done, she'd been so wrapped up with worry for Dean and his sister, and also sadness for herself, which made her feel guilty. If anyone was the victim in the situation, it definitely wasn't her.

Since parting ways with Dean on Wednesday, she'd only spoken to him three times, all via text. Once to tell him—again—how sorry she was, to which he'd replied with a *thank you*. The second time she'd reached out asking if he'd like her to deal with speaking to all of their booked vendors. To that he'd replied with, *I'd really appreciate that. Thank you so much for everything, Charlotte.* Kind enough, but she'd really hoped for something more along the lines of, *What I really need is you beside me.*

Sure, she could have been bold and offered to come over, or just shown up at his place, but something had held her back. What if she ran into Amy? Had their mutual grief and concern for the woman they felt so close to sent them back into each other's arms in a more intimate way? Pain had a way of making a person do crazy things, as she knew very well.

The third time she'd texted him was to ask when the funeral was, and to that he'd never replied. There could be an easy explanation. He was busy, he was in Georgia, or maybe he was so overwhelmed with his thoughts that he just didn't care to reply. Whatever the reason, it hurt like hell. She knew he was dealing with something tragic, but it was hard not to be angry at him for cutting her off in this way. They'd been dating, no doubt about it, and his dismissal cut her deep.

Didn't he need her?

So why did she hope to see him here tonight? That just seemed like a good way to be miserable when she should be focusing on the beauty of this couple's wedding day.

Stepping into the Stag, Charlotte inhaled the alcohol mixed with whatever delicious entrée the caterer upstairs had brought in. She glanced around, hoping to catch sight of whichever one of the guys was working tonight. Once upon a time, Dean would have been standing here waiting for her, but now she wasn't sure if his absence meant he wasn't here or he was no longer going to be that man to her. The thought was so painful her breath caught.

Her bride sat down on one of the sofas and took a deep breath. Charlotte forced a smile and walked over to her. "It's been a long day. We're in the home stretch and this is the fun part."

"I'm ready to just whisk her away to the hotel and order room service," the groom said, smiling at his wife, who gave him a saucy wink.

"Sounds good, honey, but my parents would kill us. They spent way too much on this reception."

"Why don't we take a couple of relaxed portraits here

under this chandelier? Give you guys an excuse to take a little breather. I'll even pose you on the sofa."

"Sounds good," the groom said.

Charlotte set to arranging them in a very relaxed way, almost as if they were lounging in a loving embrace, a much smaller version of the deer-antler fixture hanging over their heads. The Stag faced west, allowing a beautiful golden light to filter in the front windows, highlighting the copper still beyond them and making their skin radiant.

"Beautiful. Just lean in close, right there." She pressed her shutter several times, made an adjustment and then a few more. "These are nice."

"That looks nice," a voice said beside her. A voice that one time had been oh so right to her ears, but was now completely wrong.

Charlotte lowered her camera and turned to find John. She smiled. "Thanks. What are you doing here? Surely they haven't already forced you to take on a wedding night alone?" she asked hopefully.

He laughed. "Nah. TJ's upstairs. This is my training night. They all seemed relieved to have another person to fill in on weekend nights."

"I bet. None of them got into this business to be wedding vendors. They just got lucky."

Charlotte politely excused herself, partly because she had a job to do, but mostly because she suddenly wanted to cry. She walked over to her couple and pressed all emotion into a corner of her mind. "Ready to be introduced?"

The rest of the night went well, despite the fact that Lauren wasn't with her. Tonight she was shooting with Britt, her backup second. She liked Britt a lot. Her images were solid, she was funny, and she almost had the secret across-the-room language down. But her presence just served as another reminder that tonight was all wrong.

When it was finally time for them to grab a spot in the buffet line for dinner, Charlotte caught sight of John and TJ off to the side of the room laughing. She suddenly felt close to tears as she grabbed a plate. She didn't know Alex, and while the news had saddened her deeply, Nate's death hadn't caused Charlotte actual pain. No, the pain she was suffering from was from Dean's sadness and also his rejection of her.

Because she'd fallen in love with him. Maybe she'd loved him for a while. But it didn't matter. If he'd loved her in return, he would have turned to *her* to soothe him in his time of need. He'd have wanted—no, needed—*her* there with him in Georgia for the funeral.

When Charlotte and Britt had each filled their plates with chicken Alfredo, Caesar salad, chicken Parmesan, and garlic bread, they made their way to the little room beside the bar. Once inside they set their plates down.

"I'm gonna go grab some soda. Can I get you something?" Charlotte asked.

"Sure. I'd love a Diet Coke."

Charlotte nodded and made her way back out to the main room and got in line at the bar. She was happy to see Jen. At least one face was present to make things seem like normal.

"Hey you," Jen said. "Usual?"

"Of course." Charlotte smiled. "And a Diet Coke."

"How's Dean holding up?" Jen asked as she poured red syrup into a glass.

"Um, okay, I think."

Jen made a face as she righted the bottle and grabbed the fountain gun. "I figured you'd go to the funeral with him."

Charlotte gave her a tight smile. "I would have liked to. He didn't ask me."

Jen's head jerked back. "Why not? It's this Monday. Did you know that? Alex was supposed to arrive in Georgia today with Nate's body. Can't imagine what she's going through, and Nate's family. God . . . it's just unimaginable."

Jen's voice broke a little and her eyes had definitely gotten watery, which made Charlotte even sadder. She knew Jen's mother was battling cancer and wasn't really doing the best. Hearing about someone else's loss must have been hard.

Charlotte tried to change the subject by commenting on the DJ's choice of song for the meal. They laughed together as Jen made Britt's drink.

"A word of advice," Jen said as she slid the Diet Coke across the shiny wooden bar. "Whatever goes on—or doesn't go on—between you and Dean . . . don't let it only be up to him. He won't get it right. They rarely do."

Charlotte could have pretended she didn't understand, but she couldn't. Jen was too perceptive. Too wise. "I'll try. Thanks, Jen."

"Anytime, sister."

When she pushed open the door to their makeshift break room, Charlotte sucked in a breath when she saw John sitting there laughing with Britt. She hadn't really seen it necessary to inform her friend who John was to her, but maybe she should have. Their jovial exchange seemed innocent, but it still annoyed Charlotte. This was why she should have just told Dean not to hire John.

Maybe the time had finally come to stop referring the Stag to all her brides. It had been fun, but it would be good to broaden her horizons. For her own emotional health and sanity. Even if she and Dean continued to date, it might be healthy to get some space. Who could blame her for the thought, considering she'd now slept with two out of the four male employees.

A depressing thought, that.

Sitting down on the sofa beside John, Charlotte focused on dinner, which wasn't really difficult considering how hungry she was. The food was good, although they could have been a little more generous with the garlic, but it was hard to go too wrong with a plate of carbs and dairy.

"It's not too bad working a wedding here." John leaned forward, his elbows on his knees.

"For you I'm sure. Really, you guys just have to be in the building," Britt said.

"Yeah, that's what TJ said. It's a lot different being here at a wedding when you're not attending the event."

"I bet." Charlotte wasn't trying to be rude, but she knew she was coming off that way. Really she just wanted to eat and get back to work. She was able to get most of her dinner eaten while Britt asked John questions about his apprenticeship, and even Charlotte had to admit it was interesting. She knew some of the basics about the distilling process, but John lit up while he discussed what he was learning from Dean. It wasn't hard to see why Dean had wanted to bring him on in the first place. He genuinely seemed to find the entire thing fascinating and fun.

Was that how Dean felt about his job? It made Charlotte realize how much she really didn't know about him. The time they'd been spending together had revolved around Alex and her wedding. It was ironic and poetic that the demise of her nuptials had also been their end.

Charlotte looked up when Britt set down her plate and stood.

"I'm going to the little girls' room. Be back."

That left her and John alone, but Charlotte just picked at her garlic bread.

"I still can't believe what happened to Dean's sister." He scooted closer to her on the sofa, and Charlotte fought the urge to scoot away.

"It's horrible. I was there when he got the call. I sort of still can't believe it." Which was true. That night after it had happened, she'd woken up several times during sleep, thinking maybe she'd dreamed it.

"Are you flying down there for the funeral?" he asked, a genuine look of concern on his face.

"Uh, actually no."

"I'm sure he wants you there. I would if—"

"John." Charlotte turned hard on the sofa and put out a hand. "There's something you need to know. Dean and I . . . we haven't been seeing each other long. In fact we weren't a couple before Jason and Shelby's wedding."

His head angled a bit, bottom lip dropping open. "*What?*"

"I lied."

"Why would you do that?"

"Because. . . ." Charlotte's voice became frantic, and her hands went out as she glanced around the room in frustration. "You came into my sphere, John. I wasn't expecting you. I didn't *want* you here. Especially not when after all these years, I'm still the single girl at the wedding."

He stared at her, shocked at her outburst and obviously unsure what to say.

"I'm sorry." Charlotte shook her head. "I know I'm being rude . . . but, damn it, I really don't feel like I owe the man who broke up with me on my *wedding day* my best self."

John blinked once. Twice, and then folded his hands together. "No, you don't. What I did to you was low. Worse than low. It was selfish and cowardly."

She was not going to disagree with him, because, well,

she didn't disagree. At the same time, though, she wasn't in the market to make him pay. It served no purpose, and really there was no longer any satisfaction in it.

"It was all of those things. But while I disagree with your method, we weren't supposed to get married. You knew that, and I was in denial over it."

"You were grieving, Charlotte. So was I. Probably why I acted cowardly. It killed me to know that I would be ripping out a heart that had already been broken. But you losing the—our—baby made me realize my true feelings. And I know that makes me sound like an asshole, but we weren't meant be together. Sure, we would have stayed together had you remained pregnant. We'd have gotten married, but eventually we'd have been miserable."

She knew he was right, although it was still sad to admit it. The part he was forgetting was that while they may have been miserable after marrying each other, at least they'd still have had their sweet baby. The child in her womb that she'd felt fluttering around like a butterfly for three whole days. Did he even realize how hard you could fall in love with the feel of your own baby moving inside you? If she tried, she could still remember what those little swooshes felt like. She desperately wanted to have that again. Someday.

"Why did he go along with it?"

Charlotte turned to John. "Who?"

"Dean. He doesn't seem like the type of guy to lie about a relationship. In all honesty, it's hard for me to believe. I mean . . . he's kind of old for that."

Charlotte rolled her eyes. "He's not old."

"I didn't say he was . . . just . . . never mind."

"He went along with it for me."

John's lips quirked. "And then you two actually stayed together. Maybe you should just thank me."

Charlotte turned to glare at John. He grinned back at her. They both began to laugh.

"You can thank me that you have an awesome job now," she said.

"I do thank you for that. Seriously. I did not want to go back to what I was doing before."

They glanced at each other and then Charlotte looked down at her hands. She was a different woman now, but she could still appreciate the reasons why she'd once loved this man . . . and at one time, boy. He was never the villain in her story, although it had often been easier to label him as such. But the truth was they were just two young people who had once loved, lost, and then ultimately moved on. Nothing less, nothing more. But now she wanted that *more*, and she knew who she wanted it with.

Dean hadn't slept a full night's sleep in almost two weeks. For the past several nights, he'd lain in bed listening to Alex cry herself to sleep in the bedroom next to his. It was heart wrenching to hear. They'd been back from Georgia for five days, and not only had she not left the house, he wasn't even sure if she'd showered.

The first couple of nights he'd tried to stay with her, offer comfort, but she had always asked him to leave the room. He understood; there was really nothing he could do to ease her pain. But this feeling of helplessness was eating him up inside.

When Dean's bedside clock read one AM, he decided he wasn't sleeping anytime soon and made his way into the kitchen. Despite his occupation, Dean didn't consider himself much of a drinker. He obviously appreciated a fine whiskey, or a smooth bourbon, but he didn't drink it daily. He was more in love with the process. The science and the challenge. Watching others drink what he made, knowing they appreciated it, was what he enjoyed. Tonight, though, he pulled down a bottle of Forkhorn White Whiskey, poured a couple of fingers more than necessary, and topped it with a can of Dr Pepper just because he had it on hand. It had always been Alexis's favorite soda, so when Amy had stocked his kitchen with her comfort items she'd been sure to get a couple of cases. As far as Dean could tell, they had yet to be touched.

He used the light of the fridge to pour from the can.

"Can I have one?" a small voice said from the end of the cabinet.

Dean's head jerked up and he gave Alex a tentative smile. "Of course. Just a DP, or you want—"

"The whiskey, too. I want it all."

Dean nodded and grabbed another glass to make her one. He stood there trying to figure out what to say. Right now he felt like she was a timid animal that had ventured from its shelter and any wrong move or word would send her scampering back, and as selfish as it sounded, he needed to spend some time with her. Not only to verify she was okay—as okay as she could be—but because he was tired of her hiding away. She'd been gone for so long, and he'd missed her.

They hadn't talked much since she'd gotten back from overseas last week, and while he understood, he'd had questions. Some of Nate's family had been able to fill in the details, like the fact that the helicopter accident was just that: an accident. It had nothing to do with enemy fire or a mission. It was a technical mishap that had led to pilot error and ended with a landing so hard it had killed two of the four passengers on impact. The other two were injured, one in critical condition the last Dean had heard.

When he handed Alex her drink, Dean realized her hair was down and looked clean. He wasn't sure when she'd done that, but he hoped it was a sign that she was doing a little better.

"Thanks," she said quietly before sitting down at the kitchen table.

"You hungry? I can make you something."

"I don't know." She took a drink and winced. Then took another. "Have any mac and cheese?"

Dean almost sighed in relief. Finally, something he could do for her, even it only required boiling some water and stirring. "Of course. Amy bought like four boxes of the shells. Your favorite."

He pulled one from the cabinet and then set to work filling the pot with water.

"Why didn't you tell me about you and Amy?"

Dean turned off the sink, uncertain he'd heard her right. "What do you mean?"

"Why did you never tell me she'd been unfaithful?"

Setting the pot on the stove, he turned on the burner. "Who *did* tell you, is the question."

"She did."

Dean turned to stare at his sister, who raised her eyebrows in challenge. He shook his head and opened the box of pasta to pull out the cheese pouch. "I'm sure she explained why it was all my fault. I pushed her to do it."

"Of course she didn't. And even if she had, no one forces another person to cheat."

"We'd gone through some rough things. I wasn't perfect."

"You? Nooo." Alex let out a little laugh, and Dean smiled. It was the first time she'd joked since he'd first seen her standing in Nate's parents' driveway, waiting for him to get there like a lost little girl. She'd looked so young and stricken that day. Her shoulders slumped, eyes rimmed red, and hair in a messy ponytail. It had shattered his heart into a million pieces. This girl had gone through so much loss in her life.

"You still haven't answered my question," she prompted.

"Why didn't I tell you?" He'd known what she meant, but he was stalling. Finally, he sighed and leaned his hands on the back of the chair across from her. "I already felt bad about the divorce. I knew that in a way, Amy and I had become your parental unit. We were the only family you really had, and I didn't want you losing everything. I was afraid it would make you have bad feelings for her. You two were so close."

"So you did it because you were worried about my feelings?"

"If I'd had things my way, we'd have never seen her again. But I don't regret it, and I don't want you to stop being close to her for me."

"Did it ever occur to you that I might worry about your feelings, Dean? You're always worrying about me, but I worry about you, too."

"Alex, you're—"

"Yes I know. You see me as a child. But I'm not." There was no anger in her voice, just honesty. And she was right: No matter how old she seemed to get, in his mind she was always his little sister, fifteen years younger than he was.

"I know you're not a child, Alexis. Doesn't meant I don't want to protect you from pain. What you're going through now . . ." He stared at her eyes, which had started to glisten. "I'd do anything to change it. Anything."

"Me too." Her voice broke, and before a sob could release she sucked in a deep breath. "Goddamn, I'm so sick of crying. It's begun to hurt, crying so much. My face hurts, my lips, my head. My whole body feels wrung dry."

The sound of water boiling behind him drew Dean's focus, and he walked over to pour the little shells into the pot. He wished he knew why Amy had confided what she did in Alex. Part of his reasoning for not telling his sister at the time was at Amy's request. She'd begged him not to tell, said it would break her heart if she lost Alex over the split. He knew that as much as Amy had hurt him, she still loved his sister. And she was good to her, so it had made sense not to break either of their hearts any more than necessary.

"I hadn't seen him in two weeks. Isn't that crazy?" Alex voice was small, and when Dean turned back to her, she was staring off into the living room. "We were supposed to see each other the next day and . . . God, I was so excited. I knew our wedding was right around the corner. I'll never know what it was like to marry Nate."

"Alex . . ." He wasn't sure if her talking openly about this was healthy or if he should suggest she stop. It seemed the best action was to let her decide, so he stayed silent after that.

"You know, the hardest part about losing him is that . . . he's the person I want there, to tell how bad the pain is. He's the person I want to hold me while I cry. He's the person . . . the only person who would understand why I feel like my life is over. And he's not here." She looked back to Dean, lip trembling.

Before he could begin to process what the best response was, she pushed her chair back and within seconds she was around the table and falling against him, her arms locking tight around his waist. Deep heavy sobs ripped from her throat, her chest heaving in and out so hard he could practically feel the sound coming up from the inside of her body against his ribs. He instantly wrapped his arms around her shoulders and held her head against him, his cheek resting on her hair. She smelled like his cheap shampoo, and he knew that from this point forward he wouldn't be able to smell that scent without thinking of this devastating moment.

Dean's eyes blurred with tears, but he remained silent as she cried in his arms. He knew the pasta beside him would be done in a few moments, but there was no way he was moving. The weight of her body against him made him think her legs might give out at any moment, as if the pain was such a heavy load, it was literally pulling her into the ground.

After a long moment, her cries turned to stuttering whimpers. Finally, she moved, reaching toward the counter for a paper towel, and Dean stepped back so she could grab one.

"Oh no, I'm so sorry." She was staring down at his T-shirt, which was covered in what was definitely a mix of tears and snot. As she lifted the paper towel to her face and blew, she began to chuckle. He looked up at her and laughed a little, too.

"I guess you should have just used my shirt to blow your nose. Wouldn't really have made a difference."

Alex slapped at his arm. "Shut up."

He used the free moment to grab a strainer and finish preparing her meal. Maybe the first real food she'd eaten in days. While he stirred the goopy cheese into the noodles, she leaned her head on his arm. "Thank you for always taking care of me."

"It's my job." He reached for a bowl in the cabinet, but before he could serve her some she grabbed a fork and stuck it into the pot. He shrugged. "Or you can do that."

She gave a little smile. "Sorry. I'll use a bowl. I was just hungry."

"I'm glad. I was starting to worry about you." He scooped a hefty serving into the bowl and handed it to her.

"It's never been your job to take care of me, you know?" she said as she went to sit back down at the table. "But I consider myself lucky that you always have."

"You were thirteen. And I was legally your guardian. So yes, it was definitely my job. But I wouldn't change anything, Alex."

She took a few more bites, and Dean sat back down to his watery cocktail.

"Amy also told me you liked someone. The girl you were, uh . . . planning with. Charlotte?"

Amy had certainly been chatty. What had prompted all of her admissions? he wondered. Also, the mention of Charlotte deepened the ache in his chest. God, how he missed her. So many times he'd wanted to call her, just to tell her what was going on. How sad, but also how beautiful the funeral had been. Nate's family were members of a Southern Baptist church. The kind with the soulful choir that made you feel alive even though you were mourning the dead. It had been an incredibly moving experience, especially when all the women had circled his mother and Alexis and put their hands on them, praying out loud for them and for Nate. Dean had never witnessed anything like it, and he'd wished so badly that Charlotte had been there with him.

He'd wanted to share with her how annoying it was when they'd been laid over in Omaha on their flight back the other day. Without her, there wasn't anyone to truly share with. He'd just wanted *her*. Wanted to hold her, touch her, kiss her. But every time he'd been close to calling, he'd held back. Reminded himself of his failures. All the things he knew he couldn't offer.

He'd known what the outcome of his infertility test would be, but to hear it again after all these years had been a blow. Things were worse than they had been, his sperm quality count had dropped dramatically. No doubt him aging ten years had been the reason.

"Was she right?" Alexis urged. "Do you like her?"

"Yeah. Charlotte and I had been spending some time together, seeing how things went."

"*And?* Why hasn't she come around?"

Dean sighed. "Several reasons."

"Such as . . ."

"I guess I've started thinking maybe we aren't a great fit. For starters she's nearly a dozen years younger than I am."

Alex's eyes went wide. "Look at you, stud. But I'm not surprised. Do you know how many of my girlfriends had crushes on you? Creeped me out."

It was Dean's turn to be surprised. "What? That creeps me out, too."

"Okay, so she's younger. So what? That makes her . . ."

"Almost thirty."

Alex looked annoyed at that. "I'm pretty sure a thirty-year-old woman is old enough for you. I mean, it's not like you're seventy."

"Okay, fine, it's not a deal breaker. The other thing is that . . . I know for a fact she happens to want children, and I . . . well, I can't give her that."

His sister's eyes softened, full of sympathy and also surprise. "I always wondered why you and Amy never had a child. I used to worry it was because of me. I was too difficult. Or you were waiting for me to move out."

"No way, Alex. It had nothing to do with you. We tried. Tried for years. Amy had several miscarriages."

"Did you see a doctor? You know there are things to try."

Dean nodded. "Yes . . . to everything. I'm the infertile one, and I even went back to the doctor a couple of weeks ago to get a second opinion. The chances of conception are almost . . . zero."

Alex set down her spoon, her eyes going sad. "Dean. I'm so sorry."

He shrugged. "It happens. There are several theories on why, but . . . the outcome is the same."

"Did you tell her that?"

"I was going to. But no, I haven't. I've been taking care of you."

"Don't use me as an excuse. Dean, you're sitting here with a girl who just lost the love of her life. Do you seriously think I would have let something like infertility keep me from him? The person you love is all that matters. If you care about this woman . . . you owe it to both of you to make this decision together."

It was a little unsettling for his grieving sister to sit here giving him relationship advice. And she wasn't finished.

"I wish you'd do it for me. I'm tired of you taking care of everyone else but yourself."

"I can't believe you're sitting here right now worrying about me. This is ridiculous."

"It is ridiculous, so stop it. There's no reason that one of us can't be happy."

"Alex, you still have your whole life ahead of you. You're hurting now, but you'll love someone again."

She lifted a hand and shook her head. "Don't. I can't even think that thought. Just . . . at least tell her. Amy said she could tell Charlotte cared about you. Don't let her wonder why you're pulling away. Give her a chance to love you. For me."

Twenty-Eight

Charlotte was surprised, but happy, to see Jen at the front desk of the Stag. Today she had her dark—almost blue-black—hair curled into waves around her head, and she wore a pretty yellow dress that brought out the vibrancy in the tattoos on her shoulder. She really was a strikingly beautiful woman, and she could pull off a bright-red lip-stick like nobody's business.

"Working on a Wednesday?" Charlotte asked.

Jen spread her arms out to encompass the desk and counter. "My new domain. At least until Tara returns."

"Really? That's wonderful, and I'm sure the guys appreciate the help."

"Yeah. So far it's been great, but it's only been a few weeks. I'm better at it than I thought I'd be, though. I like working with brides and talking about their weddings. Even the distillery side of things is kind of fun."

"Good for you. What will you do when Tara comes back?"

A shadow passed over Jen's face. "Not really sure yet. Guess I'll cross that bridge when I get there."

"How long is Tara's maternity leave once she delivers?"

"Twelve weeks. So I have a while to enjoy it."

Charlotte pulled a small stack of paper-clipped documents out of her bag and laid them on the counter. "I just needed to drop off a few things for Dean to sign. I put stickies on each one indicating where he needs to fill something out and sign. Basically they're cancel contracts for the wedding. And the envelope contains several of his deposit checks and some cash that was refunded."

"They were willing to refund? That's nice."

"It is, especially since most of the deposits were contractually nonrefundable. But under the circumstances and the fact that we're in the wedding community I think they were happy to do this for him. And Alex."

"Poor Alex." Jen shook her head.

Charlotte had only one experience with loss, her unborn child. She could only imagine the suffering Alex was going through. But she did know well what it was like to think your life was headed in one happy direction, only to have that all ripped away.

"Has, uh . . . Dean been in?" she found herself asking, instantly wishing she hadn't.

"Actually he's here now. Want me to get him, you could give him these—"

"No, no. That's okay. I have to run."

"Charlotte?"

Oh God.

Charlotte's stomach fluttered at the sound of his voice. Part of her wanted to run out the front door and pretend she hadn't heard him. The other wanted to turn and head straight for his arms and beg him to explain why he'd shut her out. Trying to be strong, she turned and feigned indifference. Unsure if she would be convincing.

"Hey. How are you?"

He seemed a little surprised and unnerved by her smile. "I've been better. What are you doing here?"

Funny how a few weeks ago she'd just shown up to show him décor, or talk about a vendor choice, but now it was so awkward.

"I actually just dropped off some papers for you to sign."

"And you were going to leave without saying hi?"

Really? Her head jerked back the slightest bit, jaw dropping. She knew by the expression on his face that he could read her irritation at that comment.

"Can we talk for a minute?" He motioned for the conference room. She knew there was no way she could go in there, remembering them kissing in that room, laughing, planning.

"Actually it's not a good time. I'm on my way to a shoot." That wasn't completely a lie, but it didn't really start for an hour.

"Oh. What kind?"

Did she mistake the tightening in his jaw, or the way he shoved his hands in his pockets a little too hard? God, he looked so good today. His hair had grown a little overlong and he really should have shaved this morning, but his skin was slightly more tanned than the last time she'd seen him, and the oxford shirt he wore made his shoulders look especially broad.

"It's actually another book cover shoot. I've booked a lot of them over the past few weeks. Kind of exciting."

"Hmm. Good for you. If you enjoy it."

"I do."

His eyes narrowed a bit, and he shifted his feet. "Well then, can we get together afterward? I just . . . we haven't really been able to talk lately."

She frowned, no longer capable of holding up the pretense. "Actually, I've been very available to talk. You just haven't wanted me."

Dean's eyes darted toward the front desk, his jaw clinching. "Charlotte . . ."

"Am I wrong?" she said, looking him square in the eye.

His sigh left her worried about what his response might be. When he hesitated, she suddenly felt weak. This was it. He would tell her he was sorry but they were officially over.

"Don't answer that actually." She put up a hand. "I need to go."

Turning around, she didn't even glance at Jen as she rushed for the door. Her eyes were stinging as she stepped outside.

"Charlotte, stop," his voice called behind her.

With a groan, she wiped under her eyes and then turned. "What do you possibly need to say to me?"

Dean stopped short on the sidewalk. "First of all, I need to say I'm an asshole. I haven't handled things well, but . . . I've had a lot going on."

"Yeah. You have. And I guess I thought it might have been my place to help you with that. But if not, that really tells me all I need to know."

"I deserve your anger. But . . ." His lips clamped shut, the light breeze blowing the hair on his neck. "Please come to my place tonight. Have dinner with Alex and me."

Charlotte's mouth dropped open in shock. "Did you hear anything I just said?"

"Yes, damn it." He ran a hand through his hair. "I don't blame you for being angry, and you probably won't believe me, but I was going to call and ask you over tonight anyway. You just showed up here before I could."

She narrowed her eyes at him. "The only reason I'm even considering it is because I would like to meet Alexis. How is she doing?"

He let out a sigh. "She's doing the best she can. One hour she's able to smile, and the next she goes to her room and cries."

The sadness in his tone reminded Charlotte of what he'd been dealing with. Did he deserve her understanding? A little, but he'd said it best: He also deserved her anger. The person who deserved her sympathy was his sister.

"Every day it will get better. One day she'll get through a full day and realize she didn't cry. And then she'll feel guilty. Tell her that's okay."

Dean stared at her a long moment. Then he slowly stepped a little closer as his hand reached up and touched her jaw so quickly, it was almost a whisper. "I've missed you."

Charlotte swallowed, not sure what to think about what was happening. Her thoughts were fractured, uncertain, and she didn't trust what she was feeling in that moment. She smiled and shook her head the slightest bit. "Please don't confuse me, Dean. I'll text you when I'm done with my shoot."

Dean's brow furrowed and he nodded. "Are you going alone? I hope it's nowhere unsafe."

"It will be fine. I'll see you later." She turned, wanting out of there before she did something stupid, like talk about how much she'd missed him. Admit that she wasn't sure what he wanted from her now.

"Charlotte," Dean called out as she pulled open her car door.

She turned. "Yes?"

"No couple photos."

Staring at him, she lifted her eyebrow. "I'll *try* not to."

His eyes went wide at her response but she just got in her car and drove off. It felt good.

Dean was still nervous that Charlotte might not show up, although he'd told Alexis she was coming. His sister had been so excited, she'd offered to help him make dinner. That alone was a positive outcome. The past hour they'd hung out in the kitchen together, making pasta sauce, mixing, and layering together a lasagna recipe that Alex had found on the Internet. It had been like therapy for both of them. She'd even laughed a couple of times, although that faraway look often clouded her eyes.

He knew it would take a long time for her to get over Nate, but he hated that there was nothing he could do to make it easier for her.

Dean's phone chimed on the kitchen table, and Alex darted over to get it. Picking it up, she straightened. "It's her. She said she's just cleaning up and will be here in about twenty."

Dean sucked in a breath of relief. And happiness. "Okay. That's perfect, the timer says ten minutes."

"Then we have to let it sit for twenty."

"In the pan?" he asked.

"Yeah, I guess it helps it hold together. We can start with the salad and wine."

Dean looked around and nodded. "Okay. Whatever you say."

He'd left work right after Charlotte had driven away so he could go home and prepare. He'd called Alex to tell her and she'd immediately taken to the Internet for a recipe. Dean had run to the grocery store because although she was up for the dinner, Alex still hadn't wanted to leave the house. Baby steps, he figured. Although if she didn't leave eventually he'd have to try something. She hadn't stepped outside in over a week. Maybe more.

Alex went off to her room to change and Dean went into his own room to grab a new shirt. The one he'd been wearing had acquired a nice tomato sauce stain. Not long after that they set out the salad and wine, and Alex pulled the dish out of the oven.

"I'm glad you did this," she said as she put the bread in the oven. "It's kind of taken my mind off myself for a while."

"Good, I'm happy to hear that." Dean ruffled her hair and she scowled at him. Those moments gave him some hope that Alex would someday be back to her old self.

When a knock sounded at the door, Alex stiffened. "We didn't discuss how we're going to do this."

"Well, she'll come in and I'll introduce you."

"Oh yeah. Of course." She shook her head and followed Dean into the living room. "Should I stand? Sit?"

Dean turned to her, laughing. This was so unlike her. Maybe it was because she'd never witnessed him with any other woman but Amy. "Alexis. Chill the hell out."

He opened the door to find the most beautiful woman he'd ever known standing on his stoop. The sun was just now meeting the treetops, and her hair glowed in the golden light. It made him think of the night they'd made out next to the old Harley. The night everything changed.

"Hey, come in." Dean stood back so she could pass him and couldn't help inhaling her delicious scent.

"Hi, you must be Alex. I feel like I know you." Dean watched in awe and a deep feeling of painful satisfaction as Charlotte walked right over to his sister, without him saying a word, and gave her a long, tight hug.

He didn't mistake the quiet sound of Alex sniffling against Charlotte, but before he could apologize or say anything, Charlotte spoke first, a hint of tears in her voice.

"I'm so sorry we have to meet under these circumstances. I'd have much rather been able to show you all the beautiful things we'd planned for you both in person."

Oh no. Dean cringed as Alex cried harder, squeezing this woman she'd never met before. Charlotte only rocked from side to side gently, patting Alex's back. And Dean stood there completely dumbfounded and helpless.

"Since that isn't possible, I brought you a gift," Charlotte said quietly. "Can I show you?"

Alex pulled back, nodding her head as she reached for the one of three rolls of toilet paper she used to blow her nose, scattered around the living room. One was always near her.

Charlotte sat down on the sofa and patted the cushion next to her. Alex sat immediately, and Dean walked a few steps closer since both of the women had forgotten his existence in that moment.

Pulling a square-shaped, flat box from her bag, Charlotte laid it in Alex's lap but didn't take her hand off the top. "I don't know if you want to look at this yet. But someday you might. Throughout the planning, I took photos with my phone. They're not great, as I'd mainly done it for referencing and planning. But I've assembled them and had them put in this album. The food, the flowers, the venue, the . . . places I wanted to take you for portraits. All in here. It would have been a beautiful day, and I wanted you to know what it would have been like. You should know."

Dean held his breath, wondering how Alex would react. Was this a good idea? Wouldn't it have been better to just pretend the wedding had never been planned at all?

When Alex went still, looking down at the box and

sliding her finger across the ribbon on top, Dean felt his heart sink. "Charlotte—"

"Can I look now?" Alex looked up at Dean. "Is that okay?"

"Are you sure, Alex?" Dean asked.

"Yes. I want to. I need to."

He glanced to Charlotte, who nodded. "Okay. Open it." He walked over and sat down on the sofa beside Charlotte. He could barely keep himself from touching her.

They watched as Alex slowly untied the ribbon, opened the box, and pulled out a small album. It was no bigger than five inches square and it had the words ALEXIS & NATE written in the middle of the cover. At the sight of it, Alex lifted her fingers to her mouth and just stared for a long moment.

Finally, she glanced over at Charlotte and gave a teary smile. "I already love it."

"I'm glad," Charlotte whispered, and in that moment Dean could no longer help himself. He leaned forward and placed his lips against her head, just behind her temple. He felt her stiffen, but then slowly she leaned against him, pressing her body back toward his. In that moment, he'd never loved her more.

He loved her.

There was no denying it. He was in love with Charlotte and he wanted to give her everything he possibly had to offer. He would do whatever he could to make her happy, if she'd let him.

They watched as Alex flipped through the pages. The first was of the Stag, then a close-up of a plate of chicken piccata.

"It looks delicious," Alex said.

"It was," Dean said, remembering how Charlotte had fed it to him.

She oohed and ahhed at the images of the flower shop and the close-ups of varieties they'd chosen. Dean and Charlotte talked about each visit a bit, sharing details about the owners. Charlotte had included a picture of the cake samples and another close-up of the one they'd chosen. To the side was written the flavors of the cake and fillings and even a photo of the inspiration cake they'd liked in the photo album at Jill's house.

There were photos of the decorations and centerpieces that Charlotte had been assembling at her house, some of which Dean hadn't even seen. Then outdoor photos of scenery where Charlotte had planned to take their photos. One was a beautiful field full of wildflowers and the other a scenic path that led toward a forest.

Then Alex turned to the last page. It was a selfie of Charlotte in the dressing room of the bridal shop.

"I know that's weird. I cropped out my head, but . . ."

"I love it," Alex whispered. "I love it so much."

"Amy chose it," Charlotte said. "She did a wonderful job."

Dean watched intently as Alexis ran her fingers over the photo. She didn't cry this time, just stared. Finally, she turned to Charlotte. "It looks beautiful on you. Doesn't it, Dean?"

"Of course. I saw it in person. She looked . . . amazing." And she had. More beautiful than he'd ever seen her. He wished that moment hadn't ended the way it had, with him in a daze of pain and fear.

"This is the best gift ever, Charlotte. Thank you so much, for agreeing to plan my wedding, and for this. It means everything."

"I'm glad."

The smell of burning garlic got Alex's attention and she

jumped up. "The bread. Let's get in here and eat." She ran into the kitchen, leaving them alone.

Instead of getting up, Charlotte turned and faced Dean on the couch.

"How did you know?" Dean whispered.

A sad smile formed on her mouth. "I know it's not quite the same, but . . . when I miscarried, no one but John knew. Not my mother, not my friends, no one. And it was painful. Sometimes I wanted to grieve openly. I wanted to talk about what my baby might have looked like. What I might have named her. What might have been but never would be. I think sometimes you have to embrace the loss. Honor what you'll never have by speaking of it. I just hoped Alex might feel the same."

"I guess I've been doing it all wrong then. I've made it a point not to talk about Nate at all unless she did first. I didn't want to hurt her."

"It's a natural response. You want to protect her. But you might give her opportunities to share. I think it's healing to get it out."

Dean reached up and touched her hair. "You're something else, Charlotte."

"Dinner's ready," Alex called from the kitchen.

"You hungry?" Dean asked. "We made it together."

Charlotte's eyes widened. "I'm impressed, and yes, also starving. Photographing young, half-naked men works up an appetite."

Twenty-Nine

Charlotte laughed when Dean practically growled at her comment about half-naked men. Maybe she should have left off the *young*. She patted his leg and stood. "I'm teasing you."

She was happy to be here, and spend time with Dean and Alexis, but she wasn't completely over her feelings of betrayal. He'd turned to Amy when he was hurting. That was hard to forget.

But it was even harder to ignore how in love she was with him. How much she wanted to be here, and hoped that this meant what she thought it might. That he wanted them to start fresh. Not as pseudo-wedding-planners or flirty business associates, but as a man and a woman who wanted a relationship together.

"Charlotte, right here." Alexis pointed to a chair. "Dean, here." He was to sit next to Charlotte.

They watched as she set the bread on the table and then grabbed her already loaded plate, her new album, and a fork. "And I'm going to eat in my room."

Dean and Charlotte both instantly protested, but Alex shook her head. "I want to go spend some more time with my present—which I love so much—while you two . . . be together. Please."

"Alex, we want you here." Dean looked at Charlotte, and she instantly nodded her agreement.

"I know you do. But please, this time let me choose to do something for you. Now . . . don't let me down." Alexis gave him a wink and left the kitchen, heading down the dark hall. When they heard her bedroom door click shut, Dean turned to Charlotte.

"Well. I guess we're alone now."

"I guess so," Charlotte said.

Dean pulled the lasagna closer to them and grabbed the spatula resting on the side. "Can I serve you?"

Charlotte lifted her plate. When they both had servings, they began to eat and talk about unimportant things. She complimented the food, which truly was delicious. They discussed the wine, which Dean had chosen, and even how her shoot had gone. She was pleased that despite his obvious jealousy, Dean appeared genuinely interested.

When they got closer to finishing, the conversation became stilted. Partly because she was nervous. She knew how she hoped and wanted this evening to end, but she really wasn't confident.

She insisted on helping him take all the dishes to the sink and then put the leftovers into a dish to save. When there was nothing left to do, Dean held out his hand to her.

"Let's go sit," he said quietly.

"Okay." She took his hand, grabbed her wine in the other, and allowed him to lead her back into the living room.

She liked Dean's place. It was an apartment, but in an exclusive complex. The living area had high ceilings, a leather sofa, and some sort of dark wingback recliner. A large TV sat on the opposite wall. It was somewhat on the plain side, but she figured it was better than tacky décor. It was very him. Masculine, unadorned, but appealing.

"Is Alex going to move in with you?" Charlotte asked. Quickly she regretted the question. "I didn't mean that the way it sounded, like . . . I was fishing for information on . . . never mind. Just, it was an honest, curious question."

Dean smiled. "I know. The answer is I don't know. We haven't talked about what her plans are past the current day. But I'll do whatever she needs."

"You're a really good brother, Dean."

"Thank you."

They sat on the sofa once more. Close, but not touching, their legs angled together. "I'm glad you came over." He threw one hand over the back of the sofa cushion, and his fingers instantly touched her hair. Dean seemed to like to touch her hair, which she was just fine with.

"I have to admit . . . I was a little confused when you asked me today. I was trying to avoid you when I stopped by."

"I don't blame you." He frowned down at the leather between them for a moment before finally glancing up at her. "I acted like a dick, Charlotte. I'm sorry. I was so in my head, so . . . I don't know. Getting that news from Alex . . ."

Charlotte laid a hand on his knee. "I understand. I do. I won't say it didn't hurt me a lot that you basically stopped communicating, but I tried to put myself in your situation. I knew your sister needed you. We hadn't even been seeing each other that long so I probably shouldn't have expected so much."

"Yes, you should have. I let you down, Charlotte. Which

is ironic, because that's exactly what I was trying not to do."

"What do you mean?"

Dean suddenly felt sick to his stomach, but this was it. It was time to come clean with everything that had been holding him back. If his little sister's painful experience had taught him anything, it was that life was too damn short to worry about what-ifs.

He was going to be honest with Charlotte. After that, whatever happened between the two of them was up to her. He leaned his elbows on his knees and swallowed hard.

"Let me start over," he said, turning his head to meet her eyes. She looked confused, and almost as nervous as he felt. "I've resisted this relationship between us almost every step of the way."

Her lips pursed together, she clasped her hands. "Thanks for reminding me."

"Not because of you, Charlotte. Please understand, I've been attracted to you for years. You have no idea how many times I've adjusted the schedule so I could be the one working with you. I've fantasized about you a million times because everything about you attracts me, and the fact that I had a hard time with this is all on me."

Charlotte licked at her lips, and he could tell she was confused by what he was trying to say. He needed to make his point.

"I distanced myself from you again that day we found out about Nate."

She nodded. "Yes. You did."

"I know I hurt you, but . . . I was hurting, too. And I was terrified."

"Because of Alexis?"

Dean blew out a breath. "Partly. But . . . there's more. I haven't been completely honest with you, Charlotte."

"You haven't?" Her voice was so small and sad. "Are you still in love with Amy?"

"No!" Dean said a little too loudly. "Absolutely not. It's nothing like that."

She looked slightly relieved. "Then what have you not been honest about?"

Dean shifted, turning to face her a bit more. He reached out and touched her thumb, gently squeezing it.

"Charlotte . . . you told me about your miscarriage."

Her brows narrowed. "I did. Yes."

He nodded. "And I got the feeling that you would like to try again. To have children. You want that."

Lips parting, she huffed out a confused sound. "Yes. Of course, I would. Why?"

When he didn't respond right away, an awkward laugh escaped her lips and she looked away, toward the wall. "You're making me feel stupid."

"No, no. I'm sorry, it's just . . ." He gently pulled her face back to his. "I don't know how to say this, but, Charlotte . . . I can't have children."

She stared at him for a moment. He waited, unsure what to say next. Her mouth opened and then closed again. She glanced down at her fingers. Still she was silent.

"Do you mean . . ." she finally said quietly. "That you don't *want* to have children?"

Dean shook his head. "No. I mean that I'm unable to. I'm . . . infertile, Charlotte."

He heard her swallow, her lips twisting. A moment—that felt like an eternity—passed between them in silence. Finally she spoke. "A doctor told you this?"

"Yes. Ten years ago . . . and again a few weeks ago."

Her eyes darted up to his. "You went a few weeks ago?"

"Yes. You were right, as much as I've wanted you, my fear of inadequacy was holding me back. I was hoping . . . things had changed, I guess. You've made a few comments that led me to believe you want kids very much. I can't tell you how hard it is for me to know that I can't give them to you. So I went again. To be certain."

"So . . . you distanced yourself from me. Because you thought that . . . what? You were doing me a favor?"

Dean sat up. "I . . . maybe."

Charlotte looked over to a window, her lips closed.

"Talk to me, Charlotte. Tell me how you feel."

Her gaze cut back to him, hard and angry. But her voice was all sadness. "Talk to you? Do you mean the way you tell me how you feel when hard things weigh on your mind?"

He stared at her, stunned. She wasn't finished.

"This is two major things, Dean. A death in your family and the fact you're *infertile* and you don't let me deal with either one. How am I supposed to feel about that?"

He was speechless. "Charlotte . . . I . . ."

"You what? Think I'm young? Stupid? Emotional?"

"I don't think any of those things. And what about the fact that you didn't want to talk to me about your miscarriage?"

Her head jerked back. "First, not sharing is different from completely cutting someone off, which is what you did to me. Second, I did finally share with you, when I was ready, because I trusted you. So why don't you trust me?"

She was right, he couldn't compare the two. "I want to, Charlotte. I'm trying. But I have trouble with that." He stood up and walked into the dining area before walking right back. He suddenly felt the need to shake off all this pent-up frustration. Why did she not understand?

"What does that mean?" she asked. "You have trouble trusting *me*? Why?"

Dean plopped back down on the sofa and looked at her. "It means . . . I watched my mother leave my father for a younger man. My own wife cheated on me because I couldn't make her happy."

Charlotte shook her head. "Your mother and your ex made their own decisions. The fact that you couldn't give Amy a baby is no excuse for what she did. And do you really think I'm the same kind of woman she is?"

"No, you're nothing like her. But the fact remains that I can't get you pregnant, Charlotte."

She nodded slowly, a tear glistening in the corner of her eye. "So you were going to decide for both of us that you had nothing more to offer me than your infertility. Or that if you did, I would eventually end up resenting you and become a cheater?"

"Don't make it sound like that."

"I didn't. You did."

"Damn it, Charlotte. I like you. A lot, which means I want you to be happy."

She gave him the saddest smile. "But didn't you stop to consider that pulling away from me does not make me happy? I was really starting to think there was something special between us before that day."

"There was. There *is*."

She shrugged. "Possibly. But how would you ever really know if you didn't share your fears with me? You didn't share all of yourself."

His eyes clamped shut as he processed what she was saying.

"I think . . . I'm going to go."

Dean's eyes shot open. "Please don't," he said.

"I'm not saying we're over, Dean. I just need to think

about this." Charlotte stood up and reached for her purse.

"Charlotte, please . . ."

She lifted a hand and put it on his jaw. "You're not the only one with fears and insecurities, Dean. You got to process yours. Now it's my turn. The only thing I can promise is that I won't leave you in the dark for too long. I'll call you soon, okay?"

All he could do was let her go.

Thirty

Charlotte walked into her mother's house and was greeted by the familiar smell of homemade chicken and noodles, her father's favorite meal.

"Happy Birthday, Daddy," Charlotte said, wrapping her arms around her father's broad shoulders.

"How's my girl?" he asked over her shoulder.

"Good. Busy." When they pulled out of their hug, she handed him a plastic container and a card.

"Is this what I think it is?" He grinned.

"Of course. I'd never dream of coming without your cookies."

He chuckled and headed for his favorite chair in front of the television, popping the container open as he went.

"No cookies before lunch, Robert Linley," Charlotte's mother yelled from the kitchen.

"Okay," he yelled, his words muffled from a giant bite of cookies. He sent Charlotte a wink. "Thanks, pumpkin."

Charlotte smiled and headed for the kitchen. She'd been making her dad peanut butter chocolate cookies for his birthday since she could remember. "Hi, Mom."

"Hey, sweetie, could you hand me that tureen on the counter?" Her mother looked tired. She'd probably been up all morning cleaning and cooking for her family. Charlotte would comment that she shouldn't have, but she knew her mother would not have had it any other way.

Grabbing the large white bowl, she carried it over to her mother, holding it steady so she could fill it with the delicious-smelling noodles.

"Looks so good."

"Thank you. I haven't made it since last year so I'm a little excited myself. Can you carry that to the table? There's a lid over there. That'll keep it hot until your brother and Beth get here."

After carefully placing the stoneware lid on the tureen, Charlotte walked back over to her mother, who was busy placing rolls into the oven.

"Mom, before everyone gets here, do you think we could talk for a moment?"

She should wait, have this discussion after the meal, when they could go find some privacy. But she was afraid she'd lose her nerve. She also wouldn't enjoy being here with all of these emotions built up inside her.

"What's wrong? Did something happen?" Her mother faced her, eyes full of concern.

"Everything's fine. There's just something I wanted to tell you. It's old news actually, I should have told you years ago."

Karen Linley straightened and gave Charlotte her full attention. "Do I need to sit?"

"Uh, sure. Let's just go over here." Leading her mother over to the counter stools at the end of the island, Charlotte sat down.

Once they were both seated, Charlotte felt her palms clam up. "Mom. I should have told you when it happened, but, well . . . a few weeks before my wedding to John, I miscarried."

"Oh, honey, *what*?" Her mother hand reached out and touched her own.

"I was almost fifteen weeks."

Her mother lifted the hand to her mouth and stared, her eyes wide.

"I'm sorry I didn't tell you. We'd intended to tell everyone I was pregnant the day after the wedding. I just wanted to focus on one thing at a time, and I didn't want you to be disappointed, or think—"

"*Charlotte*, I wouldn't have been disappointed. Honey, I can't believe this. It hurts my feelings a little bit that you'd go through something so traumatic without coming to me. Why didn't you?"

"I just . . . didn't. It was supposed to be a happy time with our wedding coming up. I didn't want you to be sad, I assumed that John and I could just try again right away, and then, well . . . you know what happened after that."

"And John knew about it?"

Charlotte nodded.

"Did Roxanne Reynolds know? Why didn't she tell me?"

"No! No one did but us. But for some reason I just needed to tell you now. Sometimes I'm still very sad about it."

"Oh, honey, of course you are." Karen sat up and pursed her lips for a moment and then spoke quietly. "I've never told you, but I've had three miscarriages. So I know very well how you feel."

"Mom!" Charlotte felt her stomach drop. "When?"

"Two were before your brother was born, and then one before you. Each one was traumatic. Your poor father, it was so hard on him. I cried a lot. Our marriage suffered for a time. Sometimes I think he'd wanted to wash his hands of me just because I became obsessed with getting and staying pregnant. But he didn't, and now I have both of you."

"Oh my gosh. I wish I'd known."

Her mother just shrugged, a weak smile on her face. "It's not something I ever talk about, really."

"Why do we keep these things to ourselves?"

"I wish I knew. It's hard for a woman to talk about it, I think. People don't always understand. But it's a very real loss. Did you go to the doctor?"

Charlotte nodded. "John took me. He was there for me, the best he could be. But I know he was never quite as sad as I was."

"Don't be so sure, Charlotte. Yes, it's different for men, but they still hurt. They've still lost a child they'd expected to have, and that's devastating for anyone. But I know what you mean. They don't have that connection to a physical life growing inside them, or the hormones coursing through their body. I think more than anything they feel helpless that they can't take away the pain for you. It's incredibly emotional and tragic, Charlotte. I hate knowing that I wasn't there for you, that we were just going about our business and planning your wedding while you suffered."

The timer on the stove went off and her mother caressed her face for a beat before she got up and pulled the bread from the oven. After setting it on a trivet, she leaned her hands on the counter. "I also hate to learn that John did what he did to you after this happened."

"It was a rough time." Charlotte fidgeted with the hem of her shorts.

"Next time something is troubling you, tell me. Promise?"

"Actually . . . there's something else."

Her mother looked stricken, obviously not expecting anything right away. Charlotte held out a hand. "It's nothing serious. Well, it's serious to me."

"What is it?"

"I've been seeing someone."

"Oh?" Her mother's look of concern quickly turned into a smile. "You do keep lots of things to yourself."

"Not really, it hasn't been serious for long. Not at all. But I've liked him for years."

"Is it the man you were pretending with?"

Charlotte laughed. "Yes. We started seeing each other for real after that. But . . . we've hit a few snags. I guess you could say we each have issues."

"Oh, Charlotte." Her mother sat back down on her stool. "Every couple has issues, because every human does."

"I know." She wasn't sure how to say this. "But ever since my relationship with John, I've been kind of anti-marriage."

"I suppose that's understandable, although I'd disagree with the stance. Marriage can be wonderful."

"It's not that I haven't wanted love, but I've feared the commitment. Feared someone falling out of love with me. Which is why I've always dreamed of getting pregnant again. I knew that at the very least, a baby would be mine. Forever."

Her mother smiled. "The love between a mother and her child is special. But it's no replacement for romantic love, Charlotte. Our children don't walk through life with us."

"I know, but sometimes our romantic love interests don't, either."

"True. But what does that have to do with this man you've been seeing?"

"Well, I found out some pretty sad news." Charlotte

took a deep breath, still trying to accept the reality Dean had shared with her. "He's infertile."

Her mother's eyes widened. "Oh, honey. That's too bad. And I take it that may be a deal breaker for you?"

Charlotte sighed. "I don't . . . want it to be. But it's been difficult news to receive. I've feared miscarrying again in the future, but it never even occurred to me that I might meet a man who couldn't have children."

Her mother gave her a weak smile. "It happens, sweetie."

Charlotte nodded. "I know. Although I think I was more upset with him for not being honest with me about it. I think part of him wanted to use that as a reason to never give us a shot in the first place."

"Well, it's a very understandable fear for a man, Charlotte. Relationships and babies have gone hand in hand since the beginning of time. I'm sure he didn't want to let you down."

"He's also twelve years older than I am and has been married before."

"Oh my," she said. Charlotte waited for a protest, pleased when none came. "Well, that's not the worst thing I suppose. You know there are alternatives to natural pregnancy. IVF, donors, even adoption."

"I know." Charlotte had spent days on the internet, trying to get a good idea of what this would mean for them as a couple. The thing she kept coming back to, was that obviously Dean wanted a relationship with her. He'd been thinking long term. And while she was still frustrated with how he'd handled it, she could understand his fear of disappointing her. But what did their future look like, and could she accept it?

"Mom, would you think I'm crazy for adopting?"

"Charlotte, you can't be serious? Of course not. Your

father and I would be thrilled to welcome any child of yours into our home, no matter how they came to be."

"Thank you. I really had no doubt of that. Maybe I'm just trying to accept the idea myself."

"Oh, sweetie, adoption could be a lovely thing. But don't get ahead of yourself. Whether children come or not really is secondary to what matters most. Do you *love* this man?"

Charlotte nodded. "Yes, I love him."

"Do you want a life with him even if it includes no children?"

The thought of that sent a wave of sadness over Charlotte. This was the exact question she'd kept asking herself. There was a time she would have said no, absolutely not. But that was before she'd fallen for him. Charlotte smiled, because out of all the uncertainty surrounding them, one thing was clear. "Yes. I do."

Her mother patted Charlotte's hand and then gave it a squeeze. "Then everything else will work itself out."

Three hours later Charlotte pulled up outside Dean's apartment building. It had been four days since she'd seen him. Deep in her heart she'd known that Dean was still the one, but she'd needed some time to process this new reality that she'd never considered. Change the story and expectations in her head, because she'd spent five years imagining what her future was supposed to look like. She couldn't flip a switch and turn that off.

Grabbing the plastic container off her passenger seat, Charlotte got out, locked up, and headed up to the front door of his unit. It was a beautiful early July day, the sun bright, sky blue. Beautiful azaleas lined the walk up to the building.

After a deep breath, Charlotte knocked on the door, saying a silent plea that he would be happy to see her.

The door opened slowly, and Alex peeked out. Instantly a smile broke out on her face. "Charlotte, hi!"

Relieved at her warmth, Charlotte smiled back. "Hello. I hope it's not a bad time."

"No way, come in. But please ignore the fact that I haven't washed my hair since you saw me last."

"No judging here. Promise."

The living room of Dean's apartment was dark, the shades drawn, and the lights all off. A blanket was laid out on the sofa, the coffee table covered with glasses, balled-up tissues, and several rolls of toilet paper. Charlotte didn't comment, just stepped to the side while Alex closed the door. There was no sign of Dean.

"Excuse the mess. I'm driving Dean nuts with my hermit lifestyle. But I can't find it in myself to give a shit. Excuse my language also."

"You have every right to grieve however you want, Alex. He's just frustrated that he can't fix it for you."

"Ahhh, yes. I know." Alex sat down on the couch, her baggy sweats pooling around her feet. "He's not here by the way, but he'll back soon. Just went to get some more toilet paper and Dr Pepper for me."

Charlotte smiled and sat down. "I hope he doesn't mind that I'm here. I came unannounced."

"Are you kidding? You're all he's talked about since lasagna night. I'm glad you're here. It sucks here with us both miserable. Look at this place. It's like we're two lonely vampires."

A few moments later the front door opened, letting in a crack of light, and Dean stepped inside. He didn't see Charlotte at first.

"I bought both. Toilet paper and actual tissues. With lotion."

When no one responded, he looked up and met eyes with Charlotte.

"Hi," he said.

"Hi. Sorry I didn't call or text."

He dropped a massive package of toilet paper onto the floor, leaned to the side to lay down the case of soda, and then tossed the plastic grocery bag that had been hanging on his forearm to Alex. "That's okay. I'm just glad to see you."

Neither of them moved, and when Alex continued to sit on the sofa looking back and forth between them, Dean spoke. "Alex. Get."

With a sigh, his little sister got up from the couch, made her way to her room, and shut the door.

"I brought you some cookies," Charlotte said, holding up the plastic container.

Dean walked forward and took it from her slowly, his eyes never leaving hers. "Thank you."

"They're peanut butter chocolate. My dad's favorite. I make them every year for him on his birthday. I figured . . . I might as well bring some for the other special man in my life."

He stared into her eyes for a long time, then finally spoke, his voice low and roughed. "Do you mean that?"

"Without a doubt," she whispered.

She took the box of cookies back from his hands, set it down on a side table, and then stepped up to him, wrapping her hands around his neck. "I won't lie and tell you . . . I wasn't sad. It was a shock, and a lot to think about. But one thing you've made me realize is that, although love is scary and risky, it's worth it. Any problem is solvable . . . except being without you. I don't think I could handle that."

Dean leaned his head against hers and whispered, "I love you, Charlotte."

She bit her lip, emotion choking her up. "I love you. You alone are more than enough for me."

"I don't want you to ever stop feeling that way. I've already failed at forever once."

She laid a finger on his lips. "Your past, my past, they have nothing to do with you and me. But I do want us to promise right now that from this moment on, we deal with our problems together. Not apart."

"I promise."

"When you're worried about something, you tell me."

Dean nodded. "Yes. Agreed. Anything."

"Okay. Now you can kiss me," she said with a grin.

That's exactly what he did.

Epilogue

Charlotte held Dean's hand as they walked down the aisle of the Maple Springs Humane Society. Set after set of big round eyes stared back at them from every kennel.

"This is too hard," she said. "I want them all."

Dean released her hand and put an arm around her shoulder. After pulling her in tight and dropping a kiss on her head, he whispered, "Let's start with one for now."

She nodded, knowing he was right, even though it was so sad.

Dean had moved into Charlotte's house a month ago, in October. Much to the surprise and disappointment of them both, Alexis had gone ahead and decided to honor her commitment to deploy to Italy in July, so when Dean's lease was up they'd decided to take things to the next step. It hadn't taken Charlotte long to convince him they should adopt a rescue dog. This was their first trip out to look.

Charlotte glanced back and forth, feeling guilty every time she locked eyes with one of them. They turned a corner to go down the next aisle. The kennel to her immediate left stood open and a shelter volunteer was putting a small brown dog inside. It was shivering so badly, it could barely walk.

"Oh," Charlotte gasped. "What's wrong with him?"

The young man smiled up at Charlotte. "He's cute isn't he? His leg is injured and he's very nervous. New. Brought in by a farmer who said he and his siblings were dumped in his ditch."

With a horrified gasp, Charlotte pulled away from Dean and knelt down on the floor. The volunteer left the kennel door open so Charlotte could see the little dog better. He was no more than ten pounds with short milk-chocolate-colored fur, and little ears that flopped over into points.

"Where are his siblings?" she asked.

"They adopted immediately. He's the only one left."

"Aww." She stuck out her hand slowly, but the little pup just continued to shiver as he stared up at her with beady eyes. "What kind is he?"

"We think he's a pinscher-and-Chihuahua mix. The vet said he needs surgery to get full use of that back leg, but they won't do it without an adoption commitment. Hence him being the only one left unadopted. It's pricey surgery."

Charlotte looked over at him. "Will he die without the surgery?"

"No. He'll make adjustments in his habits, but it could cause issues down the road."

He went to close the kennel but Charlotte instinctively stuck her hand out to stop him.

"Can't I try once more?"

The young man shrugged. "Sure, but he's a timid one."

"Who can blame him?" Charlotte said. She realized Dean had knelt down beside her. "He's so scared."

"What are you thinking, babe?" he asked.

"I'm thinking his story breaks my heart," she said quietly, sticking out a hand to the shaking puppy. "The human race has let him down. He just wants to be loved."

The two little black eyes continued to stare at her for a long moment, and finally he got up off his haunches and limped toward her outstretched hand. He sniffed it once then wobbled away.

"Does he have a name?" Charlotte asked.

"The vet was calling him Fernando," the guy laughed. "No idea why."

Charlotte's heart skipped and she turned to Dean. "Oh, babe. It's fate. He's ours."

Dean raised an eyebrow. "*Okay*. But how do you know?"

She smiled. " 'Fernando' is one of my favorite ABBA songs."

Dean let out a laugh as his eyelids fell shut. Then he stood up and spoke to the volunteer. "We want him. How soon can he have the surgery?"

Five days later they drove home with Fernando, who was curled in Charlotte's lap with his leg wrapped in bandages while Dean drove. He glanced at her and their new dog as she fumbled with her phone. Within moments a song he now knew well—"Fernando"—came blaring through the speakers of his SUV.

She'd been singing it all over the house since they'd left the pound the week before.

"Aren't you excited to come home, Fernando?" she crooned to the dog. They were at a red light so he could enjoy watching the dog lick at her nose as she continued to talk to him in a baby voice. "We're gonna love you so much. Yes we are."

Dean just chuckled. She heard him and smiled up at him. "Don't make fun of me."

"Never. I love it."

"We just adopted our first fur-baby. It will be good practice for when we adopt a human baby."

Dean smiled at her. They'd been discussing it a lot lately. But he wasn't committing to anything until they finalized one more thing. Speaking of which . . .

"It *will* be good practice," Dean said as he pulled into their driveway and turned off the car. He reached into the pocket of his coat and pulled out a bag. "But first I bought you and our . . . *fur baby* a present."

Her eyes lit up, her grin wide as she took the small bag. "You did? You're such a good dad," she teased.

Reaching into the bag, she pulled out a little blue dog collar. "Aww, look, Fernando. It's so swe—" Her breath caught.

Dean watched Charlotte's eyes as she moved the collar through her fingers and touched the engagement ring attached. She turned to look at him and whispered, "Dean."

"We're a family now, Charlotte. It's time you married me."

With tears in her eyes, she reached up and touched his face. He knew what he was asking of her. To take a risk. Face one of her biggest fears. They'd done a lot of talking over the past four months about their pasts, their hopes, and their love for each other.

There was no doubt that they'd both been through what they had just to eventually find each other. And he had no interest in waiting any longer. Dean knew she was the one for him.

"You're my world, Charlotte. We'll get married in whatever way makes you feel safe, but don't you doubt for one minute that I won't show up to make you mine forever."

Her lip trembled, and Fernando climbed up on her chest to lick her chin. She laughed as the little tongue tickled her skin.

"Is that a yes?" Dean asked.

"It's a yes from me and Fernando."

Dean leaned over and kissed her. After a moment she pulled back and smiled. "I want to get married at that beach in North Carolina. It was so beautiful."

"Done."

"Just you and me. And our parents."

Dean nodded. "Whatever you want."

"And maybe Lauren, so she can take pictures."

"That sounds like a good idea."

"And then we can have a big reception back here at the Stag for all of our family and friends."

Dean laughed. "Have you already been planning this?"

"Not really." She gave him a playful shove. "But I can't wait to plan it with you."

Stay tuned for the next book by Nicole McLaughlin

MAYBE THIS TIME

Coming soon from St. Martin's Paperbacks!